Nicholas Royle was born in Manchester in 1963. He is the author of three previous novels – *Counterparts*, *Saxophone Dreams* and *The Matter of the Heart* – and more than a hundred short stories, as well as being the editor of ten anthologies. He lives in west London with his wife and two children.

The Director's Cut

Nicholas Royle

An *Abacus* Book

First published in Great Britain by Abacus 2000

A CIP catalogue record for this book is available from the British Library.

ISBN 0 349 11301 7

Typeset by Solidus (Bristol) Limited
Printed and bound in Great Britain by Clays Ltd, St Ives plc

Abacus
A Division of
Little, Brown and Company (UK)
Brettenham House
Lancaster Place
London WC2E 7EN

For Jean Royle

'The night has a thousand cameras'

Joel Lane, *The Edge of the Screen*

'When the audience and I meet in the emotional space shaped by the film, a kind of intimacy lives'

Michelle Citron, *Home Movies & Other Necessary Fictions*

1 · Beach reading

Suffolk coast, spring 1998

It starts with a woman on a beach.

You see them all along the Suffolk coast, heads bowed over the high-tide mark – women, poring over the stony shoreline. Their eyes sliding over the pebbles like so many words.

This beach has no sand, just stones. The woman is the only figure visible in either direction. She's in her early forties and could look younger but in fact looks older. She spends her time walking up and down the beach staring at the ground. Her name is Penny Burns. Her husband was Iain Burns, but he's not around any more. Hence the repeated trips to the beach. But I'm getting ahead of myself.

She first came into my jeweller's shop in Felixstowe six months ago with some stones that she'd found on the beach. That's what she said to me: 'I've found some stones on the beach.' I wondered if she was mad, a bit soft in the head. The beaches on that part of the Suffolk coast are all stony. Then I met her gaze and was forced to rethink because there was something about her eyes that made me stop and sharply take in a breath. If I say there was a haunted look about them, that's quite apt, because they've been haunting me ever since.

'I found them on the beach,' she repeated, and opened her fist over my counter. A few stones fell out with a clatter, drawing

...tention from her face. But looking at the stones, all I could see were her eyes. They were a filmy, milky blue. You could see that she had been or could still be an attractive woman behind the pain stamped on her face. Under the harsh jeweller's lights her pupils had shrunk to pinpricks.

I had picked up a couple of the stones and was automatically turning them over in my fingers. My sense of touch alerted me to what I would have spotted immediately had I not been so distracted. These were not stones at all, but lumps of fossilised resin – pieces of amber.

The beaches of East Anglia often yield amber. Originating in the Baltics, it gets washed up with the tide at Southwold and Felixstowe, Aldeburgh and Dunwich. Up and down the coast, women haunt the shore looking for lumps of the stuff. Widows, middle-aged or older, they comb the high-tide mark for hours at a stretch. You can't predict how many pieces you might find in a week. Sometimes several, other times none at all. Most of the women wait until they have a number of pieces before bringing it in, either to myself or to one of the other jewellers in town. Just about every jeweller in East Anglia has a little collection of amber; one or two devote a whole window to it. The state we receive the pieces in, you wouldn't recognise it as amber, unless, like the women and those in the trade, you had a trained eye. It's dirty, matt, unremarkable in its natural state, less striking than many of the pebbles it gets washed up with. But give it a polish and it glows.

You need to clean it up before you know how much it's worth, so, those women who bring me amber, I ask them if they can leave it with me and then I contact them later to let them know what value I've placed on their find. It occurs to one or two of them, you can see it in their eyes, that I might exploit an opportunity to be dishonest and tell them over the phone that their amber is less valuable than it actually is. Over the phone they can't see the polished material, so they still don't know if any of it contains insects or scraps of long-dead tree bark, and they can't see my face so they're unable to tell if I'm lying or telling the truth. I see these doubts pass across their eyes, one or two of them only, like clouds passing in front of the sun, when I tell them that I will phone with my report. But most of them take what I say at face value and so should they: I have never cheated one of my Amber Girls. They are far too precious to me for that.

I looked at Penny Burns's amber and saw that I would have to ask her to wait for me to phone her as well. Since she was a new client, she would need to give me her phone number, I explained, which she did without protest before leaving the shop. I felt for some time after she had left that she was in fact still there. Such was the power of her personality, despite the fact that she had said so little. I decided it was all in her eyes and, as I say, they haunted me.

So it starts with a woman on a beach, head bowed, feet shuffling. From the edge of the promenade no details are clear, but I know it's Penny. I know from the way she moves, from the length of time she stays out there, the distances she covers in a day. I have started closing the shop at irregular intervals so I can watch Penny as she searches the shoreline for pieces of amber. I know that amber is not what she is really searching for, but it is all that she will find, and when she does she will bring it to me. She will bring it to me in my shop and I will send her away and spend hours cleaning her pieces before telephoning her and sometimes asking her to come back in just so that I can tell her in person what value I am placing on the pieces she has brought me. And then I'll show her the pieces once they've been cleaned up. I sense that her need to see them is as real and intense as my own need to show them to her. Of course, she never sees in them exactly what she is looking for, but instead she sees a representation of what it is she is seeking. She subsists on images, lives by symbols.

Sometimes she casts a listless eye over the polished amber I keep under glass, the pieces brought to me by the other Amber

Girls and to which I affix price tags. Some I fashion into ear-
rings and pendants, others I leave as they are. It gets sold to
tourists. If she notices that her own pieces never seem to be for
sale, she doesn't mention it. She has only to ask and I'll usher
her into the back room and show her the separate collection
I've made of the pieces she has brought me. I pay her as much
as I pay anyone else, but I never sell Penny Burns's amber. I
have decided that I wouldn't sell it for any price, no matter how
high, because I sense that it's too valuable, even to Penny. I
sense, rightly or wrongly, that she knows I'm keeping it for her
and would give the entire collection back free of charge the
moment she asked for it.

There are a few trapped insects among the pieces she has
brought me, not that many, but then they're rarer than you
might think, pieces of amber containing anything more exciting
than a flake of bark or something similar. The collection would
be quite valuable by now, but it's not for sale.

When Penny finally comes off the beach, I follow her along
the promenade for half a mile before she cuts inland, turning
right where she always does. The only difference this time
is that I continue to follow her. What makes me do this on
this occasion, while previously I have simply watched her go,
I cannot say. The time is around five p.m. The shop can stay
closed for the day. I remain at least fifty yards behind Penny
Burns as she heads further inland. This part of the town is
all winding suburban drives lined with retirement bungalows
and the odd brace of pre-war semis. Front lawns and her-
baceous borders. Sunday mornings, all the husbands who can
still manage it are out washing the car or mowing the
lawn.

Penny Burns turns left and walks as far as the next junction,
which she crosses. The road now, at least on the side furthest
from the sea, is mainly hotels. Dire-looking places that in inner
cities would be DSS dumping grounds but for the pottery
animals in the windows and the VACANCIES signs. Each

contains a strip of see-through plastic matting in the hallway and a greasy spatula hanging from a hook in the kitchen. Opposite the Hotel Paradise, which looks no different from its neigh-bours, Penny Burns turns into a garden path on the east side of the road. I dawdle outside the Hotel Paradise while she extracts a door key from the pocket of her raincoat and slips it into the lock of her front door. I look away until she is inside. It's a semi-detached, two-storey house built between the wars. A moss-coloured rivulet running down the front of the house is evidence of a damaged gutter. The down-stairs windows are not lace-curtained, but streaky with the wind and the salt. There's some cladding on the outside of the house that I imagine Penny Burns would have always wanted her husband to remove. She doesn't strike me as the type to entertain the idea of cladding. But what the hell do I know?

At least now I know where she lives. I know where Penny Burns lives.

I went back to work, not that day, not the day I'd followed Penny Burns home, but the next. I went back to work, but I couldn't concentrate. I would be dealing with a middle-aged customer who wanted the bracelet on her gold watch repairing and I'd realise that I hadn't heard a word she was saying. I just looked at the watch she placed on the counter and then at her lips, which were moving improbably quickly, but I heard nothing of what she was saying. I apologised and asked her to leave the watch and return later in the day. As she pulled open the door, she shook her head slowly from side to side. I tried to concentrate on repairing the watch – it was a simple enough job, after all – but its minor intricacies confused me.

After two hours spent either uselessly fumbling or dealing with other customers who asked for ring trays to be produced only to screw up their noses and leave empty-handed, I realised I wasn't going to get a scrap of work done. I tried having a look at Penny Burns's amber collection to see if that would set my mind at rest, but it only thickened the treacle through which I seemed to be wading. My breathing had become shallow and my throat dry. As early as three o'clock I found myself locking the shop and walking towards the seafront. A chilly, salty breeze blew in off the sea and I buttoned my overcoat right up to my neck. My trousers flattened against my shin bones and I wished I had worn thicker socks.

I stood on the promenade and watched her familiar stoop-shouldered form make slow progress along the tidemark. In my mind I narrowed the space between us to a few yards, then a couple of feet and finally only inches separated us. I could see the fine down on the line of her jaw. I could hear the slight catch in her breathing – exertion, sea air, grief. I could see the contradictory furrows etched into her brow by hope and despair. I longed to take her hand and hold it in mine. To squeeze it, not in reassurance, but in comfort. I dreamed of feeling her soft weight subside against me. I wanted to help her, but how do you help someone whose situation is quite hopeless?

With almost no real awareness of what I was doing, I left the seafront and walked inland, taking the same route I had taken when I had followed Penny Burns the day before, but this time I wasn't following anyone. I didn't even look back to see if she was following me. When I reached the Hotel Paradise, I went in and stepped up to the formica counter on one side of the narrow hallway.

'The room on the first floor facing the road,' I said to the woman behind the little flap, 'is it free?'

She moved away briefly and returned with a key. The fob was a scallop shell with a hole drilled in it for the ring to go through.

'How long will you be wanting it, sir?' she asked, looking up at me.

'Just for tonight.'

Once inside the room, I took off my overcoat but was still

far too warm. I removed my fleece and laid it down on the powder-blue candlewick bedspread. I rolled up my shirt sleeves and stood in front of the mirror above the vanity unit. I pulled the light cord and leaned over the sink to have a closer look at the evidence of my decline. The dark shadows under my eyes were pronounced, and it never seems to matter how recently I've shaved, I always have a degree of five o'clock shadow. A few grey hairs had recently sprouted in my sideburns. My eyes, which I had always thought too close together and unusually deep set, appeared to be the colour of the mahogany wardrobe behind me, but I knew that in natural light they would have a greenish tinge to them. I looked tired, but unnaturally alert, as if I had been up all night.

I pulled the cord and turned away from the mirror, moving to the window for the first time. I suppose I delayed looking out of the window because I was frightened, both by what I might see and by the mere fact of my wanting to see it. The street was empty. I looked across at Penny's house. There were no lights on. It was still early for her to be back. I sat down on the edge of the bed and waited.

I don't know how long I waited, one hour or two. I tried to empty my mind of thought. I watched the street. If someone passed, my eyes swivelled to follow them, then returned to the point at the left of my vision where Penny would appear if she was ever going to come back. After a while the passers-by became fewer in number and eventually there were no more, so that my eyes no longer moved and I stared, quite literally, into space. An empty space a few cubic feet just to the right of where the pavement on the opposite side of the street vanished behind the left-hand edge of the hotel room window. Soon, that space seemed to phosphoresce in relation to the space around it, which became grainier and progressively darker from the perimeter of my vision inwards. Almost as if a spotlight were being trained on it.

Inevitably, when Penny Burns walked into the spotlight, I

wasn't ready for her. She moved too quickly, arriving on the scene before my evolution from sentient being to security camera could be completed. I had not yet successfully shut down all my other senses and their sudden reactivation shocked me. Sensations flooded my consciousness, chief among them the thumping of my heart, the quickening of my breathing. I felt sick and found it hard to swallow. Penny let the gate swing to after her and walked up the path. She slipped into the house as swiftly and efficiently as she inserted the key in the lock and twisted it.

Still I watched the front door, but broadened my focus in case she were to appear in one of the windows. A light went on in the half-light above the front door. Another light, a softer one, appeared on the first-floor, opposite me. There were lace curtains at that window preventing me from seeing clearly, but I made out a smudge of darkness moving about behind the nets. Then the light went off and nothing else happened for a long time. The house itself now seemed to float in a soft peachy glow while the space around it perceptibly darkened to sepia.

It grew hotter in the room. Sitting where I was, on the edge of the bed by the window, I was practically on top of the radiator. Sweat sprang out across my skull. I could have switched the radiator off but I didn't want to move. The streetlamps came on, salmon pink at first and fizzing, then gradually turning orange. The cloud line above the row of houses opposite was a black crust, the edge of night. I put my hand in the pocket of my jeans and pulled out a small, smooth lump of amber, cleaned up and polished. One of Penny's, it contained an inclusion, a tiny speck of a fly. Penny had not yet seen this piece in its polished state. I thought about taking it across the road, knocking on her door and showing it to her, but I didn't think about it for very long.

I pulled my mobile phone out of the back pocket of my jeans and looked at it for a moment before twice pressing the green key. I strained to hear the phone ring in the house across the street, but I could not. Just its ghost rattling in my mobile.

She picked up: 'Hello?'

I couldn't be sure but it seemed to me that there was a perceptible lift on the second syllable, as if life wasn't the barren desert I'd imagined for her, as if there might actually be someone she might want to speak to on the phone, as if I might even be . . . *him*—

This puzzled me. How could I be him? How could *anyone* be him? How could he even get to a phone to call her if he was buried six feet underground? At this stage, I was still making presumptions, but how could the reality be any different from my imagined version? The way I saw it, there was no room for error. The Amber Girls were widows to a woman. Tramping the shoreline day after day was something to do, something to kill the long widow's hours. The fact that among the millions of pebbles there were a few semi-precious fossils meant that they had a purpose, something to look for. They weren't just walking up and down the coastline for fun; there was an object to their search. Not only that, but if they actually found anything, they could sell it. Nothing validated a pastime like getting paid for it, hard cash in return for pebble-sized lumps of pre-history.

Penny, like the rest of the Amber Girls, was driven by the desperate and endless quest to find something to replace her missing man. What better, since the opportunity lay on their doorsteps, than to hunt for little lumps of life-preserving material. So it was only an illusion – that was better than nothing. Maybe life was only an illusion anyway. It must often have appeared like one to them. Was a perfectly preserved fly in amber any less real than a photograph of the husband they had lost? They all carried such photographs in their coat pockets. Framed pictures sat on their mantelpieces and dressing tables. If out of all the millions of stones on the beach they discovered a snipe fly in highly oxidised red amber that had been washed two thousand miles from the Baltics, did that not seem to suggest that miracles could happen? Would that not give them hope that they might actually catch sight of their late husband window-shopping in the high street on the way back from the seafront? Or that the phone might ring one cool spring evening and when they picked up and said, 'Hello?' it would be him?

'It's Wim De Blieck.'

'Who?'

I flinched and lowered my head between my legs.

'Wim De Blieck, the jeweller. Have I called at a bad time?'

'No, not particularly.' Her voice was flat, expressionless.

I lifted my head and looked across the street. She was standing by the streaky window on the ground floor. One hand in her hair, the other holding the receiver. Her face looked as if it had been flayed; it was red from crying.

'I was just calling to say that I've cleaned up the amber you brought in yesterday and wondered if you wanted to come in and look at it. Perhaps tomorrow morning at nine?'

She didn't say anything but I could hear the sound of her breathing.

'Later if that's too early,' I suggested. 'Ten?'

'Ten o'clock,' she said.

'OK,' I said, staring down into her front room. The hand in her hair moved back and forth. I could hear its gentle, stroking rasp in the receiver. 'See you at ten o'clock tomorrow morning. I'll look forward to it.'

I bit my tongue, but too late. I shouldn't have said I was looking forward to it. It was wrong. It was right, of course, in that it was correct, but it was the wrong thing to say. But I had said it. I knew for certain it had been the wrong thing to say when she said nothing in reply, only hung up. I watched her intently as she stood there for another minute, at least, immobile apart from the regular movement of her hand in her hair. I stowed the phone in my back pocket, remaining otherwise still so that she wouldn't look up and see me.

Eventually she left the room and didn't reappear in either window again all night. The bedroom at the front of the house mustn't have been the one she slept in. I guessed it was the bedroom she had shared with her husband and that she couldn't bring herself to occupy it with him gone. She would have moved her dressing table and a few things into a smaller bedroom at the back of the house. Towards midnight I lay back on the bed and immediately fell asleep. In the early hours I woke shivering and had to climb under the covers. When I stirred in the morning it was to the sound of a front door closing. I leaped to the window just in time to see the back of her legs as she disappeared in the direction of the seafront. I looked at my watch. It was half past eight.

When she arrived at the shop an hour and a half later, I persuaded her to come into the back office to look at her growing collection (she produced nothing to add to it from her morning's excursion). We talked about amber generally and after an hour I felt some hidden tension break and she slumped in the chair. I poured her a small brandy and encouraged her to drink it, saying it was getting on for lunchtime. She did so and within only several more minutes had decided to relax her grip on what she knew and what she didn't know but wanted to know. I flipped the OPEN/CLOSED sign and shut the connecting door and over a cup of tea and more brandies she told me her story.

2 · POV

It starts with a body wrapped in celluloid, like a fly in amber.

All morning Frank had watched the police crawling over the demolition site across the street from his flat. He was used to watching, and he was good at it. Watching was what Frank did for a living.

At ground level you got no impression of the extent of the demolition site, even when you walked around its perimeter. Erected to mark the precise boundary between site and pavement was a series of wooden hoardings that formed a new, temporary frontier between the empty space where once there had been a row of shops – hi-fi outlets, porn merchants, electronics dealers, a chip shop and a pub – and the empty space that had always been just empty space.

Frank knew all about empty space. He was an expert in it.

He also knew more than most people about the empty space that was being opened up across the street. His knowledge of it was shared with Harry Foxx, Richard Charnock and Angelo, three people to whom he had once been close.

The structures had gone, demolished by the hard-hats over the preceding weeks. If he was heading into Soho, Frank now invariably took the trouble to cross to that side of Tottenham

12

Court Road so he could skirt the demolition site and turn right into Hanway Street. In fact, even when the buildings on the corner of Tottenham Court Road and Hanway Street had still been standing, Frank tended to take the same route to access the square half-mile. He *liked* Hanway Street, with its succession of discount record stores and private drinking clubs, cheap restaurants and unusual bars; he preferred all that to the grim alternative proposed by Oxford Street's corresponding stretch (The Tottenham, Virgin Megastore, McDonald's, Angus Steak House).

Only from Frank's eighth-floor vantage point across Tottenham Court Road did you get a view of the site that enabled you to appreciate how far back it went, how substantial a chunk it bit out of the city.

The screensaver on Frank's PowerBook had not been wiped since it had first cut in, ten minutes after that morning's start-up. The demolition site, normally busy as an ants' nest, with men scurrying this way and that, some chipping away, others operating heavy machinery, had been besieged by police. Uniforms and plain-clothes detectives were present in large numbers, their vehicles parked in a wedge at the main gates, doors open, radios buzzing.

At the northern extremity of the site, a white tent had been erected. A uniformed officer stood guarding the tent's entrance while men in papery white zip-up suits maintained a constant stream of traffic between the tent and the parked vehicles.

Towards the end of the morning, Frank watched as they wheeled a gurney out of the tent. Whatever it was the men in white suits had found and were taking away needed to be concealed inside a black zip-up body bag.

Frank guessed it was a body.

He thought again of Harry Foxx, Richard Charnock and Angelo.

He moved away from the window and went to pick up the phone.

* * *

Harry Foxx was close. He was that close. He could feel it, he could sense it. But being that close would only mean, if the meeting didn't go well, that he would be that much more frustrated.

Harry Foxx turned to look at Lawrence Gold sitting alongside.

'Harry,' said Lawrence, with his standard reassuring smile that was about as reassuring as an air stewardess in a life-jacket, 'don't worry about it. Ritchie McCluskey is a nice guy. He also runs one of the best production companies in London. We have a good proposal. What could possibly go wrong?'

'I hope you're right, Lawrence,' Harry Foxx sighed. 'A man can't build a reputation on one film alone, even if it is *Nine South Street*.'

'Mmm, well. Just make sure your bloody phone's switched off. We don't want that going off again at the wrong moment. Ritchie McCluskey hates to be interrupted.'

'It's switched off,' Harry Foxx assured him. 'Don't worry about it.'

If Ritchie McCluskey agreed to back their proposal, it would take a lot of pressure off them and would mean they could actually get on with making the film. Harry Foxx would rather take no part in the fund-raising side and just be allowed to get on with the creative act of turning the words on the page into images on celluloid, but Lawrence, the kind of producer who operated on hunch and initiative, had insisted that Harry attend the meeting.

'Ritchie McCluskey came up from the creative side,' he'd told Harry prior to the meeting.

'He'll have seen *Nine South Street*,' Harry had said.

'Of course. That's why you have to be there. He'll see you as a kindred spirit. For once you'll actually be doing the right thing by going on about camera angles and dissolve this and jump-cut that. You will never see a cheque written as fast. I'm telling you, this is it. This is the big one.'

They'd been close to the big one before and been knocked back. Harry Foxx had made one full-length feature, *Nine South Street*, some years earlier, and had been trying to raise the money to make another ever since. Lawrence's background was in television. Commissioning, scheduling, editing – the further back in Lawrence's career you went, the closer it got to the creative coalface, as he called it. That was fine by Harry Foxx: the last thing he wanted was a producer who had his own ideas about what should go in the shot.

Ritchie McCluskey's was the third production company they had been to with the project, but Lawrence had built Ritchie up more than he had the first two. At a crucial moment in the act of parking Richard Charnock's car, half an hour before the meeting was due to start, Harry, whose day job often involved parking Richard Charnock's car and parking it in such a place that he was able to get back to it and to wherever Richard was before he could finish saying, 'Where in the name of fuck is my bastard car?', had wondered if Lawrence had deliberately set up the first two meetings as dummies, test runs, knowing they wouldn't get anywhere with them. The thought distracted Harry for that vital split second and the bumper of Charnock's S-class Mercedes (he bought his the day after Diana achieved sainthood in hers) knocked the rear end of a Series 3 BMW. Harry held his breath, waiting for an alarm and the consequent appearance of the security guard who otherwise could happily go on reading his *Mirror* in the comfort of his little hut and never know that Harry was parking illegally in the University College Hospital staff car park.

No alarm went off. Harry exhaled and slipped out of the car, making for Tottenham Court Road and turning left. The hospital car park was as near as he could get to Soho and not have to resort to an NCP job. Richard Charnock liked a quick response time and Harry needed to hang on to the chauffeur's cap. The money was useful.

So far, only Lawrence had met with Ritchie McCluskey and

he had reported back to Harry that McCluskey loved the basic concept and was happy with Harry's idea for an ambiguous ending. Moreover, he had no problems with there being no American parts and had no objection to the lack of nudity.

Harry looked across the street at the art deco apartment block next to the *Time Out* building. He knew that Frank had a flat in there, but didn't know which floor it was on. When he reached the demolition site, Harry found himself having to skirt a crowd of onlookers. Under normal circumstances he would have stopped, but given what he knew about the demolition site, the circumstances were not normal.

Harry and Lawrence met in Soho Square and cut down through Frith and Bateman Streets to get to McCluskey's.

'Shush, here he comes,' Lawrence announced, lowering his voice as a figure in a faded denim shirt and black jeans lumbered up the passage leading to the room in which they had been asked to wait.

'Ritchie.' Lawrence jumped up. 'Good to see you. Harry Foxx.'

'With two exes,' said Harry, as Lawrence rolled his eyes in the background.

McCluskey, smelling more than a little of the drinking club he had just left, grunted, shook hands and dropped a dog-eared copy of the proposal on the desk. A good start, thought Harry Foxx, hoping his phone, which of course wasn't switched off, was not about to ring. A proposal that looks as if it's been read is always better than one that looks as if you've just picked it up off the laser printer.

'Guys,' Ritchie said, 'what can I tell you? It's great. It's like really . . . great.' Harry imagined McCluskey responding similarly to a waiter at the Soho House who might have asked him what he'd thought of his salmon fish cakes. 'There's just a couple of things we need to look at before we talk about taking this a stage further.'

Harry Foxx and Lawrence stared at McCluskey in silence.

'I like the all-British cast angle, like it a lot. Very Brit-pack, very cool fucking Britannia and all that shit. I'm looking at Sean Pertwee for the lead. You've got an obvious part here for Kate, right, Kate Moss, and all that stuff's very exciting, very *now*. But—' McCluskey dragged a softpack of cigarettes from the pocket of his Levi's shirt and tapped one out, then dropped them on the table without offering them round. 'What about having an American in there? You know, I mean even if it's some loser. Let's just think American audiences for a minute. And let's see some flesh. Then there's the final reel. The ending's woolly. You've got to make it one thing or the other. Make your minds up.' McCluskey swung his right arm up to his face and dragged his thumb across the wheel of a cheap disposable lighter. He exhaled, sending a ragged stream of smoke across the table towards Harry and Lawrence.

'What about *Nine South Street*?' Harry prompted. 'I mean, no one complained about ambiguity then.'

'*Nine South Street*?'

Once they were outside in the street, Lawrence turned to Harry, spread his palms outward and said, 'Harry, Ritchie's a cunt. You know that. I know that. It's a well-known fact. He hasn't got the first idea how to make a decent movie. We may be back to square one but at least we haven't got Ritchie McCluskey to fuck it up for us.'

'Lawrence,' Harry began, his voice breaking and his face turning red, but his mobile had started to ring.

'Saved by the bell,' observed Lawrence archly.

The phone was ringing but Richard Charnock would let it ring. He knew from its tone which phone it was and that particular phone – the office land-line – could ring all day before he interrupted what he was doing to answer it. No one from the A list rang him on that phone. That was a B- or even a C-list phone. Whatever they had to say would be B- or C-list stuff.

Richard was busy. When Jenny Slade was taking her clothes

off, Richard was always busy. He leaned closer for a better view. She shrugged her shoulders free of the man's white cotton shirt and stood, tilting slightly, in her underwear. Her right hand came slowly up to the bra strap.

'Stop,' Richard said, dry-mouthed. 'Stop there.'

Having paused her, Richard sat back, looking at her still form. This was the moment when he came most alive. The moment of intervention. The moment where he said stop and leaned forward to do it for her. To lift the strap free of the shoulder, slide it down or let it fall, depending on the amount of tension in it. Then he would take the edge of the cup and peel it away from her breast like skin from an orange, his palm catching the weight of the breast as the bra fell away. Then with his thumb he would lightly brush against the nipple until it began to stiffen. Then he would lower his head until it was level with the breast, and take the nipple gently between his lips, closing on it and moving his tongue over it. At this point she would give a faint moan of approval and encouragement and Richard's free hand would alight on her other breast, which was still concealed. He would massage it softly through the material until his action caused the bra to come away and he would cup it, too, like he had the other one. Releasing the right breast now from his mouth he would retreat, just enough to see the two breasts cupped in his hands, and he would apply a little pressure, maybe bring his hands closer together to create a soft pillow on to which he would then, briefly, lower his face.

The phone stopped, and it was only then, by its ceasing to ring, that it broke his concentration. He rubbed his forehead.

Looking back at the screen, he released the button on the remote that would allow Jenny Slade to continue undressing. She did so with calculated, sly indifference.

Jenny Slade was the kind of girl who in six months' time was going to make Kate Moss wish she'd given up smoking and taken out a better pension. Cleverly, Jenny was effecting the crossover from model to actress before she'd reached anything like the peak of her modelling career. In fact, some of her best campaigns were still under wraps. By the time the film was ready, she'd be the face of this, the body of that. Richard could foresee that she wouldn't necessarily want to be doing the kind of stuff he'd got her to do for *Little Black Dress*, but the fact of the matter was that the kind of stuff he'd got her to do wasn't necessarily going to end up in the film. In fact, there was no way it was going to end up in the film, or not in the version of the film that would get shown to the public anyway. There was a small chance it might end up on the director's cut, which in this case, instead of being a slightly different and frankly inferior and somewhat self-indulgent edit of an OK film that's already had a big release in its original version and is now going to get another chance to get the tills bulging, would be very much a one-off. There would be no prints in existence. It simply wouldn't exist on film. But there might be one copy on videotape in Richard's office that only he would know about. That way he could keep good control of it. He could make sure it didn't get into the wrong hands.

Jenny Slade was lying back on the filthy floor of the disused Exhibition halls in Shepherd's Bush. Richard knew what came next, not only because he had seen the tape several times before, but because he had been there when it had been shot. He'd been the director. He'd also operated the camera. And been the lighting guy and the sound man and the focus this, that and the other. And Jenny Slade had been the cast. She wasn't stupid. She'd worked out, correctly, that this was what she had to do to remain on the film. This was the price she had to pay for getting her first decent part, lots of on-screen time and a subsequent hike in the level of fees her agent could demand next time someone came asking her to be in a movie. And after *Little Black Dress*, they would be forming a line outside Richard Charnock's office in Ham Yard all the way back to Wardour Street.

Richard felt a tickling sensation on his left buttock. His

mobile, on vibrate. Richard had two mobiles: one rather bulky, out-of-date Ericsson that didn't necessarily go everywhere with him, its number available to people on the B list, which included his accountant, his agent and Caroline, his girlfriend. The little mobile, the Samsung, the one with the vibrate facility, only ever left his back pocket when it got the shakes. The Samsung was an A-list phone and only A-list people (his dealer, his driver, and that was about it) had the number. He hoped it was only Harry Foxx wanting to know when he needed picking up. Sighing, he paused the video and flipped the talk-pad on the mobile.

'Hello?'

He listened intently to the voice on the other end of the line, his fist tightening around the phone. There was a rush of blood to his face and his breathing became fast and shallow. When the call was finished he got up from the desk and walked to the end of the studio. He stared at the floor, rubbing the side of his face. He was still holding the phone. He reopened the talk-pad and pressed a series of keys.

Angelo walked up Rathbone Place and into Charlotte Street. He crossed Goodge Street and paused outside Channel One's offices on the corner of Tottenham Street, running his hand over his shaved head and enjoying the sensation of the stubble yielding to his fingers. He remembered Channel 4 being on the same site before their move to Victoria, but long before the TV companies moved in, the site had been home to the Scala Theatre, opening in 1911 and showing movies on and off until . . . until when? Angelo took out a little red-and-black note-book and flicked past screeds of tiny handwriting, scraps of maps and little diagrams until he found the right page. Until the late 1950s, when the British Soviet Friendship Society screened Russian films. The Other Cinema had opened in the same space in 1976, showing avant-garde films and failing to attract enough of an audience to prevent its closure only a few months later, but then reopened as the Scala in 1978. Functioning as a club that required a nominal membership fee and offered a daily changing repertory programme, it closed to make way for Channel 4 and reopened in King's Cross, only ultimately to go dark there as well.

On the opposite corner, at 64a (now 69) Charlotte Street, the Fitzroy Picture Palace had operated between 1912 and 1916. Angelo was certain that not even the passage of eight decades would have eradicated all vestiges of the building's former incarnation. Some part of its original space would remain intact within the sandwich shop that now occupied the premises. It was closed. He put the notebook back in his bag and took out a compact digital video camera, which he pointed at the window of the sandwich shop. He moved up close to the glass to get the best shot of the interior.

Stroking his soft skull, he walked on up Charlotte Street, turned left then right into the cobbled mews by the side of the BT Tower. He didn't always take the same route to get there, but he invariably ended up at Great Portland Street tube.

A Hammersmith train arrived as he reached the platform. Someone had left a copy of the *Standard* on the seat next to his. He unfolded it and looked at the front page.

'FILM CLUE TO BUILDING SITE MURDER' was the three-deck headline.

'While rumours escalate concerning the condition of the body of a man discovered by demolition workers earlier today in central London, police refuse to comment,' the report started. 'Contractors at the busy site located at the south end of Tottenham Court Road in the heart of London's West End spotted the body of a man, thought to be middle-aged and to have been lying undiscovered for several years, in the crumbling foundations of a former cinema. Unconfirmed reports suggest the body was wrapped in coils of celluloid film, which could have been used to strangle the deceased. Cont. page 2. See page 3: Future of luxury development in doubt.

Page 12: The *Standard*'s Film Editor Alexander Walker on Screen Violence.'

'They don't *know* it was murder,' Angelo muttered to himself, picturing Iain Burns slumped forward on the old, sheet-covered sofa in the abandoned cinema. 'They only *think* it was murder.'

3 · The Blue Posts

London, a few months earlier – spring 1998

Back in the spring, before the body was discovered across the street from his flat, Frank drank beer with Yasmin in the Blue Posts. He also drank in the Blue Posts with Siân, who liked vodka and ice. The Blue Posts was where he used to go in the past with Sarah, who would get through a glass of wine for every pint he sank. And when he wanted to meet other women, whatever they might prefer to drink, his chosen venue didn't take much figuring out – it was the Blue Posts.

Frank's enthusiasm for women, like his appetite for drink, was insatiable, but he wasn't stupid. After all, he was nearing forty and he'd picked up a few tricks in his time.

There were four pubs around Soho that went by the name of the Blue Posts.

The film magazine Frank worked for had its editorial offices on Wardour Street in Soho, and the first woman who made an impression on Frank that spring was Siân, the picture editor of the magazine. The editor, Tom, pointed her out when he was showing Frank round on his first day, but she was at the end of a long, narrow room jammed on both sides with filing cabinets filled with movie stills, and she was on the phone. She turned around in her swivel chair, still holding the phone to her ear with one hand and twirling her hair with the other. She continued to speak into the phone and Frank met her distracted gaze for a moment, thinking that it was a long time since he had seen anyone so devastatingly attractive anywhere other than on a cinema screen. The low wintry sun, which came straight down the street and directly in through the window, set fire to her mass of auburn curls.

The next time Frank saw Siân was that afternoon. It wasn't a big office but still he felt he needed an excuse to go and see the picture editor. He had a look at the list of previews he was due to attend in the coming week, and saw that it included a new release by a young director whose name was increasingly being mentioned alongside that of Patrick Keiller, an architect whose appreciation of light and space found another form of expression in the cinema. It wouldn't be unreasonable to go and ask Siân if she had stills from Keiller's features, *London* and *Robinson in Space*. So he pushed his chair back from his workstation and made his way across to the picture desk, and when he got there, he saw that there was a man sitting on Siân's desk swinging his legs under the worktop. Siân was sitting forward in her seat, resting her elbow on the desk and grinning at the man, who reviewed new video releases for the magazine and who was called Christopher and who, as far as Frank was concerned, must be either gay or very strange if he wasn't enjoying the view down the front of Siân's top.

They both turned to look in Frank's direction. Christopher was smiling politely at him and Siân looked questioningly – she had Fanny Ardant's broad forehead and Sigourney Weaver's square jaw – obviously wondering what request he might be about to make. Frank, unusually for him in this kind of situation, suddenly felt awkward.

'Do we have any *London* pictures?' he asked, becoming flustered when he saw the baffled looks on the faces of Siân and Christopher.

'I mean the movie *London*, directed by Patrick Keiller, you know?'

Siân and Christopher exchanged a look, then she said, 'Try under L,' gesturing in the direction of the filing cabinets.

'Yes, sure. Right. L,' Frank muttered as he knelt to read the label on the nearest of the filing cabinets. 'L. Here it is. Thanks.'

He flicked through the Ls distractedly, wishing that Siân and Christopher would resume their conversation. He pulled out one cellophane wrapper after another, trying to read the titles on the adhesive labels, but all he could see was himself and Siân having sex on the sanded wooden floor between the filing cabinets, the drawers sliding open above their heads and thousands of stills spilling out and showering them, slapping on to his bare buttocks. The thought made him smile to himself as he pulled out a set of stills marked '*London*'.

'Thanks,' he said as he stood up. 'I'll let you have these back soon.'

A couple of days later, Frank was at a screening in a preview theatre in a Dean Street basement and he was just reaching for the last triangular prawn sandwich on the tray when he noticed another hand doing the very same thing. As he apologised and withdrew, he looked up and saw the owner of the other hand, a short woman with dark hair and glittery eyes, a petite, slightly *retroussé* nose and bright, shiny teeth. Her skin was olive-coloured and bore a moist sheen. 'Go ahead,' he said with a smile. 'Frank,' he introduced himself, also naming the magazine he worked for. 'I'm new. Four days a week. I used to be freelance.'

'Yasmin,' she said, holding out her hand. 'I still am. Freelance. I like being able to pick and choose. Take it or leave it. No strings.'

'I remember.'

They got a couple of beers and went into the screening together. It was a fairly standard Hollywood thriller and therefore it contained a couple of fairly standard Hollywood thriller sex scenes, during the second of which Yasmin turned her head and rolled her eyes at Frank. He returned the look and when the lights went on he leaned across and asked her if she might like to get a beer somewhere near by and discuss the movie. Yasmin said she would like to do that, so they climbed the stairs together, surrounded by the ritual murmur of film critics tiredly setting about their task.

Frank took Yasmin a couple of blocks to the Blue Posts on Berwick Street. When it came to taking Siân out, they would go elsewhere.

Yasmin was going out with a musician, she told him as they perched on stools by the bar, but he was in Europe touring with his band. She sat slightly forward on her bar stool, the better, it seemed, to show off her breasts. After a couple of drinks apiece, they were both fairly open about the fact that she was showing him her breasts and that he was enjoying looking at them. After a third drink he heard himself make a remark about them and Yasmin sat forward on her seat a little more, so that there should be no misunderstanding.

'I live very close to here,' Frank said.

Sometimes, after sex in Frank's flat on Tottenham Court Road, a girl would leave and flag down a cab to get home, either of her own volition, or because Frank let it be known that that was the way he wanted it to be. He would never kick a girl out if she was begging to stay, or at least he believed he would never do. On this occasion, Yasmin fell soundly asleep while Frank remained awake. He climbed out of bed, taking care not to wake her, and pulled the duvet up to her chin, then moved into the main room of the flat.

He made a mug of black coffee and took it over to the desk by the window. He opened up the PowerBook and hit a random key to wake the machine up. Two file icons appeared in the window of the folder marked 'New Stuff'. One was his story on the Gaiety cinema and its former neighbours; the other was more personal, an in-depth piece on visions of Heaven in the cinema (Frank intended to do a book on the subject; the feature was intended to get him started on the text). They were ideas he'd proposed in his interview for the job at the magazine, and Tom had been sufficiently enthusiastic to give them both the go-ahead. Not only that, but he also imposed a comically implausible deadline that Frank, being new in the job, sensed was non-negotiable. So now he had to write the damn things. Not that he didn't enjoy doing that kind of stuff: he'd applied for a staff writer's position at that magazine rather than certain others because he'd known there was a fair chance they'd actually want to print the kind of articles he liked to write. While the more commercial magazines were fighting over cover stories on Leonardo Di Caprio, and double-page spreads on Kate Winslet 'at home', Tom's magazine could plough its own highbrow furrow as long as the subscribers continued to lend their support. Tom had made concessions, such as Christopher's two-page coverage of video releases, and he would occasionally spend the extra half-day getting a cover line just right in order to tempt a few more sales off the news-stands, but the magazine was essentially the same creature it had been at its launch thirty years earlier.

The Gaiety piece (Frank had turned to gaze across the street) was about the first cinema to open on Tottenham Court Road, and three others in the same block. His research had taken him back to 1910. Few people who plodded through the shanty town of fast-food lean-tos and hi-fi rip-off joints that was Tottenham Court Road at the tail end of the second millennium would guess it had enjoyed such a glorious past.

The idea for the Gaiety feature had come from Angelo.

Frank had made a short film with Angelo and Richard Charnock and Harry Foxx in 1983. As far as Frank was aware, there had been little contact between any of the four of them since, although Frank and Harry Foxx had met up once or twice, and Angelo had remained in touch sporadically, urging

Frank to write something on his pet subject – cinemas that had been abandoned, disused, closed down, turned into offices, massage parlours, whatever. Since moving into the building on Tottenham Court Road in the mid-90s and researching the street's history for his own interest, Frank had been turning over Angelo's request in his mind. A piece on the history of London's picture houses did seem relevant now that the lights were beginning to go out in many of the rep cinemas.

Frank opened the window and leaned out so he could see further down the road towards the junction with Oxford Street and Charing Cross Road. A hundred yards short of Oxford Street, on the corner of Hanway Street, was another Blue Posts pub, one that Frank knew well. He decided that that would be the one where he would take Siân, when she agreed to go out for a drink with him. This particular Blue Posts didn't have good associations for him; in fact, he'd avoided entering the pub at all in the fifteen years since 1983. Going there with Siân could be just what was needed to lay that ghost to rest.

Frank's eyes moved to the right, to the row of sex shops, Greek chippies and mobile phone merchants, which were all in darkness. They'd been dark during the daytime for the past week as well – the row was earmarked for demolition. In fact, the demolition guys appeared already to have started around the back.

Yasmin departed early the next morning while Frank was still asleep. She left her phone number but no other note, which Frank decided was reasonably cool and so he thought that maybe he would see her again. It was quite a big maybe, however. To a carnal explorer such as Frank, penetration of the interior became an end in itself. Pretty immature behaviour for a guy in his late thirties, it had been pointed out on more than one occasion, but he was hardly the only man in London carrying on in this way.

He worked on the Gaiety piece most of the day after the

night spent with Yasmin, stopping by Siân's desk several times with requests for pictures he guessed she either wouldn't have or would take quite a bit of time to find. So he got to hang around her desk and talk to her. She asked him how he was settling in.

'OK – I think,' he said. 'It's going to take a while.'

'I hope we've not been too unfriendly.'

'No, it's just . . . you come into an office where everyone knows everyone else, knows who's married and who's not. Whereas, when you're the new boy, you're asking someone if they take milk and sugar, while what you really want to know is do they go home to someone or is it a different bed every night. If that makes any sense.'

'Perfect sense. You're a power freak.'

He laughed.

'In case you were wondering,' she continued, 'milk, no sugar.'

Frank laughed again and said he should get on. 'It won't get written otherwise, and I'll be back to freelancing.'

Half an hour later he took her a cup of tea (milk, no sugar) and when she looked up and smiled he asked her, 'Do you want to get a proper drink after work, grab a beer or something?'

'Or something?'

'There's a place I haven't been to for a long time and they're knocking it down. I want to see inside again before it's gone for good.'

Sometimes you just know, right at the beginning of the evening, whether you're going to end up in bed together. You see it in a multitude of signs. She sits close enough for you to feel her arm against yours when she lifts her glass. She holds a look longer than is necessary. Or she shoves a hand down your jeans beneath the table.

Siân did none of these.

And yet, it was far from obvious that the evening was a

non-starter. Even with his experience, Frank was perplexed. The signs came thick and fast, but they were contradictory. Siân kept pace with him and they both got a bit tipsy. She looked at him from under her hair when it fell over her face, but as a come-on it was not unambiguous. If she hadn't been a colleague he would probably have either cut his losses and left or made a direct play to force the issue. He didn't have much time for games-playing. Sarah had never played games. In respect of her self-possession, however, Siân did remind him of Sarah.

They were in the Blue Posts on the corner of Hanway Street and Tottenham Court Road. He mentioned the fact that his flat was just across the road, but Siân failed to come back with exactly the right response that would indicate her desire to accompany him back to it.

Deadline anxiety in conjunction with the problem of Siân conspired to give him a splitting headache and he soon heard himself making his apologies. They wished each other good-night outside the tube station (Siân lived in Camden) and he hurried back to his flat. In the lift going up to the eighth floor, he stared at his reflection in the mirror. He pinched the skin of his cheeks and pulled it away from the bone, then lifted his chin and patted the skin underneath. With his left hand he felt his stomach, which he knew could do with some attention. It wasn't that he ate too much, just that he ate badly: prawn sandwiches smeared with mayonnaise at screenings; crisps, peanuts, beer.

Frank had a broken night's sleep and he could have done without a wake-up call.

Especially one from Yasmin.

'How did you get this number?' he asked.

'Phone book.'

'I went ex-directory.'

'I've got last year's phone book.'

Alarm bells rang in Frank's head.

'What time is it, for fuck's sake?'

'It's eight thirty. I waited till I thought even you'd be up.'

'I hate to be rude,' he lied, 'but I have to go back to sleep. Will it keep?'

'I just wondered if you wanted to go for a drink at lunchtime?'

The alarm bells grew louder and Frank wondered if he might have to stop seeing Yasmin after all.

'Can't, I'm afraid. I'll call you.' He barely waited for her to react before hanging up.

Siân was off sick. Frank spent the morning wondering if he should call her at home to see how she was, but couldn't decide and so did nothing. He got through the afternoon by drumming furiously on his keyboard and by five o'clock gave up and rang Yasmin to suggest they meet for another beer.

Yasmin bore no grudge, so he ended up in the Blue Posts on Berwick Street after work. They had several beers each and took a cab back to Frank's place where they had sex in the main room. Yasmin got up on the window ledge and Frank climbed on to his chair to fuck her. His chin resting on her shoulder as he thrust inside her, he looked at the row of shops opposite where demolition had now begun in earnest. The Greek chippy had moved to new premises on Oxford Street. No one would miss the other dumps, apart from a few sad porn freaks and PC-heads dying to be ripped off on two metres of coaxial cable and a modem the speed of an Andrei Tarkovsky movie.

Within twenty minutes Yasmin had left the apartment and headed off in the direction of the tube.

Arriving at work the following day, Frank found a pile of photographs lying in a cellophane wallet on his desk. Obviously, Siân was back. He shuffled through them and to his delight realised that these were old shots of the four cinemas that had stood opposite the site of his apartment building in the early part of the century – the Gaiety (opened on 4 December 1909), Grand Central (12 February 1910), the Majestic Picturedrome (4 May 1912) and the Carlton (October 1913). The Gaiety became the Sphere News Theatre and closed in 1940. The others all went through name changes and different ownership, too, and closed within a few months of each other in 1976.

He went to see Siân.

'Siân, thanks. They're brilliant.'

'I'm so glad,' she said. 'What are?'

'The pics.'

'Oh, right. You're welcome.'

It gave Frank no special kick to be running two girlfriends (plus the odd one-night stand, which was where the Blue Posts on Kingly Street came in handy), but juggling the dates and the times and the pubs and the women seemed to be within his capabilities, so he saw no reason to stop. As long as he kept the locations within the established pattern, he felt in control. The only time recently that things had spun out of control was after he'd led a media studies workshop in a school in an unfamiliar part of London, and he had gone for a drink afterwards with one of the staff. Both of them got falling-over drunk and ended up getting a cab back to her place, where they had sex. Frank had fled in the middle of the night, running through the unknown streets until he stumbled across a cab. He'd not even asked the woman her name.

As long as he remained in control, he was fine. He didn't worry about Siân or Yasmin calling him at home, because since the morning of Yasmin's surprise phone call he kept the ringer turned down and the answering machine switched on (with the volume down).

Walking down the row of condemned shops, Frank confirmed his suspicion that demolition had started from the rear of the block working inwards, so that the façades were now all

that remained. It looked very much like a movie set. At the end
of the row, the Blue Posts curiously remained intact.

When he reached the office he suggested to Siân that
they should pay the pub another visit, as it could be their last
chance. She raised her eyebrow, as if Frank had intended some
inference to be drawn.

It was a misty night; subtle coronas clung to the streetlamps.
'I love Hanway Street,' Frank said. They passed Bradley's Spanish
Bar, a jeweller's, a shop specialising in rare vinyl, a bar that
seemed to change hands every six months. Frank pointed out
the Mondrian-styled façade of the offices of the Recorded
Picture Company, which Siân didn't need pointing out to her.
The Troy Club looked and sounded as lively as ever. Vinyl
Experience had closed down; the Japanese restaurant was
empty. The premises on the end of the row now seemed to be
used for a never-ending series of 'golf sales'. As they neared the
Blue Posts from the rear, Frank became aware that they had
missed their chance. The pub was dark. They peered through
the grimy windows. Work had already begun on tearing the
place apart. The pump handles had gone and the bottles had
disappeared from behind the bar. The chairs had been moved
to one end of the narrow room and there were already a couple
of holes in the floorboards, as if the place were crumbling away.

Frank imagined breaking in with Siân and crawling into one
of the holes in the floor to see what lay beneath. Perhaps there
would be enough room for them both to lie side by side, as if
they were children hiding from the grown-ups, and then he
would touch her, gently, and she would touch him back.

Siân's hand on his arm interrupted his reverie.

'Maybe we should do something different instead. We could
go somewhere tomorrow. Camden perhaps.'

The following day was a Saturday and Frank had already
earmarked it for working on his features, because he was
increasingly aware that time was running out, but he was finding that Siân exerted a peculiar pull over him. He couldn't

think of anyone else since Sarah who would have got anywhere at all by suggesting a trip to Camden. He felt that he'd out-grown Camden.

'OK,' he agreed. 'Look, I live across the road. Why don't you come up. I've got a bottle of Stolly in the freezer. No pressure, no hassle. Just a drink, then I'll call you a cab and tomorrow we'll go to Camden.'

Siân thought about it.

'OK,' she said brightly. 'I'm curious to see your place anyway.'

Next morning, Frank went straight to the windows in the main room. Across the street, the entire row had been flattened, with the exception of the Blue Posts, of which only the shell remained.

Siân had cabbed it home the night before. They hadn't even held hands or kissed. Frank wondered if there might not actually be something refreshing about this whole taking-it-slowly business.

He showered and grabbed a black coffee before heading out to meet Siân. They walked down Parkway, Frank scowling at the Odeon.

'Do you remember when this was the Parkway?' he asked. 'Best cinema in London. Where else would you get the manager playing the piano in the foyer, then introducing the film? Big screen, too. It was wonderful. Now look at that. Maybe Angelo's right.'

'Who?'

'Old mate of mine. Loves old cinemas. Hates shit-holes like this – you can see his point.'

'Could have been worse,' she said. 'They could have converted it into offices like they intended to. What is it with you and these old cinemas anyway?'

'It was Angelo got me interested in it. He's been going on at me about it for years. Now I'll be lucky if I make my deadline.'

'If you'd rather be at home working . . .'

'That's not what I meant.'

Frank fell silent as they passed the former Plaza.

'I didn't mean anything,' Siân said, looking at him.

The old cinema was lost behind stalls selling hand-printed T-shirts.

'I used to know someone who worked there,' he said. 'It's sad.'

They wandered into the market, where they idly flicked through racks of LPs, sorted through yellowing books, each nudging the other when they turned up anything relating to film.

It felt alarmingly like being out with a girlfriend.

4 · The House

London, spring 1998

In his house in North Kensington, Harry Foxx looked up from his desk at the wall above it. A poster for *Nine South Street* met his gaze. Gareth Sangster, who played the killer in the film, emerged from darkness hiding half his face behind a camera. Harry's eye trailed across the credits and paused at the point where it always did: 'Written and directed by Harry Foxx.'

He got up from his desk and went to the window and looked out. He saw what he always saw when he looked out of his window, a brick wall, and it hadn't changed much at all since he had last spent twenty minutes studying it.

He sat down again and looked at the laptop sitting on his desk.

Three files of interest sat on the desktop: 'Current Projects', *MPD* and Backgammon. 'Current Projects' was just a list, the contents of which would get reordered every couple of days or so according to Harry's assessment of their likelihood of ever getting off the ground. Things would get cut and pasted into a folder that lived on the hard disk called 'Current Projects (Dropped)'. *MPD* was the project to which Harry was currently devoting most of his time and energy – in theory at least. It was the only project that had a producer attached. The producer was Harry's longtime colleague Lawrence Gold, who had already had meetings with a couple of funding bodies about *MPD*, which was devised as a low-budget thriller set in north-west London. The double meaning that was subtly implicit in the title – MPD was a handy acronym for both multiple personality disorder and motive power depot – signalled the content of the script, since it concerned itself with a serial killer who hung around railway sidings.

Harry tried to have no expectations regarding their chances of securing funding from either of the organisations Lawrence had been to see, but he couldn't help having his hopes built up. It was getting pathological, but what could he do? Stop hoping for a breakthrough? Switch careers and work in a medium that didn't require millions of pounds to realise your dreams? Neither option was in fact an option. If he gave up hope, he'd lose his identity, which was bound up with being a film-maker. At thirty-eight he was beyond change. As for doing something different, he couldn't see that either. He'd earned no qualifications beyond a degree from art school, and had no talent for anything other than making films. Surely someone, somewhere, would back the director of *Nine South Street* to make a second feature. One or two of the more left-field critics in the business had argued the case, however obliquely (a few positive words about *Nine South Street*, as far as Harry Foxx was concerned, were tantamount to a campaign). What mattered was to keep going, to persevere, to work tirelessly at whatever project looked closest to fruition and then to work on the others, to build them up, to stoke their tiny, internal fires. Never stop, never give up, and above all, never get distracted.

Harry double-clicked the Backgammon file and played three games against the machine, losing each one.

He would have played on, but the phone rang. It was Lawrence to tell him that one of the funding bodies had turned them down. Lawrence then outlined a new plan: to find a co-producer.

'Who've you got in mind?' asked Harry.

'Guy called Ritchie McCluskey. Great CV. Been around a bit. Knows people. Be a good move, I think. But let's wait and see.'

When Lawrence had rung off, Harry Foxx paced up and down the futility room. He and Janine had so christened the room that would eventually be his office when they viewed the house for the first time. They had done so ironically, since they'd bought the house in a flush of confidence in the wake of *Nine South Street*'s completion. Stuck on to the back of the house and accessed via the kitchen, it had featured in the estate agent's blurb as the utility room.

Harry paced for ten minutes, put on a CD and took it off again after a couple of bars. He looked at his watch. Janine would be home in half an hour and at some point during the evening was bound to ask if he had paid the phone bill, the electric bill and the council tax, and he would have to admit that he hadn't. He hadn't paid them because they couldn't afford to pay them. Nor could they afford to take the car into a garage and get the starter motor replaced. As long as they were surviving on Janine's salary, and Harry's contribution remained at zero, the bills would mount up.

He sat down and created a new file, calling it 'Money'. In it he listed a few of the ways in which he might possibly raise some extra cash.

1. Teaching
2. Unfocus groups
3. Corporate videos
4. Sell body
5. Drive Richard's car

He'd taught courses in film studies and film-making at Bristol and would do it again if he absolutely had to. The problem was that you had to sign up for a whole course and so if one of Harry's projects suddenly got legs he'd have a problem.

Lawrence Gold ran focus groups for large commercial clients, including a number of TV companies. They were his main source of income; without them, working with Harry would be a luxury he couldn't afford. Lawrence had invited Harry to join him in planning and executing the sessions, which Harry invariably referred to as unfocus groups to reflect how much use he thought they were to anybody and anything.

'Show me a focus group that clamours for another film by the creators of *Nine South Street*,' Harry Foxx told Lawrence, 'and I'll come and join you.'

The closest Harry had come to the so-called non-broadcast television industry was having watched a few corporate videos when assessing potential cinematographers for a movie project that almost happened but of course collapsed at the last minute. They were anathema to him. They made him feel ill. There was only a hair's breadth between doing corporate work and going out on the streets and selling his body, which he knew he would much rather do than drive Richard's car.

The fact that Richard's offer had made it on to Harry's list at all, however, was an indication that he was prepared to consider it. Richard Charnock, who had not been in touch for some time, had called Harry that morning after Janine had gone to work and asked if Harry would meet him for a drink at the House to discuss a job offer.

'Do you know the House?' Richard had asked.

'If you mean Soho House, then yes,' Harry had replied testily.

Soho House was the kind of place Harry Foxx and Richard Charnock would have had strong opinions about in the old days. They would have hated it, as would Angelo and Frank. They would have hated what it was and what it stood for. They would have hated its exclusivity. Richard would have hated it primarily because it would have excluded him, while Harry would have hated it for excluding anybody. The fact that

Richard had suggested they meet there was less revealing about Richard's attitude towards Soho House than the shorthand he had used. The fact that members called it 'the House' and assumed that everyone knew what they were talking about was what, these days, Harry Foxx hated more than anything else about the club.

It made him hate Soho House more than he hated the Groucho or Black's, the Union Club or the Cobden. If you wanted to meet someone at the Groucho Club, you'd say, 'See you at the Groucho,' and that would be fine, dropping the 'Club' because it was redundant; there was no other Groucho where you might go to meet someone. But Soho House members would say, 'See you at the House,' as if there were only one house in London, when there were several million. And this one, this one so-called house in the middle of Soho, by implication thought itself more important than several million other houses. It was more important than Harry's house or Richard's house. It was 'the House' and it pissed Harry Foxx off. But not as much as the fact that he spent half his life in the place. He wasn't a member, obviously, but most of London's film community was, and five out of ten meetings would take place at the House, whether Harry Foxx liked it or not.

Harry arrived on time and settled into an armchair in the bar, a glass of lager by his hand. He contrived not to exude pissed-offness, which became increasingly difficult as the minutes ticked by and still Richard failed to make an appearance. Finally, he turned up, fifteen minutes late.

'Harry!' Richard's outstretched hand preceded him across the room. 'It's been too long.'

Harry got to his feet to return the greeting and immediately noticed Richard's clothes. Back in the early 1980s, they'd all dressed scruffily, but for different reasons. Angelo and Frank filled their wardrobes with second-hand gear from Camden and Portobello markets. Harry's former policy of shopping only at Oxfam and Mind struck him now as somewhat naive, but the fact was that he'd given more to charity fifteen years ago than he did nowadays. He considered himself a charity case, after all, and always wore one of a number of denim shirts with a pair of jeans and a deceptively inexpensive Gap leather jacket. His long fair hair was usually caught in a rainbow-patterned towelling scrunch. Richard, on the other hand, had only ever wanted to blend in, so in 1983 he'd dressed like his peers, and now he was clearly doing the same. If he didn't wear Calvin Klein pants and a Paul Smith jacket, he'd stand out in 'the House'. His hair was as thick and wavy as it had been fifteen years earlier, but now it was carefully styled. All this to remain invisible.

'Harry. Sit down. How are you? What's going on? I must get a drink. Let me get you another drink.'

Harry didn't need another drink, but when the girl came, Richard ordered a JD with ice for himself and the same again for Harry.

'Cheers, mate,' said Richard. 'It's good to see you.'

Mate.

They sat and looked at each other for a few moments. Richard rocking forwards in his chair and Harry sitting back, vaguely ill at ease.

'So, what are you working on, Harry? What's the current project?'

Harry took a swallow of his beer.

'You know how it is. Trying to get some money together to make a film. There's only so many favours you can pull in, you know?'

'Jesus, tell me about it,' said Richard. 'It never seems to get any easier.' Although, of course, it was a great deal easier for Richard than it was for Harry, as both Richard and Harry knew, but Harry was prepared to let Richard play that game if he wanted to. It didn't mean anything. It didn't humiliate Harry. Harry knew the score. He knew that the goalposts moved a little as you got to be more successful, but they didn't move that much. Someone like Richard Charnock didn't find it that difficult to raise the money to fund his next movie.

'I'm trying to work out what you want,' Harry said.

'Harry. Why do I have to want something? I know we've not been in touch a great deal, but it takes two to lose contact, you know. I've been following what you've been up to with great interest.'

'Yeah? Well, it doesn't take that much effort to keep track of a film-maker who never makes a film. Whereas you've certainly been busy.'

Richard dismissed this with a gesture. 'There was—' And he froze. Harry's one full-length feature and Richard had forgotten its title.

Harry wasn't going to help him. Instead he raised his glass ironically to Richard's humiliation and swallowed a mouthful of beer.

It had been five years ago. Hardly so long ago it existed only on nitrate stock and lived in a vault in Berkhamsted. It had had a partial theatrical release. Very partial. A week at the Everyman, plus selected regional art houses. The reviews had been mixed. Two interviews had been done, for the *Guardian* and *Time Out*. The *Guardian* had spiked theirs; *Time Out* cut Tom Charity's piece from three pages down to one and ended up running it after the stint at the Everyman had finished, changing its tone from 'New independent British film sparks industry renaissance' to 'British film industry in crisis'.

'*Nine South Street*,' Richard barked, the title somehow coming back to him. 'Yeah? I mean, that's not that long ago. It was a good movie. It did OK, I seem to remember.'

'It was what I think they call a cult hit. No one went to see it, mainly because it wasn't on anywhere, but everyone was talking about it. It played for two weeks, in cinemas the size of your front room. Well, my front room.'

Richard took his cigarettes out of his jacket pocket and lit up.

'Cigarette?' he offered.

'Given up.'

'Given up?'

'Necessary sacrifice,' Harry explained. Richard looked blankly back at him. 'Can't afford them,' Harry elaborated.

Richard dropped the pack on to the table between them.

'Look,' he said, 'I've got to have a slash. Back in a minute.'

As soon as he'd gone, Harry reached over and picked up Richard's cigarettes. Richard evidently still kept the bottom bit of the cellophane wrapper on the pack until he'd finished it. And Harry, for all Richard's having taken an age to remember the title of his only film, would still gain a shred of enjoyment from removing it and slipping it back on over the top of the pack. He replaced the pack on the table and looked out of the window. A line of black cabs waited to cross Old Compton Street, nosing forward out of Greek Street. Cycle couriers leaned this way and that, irritating pedestrians, slaloming around angry drivers.

Richard returned from the loo and stubbed out his cigarette.

'I've seen your name about more recently as well. You've certainly been in the news with something. Is there a new film or what?'

'There's no new film, but not for the want of trying,' Harry replied. 'Well, yeah, there's a new film, there's always a new film, but there's no money to make it. The money from the last teaching job I did has just about run out and I'm going to have to go out and find another one. So far I've sunk about four grand of my own money into this bloody film. You've no idea, Richard, no idea.'

Richard said nothing for a moment, but just watched as Harry recomposed himself. Before replying, he reached for his cigarettes and immediately realised what Harry had done.

'Very funny, Harry. Very funny,' he said. 'Just like old times. Look, I've got an offer to put to you.'

Harry, feeling a lift inside his chest, cautioned: 'Look, Richard, you know our ideas about film are very different.'

'Not that kind of offer.'

Deflated: 'Oh.'

'Do you still enjoy driving?'

Harry looked puzzled.

'I seem to remember you giving me lifts places, bombing about in that death trap.'

'I got rid of the Mini a while ago, but yes, I still like driving. Janine drives an old Volvo. I drive that now. Or I do when it goes.'

'Janine?'

'My girlfriend. We've been together six years. You met her when the ICA did that thing on snuff movies three years ago. Remember?'

'I prefer to forget.'

Richard fumbled the cellophane off the top of the pack and got out a cigarette and lit it, his sudden briskness signalling a more businesslike approach. As if he had another meeting to get to.

'OK, look,' he said, knocking back the rest of his Jack Daniels and leaning forward. 'If you remember, in the old days the reason you gave me lifts places occasionally was because I didn't drive. Well, I still don't drive. So I need a driver and I'm thinking do you want the job? Do you want to be my driver? Good pay, shit conditions – you'd be working for me. What do you say?'

Harry thought about it while Richard went to the loo. The worrying frequency of Richard's trips to the gents' notwithstanding, Harry tended towards acceptance, but couldn't make up his mind. As soon as Richard came back, wiping his nose, Harry asked him to define 'good pay'. Richard quoted a figure that he would have known would be more than enough to keep Harry happy, but Harry looked doubtful.

'I don't know. It's a difficult decision. It's not the money.'

Richard reached for a cigarette and raised the offer by twenty per cent.

Harry said he'd think about it.

By the day's end, when Janine came home, Harry Foxx had decided, despite its place in fifth position on his list, to accept Richard's offer. For one thing, because Richard had said Harry could keep the car whenever Richard wasn't going to need it, it meant they didn't have to get the Volvo fixed. Besides, Harry couldn't deny that he was a little fired up at the prospect of driving the S-class Mercedes.

5 · The disappearance

Suffolk/London, 1982

Iain Burns had always been an undemonstrative man, which was ironic, his wife Penny told me in the back of my jeweller's shop, when you considered what he did for a living. Six days a week at five thirty p.m., he would get into his family saloon (another irony) and drive twelve miles to Ipswich. He would leave the car by Christchurch Park and walk to the Ipswich Eye Cinema where he would wish the day manager and the box office staff a good evening. They would return the greeting and he would shut himself in the projection booth to prepare the reels for that evening's programme.

Iain Burns had been the Eye Cinema's chief projectionist ever since the original cinema, in Eye, had been forced to move south in search of bigger audiences. That had been four years earlier, in 1978. Burns had been the assistant projectionist at Eye, working under Irmin Hegel, a former German prisoner of war who had elected to stay in Britain after 1945. With the closure of the Eye, Hegel retired to a seafront maisonette in Southwold, and Burns was promoted. It was ideal for him, with the wages rising and Ipswich being closer to home.

Iain and Penny lived quietly in Felixstowe, in their pre-war semi. Iain enjoyed driving and Penny liked being driven, so on a Sunday they would speed down to London and spend the day driving around the deserted City, criss-crossing the Thames, taking in a film at the NFT or the Everyman, and returning home in the dark. Iain was not much given to displays of affection, so when he did place his left hand gently on Penny's knee in the car it meant all the more to Penny. Her eyes reflected the glimmer of the dash. Towards the end he started to do this sort of thing more. His upbringing (Iain's father, a Londoner who moved to south Birmingham when he entered the church, was strict) had contributed to a certain reserve. As a teenager he had only ever felt free in one place: the dark. The dark of a smoky picture house, of which Birmingham had many. Alone in the dark, he had felt the emotional straitjacket loosen a few notches. In certain old movies he even cried, but this was a secret he shared with no one until he met Penny, and even then he only told her once, late at night as they lay in bed watching the moon's reflection in the windows of the Hotel Paradise across the road from their house.

Also as an effect of his upbringing, with its bleak domestic routine, Iain suffered from low self-esteem. Penny demanded little of him, but a small part of Iain always felt unworthy of his wife's devotion. He never forgave his family for the stand they made by not attending his wedding. Penny had not wanted to marry in a church, and they had gone ahead with a civil ceremony in Ipswich, Iain's former boss Irmin Hegel coming down from Southwold to be best man.

Iain was prey to a nagging belief that he was a dis-appointment to Penny. It was not true and whenever she became aware of the problem Penny would make the point to Iain with passion and vehemence.

'How can you be happy,' he asked her, 'with a projectionist?'

Penny had been an academic at Aston University (they met at the Imperial on Moseley Road in Balsall Heath) and had given it up to move to East Anglia and start a family with Iain, only to find once they had left jobs and moved south that they were unable to have children, following which, Penny drifted into a life of dependence upon Iain.

'I'm perfectly happy,' she told him. 'I've got everything I need.'

This was as much as Penny knew and therefore as much as she was able to tell me after we started meeting up and talking in the spring of 1998. She didn't know about the first appearance of Iain's symptoms. He didn't tell her about the occasional clumsiness, the sudden weakness in his hands and the vision impairment. He took the trouble to conceal it from her when shooting pains attacked his arms and legs. She didn't know that when he said he was going to London to an EGM of the Cinema Projectionists' Guild (she wasn't sure of the name; in fact, no such body exists), he was actually keeping a second appointment with a Harley Street neurologist.

I know all of this because I talked to people, later. Afterwards.

He'd been for tests two weeks previously, having ostensibly travelled down to see an extensive collection of old projectors at the Muswell Hill Odeon (he saw the collection in the morning, then drove down to Harley Street and parked on a meter. The neurologist took a history, examined him, checked his reflexes and took samples of blood and cerebrospinal fluid, and asked him to come back in a fortnight).

If it turned out to be bad news, he wanted to make sure that no one knew, no one who might tell Penny. If he went to see his GP in Felixstowe and had his worst fears confirmed, he was worried that the doctor might tell Penny, Hippocratic oath or no. (His judgement had already started to be affected.) If he had MS, as he suspected, he didn't want Penny to know, because there was nothing to be gained by her knowing. His decline would be inevitable, perhaps swift, and it would be better dealt with in his own way. His father had succeeded better than he would ever have believed in drumming into Iain the belief that he should stand on his own two feet. He would die on them, too.

Making the return visit to Harley Street, Burns knew the news was bad as soon as he entered the doctor's consulting room. The doctor wouldn't look him in the eye at first and appeared uncomfortable.

'I'm very sorry,' the doctor said, looking down at his hands.

'I was right, wasn't I?' said Burns. 'It's MS. I've got MS.'

The doctor told him that he did not have MS; he had tertiary syphilis. Burns stared at him, aghast. Finally, the doctor held his gaze.

'I'm afraid there's no question of a misdiagnosis,' said the doctor.

There was a long silence. Finally, he asked Iain if the diagnosis made any sense to him at all.

'National Service,' Burns said quietly. 'I wasn't the only one . . .'

'You were unlucky.'

'This is worse than MS, isn't it?' Burns asked.

'These are not diseases you can really compare.'

'It's worse.'

'It can be treated, but any existing damage cannot be repaired.' The doctor paused. 'You do have some existing damage.'

'Worst-case scenario?'

He told Burns about lesions that would undergo mucoid degeneration, papilloedema that were already causing visual disturbance and would get worse. Ataxia, dysaesthesia, anaesthesia. Aortic aneurysm. Burns listened in stunned silence. Decline in memory and judgement; dementia. Iain might suffer bouts, like the recent spate of symptoms, and at some point they would begin to get worse. He might be well for intermittent spells, but the symptoms would return. By the end, he would be dependent and in constant pain. It was likely that he would go blind. Indeed, his vision could be one of the first things to go.

The doctor asked what he did for a living and Iain told him.

He shook his head slowly and said once more that he was very sorry.

'If you see your GP,' the doctor said, 'he will give you a referral. Treatment will ensure a much greater degree of comfort.'

On leaving Harley Street, instead of collecting the car from beneath Cavendish Square and driving straight home, Iain walked down to the South Bank. He browsed amid the bookstalls by the NFT and bought a paperback, then sat on a bench and gazed out at the great swirling river. As soon as he realised that there were tears rolling down his cheeks, he got up and left. Climbing the steps to the higher level, he passed the Royal Festival Hall and walked up on to Hungerford Bridge. He stopped halfway along the bridge and looked back at the skyline behind him, wondering if it was the last time he would see the grey boxes of the National Theatre and the gaudy tubes of the Hayward Gallery Neon Tower. Having never lived in London, he suddenly wondered if it was necessarily the case that he had missed his chance.

He leaned against the railing until people started offering him money. He looked down at the book he had bought: an edition of *Sweet Bird of Youth*. He had no interest in Tennessee Williams, none whatsoever.

Three weeks later, he disappeared.

Iain's disappearance took the form of his not returning home from the Eye on a Friday night. When Penny called the cinema, no one answered. It was too late; they would be closed for the night. She had waited until he was an hour late before doing anything, and phoning the cinema was the first thing she did. Having done that, she waited another hour before calling the police. They said he hadn't been gone long enough to be a missing person. She tried to remain calm but could not. She pictured the car, out of control, veering off the carriageway at the top of the unfinished Orwell Bridge and smashing through the concrete wall to fall, boot over bonnet, into the estuary. At

the back of her mind was the knowledge that he had been acting strangely in recent weeks: periods of introspection alternating
with spells of manic activity.

Mid-evening on the first Friday in October 1982, Burns
slipped out of the Eye having rigged up his final reel. He walked
to the car and drove slowly down to the docks. Never busy in
those days, the docks were deserted when Iain pulled over and
killed the lights. He left the engine idling while in his mind he
went over his plan for the last time.

Close to the level crossing there were gaps where no wall or
bollard would prevent a car rolling directly into the dock. Iain
didn't know the depth of the water, but it was deep enough for
the small freighters that swayed gently at the quayside.

Iain Burns boarded the last London-bound train of the
evening, having slipped on to the platform without buying a
ticket, so that no one would remember a man of his description
travelling from Ipswich that night. By the time the train pulled
out, the wheels of his car would have become embedded in
twelve inches of mud under several feet of water. Keeping on
the move, Iain avoided any inspectors. There was no control at
Liverpool Street. He pulled up his collar and passed swiftly to
the Underground, where he hopped on a westbound Central
line train, changing at Bank and heading for the Northern line.
At Camden Town he exited the system, intending to look for a
convenient doorway. Having taken no more money than usual
out of his account, he didn't have a lot of cash and a hotel
was out of the question. His credit and cashpoint cards he had
snapped in half and dropped in a bin.

Across from the tube station was the Camden Plaza, as good
a place as any to bed down for the night. In fact, he realised, as
he leaned back and bent at the knees and began to drift off to
sleep, it was appropriate in that he'd not long ago screened
Christopher Petit's first feature, *Radio On*, as part of a road movies
season he'd programmed for the Eye. As he tried to get comfortable, he imagined he saw the lead actor in *Radio On* parking

his car outside the tube station and walking across the street to the Plaza. The film contained scenes both outside the Plaza and upstairs in the Artificial Eye offices. Iain imagined Petit himself coming back, three years after making *Radio On*, to find a stranger dossing down on the set of his movie. He'd park his car across the street, just like the character in the film, and cross over, an 8mm camera in his hand. He'd shake Iain's shoulder and wake him up, proposing a sequel in which Iain would play a cinema projectionist living under a death sentence. Iain would prevaricate – he didn't know if he was cut out for performing, he'd explain. He'd get back to him.

He was trying to work out whether he would prefer it to be black and white or colour when consciousness left him altogether.

6 · The conversation

London, spring 1998

After offering Harry Foxx a job as his driver, Richard Charnock had two more meetings before he could go home. He went to see a casting agent in Marshall Street and some TV people at the Groucho, after which he returned to Holland Park by cab.

As soon as he crossed the threshold he saw that there was a look on the face of Caroline, his girlfriend. It was a look that said don't bring me any of your so-called problems. A look that said I've been looking after two kids all day, so I don't want to hear whatever film industry bullshit it is you think you've just got to tell me.

'Hello, Caroline.'

Caroline swept by the bottom of the stairs after one of the children.

He removed his jacket and hung it up in the corner of the hall.

'What was that?' Caroline had reappeared, her granite face poking round the kitchen doorway.

'Nothing,' he said, staring at the creases in his coat where it hung from the hook. 'It can wait till they're in bed.'

'Can't you bear to spend any time with them at all?'

'Sorry?'

'You don't see them all day, then as soon as you come home you want to shoo them off to bed.'

He wanted to say that they weren't his kids, which they weren't, but that never seemed to work for some reason. Surely it was enough that he put a roof over their heads.

'We'll talk about it later.' He looked up at her. Her mouth was twisted like a hot wire. 'How are the kids? Did you have a good day?'

'Don't change the subject. What was it you wanted to discuss?'

'Nothing. It can wait. It's not important.'

In the kitchen the noise level was rising.

'Don't you think you should go and see if they're all right?'

'I don't know how you've got the gall to tell me how to bring up my children when I spend all day doing just that while you're out at your so-called work.'

'If it wasn't for my so-called work, do you think you'd be living in a place like this?' Richard indicated the size of the kitchen with a sweep of his arm. 'Do you think places like this are just *given* to people?'

Caroline turned away to attend to her two boys.

Later they sat watching television, not exactly at opposite ends of the sofa, but with daylight between them. Or artificial light, since the natural light had gone for another day and Caroline had drawn the curtains on Holland Park and all their diplomatic neighbours.

'Sorry about earlier,' he said.

'Mmm,' Caroline responded, finally adding: 'So am I.'

Richard said, 'I've been thinking of offering Harry a job.'

'Harry? Harry who?'

'Harry. You know. *Harry.*'

Caroline turned to look at Richard.

'You mean Harry Foxx?'

'Yeah, of course I mean Harry Foxx. How many Harrys do I know?'

'You hardly *know* Harry Foxx.'

'True.'

'What's the job?' Caroline asked.

'My driver.'

'Your driver?'

'Yeah, driver. Chauffeur.'

'Why would you want Harry to be your driver?'

'Why would I want Harry to be my driver? Because Harry can drive, darling. Harry can drive and I can't.'

'What I mean is, why not get a professional? Get a chauffeur.'

'Harry's a good driver. You know I don't trust professional chauffeurs. I mean, did you like Robert? Of course you didn't. He was shifty and small-eyed. What did you call him, a sloper?'

'He wasn't very bright. But a chauffeur doesn't need to be bright.'

'No, but they need to be reliable. I need to know I can trust my driver. These guys in their blue blazers and their caps – they're crooks and swindlers. They've no reason to be loyal to me. I'm a rich man. I don't get respect from these guys, just resentment. Working-class boys made good – only they never did. They're working for wealthy execs – how do you think that makes them feel? It makes them more resentful. I can't trust them. I need someone I can trust.'

'I didn't realise you were such a snob.'

'I just can't talk to them. We're from different backgrounds. We live in different parts of town. They're like coppers. Every time they call you "sir", it's so loaded you want to hit them. Whereas I know Harry. I can talk to Harry. Anyway, he needs the money. I'd be doing him a favour.'

'Exactly.'

'What do you mean?'

'You'd be doing him a favour. He'd be beholden to you. Harry would resent you every bit as much. Face it, Richard, everyone hates the rich. Everyone in this country anyway. Your driver will resent you whoever he is.' Caroline drained her wine glass and placed it carefully on a coaster on the glass-topped table. 'Anyway, we're not rich.'

'You're not doing badly. How many times have I offered to employ an au pair?'

'I'd rather raise my kids myself.'

'Well, anyway,' Richard said, 'we're rich compared to Harry. Maybe I owe him one.'

7 · The projectionist

London, October 1982

When Iain Burns woke in the doorway of the Camden Plaza after his first and, he hoped, last night spent on the streets, he ached so badly that all of his other worries were eclipsed by the immediacy of his discomfort. He tried to brush aside thoughts of Penny. She would be going mad with worry and it caused him almost unbearable pain to know that and to do nothing about it. But he repeatedly rationalised his decision. In the long run, doing it his way would cause Penny the least distress, he believed. It would hurt her less than forcing her to witness his inevitable and terrible decline. If he wrote or called, it would only make her determined to come and find him. If there was anyone who could be more stubborn than him, it was Penny.

He stretched and read the Now Showing poster for Werner Herzog's *Fitzcarraldo*, then walked off at a brisk pace down Camden High Street.

From Camden, he walked east, then south. He entered the foyer of the Scala Cinema, a grim, forbidding cathedral to the dark art of cult movies, and helped himself to a copy of their fold-out programme. Leaving King's Cross, he headed south; he wandered down Dickensian alleys, drifted through Inns of Court, chanced one-way traffic systems where the cars, taxi cabs and motorbike couriers showed little mercy. Rain was a constant threat with the looming sky the colour of asphalt. Eventually the tension broke: a few fat drops spotted the pavement ahead of him and Burns ran for cover as the downpour began.

He stood in a doorway on a thoroughfare he couldn't recollect seeing before, whether on foot or through the windscreen of his car. The dark clouds unleashed movie rain, splashing from the pavement into the doorway. Burns watched pedestrians hurry past as they clung to umbrellas. Buses hissed through puddles and black cabs squealed to a halt in long lines of red tail lights and swishing wipers.

I'm going to die, thought Iain. That's my death sentence. I'm going to die.

He gave a bitter little laugh as he hugged himself to keep warm.

I only have twelve months to live. Another death sentence. He stamped his feet. I only have six months to live. Three months. Six weeks. The rain started to ease off slightly. Whatever, he thought.

In fact, like most people, he had no way of knowing how long he had left. And, he had to admit, as a passing bus splashed water over his shoes, he did, for the time being at least, feel alive.

Iain spent his second night in London in a hostel. He had bought a coffee at the NFT and lowered himself on to one of the long, low, moulded seats in the bar. When it grew dark, he moved outside and scavenged leftovers from plates left lying on the long wooden tables.

Instinct took him away from the West End to Brick Lane in search of a cheap bed for the night. Commercial Road yielded a Victorian hostel for men. The following day he walked for miles, from the East End to St Paul's and the Barbican, then London Bridge, Waterloo, all along the South Bank and over the river by Vauxhall Bridge. He stopped at the Tate to see the De Chirico exhibition.

He felt a greater affinity with the artist's skittle-head dummies than with the gallery-shufflers around him. The long shadows cast by doorways and corners and trains seemed pregnant with significance.

On the long hike back to the hostel, Burns noticed that he was walking like a drunk.

The following day, Burns walked back towards the West End. He veered right at Old Street and fetched up in Islington. A few blocks after the Screen on the Green he went left, towards Camden and the offices of Artificial Eye, where he scored a minimum of three shifts a week projecting at the Plaza.

One of the other part-timers at the Plaza had a friend who knew someone who was looking for a lodger. The flat was at Archway; the room was tiny, but the rent was low. Burns took it sight unseen: it couldn't be worse than sleeping with two hundred meths-drinkers in a draughty dorm that stank of stewed carrots and disinfectant.

Burns pressed his thumb against a grimy buzzer and stood back looking up at the windows to see a corner of curtain fall back into place. Presently he heard footsteps and a light came on above the door, which was then opened by a short, wiry man in his mid-twenties. His hair was not quite long enough for the ponytail in which it was tied back. He had uneven, gingery whiskers that looked as if they had been scattered across the lower half of his face like crumbs; eyes that were used to darting over shoulders and round corners for ticket inspectors, housing benefit officers, unattended stage-door entrances. He checked out the street behind Burns, then finally met his gaze.

'My name's Iain Burns.'

'Andrew Kerner,' the man said. 'Come up.'

Iain followed Kerner into the orange hallway. The orange was from a bare bulb, the kind used in log-effect gas fires; the walls were a dirty white, the brown carpet thin, damp and bobbly.

'It's just up here,' Kerner called back over his shoulder as he climbed the steep stairs three at a time. 'It's not a big room, you know.'

The first thing they looked at when they got inside was a cupboard.

'I told you it wasn't very big,' said Kerner.

Burns didn't care. Space was a luxury he couldn't afford, but nor did he need it.

'A week's rent in advance,' Iain said, offering Kerner three notes, which the younger man folded into his back pocket.

'Bathroom,' Kerner declared, pushing open the door nearest to Iain's room. A brown bath mat trodden so flat it was indistinguishable from the carpet; a perished rubber shower attachment coiled in the avocado bath; a collapsed blind, its fabric beginning to bear fruit.

Kerner led Burns down a short corridor, the walls of which were covered with clip-framed black and white photographs: derelict buildings, blighted cityscapes, blurred portraits. They walked up three steps into a kitchen dominated by black and white prints on the walls.

'That's my room through there.' Kerner indicated a doorway on the far side of the kitchen. Iain caught a glimpse of a desk covered with cameras and lenses, photograph wallets and more loose prints, before Kerner pulled the door shut and shoved his hands in his pockets. 'So you work at the Plaza?' he said.

Burns nodded. 'Part-time. The rest of the time I won't be around that much. It's really just somewhere to sleep.'

'Well, there's just about room for that. Never get a double bed in there, though, if you know what I mean.'

'That's fine,' Burns said. 'I'll leave you to get on.'

'I'm kind of in the middle of a job,' Kerner said. He looked down, prodded a piece of food with the toe of his Chinese slipper.

'Kerner's an unusual name,' Burns persevered.

The young man nodded, then turned and disappeared into his room.

Burns surveyed the miserably appointed kitchen – the 'before' picture in a DIY magazine feature – then turned to examine the dozens of photographs on the walls. The majority were portraits, often artistically fuzzy, sometimes, Burns suspected, blurred simply through incompetence. But the photographer clearly had an eye for what he was doing. It was obvious that he was at best single-minded, at worst an obsessive, from the number of times particular people or backdrops cropped up. There were a lot of shots of a man in his early twenties with wavy, dark hair, intense eyes that looked alternately sad and half amused. There was a mole on the left-hand side of his face, near the base of the nose, and a strong, square jaw. He seemed a good subject.

Another face that appeared frequently was that of a man about the same age. His face was thinner with a high forehead and long, wispy fair hair. In some lights his cheekbones were accentuated, giving him a gaunt look that was enhanced also by his perpetual stubble. His eyes looked dreamy, his pupils dilated, as if he'd just woken up after a long, comfortable sleep, or as if he'd spent the ten minutes before each picture was taken smoking strong weed.

There were a few pictures of both these characters together in a group with two others – a very good-looking man, again in his early twenties, with thick, black hair and bright, piercing eyes, and a younger-looking man with short, square-cut fair hair and fine, almost feminine features. In a couple of these group shots, there was some larking about; the bright-eyed man was framing his view of a couple of the others with his hands like a film director; the long-haired, thin-faced man was cupping his hands about his mouth as if shouting to someone out of shot. There seemed to be an easy chemistry between the four of them. And between the four of them and Kerner.

* * *

Burns worked three shifts a week at the Plaza, sometimes four. The rest of the time he haunted rep cinemas, where he got to know the staff and they sometimes let him in for free. He drifted between the Everyman, the Roxie and the Scala. He also went to the NFT; sometimes he just hung out in the bar or read the notices pinned up on the board. A few offered translation services, others script-doctoring. Several individuals desperately needed rooms, bedsits, studios. Under the heading 'Destiny Beckons', a quartet of film-makers calling themselves *auteurs* begged for film stock, cameras and lights in order to make their first short film.

The Roxie was the one place where he'd always happily pay to see a film. It may have been small, but the seats were so big and fat and soft you'd be happy to sit and watch even the slowest Eric Rohmer, the most incomprehensible Marguerite Duras, although the programming actually tended towards the more cultish art-house movies such as *Performance* and *The Shout*, while casting its net in the direction of the mainstream as far as Pink Floyd's *The Wall*. In place of hard rock, the Everyman offered rock-hard seats and a bum-numbing programme that ranged from *Ai No Corrida* to *Zazie dans le métro*. At the Scala, Burns sat through all-nighters featuring the work of Ed Wood, John Waters and the astonishingly explicit George Kuchar.

As he had promised Andrew Kerner, he spent very little time at Archway. One night he came back to the flat after an evening screening to find the kitchen full of young people. The air was thick with smoke and the tireless shuttle of alcohol talking. Since the subject was film and because he recognised them instantly from Kerner's photographs, Burns didn't head for his room but, invited by a gesture from Kerner to stay, filled the kettle and leaned against the sink.

At a break in the conversation, Kerner introduced Burns. 'Everyone, this is Iain Burns. Iain, this is – everyone.' This produced a laugh and the odd grunt. Someone offered Iain a beer, which he accepted. 'Hang on, then,' continued Kerner, 'Richard Charnock. Sarah. Frank. Harry Foxx. And Angelo.' He pointed out each one in turn.

Richard Charnock looked about the same age as Kerner, early to mid-twenties going on thirty-five: they both looked tired, strained, burdened. Burns recognised Richard's wavy, dark brown hair, his mole and his square jaw from the first of the photographs he had studied on his first visit to the flat. His intense eyes suggested a lively intelligence that the photographer had not managed to capture. A cigarette rested in an ashtray next to Richard's hand but was left largely untouched.

Next to Richard, sitting on a swivel chair that had been brought through from Kerner's room, was Sarah: her long, shining auburn hair framed an oval, freckled face, hazel eyes and a slim nose. In one hand she held a can of lager, while clasped around her other was the hand of the man sitting next to her on one of the plastic kitchen chairs. With unusually bright blue eyes, unruly, thick, dark wavy hair and heavy eyebrows, this was Frank, the good-looking man from the photos. Frank looked about the same age as Richard, Sarah perhaps a year or two younger, but they looked very much an item.

While Richard, Sarah and Frank were sitting around the kitchen table, Harry Foxx was leaning back on an old wooden chair, the back of his head resting against the wall. He appeared detached, but that might have been the effect of the reedy-looking joint he held between forefinger and thumb. About the same age as Richard and Frank, he had unfashionably long, straight, fair hair and wore a leopard-print shirt. His cheekbones and high forehead were less pronounced than Kerner had made them seem. Every few seconds he lifted the joint to his mouth, inserted the damp roach delicately between his lips and sucked hard enough to produce a wince.

Angelo was perched on an incongruously high four-legged stool, in the middle of the kitchen, directly underneath the single bare bulb. The youngest-looking person in the room, he could still have been the same age as the other men (in fact, he was). As Burns would find out later, his real name was Michael, but as a fan of the Italian director Michelangelo Antonioni, he had acquired the nickname Angelo. His appearance was as striking as Frank's but less rugged, his fair hair razored into a straight line that stood up from his forehead.

Frank asked Burns what he did and he told them.

'Have you seen *Hammett* yet?' asked Sarah.

Wim Wenders' new film had been chosen to open the Lumière on St Martin's Lane on a Thursday at the beginning of October. A favourite with the black-turtleneck-collar brigade, the Lumière was run by Artificial Eye, who ran the Plaza, so Burns got in free.

'Disappointing,' he said. 'Confused and, to be honest with you, a bit confusing.'

'We thought it was brilliant,' said Frank. 'Didn't we?' He squeezed Sarah's hand.

'Nah,' said Harry Foxx, 'he's lost it.'

'Who?'

'Wenders.'

'What about *Fitzcarraldo* anyway, what's that like?' asked Richard Charnock.

'Let's just say it doesn't repay repeated viewing,' said Burns, who had projected it a dozen or so times at the Plaza.

Richard retorted: 'But what would?'

'Anything by Tarkovsky,' interjected Frank. 'Resnais. Antonioni.'

'Antonioni – repeated viewing? I don't think so,' said Harry Foxx. 'I fell asleep watching *Zabriskie Point* on the telly. Good soundtrack, though.'

'I fell asleep watching *Mirror*,' said Angelo.

'And as for Resnais,' Richard cut in, 'what's *Last Year at Marienbad* if it isn't a load of pretentious old wank?'

'Oh yeah, sorry. I forgot about the subtitles,' Frank said. 'They can be *so* hard to read.'

'How come you're all so into movies?' Burns asked.

'That's what we do,' said Frank. 'We make movies.'

Burns raised his eyebrows. 'All of you? Together or individually?'

'Don't include me. They wouldn't,' Sarah added. 'I'm a critic. I just write about movies.'

Burns marvelled at the confidence of this girl barely out of her teens calling herself a 'critic', and of course the 'just', as in 'I just write about them', was for the benefit of the others – but would they appreciate the irony? She clearly didn't *think* her role as a critic was beneath theirs as film-makers, but she was sufficiently aware to see that they certainly did. With Frank as the one possible exception.

'Who do you write for?' Burns asked her.

'My college newspaper. It's great – I just go to screenings all the time.'

'Sounds good. So you sit with the Barry Normans and the Derek Malcolms and the Alexander Walkers of this world?'

'It's a price worth paying. Anyway, if I aspire to be the next Pauline Kael, I should be able to hang out with those few British critics who manage to be household names. I'm doing a piece on Fraser Munro that I'm going to try to freelance to one of the nationals.'

'Fraser Munro?' queried Burns.

'Scottish, avant-garde, short films mainly. Very weird. He started off making documentaries, nature films, Highland landscapes and stuff like that. Very traditional. Nicely shot but a bit bland. Then he changed direction so utterly and drastically that you want to find out what happened to him.'

'I'm afraid I've never heard of him,' Burns admitted.

'No, well, he's never been very mainstream, either before or after the change of direction.'

'The new stuff was really weird, wasn't it?' Frank chipped in.

'At first it was like he wanted to subvert the early stuff, mixing footage of mountains with shots of partially dissected cadavers. Very weird and strangely meaningless. It doesn't even seem pretentious: you don't get the impression he wanted it to seem like it had depth. Then it just gets weirder, but in a sense more conventionally avant-garde.'

Burns saw that Sarah's enthusiasm, while arousing support from Frank, seemed to have slightly alienated at least two of the group. Harry and Richard stared into space, looking bored.

'Is he still around?' Burns asked.

'He's a recluse apparently. I couldn't track him down. In any case, I'm not that sure I'd like to meet him, having seen his films. To say that he seems obsessed with death would be an understatement. In fact, I know I wouldn't like to meet him. I'd worry about ending up in one of his films.'

Burns changed the subject: 'What's the best film you've seen this year?'

'I don't know. It's not been a great year. *Diva*? I love that aria.'

'*Christiana F*?' Frank suggested.

'You two haven't just met since starting college, I take it?'

'We were at school together,' explained Frank, grinning at Sarah.

'Childhood sweethearts,' smirked Richard from his corner.

'What about you, Richard?' Burns changed tack again. 'What's the best film you've seen this year?'

'I don't go to the cinema any more,' he replied darkly. 'I don't want to compromise my own vision.'

'Oo-oh,' mocked Harry Foxx lightly, finally dropping an eighth of an inch of sodden grey cardboard in the ashtray.

'You make films then?' Burns asked Richard.

'We all do. That's what we do. How we know each other.'

'We want to make a film together,' Frank elaborated. 'Pool our talents and resources. Well –' he looked around at the others and laughed, 'our talents anyway. We haven't really got any resources.'

'But we're getting some.' Harry had brightened up since no

longer having to concentrate on wringing the last gasp out of his joint.

'Yeah?'

'Yeah, I can get some stuff from college. Frank knows someone who's going to lend us some lights, I think. Am I right, Frankie boy?'

'Yeah, I can get lights. You still got that joint?'

'No, it's finished.'

'Yeah, you finished it.'

'All six of you?' asked Burns. 'You're all going to work together.'

'Leave me out of this,' said Sarah, shaking her auburn hair back.

'You can review their film when they've made it,' Burns joked.

'Yeah – and you can show it,' retorted Sarah.

'What about you, Andrew?' Burns turned to his landlord. 'You could photograph them for *Vogue*.'

'Andrew's our stills man,' said Richard Charnock. 'He's the best.'

'They're excellent photographs,' Burns agreed, gesturing at the walls.

Kerner acknowledged the compliment with a small nod.

'Who's the scriptwriter?' Burns asked.

'We haven't got a script,' answered Frank, his bright eyes shining with enthusiasm. 'Scripts aren't really our thing. We're waiting for the right idea, you know? Anyway, Kerner is our mentor and patron as far as ideas are concerned.'

Everyone laughed at this, including Kerner.

'Well, I'm your host if nothing else,' Kerner announced. 'So who'd like another drink?'

More alcohol was produced. Burns made coffee for himself and Richard. The conversation rolled on for another hour.

Finally, Frank said, 'We should be making a move if we're going to get the last tube.'

'You're not getting the tube,' said Harry Foxx.

'Why not?'

'Don't you watch the news? The tube killer – the Hammersmith Tube Murders. I'll give you a lift.'

'It's not on your way.'

'I don't care. It would be on my conscience if you got hacked to death when I could have given you a lift.'

Burns guessed that Frank and Sarah were less worried about the Hammersmith Tube Murders than about the number of joints Harry had smoked. But they accepted a lift all the same. Harry's Mini was parked outside the flat. He had already offered to sort out Richard and Angelo.

Next morning, Burns was getting some breakfast when Kerner entered the kitchen, which in itself was unusual since the man tended to keep out of his tenant's way.

'What did you think of the boys?' Kerner asked, opening the fridge and taking out a carton of milk, from which he drank directly.

'The boys?' asked Burns.

'Sarah's not really one of the group. She hangs around with Frank.'

'I got the impression she does more than hang around with him.'

'Yeah, I mean, like the man said, they're childhood sweethearts.'

'The man?'

'Fucking hell, you can be hard work, can't you?'

'Sorry,' said Burns, stirring his coffee. 'But Sarah's not part of the group? I can't see her face on your wall.'

'It's just the four of them,' said Kerner, sticking the milk back in the fridge. 'They've got this idea they're going to make films together, but so far it's all talk. Richard and Harry have already done one or two things individually, but nothing that amounts to very much, and they haven't worked together yet. They seem determined.'

'How do you know them? What did they say you were – their mentor and patron?'

'I knew Harry first and he introduced me to Richard and the others. They meet up here because it's neutral territory. I don't know if they get together at Richard's or Harry's. Harry's place is a bit far out. I haven't been to Richard's. I don't know about Frank and Sarah – they live together somewhere, obviously, but I don't know where. Angelo's got a bedsit somewhere near Paddington, but it's really small.'

'He seems younger than the others.'

'He's very pretty – he'd look good in front of the camera instead of behind it. I don't think he is younger. He just looks it. Full of ideas.'

'And you're not interested in being part of the group?'

'That's not how it works. They don't need anybody.'

'Unless it's somone with money, perhaps. Or a place where they can meet up and talk about the film they're never going to make.'

Kerner looked at Burns over the ash-stained, can-ringed melamine and smiled mirthlessly, his head moving slowly to and fro.

'I see the role of stills photographer as being very much to one side. You stand to one side of the movie camera and shoot from a slightly different angle. My point of view is different from theirs, but they'll make their film, you'll see. I'd put money on it. Not only that, but it'll be quite a film. A statement. I think they're right to wait until they've discovered what it is they want to say.'

'I just don't know how four people will ever agree on anything.'

'That's the challenge, isn't it?'

'I hope they do. They seem quite idealistic, for all their attitude – well, Richard's attitude. But I think the way Frank and Sarah are with each other is, so far at least, the clearest statement they make about that idealism. On the basis of one night

in their company, I admit,' Burns conceded. 'Listen to me –
what do I know? A middle-aged projectionist living on borrowed
time. I'm history. They're the future.'

That night, Kerner and Burns ended up in the kitchen drinking whisky together and talking about films and talking more
about Kerner's friends and Kerner asked Burns what he'd meant
when he'd said he was living on borrowed time. Burns told him.

'I can't believe I just told you that,' Burns said a few minutes
later as Kerner poured him another Scotch. 'I haven't even told
my wife.'

'It's your business, isn't it?'

'She has a right to know.'

'You've got your reasons.'

Burns explained the situation.

'Maybe they can do something,' Kerner said. 'I mean, you
look well enough to me.'

'It's all fucked up inside.'

'Can't they treat it with penicillin or something?'

'The disease, yes, but not the damage that's already been
caused.'

Unembarrassed, Kerner asked: 'How long have you got?'

Burns swallowed his Scotch. 'I've been reading up about it.
Let's just say we'd better stick to a weekly contract for the rent.
To take the room for six months, say, would be a bit silly.'

'You seem pretty calm, considering.'

'There's nothing you can do. You adapt.'

'I'm not sure I'd adapt. I'm frightened of dying.'

'Who isn't?'

Kerner poured a couple more Scotches. 'From where I'm
sitting, you're doing a good impression of a man not frightened
of dying.'

'Look at it this way. It's more frightening not knowing, in
a way. It's more frightening getting on a plane or having an
operation. You don't know if you'll come out the other side.

Whereas I know I'm not going to. This is it.' Burns downed the Scotch and positioned his glass so Kerner could refill it. 'My library book's due back and I can't borrow any more. My club membership is about to expire and renewal's not an option. All those with a future ahead of them, take one step forward: Iain Burns, where the fuck do you think you're going?' Burns fingered his glass. 'Sorry,' he said. 'I'll leave if you like. Get another place. Who wants to live with a condemned man?'

'There's no need to go,' Kerner said, upending the bottle. 'And every need to have another drink. In fact, I'd quite like to do some pictures with you, if you don't mind.'

'Death-mask shots?'

'You've got a good face. The camera likes faces like yours.'

'Whatever. We can do some pictures.'

(They never did.)

8 · The bed-sitting room

London, spring 1998

Angelo came back from lunch to find a padded envelope on his desk. Padded envelopes were not an uncommon sight in the dispatch room, but ones with his name on were. In the top right-hand corner were the handwritten words 'By Bike', and in the centre of the envelope was an address label on which had been written, in printed capitals, his name and the name of the production company. Angelo tore open the padded envelope. Inside was a video cassette. VHS, in a simple cardboard sleeve bearing the name of a duplication bureau.

As he handled the cassette, his actions were performed slowly and with exaggerated care. He would examine every inch of it before placing it anywhere near a VCR. It was a C30, he noted. TV industry standard. The facilities houses handled a lot of stuff for TV, but they handled a lot of stuff for film as well. There was no label on the front of the tape, but there was a label on the spine, which he had been trying not to look at because he had seen what it said and he didn't like it very much. It said *Ghost Train*.

There were no other markings on the cassette. He didn't like what was written on the spine, but he liked even less the idea of putting the cassette back in the padded envelope and hiding it in a drawer and never watching it. It was possible that, unwatched, the thing would have even more power over him.

Right at the back of Angelo's desk was an old monitor and a VCR for the rare occasions when Angelo had a genuine, work-related reason for checking tapes. He ejected the tape that was in the machine (something about disused tube stations he'd bought at the Transport Bookshop in Cecil Court and never got round to taking home) and slotted in the new tape. He picked up the remote.

There was nothing on the tape. Just white noise. Snow. Static. Interference. Whatever you want to call it.

Angelo fast-forwarded and pressed play. The same. He ran the tape on both play and fast-forward until the end, so he could be sure that there was nothing else on it. The tape reached the end. He let it rewind back to the beginning and ejected it, slipping it back into its cardboard sleeve. He dropped it into the pocket of his jacket to take home, where he would watch it properly, at the end of his shift.

When he next saw Loz, the dispatch rider, he asked him if he'd delivered the tape. The man's helmet shook from side to side.

'Must have been an outside job,' he said, his voice muffled.

Angelo saw a lot of Loz and trusted him as far as he trusted anybody, which was not all that far.

'What is it?' Loz asked, removing his helmet and reaching for his bag of rolling tobacco.

Angelo dismissed the enquiry.

'You handle hundreds of tapes. What's special about this one?'

As the dispatch clerk, Angelo saw hundreds of tapes and thousands of cans of film.

'Nothing. Look,' he indicated a pile of U-matics on the corner of his desk, 'these are for you. As soon as you can, according to upstairs.'

'Upstairs can wait till I've had a fag. Anyway, it's Friday afternoon.'

'Yes.'

'No one works on Friday afternoons in this business. The tapes are just going to sit on someone's desk till Monday morning.'

'Yeah, well.'

'What you doing over the weekend, then?'

'Dunno. Nothing much.'

This wasn't true. Angelo did know what he'd be doing. First thing Saturday morning he'd pay another visit to the vintage poster gallery he'd discovered the previous weekend.

He didn't want to tell Loz. What if Loz followed him and found out where he lived? Angelo was very careful about who came to Gloucester Terrace. It was his private space. It was where he kept his maps and charts. It was where he kept his various collections.

He'd come across the vintage poster gallery by chance while walking back from the former Twentieth Century Theatre, a disused cinema located above an antiques showroom on Westbourne Grove. The gallery, next door to a TV and hi-fi shop on Talbot Road, required you to ring a bell to gain admittance. He instinctively disliked such places but was attracted to this one by the framed movie posters on the walls. He knew that the attractive girl sitting behind the desk at the far end of the room would instinctively dislike him.

Posters for *Vertigo*, *Performance* and *Some Like It Hot* could be seen from the street through the plate-glass window. The prices were printed far too small for him to read without going in. He pressed the buzzer.

The girl looked up and operated a switch. He pushed open the door and slipped inside as a gasp of air escaped past him into the street. He avoided the girl's gaze by turning to the nearest exhibit, a set of lobby cards for *Point Blank*. As he moved forward to read the price he glanced left towards where the girl was sitting. Her head was bent over the desk, her face concealed by a dark, twisting curtain of velvety hair. He could see her ankles and feet under the desk. She raised one foot and crossed it slowly behind the other.

There were three other men in the gallery. They all held the same position in relation to the walls of the room. Each was standing straight, head back, chin up as he examined the poster in front of him. Their hands were either clasped behind their backs or kept close by their sides. The ambience was one of silent reverence.

The girl uncrossed her ankles. Angelo glanced at her and saw that she was looking directly at him, her hair sliding down over her forehead. He looked away, heart thumping, and concentrated on the *Vertigo* poster. The card on the wall revealed that it was linen-backed and priced at £2,000. It made Angelo dizzy just to imagine handing over that amount of money. It made him dizzy to imagine ever owning that amount of money. But it made him even dizzier just to look at the girl.

She reminded him of Naomi.

As he moved deeper into the gallery, stopping to admire a poster for Alain Resnais' *Last Year at Marienbad*, card-backed at £800, Angelo became aware of a presence. He turned around to see the girl standing close to him. She leaned even closer to speak and he saw that she had an overbite and that her bottom lip was heavier than her top lip. The tip of her tongue was bubblegum-pink.

'We have some special items in the back.'

Angelo swallowed. She even sounded a little bit like Naomi.

'Special items?'

'Follow me.'

She turned on her heel and stilettoed across the blond-wood floor, the staccato reports ricocheting off the white walls, towards a staircase ten yards away. How could Angelo not watch her legs and the way her skirt moved as she crossed that short distance? He followed her up the half-dozen steps, mesmerised by the sway of her hips.

With an ironic flourish, she showed him a glass case filled with ticket stubs, velvet swatches, thimblefuls of carpet dust and cigarette ash. Angelo pointed to a frayed square of white canvas.

'From a screen?'

'Coliseum, Harrow Road. Closed 1956, site redeveloped.'

'Very nice,' murmured Angelo, looking more closely at the brass upholstery studs, obsolete lenses and strips of 35mm advertising trailers.

The girl turned to look towards the front of the gallery. He sensed that she was bored. She'd misjudged him, had thought he might be a genuine collector, his scruffy attire the signature of the eccentric.

'Everything's for sale?' he asked.

'This kind of stuff is currently fetching very good prices,' she pointed out. 'I'm sorry, I must be getting on.'

The mild flirtatiousness had vanished. Angelo realised his viewing of the special collection was over. He turned to meet her gaze.

'If you wouldn't mind,' she said, gesturing towards the shop.

He negotiated the steps and stopped by two more posters – *Get Carter* and *The Lavender Hill Mob*, each conservation-paper-backed and priced at around three months' wages – before opening the door and stepping into the street.

Back at 208 Gloucester Terrace, Angelo sat by his window watching the railway lines that fanned out of Paddington. One train after another pulled out of the station, blundering through the forest of points. Passengers rocked in silhouetted rows, cut-outs against the tawny light pouring past them.

There were Great Western 125s bound for Bristol, Cardiff or Penzance, diesel multiple units terminating at Reading but stopping at every station in between, six-car Hammersmith & City line tubes that would henceforth remain above ground all the way to Hammersmith. From his magnificent vantage point, it seemed almost as if a single word from him would bring them all to a grinding halt.

Sometimes he rode on the trains. He went down to Paddington or Royal Oak and stepped on board. He'd been to Bristol, visited Swindon. He'd travelled to the airport and back on the Heathrow Express. And many times, late in the evening, he'd taken the Hammersmith & City line round to its western terminus.

Returning home to Gloucester Terrace late at night he'd always manage to find a vacant carriage where he'd sit and wait to see who would get on at the next station. One night a young woman boarded his empty carriage at Ladbroke Grove and sat down on the opposite side one row of seats down. He closed one eye to compose the shot, but she switched to the next carriage at Westbourne Park.

She, too, had reminded him of Naomi.

As Angelo sat watching the trains outside his window, he kept thinking about the girl from the gallery. He saw her head silhouetted in every frame.

He turned away from the window and trailed his fingers along the video boxes lined up on one of his two bookcases – the one with white shelves. Meticulously labelled and sorted, the spines of the sleeve-inlays announced their contents, but not a single one promised distraction from the enduring image of the girl. The way she leaned forward to tempt him, then withdrew almost as abruptly – pure Naomi. He picked out a video box from the top row and opened it very carefully just wide enough to sniff inside, then snapped it shut and replaced it, his index finger lingering on the neat lettering under the plastic sleeve on the spine.

The flat was in darkness, as usual when he was not working.

There was enough of the city's ambient light coming in at the window to cast shadows behind the few things he had in the flat and so make them stand out. A dust–furred cooking ring, filthy sink and minibar-style fridge. The bed. A large pile of empty video boxes on the floor. A table bearing the ancient Remington typewriter on which he wrote the endless letters that he hand-delivered to the BFI, the Film Theatre Association and English Heritage. Also on the table, his maps of London, his press cuttings about old cinemas and his digital video camera. Finally, leaning against one of the two walls perpendicular to the window, the white bookcase that held the video boxes with the neatly inscribed inlays.

The window was kept shut, even in summer, and a substantial draught excluder lay along the bottom of the door that led to the stairwell and the shared bathroom. Beyond the window, against the wall facing the wall with the white bookcase, was a black bookcase. Its dimensions equalled those of the white bookcase and its contents looked similar but were in fact different. The black bookcase contained thirty or forty video cassettes in cardboard sleeves, each one labelled *Ghost Train*. Angelo had kept the tapes since they'd first begun arriving in the mid-1980s. Some had been posted to him at Gloucester Terrace, others couriered to him at work, like today's.

Night-times, if he wasn't out riding the trains or tramping the streets in search of abandoned cinemas, he would watch the tapes and they would speak to him. He would watch the static as it effervesced and he would remember Iain Burns and he would recall with regret and cumulative unease his part in what had happened to him. By the end of each thirty-minute tape, Angelo was convinced he was a murderer.

He woke in the morning curled up on the mattress clutching two video boxes from the white bookcase. Both, he saw, were tightly closed. It was early. The light from the window, which faced north, was weak. He could hear the constant rattle of the daytime commuter trains, which were of little interest to him. This was how he knew he wasn't going mad: he was capable of discernment. Night trains – interesting. Day trains – not interesting. It was all to do with the light.

Huddled over the table with a lukewarm cup of coffee,

Angelo pored over the west London maps. He had yet to plot the abandoned cinemas on the Harrow Road that he had been on his way to find when distracted by the vintage poster gallery. That his research and a possible harvest had been slightly delayed was not a major problem. He could even spare the time to go back to the gallery. He plotted the rough locations of the demolished Coliseum, the Prince of Wales (bingo hall) and the former Regal, all of them on Harrow Road, and extended lines from them across to the sadly unplugged Electric on Portobello Road, the Gate, the Coronet, and the former Twentieth Century Theatre, restored and Grade 2-listed, but bereft of seats and screen.

His red pen came back to the Electric and hovered. He remembered going there with Iain Burns. It had been on that night that the former projectionist had impressed Angelo with the vehemence and sincerity of his belief that where a film is shown is more important than where it is shot. The Electric, of course, was also where John Reginald Christie had been employed as relief projectionist during World War II. Four years after the war's end, Christie was found to be a mass murderer, having killed at least six women, and hanged.

The red pen continued to Edgware Road, just below the junction with Old Marylebone Road. At 194/6 Edgware Road, where the Edgware Hi-Fi Centre and the Hubbub Express sandwich shop now stood, the Blue Hall had previously entertained up to a thousand film fans a night. The Blue Hall, closed in November 1956 and later demolished, was part of an early chain opened by Enrique Carreras, co-founder of the Hammer film company. Other Blue Halls had existed at 207 King Street, Hammersmith (now the soulless multi-screen Virgin Hammersmith), and in Upper Street, Islington. Angelo had so far been unable to establish the exact location on Upper Street. All he knew was that it had opened, as the Berners Hall for concerts, in 1869. In 1908 it was renamed the Palace Cinema and later became the Blue Hall before being rechristened the Gaumont in 1951. It closed in January 1963, its use switching to bingo until 1975. Ten years later it was demolished.

Tantalisingly, from King Street to Edgware Road and then on to Upper Street was more or less a straight line. If once the exact location of the Upper Street Blue Hall could be plotted it did indeed allow a straight line to be drawn linking the three former cinemas, that would be an indication that order existed where chaos was perceived. This excited Angelo almost as much as the image of the girl from the gallery.

He picked up his coffee and withdrew the tape from the pocket of his jacket, which was draped over the chair. He slotted the tape into the VCR. The apparent chaos of snow filled the screen; Angelo sat down in front of it and waited for order to coalesce.

9 · The shooting

London, winter 1982/83

No one seemed to know whose idea it was – Burns's, one of the group's, or even Kerner's. The photographer had been busy acting as middleman.

Once Burns had decided to take his own life, it seemed only a short step to the idea of doing it on film. Committing his suicide to celluloid. Whoever had had the idea in the first place, Burns saw it as his chance to take control right at the end.

'How would we do it?' he asked.

'However you wanted to do it,' said one of them.

'Are you sure this is a good idea?' said another.

'You'd be accessories to a suicide,' he acknowledged.

'It's not that. It's that surely there must be an alternative. I thought you said it could be treated.'

'It can, but existing damage is irreversible.'

They met in Kerner's flat or in a rundown pub in Finsbury Park. The group still made a certain effort to talk him out of it, passing the baton of responsibility for this from one to another. Sometimes Burns wavered; on other occasions, when the pain was bad and his vision impaired, he didn't question for a moment that they should proceed. He sensed that whenever they were away from him the four were busy pulling in favours, giving it a lot of talk and blagging the necessary gear. He sensed that *they* sensed that this was their big chance.

For their first meeting of the new year, Burns turned up early. They were marking the tail end of the festive season with a curry at a cheap South Indian vegetarian restaurant in Stroud Green. Twenty minutes before the appointed hour, Burns turned up with a clutch of beers from the off-licence across the road. Seeing that Angelo was early, too, he took his bottles to the counter to get two of them opened and to order some poppadums, then joined him. For a while, neither spoke.

'Good Christmas?' Burns asked.

'OK,' he shrugged.

'Did you go to your parents'?'

'No.' Angelo snapped off a larger piece of poppadum than he'd intended and tried to break it further without using his other hand. 'My parents are dead.'

'I'm sorry. I didn't know.'

'No, well, I don't talk about them much.' He sipped at his beer. 'There's not much to say.'

Burns watched the young man.

'I never knew my mother,' Angelo continued. 'My father died years ago. But not before time.'

'What did he do?'

'Not much.'

'I mean what did he do to you?'

Angelo hunched over his plate, studied the label on his beer bottle. There was sadness in his eyes, and loneliness; above all there was hurt.

'What do you remember?' Burns asked him.

'I remember sitting and watching trains go by. I sat and watched the trains, night and day, through the bars.'

'What bars?' Burns asked.

'I don't know,' he admitted. 'My cot, perhaps, or the window.'

At that moment, the door swung open, admitting Richard, Harry and Frank and a blast of cold air from the street.

'Why did you watch the trains?' Burns asked quietly, but the shutters had come down. The conversation was at an end. Burns wondered who out of the three made Angelo nervous to carry on.

'I hope you're not leading him astray,' said Richard Charnock as he swung into the empty seat next to Angelo.

'What with?' Burns enquired. 'Tales of provincial decadence? My adventures behind the projector? I should imagine Angelo has far more interesting tales to tell.'

Burns stared at Angelo, who looked up and caught Richard's eye.

'Anyway, Iain, how are you feeling?' Richard asked.

'Better than you'd like,' said Burns, with a little smile to show he wasn't being serious, but with a curl to his lip to show that he was.

'Let's call it off,' Frank said. 'It's what I was thinking to my-self over Christmas and if you're not sure, then we shouldn't go ahead.'

'No,' said Burns firmly. 'We do it.'

Harry ended the awkward silence: 'You will give us plenty of notice, won't you?' Harry could be quite direct when he hadn't just had a smoke. 'No offence,' he added.

'None taken. What I'd recommend is that you get your-selves to a state of near readiness so that you can go with a day or two's warning.'

Angelo was the only one of the three not looking at Burns as he said this; he was looking down at the remains of his poppadum.

'The whole point of me doing this – or part of the point – is that I get to avoid the worst of the pain, so if the pain suddenly gets really bad, I'm not going to want to be hanging about while you hitchhike to Nottingham to pick up a camera.'

'Don't worry about it,' said Harry. 'We've got the gear. We're ready to go at any time.'

'Do I detect a slight note of impatience, Harry?'

'Oh, come on, man – this is difficult enough for us as it is.'

Burns just stared at Harry Foxx without responding to this.

'I think,' said Richard pointedly, 'that it's probably a lot more difficult for Iain than it is for us.'

'Shit, I'm sorry.' Harry shook his long hair out of his face. 'Sometimes I just don't think before I open my big mouth.'

'As you say,' Burns advised the embarrassed would-be co-director, 'don't worry about it.'

The quartet had explained to Burns, at his request, how they were going to go about filming him. Because all four wanted to direct, they would all assume equal responsibility and each would co-direct. Harry Foxx had come up with the film's title, *Auteur*, which Richard had objected to on the grounds that *auteur* theory was predicated on the belief that the director was regarded as the chief creative force behind a film, indeed as the author of the film, and on this film, their first proper outing as directors, the four would share the credit. Such collective unselfishness hardly recalled the spirit of Truffaut's 1954 article in *Cahiers du Cinéma* marking the first use of the term *la politique des auteurs*, best translated as '*auteur* theory'.

'Maybe Harry realises that and is being ironic,' Frank had argued.

'Harry doesn't know what ironic means,' Richard had scoffed.

'Anyway, what does it matter,' Angelo had wondered, 'since the film will never be released?'

Harry Foxx had remained silent during this exchange. In 1982 the discreditation of *auteur* theory had yet to become widespread and he for one admired the work of Truffaut and Godard and took the theory on board without reservation. Out of the four, he was perhaps the one who dreamed most vividly of being recognised as a genuine *auteur* himself. If he was unhappy at the prospect of sharing the director credit with the three others, he kept it well hidden.

They were keeping an open mind as to length, format

and general approach, believing that the ideal solution would suggest itself when the time came. No one had yet asked Burns what method he intended to employ, yet he could tell that the question buzzed in the heads of the group like a wasp in a jar. At times he thought about teasing the quartet by announcing a chosen method and then changing his mind and repeating this until they could no longer hide their frustration.

Angelo was the only group member already actually working in the film industry. He had got himself a job as a runner with one of the smaller Soho-based production companies some four months earlier. Their offices were on Beak Street, right across from an Italian café with tubs of seafood salad and steamed-up windows. Burns wiped an arc in the condensation with the back of his hand as he sat with a tuna sandwich and a cappuccino. He didn't have to wait very long before Angelo appeared, darting out of the doorway and turning to head towards Lexington Street. Burns grabbed his polystyrene cup and left the café. Angelo was only a few yards ahead, looking in a shop window. Burns halted, then reconsidered and got back into his stride.

'Angelo,' he called out. 'Fancy seeing you here.' He placed a hand on the young man's shoulder.

'I work here,' Angelo said. 'Just down there.' He pointed back to where he'd come from.

'Where are you off to? I'll walk with you,' Burns offered.

'Over to Rathbone Place to drop something off. I'm a runner.'

On the way, Burns asked about Harry Foxx: 'Why the double ex?'

'You know John Foxx, the musician? Used to be in Ultravox, then went solo. Harry changed his name: he said it was an *hommage*.'

'What was it before?'

'Fox with one ex.'

They had reached Rathbone Place. Angelo went into a print shop to drop off his job while Burns waited outside.

When Angelo emerged he pointed towards the end of the street, where it split three ways.

'Do you know what they filmed here?' Angelo asked excitedly.

Burns saw something ignite in the younger man's eyes.

'Tell me,' he said.

'Come to the end of the street. Look!' Angelo pointed to the upper floors of a building on the corner of Rathbone Place and Percy Street, above a newsagent's. '*Peeping Tom*. Michael Powell's *Peeping Tom*.'

'I know.' Burns enjoyed seeing Angelo so excited.

'They filmed the exteriors down there.' He gestured towards Rathbone Street. 'In the alley by the Newman Arms.' Angelo placed his hand against the brick wall. 'Michael Powell might have stood here. He could have touched this wall right where I'm touching it.'

'If you like Michael Powell,' Burns said, 'you might like Georges Franju. *Les Yeux sans visage* is showing at the Electric tonight. Nine fifteen. Have you ever seen it?'

'No.'

'It's dreamlike and creepy. I think you'd like it. Do you want to go and see it? I can get free tickets.'

'Er, yeah. Why not? The Electric's not far from me.'

'Which is where?'

'Two-oh-eight Gloucester Terrace, near Royal Oak tube.'

'I'll pick you up at eight.'

'OK.'

Gloucester Terrace seemed infected with negative emotions. Loneliness, disappointment, sadness, desperation. The crumbling stucco, the peeling paint that had once been white, the anonymous doorways with their columns of bell-pushes. There was no evidence of love, inside or out. The only sign of life was a stick-thin middle-aged woman who scuttled past Burns and ducked, key at the ready, into the doorway she shared with a dozen others. Life here did not flourish; it clung on.

Burns stopped at the number he'd been given and searched among the names for Angelo's, realising he didn't know his surname. A few of the bells were unnamed; the top bell was one. Burns tried it. Half a minute later, he heard footsteps. The door was opened.

'I'm not quite ready,' said Angelo.

'I'll come in and wait then.'

Angelo seemed reluctant to admit him.

'I won't bite,' Burns reassured him.

'No one comes here,' the young man said, looking vulnerable.

'Look, it's cold. I don't fancy waiting in the street. Let me come in. I won't touch anything.' Burns was curious to see Angelo's place.

Angelo acquiesced, and after climbing several flights of stairs, Burns followed him into a tiny bedsit dominated by the view of the railway lines. Furthest away was the overground tube line, with a train slowing down to stop at Royal Oak. In the foreground a BR electric multiple unit rattled across several sets of points, and for a moment the two trains travelled side by side at the same speed, a double exposure, before the commuter train accelerated away and the tube jerked to a halt at the empty platform. No one got off, Burns noticed, and no one got on.

'I won't be a minute,' Angelo said.

'Nice little place,' Burns said.

'It's cheap.'

It wasn't a nice little place at all. The bedsit was airless and had an atmosphere of tension. A number of weathered paperbacks stood upright on the window ledge – *Samson and Delilah* by Felix Salten, Walter Tevis's *The Man Who Fell to Earth*, John Burke's *Hammer Horror Film Omnibus*. Stacks of assorted true crime acted as bookends.

'You read much?' Burns asked.

'I'm ready now, let's go.' Angelo was holding the door open.

They walked. Big Edwardian houses filed past them silently, family homes for the comfortably well-off. Lamps glowed softly in golden shades, highlighting rows and rows of white-spined Picadors, orange Penguins and eggshell-green Modern Classics in shelved alcoves.

'How are the rest of the group?' Burns asked, for something to say. The group member who interested him most was currently walking two steps ahead of him.

'OK.'

Behind the high brick wall, trains could be heard clattering over intersecting lines.

'What are they up to?'

Angelo shrugged. 'Nothing much. Frank's doing what he's always doing: working on script ideas. Sarah's trying to write her article about Fraser Munro and doing lots of reviews, as always.'

'For her college paper?'

'Yeah, but most things she writes she sends to the newspapers or film magazines as well. One day someone'll call her back. Richard and Harry just . . . well, I don't know . . . they're not doing much. Just hanging around. Talking about stuff but not really doing that much.'

It was only when they reached Powis Square that Burns understood why they'd walked instead of taking the tube. Angelo pointed out the big house on the north-west corner.

'Look,' he said reverentially. 'Where they filmed *Performance*.' He stepped closer and touched the gatepost.

'You know they never filmed inside,' Burns said. 'The interiors were done in Belgravia.'

Angelo turned a desolate, betrayed gaze upon Burns.

'What?'

Burns instantly regretted his insensitivity.

'I'm sorry,' he said, 'but it's true.'

Angelo walked on disconsolately and turned into Portobello Road near the Electric. When he realised that Burns was no longer following, he looked back. The older man was leaning against a wall, his face contorted with pain.

'Are you all right?'

'Give me a minute.' Burns put out an arm, resting his hand on the other's shoulder. Angelo stood awkwardly, hands by his sides.

'Look, Angelo.' Burns used his free hand to massage his leg. 'That house in Powis Square is just a location. It's where they shot part of the film. Like they shot *Blow Up* in Maryon Park and, as you pointed out earlier, *Peeping Tom* in Rathbone Place. I just don't believe that locations are significant. This –' he pointed across the road to the Electric, 'is more important. This place will never lose its significance. It'll never lose its ghosts. As long as it's standing, even if they close it down at some point in the future, it'll always be a special place.'

'What do you mean?'

'I mean, this place has some kind of power. So many films have been shown here to so many audiences – you can't under-estimate the effect of that kind of concentrated exposure to human emotion. The walls and ceiling of the place will be dripping with it. The screen may appear two-dimensional, but in fact it's like one of those billboards with countless posters pasted one on top of another. Peel one off and there's another one underneath.'

'But this is just where people *watch* a film. Back there –' Angelo indicated the way they'd come, 'is where they *made* one.'

'Imagine a film that gets made that nobody ever sees. What does that amount to? Would you haunt its locations if you'd never seen it? Would Powis Square mean anything if you'd never seen *Performance*?'

Angelo frowned.

'This is what's important. This place. This is where the love affair is consummated. Between you and what's on the screen and in the air all around you. Believe me, this place and others like it – they're the ones that have the power. They'll never die.'

'What about television? Video? The effect video's going to have?'

Burns looked disgusted. 'I hope you're joking,' he said. 'This film we're going to see, *Les Yeux sans visage*, on television it's an unusual little film. Here, or at any other decent cinema, it's a magical experience. But I don't need to convince you of that.'

After the screening, Angelo needed little convincing.

Burns offered to walk home with him, but Angelo snapped back, 'I'm not a kid, you know.'

'Sure. OK,' Burns agreed.

A week or so later they were at the Gate Bloomsbury in the Brunswick Centre for a screening of Barry Levinson's first film as director, *Diner*. This time, Angelo accepted Burns's offer to share a cab after the film. They'd been out a few times since seeing *Les yeux sans visage*, firstly to a press show of the Plaza's forthcoming feature, Wim Wenders' *The State of Things*. At the weekend they had been to the Scala for one of its most frequently programmed double-bills, *Performance* and *Don't Look Now*. The following Tuesday, Burns went to the Roxie on Wardour Street, alone, for an evening screening of *Death in Venice* and sat through it with tears streaming down his face, since the dying hero's fate echoed his own to an uncomfortable degree. The nature of Burns's pursual of Angelo might have been different to Von Aschenbach's of Tadzio, but the dynamics were similar. The next night, he and Angelo went to the Gate to see *Diner*. After the film, Burns suggested they walk up to Euston Road and get a cab. But just the effort of leaving the cinema brought him to a standstill. 'I need to rest,' he said, and they sat on the bench by the bottom of a set of steps that led up to the Brunswick Centre flats. 'Get my breath back,' he puffed. 'Do you recognise this place?'

Angelo looked blank.

'You must have seen *The Passenger*?'

'Of course.' Angelo had seen all of Antonioni's films at least once.

'At the beginning,' Burns said, 'where Maria Schneider comes down those concrete steps and meets Jack Nicholson. Or is it Jack Nicholson who comes down the steps? I can't remember now. Anyway, that was filmed right here. One of them sits on this bench, the other walks down those steps.'

'Really?' said Angelo. 'But, surely, what's more significant about the Brunswick Centre is that it's got its own cinema.'

Burns looked at him and laughed. 'You're learning.'

'Anyway,' Angelo said, 'it was Jack Nicholson who came down the steps. Maria Schneider was sitting on the bench. You must be able to remember that?'

Burns tapped the side of his head. 'It's being eaten away up here. Slowly eaten away.'

Angelo looked down.

In the cab, neither of them spoke. Burns, looking blankly out of the window at the passing antiques shops, curry houses and late-night supermarkets, was lost in his thoughts. Angelo was trying to imagine what they might be. When the cab turned into Gloucester Terrace and pulled over, Angelo turned to face Burns as he was getting to his feet.

'You know when we do the film?' he said, hesitantly.

Burns nodded.

'Will where we shoot it be less important than where it gets shown?'

Burns half smiled. 'Depends,' he said.

'On what?'

'On your point of view, I suppose. But yes, I think so. You could shoot it anywhere. What I'm going to do I could *do* anywhere. What matters is who sees it and where.'

Angelo frowned, trying to understand. The cab driver sat patiently, the back of his neck marked with soft wrinkles.

'Give me your hand,' Burns said to Angelo.

The young man complied and Burns held it in his two hands.

'We're going to have to do it quite soon, I think,' Burns said quietly. 'You're going to have to work out if you're ready.'

He was still holding Angelo's hand.

'*I'm* ready,' said the younger man gruffly, looking away, his manner prompting Burns to infer that the opposite was the case.

'I've got to go,' Angelo said.

Burns let go of his hand and Angelo started backing out of the cab. If he'd have looked up at that point, he'd have seen the older man smiling at him with a strange light in his eyes.

'Archway?' the driver asked, half turning round.

Burns watched row after row of Georgian terraces as they were drawn past the north-bound cab. Newsagents, beauty salons, overpriced grocery stores. Video shops, mini-cab firms and disused electricity showrooms. The taxi rattled up the Holloway Road. The Coronet, formerly the Savoy and then the ABC, was showing *First Blood*, to be followed on Sunday by *Airplane II*. Burns wouldn't live to see the Coronet's closure, five months later, with *Blade Runner* and *Body Heat*, and subsequent conversion to the New World Snooker Club.

What he had told Angelo was the truth. It wouldn't be long now.

The following morning, Kerner was in the kitchen making breakfast when Burns staggered in from his end of the flat.

'Not good?' Kerner asked.

'Not good,' Burns confirmed through gritted teeth.

'That was them.' Kerner looked at the phone. 'Did it wake you?'

'No, the pain in my leg woke me.'

Kerner paused. 'They're ready when you are,' he said. 'No pressure, but they've found a place.'

'Where?'

'I don't know.'

'I'll call Angelo.'

'Call Harry. I'll give you his number.'

Burns called Harry Foxx.

'I gather you've found somewhere,' Burns began. 'Just in time.'

'What do you mean?'

'It's getting close.'

'I'm sorry,' Harry Foxx said softly. 'I didn't realise.'

'No, well, we haven't spoken for some time, have we?'

'I think we all feel a little awkward.'

'If you don't want to go through with it . . .' Burns quipped.

'Are you sure *you* do?'

Burns looked down at his free hand. It looked different. No longer able to thread 35mm film through a Bell & Howell.

'I've no choice.'

'But the filming . . .' Harry's voice tailed off.

'Yeah, let's do it.'

'If you're sure.'

'I'm sure,' Burns growled. 'Where're we doing it?'

'There's a place off Tottenham Court Road that's just right. I think you'll like it.'

'Do you think that's important?'

Harry was silent for a moment. 'No offence,' he then said.

Burns signed. 'No, I'm sorry. It's just a bit weird.'

'I can imagine.'

'This weekend,' Burns said quietly.

'This weekend?'

'Saturday. Why not?'

'I'll tell the others.'

'Yeah, right. *Action*.'

Burns had two further phone conversations with Harry Foxx on the Friday to stipulate certain conditions, and he spoke briefly to Richard Charnock. On Saturday morning he woke in the early hours after a dream in which he was trying to get into his house in Felixstowe. He approached another house. The door swung open and a light came on, prompting him to flee. But then he must have returned because he had pene-trated either that house or another and it was unfamiliar to him. He went upstairs and couldn't orient himself. It was not like a house, more like some kind of abandoned institution.

In another part of the dream, Burns found himself with an old girlfriend, someone he'd known before Penny, and he was tempted to go to bed with her. At first he wouldn't, then he would. Then possibly she wouldn't let him, or someone else there was going to betray him. He couldn't remember. She lived in a shared flat with at least one other girl. There were other women in the dream. One dark, suntanned woman, whose breasts he scooped out of her low-cut top and fondled and kissed and sucked. Then there was a younger woman with small, hard breasts. He found to his surprise that he was having fun.

Then he woke and the pleasure of the dream didn't immediately fade, even when he remembered what day it was. He was unable to prevent certain thoughts entering his head – this is the last time you will lie here dozing – this is the last time you will lie in this bed – but he found that beyond them lay nothing. Neither stark terror, nor the curiosity he'd always felt about what might follow death. He held no religious or spiritual beliefs. All that lay beyond the promptings and questings of his mind on that last morning was a single question mark. So what? Not what would there be? What would he see or feel? But so what?

Then he wondered if the abandoned institution in his dream might be a hospital. Perhaps if he sought help now and prevented further deterioration, he could salvage some kind of a life. He could go back. But he'd already gone too far down this road to turn round and go back, hadn't he? Well, hadn't he?

If the institution had indeed signified a hospital, it had been abandoned for a reason. And, anyway, since when had he looked for the answers to life's questions in his dreams?

The location was accessed via a nondescript doorway between an Indian restaurant and an abandoned printing business on

Hanway Place, off Hanway Street. The door was locked from the inside and Frank had to knock.

Burns had expected them to send Angelo to fetch him, but when Frank had turned up at Kerner's flat in a black cab, it made more sense. Sending Angelo would have been risky, given that he and Burns were the two people most likely to bottle out at the last minute. To give him his credit, Frank did ask Burns if he was sure he wanted to go ahead with it, but he waited until they were walking to Hanway Street from where the cab had dropped them off. Burns made no response other than to keep walking.

Richard Charnock opened the door and glanced nervously up and down the narrow street while they entered. At the end of a short corridor, they went left then right into what looked as if it had once been a backstage area. Tea chests, cardboard boxes and bundles of old rags or clothes were dotted about on the dirty floor. Broken mechanical parts, a few scattered film cans and the mildewed remains of an old screen were Burns's first clues that the premises had once been a cinema.

'I get it,' he murmured, directing this at Angelo, who looked away. Turning to Harry Foxx, he said: 'You got the things I wanted?'

'Iain, we've got everything. Don't worry about it.'

An old sofa draped with a clean white sheet sat in the middle of a cleared area. A 16mm projector sat on a stand by the far wall. There was a TV and VCR near the sofa. On the floor by the sofa was a tray, the kind you get in cafeterias, bearing two bottles of Scotch and one heavy tumbler. Burns noticed more glasses and another bottle on a trestle table near the projector, plus a canvas hold-all that he imagined concealed the drugs. A small fan heater, plugged into a multi-extension socket, was belting out enough hot air to warm up the damp space. Several old velvet-upholstered cinema seats were scattered about.

But these were details. The significant thing about the place was its atmosphere.

'Can you feel it?' Burns whispered. Angelo, who was standing nearby, looked up at Burns for the first time and held his gaze. His eyes already had a haunted look about them. His shoulders had slumped under the weight of the guilt that had already settled there. 'Can you feel it?' Burns repeated.

Angelo nodded. He thought that he could feel it. A multiple exposure in three dimensions. A collection of echoes in an airtight concert hall.

'Your choice?' Burns asked him.

Angelo shrugged.

Burns limped across to the low-slung sofa and sat down. He reached for the first bottle of Scotch and unscrewed the cap.

'There's more,' Richard said, pulling up one of the old velvet seats and sitting down opposite the sofa.

Burns just nodded. He was still reacting to the set dressing. A few lights had been positioned but not switched on.

'This place has electricity?'

Richard shook his head. 'We ran an extension lead through from one of the sex shops for a small consideration.'

'You told them you're making a film?'

'I think they're expecting something a bit different.'

'But you won't show it to them?'

'They're not our target market.'

'Who is?'

Again Richard shook his head. 'Cinema historians?' he suggested. 'Film students. Not Leslie Halliwell anyway.'

'In the bag . . . ?' Burns indicated the hold-all on the trestle table.

Richard just nodded. By now the others had gathered around. Harry Foxx was perched on an old seat alongside Richard. Frank and Angelo stood somewhat awkwardly. Clearly no one felt comfortable sharing the sofa with the condemned man.

'I think we all need one of these,' said Burns, raising his glass of whisky.

Frank fetched glasses from the table and sat down on the sofa next to Burns. Angelo crouched down and Harry Foxx took the bottle and poured everyone a generous measure. Richard Charnock announced a toast – 'To Iain Burns' – and they all touched glasses and drank.

The atmosphere improved. Burns slowed down on the Scotch and Harry Foxx and Richard Charnock busied themselves getting the cameras ready. Frank was attending to the lights and Angelo was fiddling with the sound gear.

'Let's do a test,' Richard called out.

The four film-makers suddenly started to move together like parts of a machine. This was either rehearsed or instinctive. There were two cameras, an 8mm model that was owned jointly by the group and a knackered-looking 16mm job on loan from Harry's art college. 'Technically we're hiring it by the day,' Harry explained, 'but I don't think anybody expects us to pay.'

'Iain,' Richard shouted, unglueing his eye from the eyepiece of the 16mm camera. 'Do you mind if we get some stills?'

'Be my guest,' he mumbled.

If Burns was surprised when Andrew Kerner appeared from behind one of the bright lights, he didn't show it. Kerner stood just to one side of each of the cameras and took several shots of Burns on the sofa. Burns watched him move into the background and get some pictures of the quartet as they worked at their respective tasks. Like all good stills photographers he blended into the background and irritated nobody, got in no one's way. He blended in so well, he'd been gone some time before Burns realised he no longer seemed to be around. Richard Charnock fetched the black hold-all from the trestle table and placed it on the floor by Burns's feet. The two men exchanged a glance.

'You know what you're doing is illegal?' Burns said in a hoarse whisper.

'Of course. Don't worry about it.'

'I assume you're only filming me and that if any of you are caught on camera, you'll edit it out, but what about the stills?'

'Andrew's going to give us the negs. We only have to release what we want to release. We'll shoot the film and then, afterwards, we'll take a view on what to do with it. Our intention is to show it as widely as possible. It's going to be a talking point. It could be very controversial.'

Frank came over and sat next to Burns again.

'How's it going?' he asked. Of the four he appeared the most relaxed. The wheels were in motion, no point playing games now. Richard Charnock, on the other hand, maybe seemed a bit defensive. Harry Foxx was absent most of the time, hanging around on the fringes like a shadow. And Angelo was visibly distressed, which upset Burns.

Burns shrugged. 'What can I say?'

Harry Foxx squatted down at the edge of the pool of light cast by the lamps Frank had set up. Angelo was studying the 8mm camera.

'Look,' Burns said, 'this doesn't feel right. Something's wrong about it. I don't know what, but something's not right.' He paused. No one reacted as they waited for him to finish. 'I'm not going to be able to do it with you all here watching.'

The four stared at Burns, who looked back at each one in turn.

Harry Foxx was the first one to break. He stood up and walked away from the group, his boot heel crunching grit.

'There's got to be a way round this,' said Frank, running a hand through his thick black hair. 'There's got to be. Unless you want to call the whole thing off?'

'I don't know.'

'You don't know!' snapped Harry Foxx on his return from the shadows. 'Well, I'm sorry, but it's time you did. We can't fuck about any more. You've got to make your mind up once and for all.'

'Harry, that's enough,' advised Richard, stepping forward and resting a hand on his forearm. 'Iain, look, Harry's just not responding very well to the pressure we're all under. You're absolutely right to question how we do this, and I'm sure there is a way round it. After all,' he went on, looking at Burns, 'what you're doing is a personal thing. You don't want four blokes hanging round watching. I can understand that. I'm sure we all do. Right?' He looked at the others.

Frank said, 'Of course.'

Angelo nodded.

Eventually, Harry Foxx muttered, 'Sorry, man. No offence.'

'But,' Richard continued, 'the cameras will only run for fifteen minutes before the film needs changing. We're not short of stock – we've blagged tons. The cameras will run on their own, but someone will need to be around to replace the film. So either one person stays all the time, or we all leave you and one of us comes back at intervals to reload. We could take it in turns. What do you say?'

Burns was staring at the floor, his forehead grooved in bitter concentration. His vision was fading in and out and he felt woozy.

'There's a pub on the corner,' he managed to say.

'The Blue Posts,' said Frank.

'We could wait there,' Richard suggested.

'Set everything up,' Burns said, the tension falling away from him. 'Just come back to change the film. No more.'

Angelo trapped the sound boom between two big boxes just out of shot. He raised his head and caught Burns's attention without looking him in the eye.

'Can you just say something for level?'

'Yeah. Look after yourself, kid. Take care.'

Angelo bent over his sound gear and made a few adjustments, but he couldn't bring himself to look directly at Burns.

Frank was standing to one side framing the sofa through a viewfinder made of his hands and thumbs. He discussed moving one of the cameras with Angelo and Harry Foxx, and together they shifted it a couple of feet. Angelo leaned into the camera and got his first good look at Burns. He adjusted the focus.

Richard Charnock asked Frank a question about the lighting and the two agreed to make a couple of changes to Frank's arrangement. Meanwhile Angelo and Harry Foxx talked briefly about whether the sound from the monitor and speakers would drown out any other sound they might want to pick up, such as anything Burns might say. One of Burns's conditions, outlined to Harry Foxx on the phone in the previous week, had been that the group provide two films for him to watch and the means on which to watch them. Consequently, there was a monitor connected to a VCR that contained a VHS copy of Louis Malle's *Le Feu follet*, while an ancient projector had been called into service to screen a 16mm print of Nicolas Roeg's *Bad Timing*. The significance of the two movies hadn't been lost on the group – both dealt with suicide.

The tape was in the VCR, the projector was ready to roll.

'Time to go,' Burns said suddenly, pouring himself another drink. 'Someone – Angelo, please – start the projector. And pass me the remote for the video.'

Angelo did as he was bid and Harry Foxx placed the VCR remote-control device in Burns's hand. Frank set both cameras running while Richard did a final check on the lights and the sound gear. Then as a group they moved gradually towards the exit. Frank broke away and crossed the floor to speak to Burns.

Awkwardly he held out his hand and Burns looked up at him, considering the hand for a moment before he took it.

'If we seem not to know what to say,' Frank said quietly, 'it's because you humble us.'

'Bollocks. Get out of here.'

'See you later.'

Burns gave a little laugh. 'Yeah.'

There was a general, mumbled valedictory chorus from the other three, whom Frank now rejoined and together they moved towards the exit.

* * *

When they reached the end of the corridor and Richard unlocked the door, the wintry daylight, even in the dim recess of
Hanway Place, seemed shockingly bright.

'Blue Posts?' Frank addressed the group.

They sat around a table, Frank and Harry Foxx on the bench
seat, Richard and Angelo on stools. Richard got a round in
and they sat staring at their drinks, occasionally looking up and
catching another's eye, which would prompt a raising of the
eyebrows or a pursing of the lips, and then they'd look down
again. Harry Foxx flipped his beer mat repeatedly on the edge
of the table until Frank snatched it out of his hand and tore it
in half and dropped the pieces in the ashtray, at which point
Harry lit up the first of a chain of cigarettes. After fifteen
minutes, Frank, checking his watch, got to his feet.

'Is there any particular order we should do this in?' he asked
to a general shrugging of the shoulders. 'Well, someone needs
to go first. Keys, Richard?'

Richard Charnock handed over the keys and Frank slipped
out of the bar by the side door.

The atmosphere changed little in his absence. Harry Foxx
lit another cigarette from the butt of his last one; Angelo fiddled
with the faulty zip on his cheap bomber jacket; Richard Charnock
went to the bar and came back with a single packet of crisps,
which he tore open and dumped in the middle of the table. No
one apart from Richard touched the crisps. Angelo stopped mess-
ing with his zip when Richard slapped his hand irritatedly, and
Harry Foxx lit a new cigarette with his lighter while what remained of the last one was still stuck between his lips. Finally,
Frank came back in and everyone looked at him expectantly.

'What?' he said innocently.

'What's going on?' Harry Foxx asked.

'Not much. Theresa Russell and Art Garfunkel giving each
other a hard time. Some French guy in black and white looking
depressed.'

'Don't be a twat, Frank.'

'He's just sitting there drinking. As soon as his glass is empty he fills it again. I mean, I just don't know how he can do this. I suppose I never thought he'd go through with it, or that we'd allow him to do it.'

'Is everything all right?' Harry Foxx asked.

'I don't feel good about this,' Frank said, shaking his head.

'I said, is everything all right?' Harry Foxx repeated.

Frank looked at him. 'I changed the film and checked the cameras, if that's what you mean.'

'That's exactly what I mean.' Harry Foxx looked away, stubbed out his cigarette.

'Sit down, Frank,' said Richard. 'Look, we've got to be together on this. OK?' His attitude was more sympathetic but firm. 'We've started now, we can't very well go back.'

Frank looked at him, then at Harry, who was lighting another cigarette. Angelo said nothing.

'Yeah, OK,' Frank agreed in a low voice. He picked up the empty crisp packet and screwed it up into a tight little bundle, placing it in the ashtray. It immediately started to uncrumple itself.

'Do you think he's . . . you know . . . yet?' asked Angelo.

'Couldn't tell. My round?'

'Is he actually going to do it?' Angelo persisted.

'He's got to,' Harry Foxx said.

'He's come this far,' said Richard, 'he'll go all the way.'

Frank went to the bar.

'So who's going next?' Angelo asked the remaining two.

'Why don't you go next?' Harry Foxx suggested.

Frank came back with a round of drinks. Richard went to find the gents'. When he came back and they were all sitting around the table once more, Angelo asked another question.

'What are we going to do with him afterwards?'

Richard snapped: 'When are you going to stop asking so many questions?'

'That vault, remember?' said Frank.

Angelo flinched, angled his head even lower. The group fell silent.

'Time for you to go,' Frank said eventually, nudging Angelo, who looked up to find all three of them looking down at him.

'Can you do this?' asked Richard, gentler than before.

'Of course I can do it,' he responded as he got up.

Once Angelo had left the pub, Harry Foxx asked, 'Do you think he's up to this? I mean, are we safe?'

'Do you mean is he going to go crying to the police?' retorted Richard Charnock. 'No, he's not. Look, you know Angelo. It's going to be hard on him.'

'What effect is it going to have on him though?' asked Frank. 'In the long term, I mean. What effect is it going to have on any of us?'

Richard and Harry Foxx both looked at Frank, then at each other.

'Look,' Harry Foxx said, setting his pint down on the table, 'we all want to direct and for the time being we want to direct together. Not only that but we've known for some time what kind of film we want to make. This is an opportunity. We're not forcing him to do anything he doesn't want to do.'

'The police might not share our point of view,' observed Richard. 'We've got to think carefully about what we do with the film afterwards. Not only how we cut it and everything, but what we do about showing it. It's going to be very sensitive.'

'Unless,' Harry Foxx interpolated, 'we don't say it's a guy killing himself. We don't admit it's a film of a real event. We put it out like any other short film – a film about suicide. Like *Le Feu follet*.'

They were all considering this when Angelo returned, looking grey.

'He's getting drunk. Apart from that, not much to report.'

'I think we should join him,' declared Richard.

Harry Foxx started to protest.

'I mean we should get drunk.'

'I think I already am,' added Frank miserably.

'I'll get a round,' Angelo suggested.

'If they'll serve you,' quipped Harry Foxx.

'If they serve you, they'll serve anyone,' said Richard to Harry, and Harry picked the screwed-up crisp packet out of the ashtray and threw it at Richard.

'I'm going to the loo,' said Richard, dodging the missile, 'and when I get back I'm going next door.'

'It's not time yet,' said Frank.

'It will be by the time I've finished in there.'

Richard blundered towards the loos.

Someone else got another round in while Richard was off on set, and they were ready for another by the time he returned.

'So?' asked one of them.

'I don't know. I don't understand this guy. There he is, he's got the choice of watching Theresa Russell getting her kit off to a Stanley Myers score, and he'd rather watch a black and white film with subtitles and a dodgy piano soundtrack.'

'That dodgy piano happens to be Erik Satie,' Frank pointed out.

'Whatever. He's completely wrapped up in it.'

'Has he taken the insulin?'

'Couldn't tell. Didn't feel like asking.'

'How are the cameras and that?'

'No problem.'

'Does he look pissed?'

'Suppose so.'

'What – as pissed as us?'

'Don't know about that.'

Another round.

'Are we still going to be able to operate all the stuff this pissed?'

'It's not as if we've got to do that much.'

'What about – you know, *after*?'

'I think being pissed will be a positive advantage.'

'It's got to be my turn,' said Harry Foxx.

'Guess so.'

Harry Foxx tried to push the door rather than pull it, producing a resounding crash and jarring his arm.

'For fuck's sake, Harry,' muttered Richard.

'I don't think he did it on purpose,' said Frank.

'We could do without attracting attention.'

'I don't know. I think being as pissed as a fart in here at the time of death is a pretty fucking good alibi, don't you?'

'I'm sort of hoping it won't get as far as alibis.'

'Me too.'

'It won't, will it?'

'Not if we're careful.'

'What are we going to do with the film?'

'We'll see.'

'Who's going to edit it?'

'We'll see.'

'*We'll see. We'll see.*'

Harry Foxx came back into the pub. He looked pale, but then he always looked pale. He sat down.

'What?'

Harry seemed unable to speak.

Everyone seemed to sober up.

'He's gone,' Harry said eventually.

'Oh fuck.'

'Jesus.'

'He finally screwed up the courage, then.'

'Are you sure?'

'Of course I'm sure.'

'You checked?'

'Course I checked. There's no pulse. No heartbeat. He's not breathing. I mean, how thorough do you want me to be?'

'Keep your voice down.'

'I didn't think he'd go through with it.'

'We'd better go.'

'No. Not yet. We should have another drink.'

'What?'

'One more round – and we should drink in his honour. To his memory. Whatever.'

'Harry's right. Frank? Your round?'

'Why not? Every other round's been my round.'

Frank got another round in, nevertheless, and they clinked their glasses as they murmured Burns's name.

Someone else made another visit to the bar and the time passed swiftly. Before they knew it, an hour had gone by since Harry's visit. More drinks and a further half-hour. Eventually they gathered themselves together and left, by the side door, as unobtrusively as possible, which was difficult as they were by now quite drunk.

The false, alcohol-fuelled bravado vanished in the transition from the warm glow of the pub to the chilly darkness of the back street.

'Keys?' said Richard.

Harry Foxx produced the keys and Richard dealt with the lock, and within moments they were back in the close confines of the set. The take-up reel on the projector was still turning, the loose end of the film flapping against the casing; the lamp inside the machine threw a blank white square on to the wall. Richard switched off the projector and stopped the reel with his hand. He picked up one of the finished reels and looked at it, then put it down on the trestle table and went to switch off the two cameras while Frank and Harry Foxx took care of the sound and lighting gear. Angelo knelt down in front of the TV monitor, which was fizzing with white noise and snow. Next to him, on the sofa, slumped forward and leaning drunkenly to one side, was Burns's body. Angelo was close enough to touch him, yet appeared unaware of his proximity and was instead mesmerised by the screen. Frank knelt down next to him and asked him how he was doing, but Angelo made no answer. Richard gathered up the hypo and the insulin and any other incriminating bits and pieces and stuffed them into the hold-all. Harry Foxx, meanwhile, was toying with one of the reels of *Bad Timing*. Frank came over and asked him what he was doing and Harry said that since there was no need to return the film (it had been hired under a false name), they might as well make good use of it. Richard heard this and asked what Harry had in mind.

'Let's wrap him up in it.'

They called him a wanker, but Harry Foxx said that he was serious.

'Why not? Let's do it.'

'Look around you,' said Richard. 'This is not Egypt. We are not in a fucking pyramid.'

'Maybe it's what he would have wanted,' Harry Foxx argued. 'Why else did he ask for film and not video. I mean, videotape, I grant you, would be a bit crap, but film is a sign of respect. Come on, let's fucking do it.'

'Whatever,' said Richard.

Frank voiced no objection. 'What about him?' Frank asked instead, looking at Angelo. 'We mustn't let him go to pieces.'

Richard went over and crouched down next to Angelo, placing an arm around his shoulder and talking softly to him. Harry Foxx and Frank got the reels of Roeg's movie and unspooled a few dozen feet of film on to the floor. Richard persuaded Angelo to get to his feet and led him away from the monitor. Harry Foxx unplugged the TV and video and pushed them out of the way, then he and Frank manhandled the corpse on to the floor in front of the sofa.

'We're not undressing him,' Frank said.

'No fucking way,' agreed Harry Foxx, reaching for Burns's unfinished bottle of Scotch. 'No sense in wasting it.'

'Dead right.'

Harry Foxx passed it to Frank, who swigged from it and passed it back. They rolled Burns's body on to the celluloid. He was a big man and it required the efforts of both of them to shift his dead weight. Slowly and methodically, with the extraordinary level of concentration you see in drunks trying to settle a bill at the end of the night, Harry Foxx and Frank wrapped Burns's body in the gradually unspooling film. Richard persuaded Angelo to help, and between the four of them they managed to hide Burns's body completely from view. Harry Foxx tied a couple of the loose ends together. The celluloid slipped and slithered as they manoeuvred the bundle and tried to pick it up between them.

'If this were a scene in the film,' Frank observed, 'I think the camera would now pull back, tastefully, sparing us and him both the indignity.'

Richard Charnock grunted an acknowledgement. Harry Foxx grunted with the effort of trying to remain upright. Angelo hung on, grim-faced.

From above you would have seen four grown men grappling unsuccessfully with a giant, glistening larva casing bigger than any one of them. What could be going on? The disappointing climax to a bad science fiction film? Or a farcical remake of *The Trouble With Harry*? Struggling, two men at either end of the mummy-like form, they think they have the better of it, when Frank steps backwards on to one of the film cans and slips, falling on to his backside, and the other three are unable to hold on to their burden. But once Frank gets to his feet, we're finding it harder to tell any difference between the four of them. The camera tracks back further, drawn through one of many gaps in the crumbling ceiling into a cobwebbed attic space crisscrossed with searchlight beams of the city's night light slicing through holes in the roof. From above the building you wouldn't guess it contained the remains of an old cinema. Just one patch in the amorphous mass of jumbled brick and pitched roofing material covering a huge shanty-like agglomerate hemmed in by Tottenham Court Road and Hanway

Street and Hanway Place. Fifty yards up Tottenham Court Road the Classic is showing *The Return of the Soldier*, *Party Party* and a British film industry double-bill in cinema three – *Chariots of Fire* and *Gregory's Girl*. Doubling back to Oxford Street, another Classic has *Airplane II – the Sequel*, *First Blood*, *Eating Raoul*, *Diva* and *Missing*. Drifting over to the ABC Shaftesbury Avenue, cinema-goers are lapping up *First Blood* and *Airplane II*, while further north at the Gate Bloomsbury in Brunswick Square, a more refined programme offers *The Battle of Algiers* or *Diner*. Passing over the white tower of the Scala at King's Cross, where a *Prisoner* weekend is in progress, we come to Camden Town, where one of Iain Burns's colleagues is projecting *The State of Things* at the Plaza, while on Parkway the Gate 3 has stood dark since the previous summer and will not reopen, as the Parkway, for another four months. Heading north-west, skirting the mossy-green expanse of Regent's Park, the lights on the Outer Circle a glittering crown. The Screen on the Hill grips and perplexes its audience with one man's obsessive imposition of patterns on to the landscape in *The Draughtsman's Contract*. Rainer Werner Fassbinder holds court at the Everyman with *Lili Marleen* and *The Marriage of Maria Braun*. West to the Classic, where *ET* teases out tears from hardened Kilburnites; floating high above the flickering ribbons of the Westway and a fan of railway tracks heading out of Paddington, each train a strip of celluloid with its lighted window frames and silhouetted actors; then down to the Electric with Wim Wenders' *Hammett* proving a puzzle to the trustafarians of Notting Hill. South now, over the Coronet and the Gate to Drayton Gardens, where the Paris Pullman is on its own last reel, set to close within months. Against even the glittering headlamps of several thousand taxi cabs and the burning ruby light clusters of a million private cars, the cinemas of London are its beacons – even when they're dark. The Odeon on King's Road may have closed in 1981 but it will reopen as the Chelsea Cinema in September 1983 with

Andrzej Wajda's *Danton*, until which time it lurks in the heart of Chelsea, a barely glimmering presence of dark matter. By the time we reach the National Film Theatre, the immovable star at the hub of this glittering constellation, which tonight is showing Alain Resnais' *Last Year at Marienbad*, the four *auteurs* of Tottenham Court Road have gone their separate ways, each pursuing their own long, slow tracking shot down the corridors of memory, each embarked on their own personal journey either to forgetting the past or to re-editing its narrative to suit their own conscience.

10 · The Troy Club

London, Friday 10 July 1998

Frank had to call someone. When he saw the gurney emerge from the police tent at the demolition site across the road from his flat he had to call someone and tell them what he'd seen. He couldn't call Siân because he hadn't told her about Iain Burns, or about *Auteur*.

He had to call one of the group. They might no longer be a group, but he imagined they must all have been as nervous as he had been over the past few weeks with the demolition team working on the Tottenham Court Road site. Provided they were all aware of it. He knew that Angelo was up to speed, because they had been in touch. Angelo had not long before made one of his recurrent requests that Frank write about old cinemas: the death of the repertory circuit and the curse of the multiplex. Frank had even arranged to meet him in the Blue Posts on Newman Street. They'd met just a few weeks before the discovery of the body.

'The Blue Posts,' Angelo had begun, looking doubtfully around the interior of the pub. 'This isn't where . . .'

'No, that was a couple of blocks that way.' Frank pointed east.

Frank hadn't seen Angelo for a few years. His face looked thin and drawn, etched with fine lines around the eyes. His hair had turned silvery grey and was cropped close to his skull. It was like the head of a racehorse, too big for its lean body. His skin was pale, as if he divided his time exclusively between his basement dispatch office and the dark, mildewed spaces of London's abandoned cinemas.

'I didn't know there was another,' declared Angelo.

'Well, no, I didn't either until recently. I didn't know about this one. I mean, I know about a few others. Do you have to jiggle your leg like that?'

'I didn't know I was.'

'Yes. Really quite fast.'

'Sorry.'

Frank looked at Angelo and immediately regretted what he'd said. He was sure that if he'd made a comment like that in the old days, Angelo would either have dismissed it or told him to fuck off. Frank wondered if his sense of humour had been a casualty of the Burns episode.

'No. I'm sorry,' said Frank. 'I've been feeling tense lately. I don't know if you know but they're doing building work on Tottenham Court Road. At the bottom, between Stephen Street and the Blue Posts. The Blue Posts that you were thinking of. The one we went to.'

'You mean just south of the ABC? Former location of the Carlton, the Gaiety and the Grand Central? Across the street and a little way up from the Dominion?'

Frank studied Angelo's face but it revealed no trace of irony.

'Angelo, you know very well where I mean. Where we shot our film.' He lowered his voice. 'Where we made *Auteur*. Remember?'

Frank invested his pronunciation of the title with enough sarcasm to make it clear he for one had outgrown the artistic pretensions they had shared as young men. Angelo's face, however, registered nothing. He merely looked out of the window, then moved his head to take in a line of drinkers at the bar. Eventually, he looked back at Frank.

'How come there are two pubs called the Blue Posts so close to each other?'

'Angelo. Look. They're knocking down all of the shops on that stretch of Tottenham Court Road. And the Blue Posts on the corner with Hanway Street. And all the Indian restaurants on Hanway Street and Hanway Place. So you know what that means, don't you?'

'You'll no longer be able to get a decent curry in central London?'

Frank stared at Angelo, who gazed back impassively.

'I'm going to get another drink.' While Frank waited to be served, he watched Angelo. He had started to jiggle his leg again.

Clearly, Angelo had taken a wrong turn somewhere in the past fifteen years. Or he simply hadn't moved on in the way Frank and the others had. Frank didn't need to have kept in close touch with Richard Charnock and Harry Foxx to know what they'd been up to. They'd both done well. At least, Richard had. He'd made some big films and some big money. He'd sold out, sure – the films were crap, sub-Michael Winner, but they'd made him some money. Harry Foxx had done less well, but he'd still made a film. As for Frank, he'd figured out he'd rather write screenplays than make movies. He'd spent years writing scripts that agents and production companies had sat on for months before realising they were sitting on them at all, and on realising it they sent them straight back. He started writing the odd review, the occasional feature, and before he knew it, he was a hack, the screenplays forgotten. Then he took the magazine job.

When he looked back at the screenplays he realised they were all about loss. They were about losing someone you loved. They were about Sarah. They were about the hole in his life. The journalism – and his book – was a way of keeping her memory alive. As long as Frank and Sarah had been together, she had known that film journalism was what she wanted to do, and she had done it with flair.

Angelo, however, appeared to have been shunted into a siding. To be in his late thirties and still working as a dispatch clerk for a B-list production company showed there had to be something wrong.

Frank picked up the drinks and carried them back to the table.

'Frank,' Angelo said, turning to face him, 'are there any other Blue Posts or is it just the two of them?'

So, as soon as Frank saw the body bag being wheeled out of the demolition site, he went straight to the phone and keyed in Angelo's number. When his call was answered by a machine, he realised Angelo would be at work, a number he didn't have, and nor could he remember the name of the company, so he left a brief message.

Frank stood holding the receiver and looking out of the window, trying to work out what to do next. He turned to his PowerBook and opened its address book to find Harry Foxx's mobile number, hoping it hadn't changed in the year or so since they had last spoken.

It hadn't.

'Harry?'

'Who wants him?'

'It's Frank. Listen, we've got a problem. Can you talk?'

'Hang on.' Harry turned to Lawrence Gold. They were on Wardour Street, having just left Ritchie McCluskey's office. 'Lawrence,' Harry said to his so-called producer. 'Listen. I disliked Ritchie McCluskey so much I'm going to have to go home and lie down. But first I'm going to take this call. We'll talk later.'

Lawrence held his hands up in acknowledgement. 'Who needs him?' As Lawrence backed off down Wardour Street, Harry turned away, unable to watch without wanting to run back and belt him. He wasn't sure how many more of Lawrence's fuck-ups he could take.

'Frank. Long time no hear. What's the problem?'

'Have you been down Tottenham Court Road lately?'

'About an hour ago, as it happens. Yeah. Why?'

'Did you see what was going on?'

'What do you mean?'

'They've found his body. They've found his fucking body, Harry.'

'Shit,' he said. 'Shit, shit, shit, shit, shit.'

'I'll take that as a don't know, shall I?'

'I'll call Richard. You call Angelo.' Harry Foxx cleared the line with his thumb on the red button, cursed and keyed in Richard's number.

'Who is this?' Richard answered.

'Who do you think?' retorted Harry.

'Who *is* this?'

'It's your bloody driver.'

'All right, Harry. No worries. What's going on?'

'According to Frank, they've found Burns's body.'

There was silence on the other end of the line.

'Richard?'

'I heard you,' came Richard's voice. 'I suppose it was inevitable.'

'What shall we do?'

'You'd better come and pick me up,' Richard said finally.

'I'm on my way.'

When he had read the story on the front page of the *Standard* right through to the end, Angelo read it again then folded the newspaper into his jacket pocket and waited for the train to pull into Paddington, where he got off. Some nights he travelled on to Royal Oak, looking up at the rear of his building from the train, pretending that he didn't live there and that someone else did. But tonight he got off at Paddington. It meant a longer walk, but he liked walking almost as much as he liked riding on trains.

He reached 208 Gloucester Terrace and climbed the stairs. Although it was still light outside, it got darker inside as he climbed. He had the feeling no one other than him ever came up as high as the sixth floor. Certainly no one else had entered his flat since Burns's one and only visit. Deliveries were left in the hall. No landlord came knocking: Angelo paid his rent to an agency in Praed Street. He had never seen his nearest neighbour, only heard him coming in late, and, on one occasion, conducting a lengthy, one-sided argument in the middle of the night. On the phone, he sort of hoped.

Once inside his flat, Angelo unfolded the newspaper and read the story a third time. He turned to Alexander Walker's piece on the relationship between screen violence and real life. Angelo read the first paragraph then tossed it aside. None of these people knew anything about Iain Burns. They didn't know how much pain he'd been in, nor how kind he'd been. Yet they filled their newspaper columns and magazine spreads with such authority, as if they knew something when in fact they knew nothing. They didn't even want to know the facts if they didn't fit. Angelo had followed Frank's irregular appearances in *Sight & Sound* and *Time Out*, *Empire* and *ES Magazine*, and had never let up in his efforts to get Frank to write about the dying rep scene. At their last meeting in the Blue Posts on Newman Street, Frank had finally agreed to do a piece on disused and threatened cinemas.

Angelo noticed that the red light on his answering machine was flashing. He had considered getting rid of the machine, since it attracted so few messages, but here was one and he could guess who it was from and what it would be about.

As the machine played Frank's message, Angelo stood by the window watching the trains. Then he picked up the phone and dialled Frank's number but said nothing when Frank answered.

'Angelo?' Frank guessed.

There was a further pause and then Angelo said, 'I got your message. I saw it in the paper. Why do they say he was murdered?'

'I don't know, Angelo. I guess because a dead body being rolled up in several hundred feet of celluloid doesn't look a lot like suicide.'

'No one murdered him.'

'I know. The four of us should get together and talk. I talked to Harry Foxx. He's calling Richard. What do you say? Do you want to meet up?'

'There's no point digging up the past, and anyway, I'm busy.'

'They've dug up the past already. They dug it up today. Give me your work number. This is important.'

Angelo gave him the number and Frank rang off, leaving Angelo to go back to watching the trains.

It took most of the weekend, during which time further lurid reports appeared in the press, but finally a meeting was fixed for the following week. Frank, Angelo, Harry Foxx and Richard Charnock would meet on Tuesday night at the Troy Club in Hanway Street. Frank could hardly believe that a meeting had actually been set up, and he wouldn't believe it was really going to take place until he was sitting there, with the other three, in that grim space not a hundred yards from where they had filmed Iain Burns taking his last breath.

Frank had been to the Troy Club before, with Harry Foxx, some years previously.

With the exception of Angelo's overtures to Frank, and Richard's recent hiring of Harry Foxx as his driver, the four film-makers, the self-styled *auteurs* of 1983, had been out of touch with each other for much of the past fifteen years. On a few occasions, one had bumped into another. At the ICA's symposium on snuff movies, for example, Richard Charnock had found himself at the bar standing next to Harry Foxx and his girlfriend, Janine. At a party to celebrate the completion of Harry Foxx's only full-length feature, *Nine South Street*, Richard, Frank and Angelo had all agreed to turn up, but Richard never showed and Harry played the joker by failing to appear at his own party, so Angelo had used the occasion to harangue Frank about the closure of the Electric Cinema, as if Frank were somehow involved.

'You are,' Angelo had insisted. 'You're part of the establishment.'

'Jesus,' Frank had replied. 'If I'm part of the establishment, the British film industry's in deeper shit than I thought.'

No more than two of them had been in the same room together at the same time since Iain Burns's last night alive.

Harry Foxx had made an effort to stay in touch, at least with Frank. He'd sent change-of-address cards. Christmas cards. He'd stumbled across Frank's name on the Internet when Frank had been writing reviews and gossip, unpaid, for one of the early movie web sites, and since there'd been a link to Frank's e-mail, he'd sent him a message. This was before the completion of *Nine South Street* in 1993, but not so long before that Frank hadn't heard of it. It was his job, after all, to hear of things before they happened. So when Harry Foxx's name had popped up in his incoming mail he wondered if Harry was getting in touch just because of the film. Even so, Frank decided, that was fair enough. It was a big deal having a film come out and Harry would have a lot riding on it. So Frank had replied to Harry's e-mail and the two of them had finally fixed to meet up for a drink in the Troy Club.

'So, what are you working on?' Harry asked once they'd fought their way to the bar and got a couple of drinks.

'I'm doing a book. Or trying to.'

Harry asked him what kind of book.

'A book about visions of heaven in the cinema.'

'*It's a Wonderful Life*, *A Matter of Life and Death* . . .'

'*Jacob's Ladder*, *Les Jeux sont faits* . . .'

They both took pulls on their bottles of Beck's. Frank looked around at the other drinkers and saw fear and desperation in their eyes. Frank knew what kind of place this was. It was full of people who had either been somebody or were going to be somebody. No one there actually was somebody, not at the time that they were there.

'You used to talk about writing scripts,' Harry reminded Frank.

'I've written tons of scripts. None of them got anywhere. Didn't even get past first base. I'm trying to get a commission to do this book.'

'Well, good luck.'

'Yeah. What about you? I gather you've made a film.'

Harry flapped his hand dismissively. 'Low-budget thing,' he said.

Frank remarked, 'That's how we started out, isn't it?'

'Yes,' Harry assented quietly, looking down, not meeting Frank's gaze. Then he looked up at the scrum around them, focusing on one dead, waxy face after another. 'Do you miss Sarah?' he asked.

'What?' Frank said incredulously.

'Do you ever think about her?'

'Do I ever *think* about her? Of course I fucking think about her. Only *all the fucking time*.' Frank had moved round to face Harry while he shouted this response.

'All right, man.' Harry sensed his mistake. 'No offence. It's just that I do too, you know. So I don't know what it must be like for you.'

An uneasy silence settled over them.

'*Heaven Can Wait*,' Harry said finally. '*Ghost*.'

Frank's overriding wish was to avoid further confrontation, but he had yet to recover his balance following Harry's remarks about Sarah.

'I've seen neither, but I suppose I should,' he conceded. 'I've never even seen *It's a Wonderful Life* all the way through. It's always on at the wrong time of year, *if you know what I mean*.'

'Christmas.'

'Not a great time for widowers.'

'You should see it,' Harry urged.

'I will one day.'

There was another pause. Caught up in their own thoughts, they drank silently.

'I do miss her, you know,' Harry said. 'We all do.'

'Yeah, right. Can we change the subject? Tell me about this film.'

Harry Foxx sparked into life as he delivered a brief synopsis of his forthcoming film. Frank listened with one ear, knowing that he wouldn't remember anything of what Harry was telling him no matter how hard he concentrated. He would ask him to e-mail him some stuff about it the following day. While Harry was talking, Frank turned over in his mind what Harry had said about Sarah – how all the group missed her. For some reason it had struck Frank as an odd thing to say and it remained with him after the evening had come to an end.

Frank hadn't been back to the Troy Club since that night with Harry Foxx in 1993, and it wouldn't have been his choice of venue, but he accepted it as a *fait accompli* (Harry had agreed the details with Richard Charnock and passed them on to Frank by phone on the Saturday night, the day after the discovery of the body). Frank called Angelo on the Sunday to give him the details. Angelo put up a fight, saying he didn't have time, he had tapes to watch, trains to catch and abandoned cinemas to break into.

'All that can wait,' Frank said, shaking his head. They argued some more, Frank insisted and Angelo finally gave in.

Frank realised why he found it so hard to believe they were all going to meet up again: he didn't *want* to believe it. The prospect made him tense and nervous, and Angelo was acting so weirdly Frank was beginning to wonder if Burns's death *had* been suicide.

11 · The dead

Scotland, 1979

The day Fraser Munro finally decided he would be a film-maker rather than a surgeon was the day he took his 8mm movie camera into the anatomy department at Stirling University Medical School and shot footage of the cadavers.

Munro had shown promise and few students went into medicine without intending to carry it through. Several months into his first year at Stirling, however, Munro the medic realised he owed it to Munro the film-maker to commit to celluloid some of the extraordinary sights he saw every day and had started to take for granted. Although he knew he would never forget the sight and smell and touch of the bodies they worked on day after day, no matter how old he lived to be, he increasingly felt that it was essential he shoot some film of the stiffs.

Morality didn't come into it. Anything that could be filmed – anywhere at any time – was up for grabs. Anything that reflected the merest glimmer of light was there to be recorded. It was a black-and-white issue, no need for debate. Indeed, Munro's point of view was that something so terrible and beautiful as a partly dissected corpse *ought* to be filmed. And so, one unseasonably warm April morning in 1979, Munro took his camera into the medical school. He didn't carry it around and show it off. He didn't announce his intentions to his fellow

cutters, to the Teaching Services Manager or to the Professor
of Anatomy, but concealed the camera in his locker outside the
dissection rooms and treated the day like any other.

The students were divided into groups of six and each
group was assigned a single body and a demonstrator. At some
medical schools, the demonstrators did all the cutting and the
students merely watched. At Stirling in the 1970s, however,
the students got stuck in. They got their gloves dirty. By April,
they were up to the head and neck. When the students entered
the room, where the demonstrators had already been at work
for half an hour, bent industriously over the uncovered heads
of twenty bodies, it was like walking into an open-plan trainee
hair salon. But you soon became aware of the inexpertly shaved
skulls, the uniformly grey pallor, the hanging skin flaps.
You accepted that the demonstrators' fingers and tools were
dabbling not over a customer's fringe, but in the void that is
unkindly exposed when the skin is peeled back from the
cheek and throat and the subcutaneous tissue is sliced away.
You became aware once more of the powerful smell of the
formalin. On crossing the threshold of the dissection room,
you moved out of the real world and into this mysterious theatre
of the absurd, where mannequins were substituted for human
beings and you were allowed to plunge your hands into their
desecrated spaces and grab hold of a lung, a liver, a heart.

Munro's group was assigned the body of an elderly man,
unclaimed at his death and so, according to the Anatomy Act
of 1832, transferred from the morgue to the medical school.
Most of the cadavers had been bequeathed to the university,
but Munro's sextet had been assigned one of the few unclaimed
bodies. Not that it made much difference to him. Not, in fact,
that it made any difference to him.

There was the usual amount of chatter and laughter in
the dissection rooms that day. Although the students exercised
proper respect for the dead, the dissection rooms were a social
environment. Cold, certainly, but hardly the morgue. A place

of enlightenment. A place where, in addition to acquiring the most in-depth and accurate knowledge of human anatomy there is to be had, students would also assume the ability to make a clinical distinction between the living and the dead.

Fraser Munro worked through the morning and again in the afternoon. He didn't make a big effort to join in with the social interaction, but neither did he shun the other students. The level of contact between Munro and everybody else on that day was normal. He spoke to his demonstrator when he needed to, even addressed a few remarks to the Professor of Anatomy when he appeared in the late afternoon. When the students left, Munro departed also, but he didn't leave with anyone else. He went into the lavatory block and locked himself into a cubicle, where he waited half an hour. Running through his head was the series of shots he planned to take in the dissection rooms, a dizzy variety of angles, close-ups, long shots – the works.

The cadavers were left out at night with just wet, greasy paper and a white plastic sheet pulled over each one. With the temperature at eighteen degrees there was no need to return them to the holding area and preparation room one floor down, where the air was kept a chilly ten degrees cooler by a noisy refrigeration unit.

Munro silently unlocked the cubicle door and slipped back into the corridor that led to the dissection rooms. He collected his camera from the lockers and tried the door to the Teaching Services Manager's office, which was left unlocked so that the first aid cupboard could be accessed at all times. The hinge squealed, but the door opened. He closed it behind him, then opened the first aid cupboard and removed the key that was hanging there. There were two main entrances to the dissection room, one directly off the corridor and the other via the office of the Teaching Services Manager, where he was now. Munro used the key to open this door.

It swung open easily.

Munro held his breath, sniffed the formalin on the air and waited, then, hearing nothing, advanced into the room, the breath that he'd held now clouding in the air around his head. He guessed the temperature dropped below eighteen degrees when the interior lights were off and no one was around. He closed the door behind him quietly. The only available light came from a series of high narrow windows, creating a crepuscular effect. He swung his camera up to his eye and pressed the trigger, executing a slow pan from one side of the room to the other. The sheeted mounds had the vague, ghostly quality of sand dunes by moonlight. The electric sockets that dangled from the ceiling on long black flexes looked like cobras. Munro stepped close to the nearest table and lifted a corner of the white plastic sheet with his left hand, while still filming with his right. He gave the sheet a tug and allowed it to slide off the body, that of an old man, grey, cold, half scoured. Munro removed the greasy paper and focused right in, exploring the anatomy from as close as the poor light would allow. He wheeled back and pointed the camera at the windows, then pivoted back and zoomed in on the old man's body once more.

He moved across the room to the body he'd been dissecting, the one he liked to think of as his. His own property. After all, the man had had no surviving relatives to claim the body, and once the man himself had died, it no longer made any sense at all to refer to the body as the man's. It was a nonsense, an illogicality. There was no one for it to belong to – except the university, or Munro himself. He was the one taking it carefully, lovingly apart. He was the one caring for it, now that no else was. He was the one filming it, establishing a final, living record of the place where – the body in which – the man had lived. A man, of course, whose name he didn't even know. But he didn't *need* to know it. This wasn't the man, this lump of grey meat on the table. The man was gone, he no longer existed. An idea, a memory. A wisp of smoke. Particles on the air. If that.

Munro had climbed up on to the table and was straddling the man's legs, filming his caved-in torso and semi-demolished head in the fading, grainy light from the high windows, when the squeal of a hinge broke his concentration. The smell of formalin suddenly receded, swept away by the taste of fear, the terror of discovery. The guilty rush. Instant shame. He knew he was doing nothing wrong, but who would agree with him? Neither the Professor of Anatomy, nor the university authorities. Certainly not the security guards.

He stayed very still.

A shadow passed across the frosted glass in the door leading to the Teaching Services Manager's office. Munro stayed still in the hope that the guard would not bother to try the door.

The guard tried the door.

Munro agilely hoisted himself off the table and knelt down behind it, his eyes on a level with an arthritic hand that had strayed clear of the paper and plastic sheet. Its nails were gnarled and greyish-yellow, the skin long gone, revealing the bones and tendons fanned out like a grass rake. The security guard had entered the dissection room and was poking around the far end. Munro assessed his options. They included showing himself and inventing a story about a forgotten textbook, dashing to the other door to the corridor and hoping he could unlock it before the guard reached him, or keeping his head down and retreating from where he was as far as the exit leading to the holding area on the next floor down. He knew which offered the best chance of his film not being confiscated, and so he started to creep backwards, but couldn't avoid making a few tiny scrapes and scrunches that had the guard pricking his ears. Luckily for Munro, the acoustics in the dissection room were such that it would have been difficult for the guard to tell from which direction the noises were coming. That, plus the fact that the room was full of corpses, seemed to spook him. When he called out, 'Hello? Who's there?' his voice wavered. Munro froze, but the guard turned to check out the little open-access store room. Munro wondered if he would be tempted to open the huge steel trunk that once upon a time would have been filled with formalin and was now used as a receptacle for discarded heads and severed torsos awaiting cremation. Munro took advantage of the guard's back being turned and scuttled backwards as far as the concertina doors that led to the steps down to the holding area. There was also a dumb waiter in which cadavers were brought up from down below – the students called it the stiff lift – but operating that would make too much noise. Munro was able to ease the door open just enough to slip through without the guard noticing. He tiptoed down the stone stairs and pushed open the heavy door at the bottom. Grit crunched under the door, but it was the noise from the refrigeration unit that would be more likely to drift back up the stairs. Munro pushed the heavy door closed behind him as quickly and quietly as possible and hit the light switch. He was in the basement, the holding area. A sign on the next door said 'Preparation Room', a somewhat colourless description of the activities that went on within. Munro tried the door: it was unlocked. No one inside was going anywhere, after all, and any intruders who might penetrate this far, Munro supposed, would get what they deserved.

He closed the door of the preparation room behind him. The fluorescent light flickered and buzzed. He wasn't sure what effect that would have on his filming, but he certainly intended to find out. The preparation room, in fact, was divided into two areas, but no door filled the square archway separating the two. In the smaller ante-room, two bodies dominated the space. An obese male cadaver lay on a table to Munro's left, the back of the head resting on a wooden block. The whirr of the camera competed with the chugging of the refrigeration unit. No cutting had yet been performed on the body. The skin had started to blacken in places, from the settling of the blood, but it was fresh, or fresher than any of those upstairs, which had been in the department for up to two years. The other body

was covered by a white plastic sheet, which Munro lifted to see
the blotchy, bloated corpse of an elderly woman. The body was
newly arrived, the skin very smooth, stretched taut and inflated
by the process of embalming that had clearly been started that
afternoon and would be resumed the following day. An orange
rubber tube entered the femoral artery. When the machines
were switched on again in the morning, the body would be
pumped up further with preservative solution: formalin and
glycerol, phenol to act as a disinfectant, and methanol to aid
the dispersal of the formalin. Some medical schools removed
the blood before embalming; at Stirling they retained the blood,
with the result that cadavers generally put on two stone before
they reached the cutting-room floor.

Munro executed a tracking shot the length of the body.
He dwelt on the site where the tube entered the artery, drifted
over the genitals, one of the few details, along with the
face, that ever elicited much of an emotional response from the
majority of students – nervous sniggering.

He heard a noise behind him and snapped off the camera.

A footstep.

He shot out an arm and hit the light switch.

Another footstep.

Munro carefully replaced the sheet on the woman's body and
crept into the second room. From what he knew of the second
room, he thought it unlikely that the security guard would
follow him in, if he thought there was even the slightest chance
he'd been mistaken about the source of the noises. It was completely dark in the second room and Munro navigated by touch.
It didn't make much difference to Munro whether the light was
on or off, the contents of the second room didn't spook him.
From previous visits during teaching hours, he knew that there
were two long tables down either side of the room and that
bodies would be lined up on them next to each other wrapped
individually in transparent, heavy plastic, heads pointing to the
middle of the room, feet to the wall. His hand alighted on a bag

now. The noise produced by the refrigeration unit masked any sound he was making by moving towards the far end of the room. Above his head, he knew, an inverted miniature railway was suspended from the ceiling. Its rails and metal arms and points meant that the heavy, clanking chains, which looked as if they'd come out of an abattoir, could be manoeuvred over any cadaver in the room. The system allowed the bodies to be moved by a man working on his own.

Munro reached the back wall and pressed himself against it. The guard had reached the ante-room and switched on the light. His progress was slow, methodical. Munro had twenty seconds at most. He looked. The metal harnesslike contraption that ran on the rails was parked above his head. He let out his belt and squeezed the camera down his waistband. As the guard entered the room, Munro launched himself at the metal harness. He caught it and lifted his legs clear of the bagged cadavers, waiting silently like so many rolled-up carpets.

Munro's weight gave the device enough momentum to cover the length of the room. The points were in his favour – a turn-off to either side wouldn't have helped – and he aimed at the space between the guard and the door. The man ducked to avoid getting Munro's boots in his face and Munro landed behind him, recovering quickly and darting out of the ante-room, slamming the door after him.

Munro was at the top of the steps leading back to the dissection room before the security guard had reached the bottom. He heaved the concertina door shut after him and crossed the dissection room in seconds, colliding with a dissection table and narrowly failing to upset its freight. He nipped through the door, took a few precious seconds to lock it after him and replace the key in the first aid cupboard, then was out in the corridor, breathless and abruptly resuming normal walking pace. Many of the corridors at Stirling were lined with windows that faced directly on to the campus, so that people could see out and appreciate the beauty of what was almost certainly the prettiest university campus in the British Isles, but with the result also that people could see in and spot any inappropriate behaviour – such as tearing out of the anatomy department carrying an 8mm movie camera.

The medical school was located in an annexe to the Pathfoot Building, squeezed into the top left corner of the campus. Munro entered and moved through the Pathfoot Building as swiftly and unobtrusively as possible. Exiting by the English department, he made his way towards the foot of the wooded slope where squatted the great shining blocks of student accommodation. Munro did not have a room among them, but rented a bedsit above a butcher's shop in the town. He made his way towards the link bridge over Airthrey Loch, then through the MacRoberts Arts Centre, his trainers squelching on the smooth white linoleum. Although it was late, plenty of under-graduates were still moving through the area. Three streams of students crossed and merged outside the theatre, silhouettes against the pastel walls. Munro moved among them and walked towards the exit. Passing through the doors, he skirted the Cottrell Building until he drew level with the sports centre, where he cut across the fields. Looking back, he saw that no one was following him. Whether it was the locking of the door or his having taken a circuitous route, it certainly seemed to have wiped his trail clean. He would get to keep his film.

Within five minutes he was walking down the road into Stirling, his only pursuer the overshadowing form of the Wallace Monument at the top of the steep crag to the left. He didn't expect ever to see the university again. The decision had been made. While surgery would have earned him a good living and provided the right kind of challenge to his intellect, making movies was what drove his heart – it was his ambition, his vocation – and nothing would stand in its way.

Munro, of course, was already a film-maker. He had been a film-maker for some time, ever since he had first picked up a movie camera. As a boy he had been an obsessive recorder of data. He lived with foster parents on the island of Mull, where he recorded anything that moved – birds, farm animals, wild animals, clouds, cars, car numbers – and lots of things that didn't – plants, trees, shells, types of rock. Anything that was listed in an I-Spy book or an Observer's book. And lots of things that weren't. He filled little pads with columns of numbers and pages of notes. He travelled to the mainland and down to Glasgow and Edinburgh to look at trains and buses. He had books that contained their numbers and as he saw them he underscored each one in red ink.

When he watched television, which he did most evenings until closedown, he listed the films in a series of blue-backed exercise books, grading them from A to D and ranking all the films he saw in a month.

When he realised that the only difference between a top film director with all the very best equipment at his disposal and him – or someone like him – with, say, a Super 8 camera was a difference of scale, he decided he had to have a Super 8 camera. His foster parents had a hard time making ends meet and any presents he ever received were inexpensive, so Fraser decided he would save up and buy a camera himself. He did some gardening in the evenings for a retired English couple and went caddying at the Tobermory golf course. It took him a year but he saved enough for a second-hand Super 8, his foster parents having told him that if he paid for the camera, they would buy him some film to go in it. But when it came to it, they said they couldn't afford it. Times were hard. So he worked for another month and bought some film. He soon mastered the basics of the camera and filmed his foster parents as they slept, as they rowed with each other, as they sulked and slammed about the house. The important detail was that they weren't aware. If they became aware he would stop and pretend he'd been film-ing something else. Even if they knew, they imagined they were only part of the scenery, like the nest of occasional tables and the antimacassars, because it wouldn't have occurred to them in a million years that Fraser would be spying on them. Not because he was considered the best-behaved boy in all of Scotland, but because filming them, spying on them, would have represented the most blatant and aggressive invasion of their privacy, and they were very big on privacy – he knew that, it had been drummed into him.

Munro knew that his foster father had bored a hole in the wall separating the airing cupboard from his foster parents' bedroom. One night, getting up to go to the toilet, Fraser had crept into the bathroom – he always crept about the house, partly out of a desire to go unobserved, partly to avoid incurring his foster father's wrath by making too much noise – and heard a noise from the airing cupboard, which was situated between the bathroom and his foster parents' bedroom. The way the airing cupboard was partitioned off from the bathroom, you could see into it if you stood on tiptoes on the end of the bath, so Fraser did just that, taking great care neither to upset any of the bottles of his foster mother's bath oils, nor to pop his knee joints, and when he peered over the top of the divide between the bathroom and the airing cupboard, he saw his foster father crouched down in the airing cupboard with his eye pressed to a hole in the wall. A faint glimmer of light from the room beyond pooled in the socket of his foster father's eye. The only reason his foster father hadn't heard him climbing up was that with the way his hand was going he was making enough noise himself to cover any that Fraser had made.

Fraser's first thought was to get down very quietly and go and get his camera, but while he did get down, he didn't go and get his camera. Instead he stored away the knowledge of the spy hole and the next time he heard his foster parents at it, he wrapped a blanket around his camera to muffle the noise of its mechanism and stole into the airing cupboard. The hole was in such a position that the observer had, under less than ideal circumstances, the best possible POV on the bed. Fraser filmed his foster parents at it for ten minutes, during which time they got at it in a variety of different ways, concluding with an act that reminded Fraser of two dogs he had seen on one of his trips to Glasgow. Finished, his foster father got up from the bed and walked to the door. Fraser froze to the spot and held his breath, so that his foster father wouldn't hear him while he went to the bathroom, presumably where he was headed.

The airing cupboard door opened – it wasn't flung open, it was just opened quietly in the normal way – and Fraser was confronted by the naked figure of his foster father. He should have been devising ways to avoid being beaten, when in fact the thing that was bothering him was that he was unlikely to exit this situation with his film intact.

One will never know how Fraser's life might have panned out if he hadn't been raped and then beaten and then raped again by his foster father that night. There's no way of knowing if what Fraser would go on to do was in any way connected to what had been done to him. Some people believe that we are what we are, while others think that what we are is beaten into us at some point in our childhood.

Fraser left the next day. His foster mother wanted to take him to the doctor, but Fraser was making his own decisions now and he decided to hell with the doctor. He took his camera (minus the film he'd shot the night before, but with cans containing footage of his amateur rodent dissections, a dead sheep, close-up studies of parts of his own body) and a bag full of clothes and his Post Office Savings book and hitched a ride to Craignure, where he waited for the ferry.

He was sixteen. He found a room in a squat in Glasgow and entered a sixth-form college, where he studied sciences. In between studying for his A levels and poring over a stolen *Gray's Anatomy*, he filmed his housemates through holes in the walls and floors – the squat was in a poor state of repair and privacy was the last thing anyone could take for granted. Still working part-time to buy the film stock he needed to sustain his habit, he worked hard, determined to outperform the world's expectations of him. His teachers advised against medicine, suggesting engineering or, grudgingly, since they knew of his passion for film, the technical side of the film industry. A kid with his background going into medicine was unthinkable, was how he imagined they reached their position on his career prospects.

Privately, he reassured himself, I want to cut, I want to cut. I *will* cut, I *will* cut, he promised himself.

He got the grades and a place to read medicine at Stirling.

When Fraser Munro failed to show up on campus the day after the incident in the dissection rooms, the authorities tried to reach him at home, but by ten a.m., Munro was standing in a lay-by overlooking Loch Ness waiting for his next lift.

He didn't have to wait long. A green Mini indicated left and pulled in, the driver leaning across to push open the passenger door.

'Nice one, pal,' said Munro, swinging his gear into the car.

'Where you heading?' asked the driver.

'Inverness.'

Munro had already made his decision to quit before he filmed the cadavers.

Lying in bed in the early hours of the day that would be his last at the university, Munro's brain gnawed away at an old problem. The problem of the other Fraser Munro.

There was already another film-maker called Fraser Munro.

The other Fraser Munro, being a few years older, had a head start.

Unable to sleep, Munro got up, made a cup of tea and took down from the shelf at the top of the wardrobe a blue-backed exercise book, like the ones in which he used to write lists of the films he saw on TV. He took the exercise book to his desk and switched on the lamp. Pasted to the first lined page was a brief item clipped out of the *Scotsman*:

Inverness man saved on Ben Nevis
Fraser Munro, 25, of Rose Street, Inverness, was found 500 feet
from the summit of Ben Nevis by a mountain rescue team yesterday.
Munro, suffering from mild exposure, was taken to Inverness
General but allowed home after treatment. Munro, an aspiring film-
maker who had been 'scouting locations', thanked the rescue team
for their efforts. Gavin Irvine, of Ben Nevis Rescue Team, repeated
warnings for walkers and climbers to be fully prepared . . .

On the next page was a page torn from the programme of
the Aberdeen Film Festival:

MAN & MOUNTAIN –
the short films of Fraser Munro.

Munro's short films, shot on Super 8, join a tradition of
Scottish film in which landscape is just as important as
character and narrative. The AFF is pleased to present a
programme of recent work, including *Pinnacle of
Achievement, The Witches* and *Touching the Sky*.

Munro reread each item carefully, although he was already
intimately familiar with the content. He drank a mouthful of
tea and turned the page, where he reread this short item from
the *Press & Journal*:

Young director bids to join movie greats
Documentary film-maker Fraser Munro, 27, aims to film all of
Scotland's mountains over 3,000 feet, or 'Munros'. Currently
moving between Aberdeen and the Highlands, Munro expects
his new project to take him at least a year to complete, if
funding is forthcoming. *Munro-bagging*, the title he is giving to
the mammoth project, is not expected to gain a theatrical
release. Munro is pinning his hopes on festivals and TV. Asked if
he sees himself as a 'Jock' Cousteau of the rain-sodden

Highlands and Islands, Munro acknowledged a debt instead to director Michael Powell: 'If you watch *The Edge of the World*, you'll see I'm doing nothing new.' Powell, whose powerful film about the harsh conditions faced by Shetlanders was made in 1937, went on to direct *A Matter of Life and Death* (1946) and the controversial *Peeping Tom* (1950).

Munro, his namesake's address tucked into his back pocket, had the driver of the Mini drop him off by the bus station in Inverness. The address didn't take long to locate on foot. A small terraced house, it had the forlorn look about it of a space that had not been entered for a week or more. Since the rear overlooked BR's Inverness motive power depot, Munro sneaked on to railway land to gain access. No one was about. A couple of 08 shunters sat waiting in the sidings, and the blunt snout of a Class 37 diesel poked out from the entrance to the loco shed.

Munro stood perfectly still in the tiny kitchen, holding his breath. The back door to the house had been unlocked; it was that kind of place and that kind of time. An unwashed mug stood on the draining board; otherwise the kitchen was unremarkable. He strained for any sound but heard nothing. The house smelled of the outdoors – of thick hiking socks and heavy boots, waterproofs, old maps – as well as film.

Munro moved into the narrow hall and checked out the two tiny rooms downstairs. They looked unused, except as store-rooms for walking gear and maps. There was a dining table that would seat two at a push and, in the front room, a settee that looked as if it hadn't been sat on for at least a year. Orange light sifted through the lace curtains.

Upstairs was where the other Fraser Munro planned his operations. There were two bedrooms. At the front was where he slept whenever he was at home, which wasn't often by the look of it. The back room was where he worked. There were more maps thumbtacked to the wall, some familiar stills – an image of a fireman from Humphrey Jennings's wartime documentary *Fires Were Started*, a shot of the distinctive Mull landscape from Powell and Pressburger's *I Know Where I'm Going!* – and a few unrecognisable ten-by-eights that could have been from the other Munro's own work, grainy shots of mountains, their tops lost in cloud, plus two snaps of the depot taken from the window behind where Munro was standing. On a cheap shelving unit stood a series of film cans. Munro opened one and sniffed the contents. He uncoiled some film and held a strip up to the light. More mountains.

There was also a ring binder on the shelf, which Munro took down and laid on the desk. It was filled with well-thumbed pages of lined A4, many of them covered in his namesake's untidy handwriting. It seemed to be mostly script ideas and notes to himself. In a loose-leaf folder on the desk itself Munro found a photocopied list of Munros – mountains in Scotland over 3,000 feet, named after Hugh Thomas Munro, who published a list of them in 1891. Breathing faster, Fraser leaned over the desk. Some of the names had been crossed out, others underlined. On a separate sheet was a list of the Munros that Munro had bagged so far, in what was presumably chronological order from one to two hundred and thirty-three. Number two hundred and thirty-four was written in lightly in pencil and when Fraser looked closer he could see that the preceding two hundred and thirty-three names had also been written down at first in pencil before being inked in later.

Number two hundred and thirty-four was 'Ben More (3,169)'.

Fraser Munro, while more common in Scotland than elsewhere, is still an unusual pairing of names, family and given. The phone directory lists only four F. Munros in the Edinburgh district, and not one of those initial Fs need stand for Fraser.

Since picking up a movie camera, Munro had known that he wanted to make films and he knew that he wanted his work to bear his name. It would both enable him to escape from his past and help him to establish his own identity. Discovering that another man with the same name was already embarked on the same course threw him into an existential crisis. In purely practical terms he was faced with a dilemma: should he stay at medical school or should he go?

The dilemma nagged at Munro night and day. While he stripped fat and flesh from veins and tendons he wrestled with it and when he lay down himself, in unconscious imitation of the partially dissected body on his table, the dilemma fought back, preventing sleep. The existence of the other Fraser Munro was, he felt, a bar to his becoming a successful film-maker in his own right. Even if they both, so to speak, made a name for themselves making movies, he would never just be Fraser Munro the film-maker, but Fraser Munro of Fraser Munro and Fraser Munro, the coincidental double act of Scottish cinema. They'd be a novelty turn, an item. The publicity might help their careers, but in a way they'd only have one career between them. Their fates were inextricably linked by an accident of birth and vocation.

So, the day that Munro took his movie camera into the dissection rooms, he took not one life-changing decision, but two. As in, decisions that would change two people's lives.

There are two Ben Mores among the Munros, but Fraser Munro didn't need to study the map to find out where his namesake had gone to commit his next mountain to film. Anyone who lives on an island knows its highest point. Fraser knew without having to check that Ben More on Mull was 3,169 feet above sea level.

He returned to Mull and asked around. Careful to stay away from his foster parents' corner of the island, near the miniature railway that ran between Craignure and Torosay Castle, he camped outside Tobermory where he wouldn't attract attention. He courted rumour in the bars and pubs along the harbour front, but no one knew anything about a lad with a movie camera filming the mountain. He headed down to Salen, the tiny village at the island's tightly corseted waist. It was at Salen that you turned off if you were going to Ben More. The landlord of Salen's only pub remembered serving a laddie who said he was going up the mountain with a camera. Munro explained that he was supposed to be working with him and had been delayed. Hadn't the film-maker rented a wee croft? the landlord asked a strawberry-nosed bundle of tweeds at the bar, who nodded his assent. A couple of whiskies produced directions to the croft and Munro was on his way.

He studied the croft from the road. Fifty yards down a rutted track, it would have been easy to miss had he not known exactly where to look. A light burned in the only north-facing window.

Munro.

Fraser Munro.

The other Fraser Munro.

Fraser Munro – Fraser Munro, the abused child turned corpse-cuddler – pitched a one-man tent on a hillside a quarter of a mile from the croft. Sitting inside the tent with the flap held back, he could see the tiny cottage that contained his quarry. He sat and watched the cottage until the light in the window winked out at eleven fifteen p.m. He slept shallowly, the thin groundsheet little match for the tussocky grass, and forced himself awake at dawn. The light in the cottage was back on. The other Fraser Munro was an early riser. At eight thirty the door opened and Munro stepped out, camera in hand. Fraser felt his breath catch, his heart thump. His mouth dried. He reached behind him for the backpack he had prepared and crawled out of the tent. He kept a steady two hundred yards behind Munro, a dark green cagoule the hunter's only camouflage if his quarry were to look back.

The two men headed west along the road that would eventually skirt Ben More. There was a fresh breeze and a swath of low grey cloud. Fraser hung back when the forest on either side of the road started to thin out, exposing him, and so missed seeing

Munro leave the road, but then he spotted him striding up one of the easier routes up the mountain. Fraser followed. The summit was not visible from this angle, but Fraser guessed it would be cloudbound as usual.

Most of the climb was simple. Fraser had done it before many times. He knew that three-quarters of the way to the top they would hit a brief steeper section, then cross a gently sloping boggy area before hitting the steep scree slope. Beyond that was a ridge that was less steep but more treacherous. Reach the top of that and you're home.

As he climbed, he was aware of the clouds settling over the summit ahead, which was bad news for his quarry in more ways than one. Fraser waited at the start of the boggy slope until his namesake had crossed it and had a little rest before starting to scramble up the scree slope. He jumped up and trotted across the bog, jumping from tussock to tussock. When Fraser reached the scree, the older man was only a hundred yards ahead and still oblivious.

Fraser stopped for breath and turned for the first time to look at the view, so intent had he been on not taking his eyes off the blue cagoule in front. Straight ahead was Loch Na Keal, to the left the island of Ulva. The sun was bright and clear, and the speed of his ascent had brought Fraser out in a sweat. He turned and looked back up the scree slope. The blue cagoule was making slow but steady progress. Fraser knew he didn't have time to waste and set to his task once more. The cloud layer, Fraser's ally, was very close now, but it could only be his ally if he didn't delay reaching it himself. Leave too long a gap between Munro's penetration of it and his own and he'd be in trouble. It was such a simple detail and yet he'd only just thought of it, when it was harder to accelerate than on the easy reaches of the lower slopes. It was a mistake and it irritated him. If he was carrying out his destiny, he mustn't let himself down. He wouldn't get another chance. Looking up, he saw that the blue smudge had already been erased from the slate mountainside by the felt-grey duster of cloud. Fraser felt his destiny beginning to slip away and at the same time experienced a surge of adrenaline that gave strength to his calf muscles. His quarry was fitter and more used to climbing mountains.

He was aware as he hurried up the slippery scree that the hardest part was still ahead – the narrow ridge leading to the summit. What tended to happen as soon as you hit the ridge was you got buffeted by fierce, freak winds from the north-east that came tearing over the ridge like galloping horses and threatened to kick you off the mountain.

Above all, Munro mustn't be allowed to reach the summit before him. If he did, Fraser sensed, the impetus would be lost and with it would go his future career, his identity, his life. He had embarked on a major creative act and had to see it through. Fail and he might as well fling himself from the ridge to certain death on the rocks that dominated the mountain's north-east side.

He entered the cloud and immediately hit the next section – the ridge. The wind was relentless, implacable, indifferent to his fate. When he'd been up here in the past it had been bad but not this bad. With visibility down to a few yards he kept his eye to the ground, checking that he didn't stray too close to the edge. There was no question of observing Munro. Within half a minute of getting into the cloud, Fraser had become completely soaked through. His hair was plastered to his head, loose strands ripped free by the wind. He was bent double for safety, but couldn't have straightened up if he'd tried. He thought about giving up and going back, but knew that there was no way back. Defeat would mean the end of everything. Confronting Munro would signify the beginning of something unknown and terrifying but without question creative. It was the only option. Fraser Munro would be the name on his movies, not his and those of some other guy with the same name. If his CV had to inherit a few documentaries about rural life and short films about high mountains, so be it.

The wind intensified and the little knives of the driving horizontal rain stabbed right through to his bones. He pictured his foster parents in their little stone house only a few miles away. He felt he knew at last why they had fostered him: not to save on ashtrays, as he had once suspected, by stubbing their cigarettes out on his arms, but to be a psychic sponge to soak up the turbulent emotions of their marriage. To ensure they didn't beat each other to death in their stubborn and perverted battle of wills. It was a survival mechanism, but only for them. The boy designed one for himself in the shape of a movie camera.

Deafened by the wind and numb with cold, Fraser staggered off the ridge on to the last section, a stroll to the cairn itself. For whatever reason, as soon as you step off the ridge on to the final straight, the wind falls away completely. It makes no sense at all, since the summit is the highest point on the island and cannot therefore be sheltered, but those few degrees to the east you turn through to reach the summit are enough to take you out of the wind. Fraser had never understood the phenomenon, but he was thankful for it now. The cloud was just as thick, but in the sudden stillness the moisture hung heavily in the air like sodden drapes. The conditions were less inhospitable, but it was no easier to see anything more than ten yards away. A trail of regularly spaced knee-high cairns kept you on course for the summit.

Fraser advanced slowly as it dawned on him where Munro would be. The big cairn at the summit was hollow, like a miniature castle keep with no roof. Two climbers could sit comfortably within its walls and rest before making their way down the mountain. Even as he remembered this detail, Fraser saw the cairn looming up through the cloud. He approached it very slowly until he could reach out and touch the stones in its wall. Through the gaps between the stones, he could make out a dark shape inside.

Fraser crouched down, but could hear nothing above the soft, muffled billowing of what little wind there was. The steps up that enabled you to climb inside the cairn were around the other side. He held his breath, but still couldn't hear anything over the wind, neither the rustle of a cagoule, nor the whirr of a camera. The time for waiting was over. He rose to his feet and circled the cairn, not looking over its edge until he reached the far side and the steps up. There he stopped, his left foot already on the first step.

Pointed straight at him from inside the cairn was a Bolex 8mm movie camera, its single black eye filmed with moisture. Fraser knew his image on the film would be blurry, but his being caught on film was an accident. Munro couldn't have been expecting him.

Munro lowered the camera and Fraser stepped into the cairn.

Munro said, 'Hello.'

Fraser grunted.

'Hard to believe the sun's shining halfway down the mountain.'

'Aye.'

'That ridge is a bit of a bastard.'

'Aye, it is.'

Both men fell silent and looked out over the edge of the cairn.

'Taking a souvenir, are you?' Fraser asked, looking at the camera.

'Something like that. I make films.'

'Aye well, there's a coincidence, so do I.'

'No.'

'Aye.' Fraser sat forward and worked his backpack free of his shoulders. He untied the drawstring at the neck and stuck his hand inside, pulling out his own 8mm camera like a rabbit from a hat.

'Nice camera,' said the other.

'It'll do till I get a better one. Yours is nice. Maybe I should have that one.'

Munro laughed, possibly nervously – it was hard to tell. He

was about the same size and weight as Fraser, but his hair was longer and untidier. He looked as if he hadn't shaved for a couple of days. Hair continues to grow on a dead man for thirty-six hours.

'What do you shoot with it?' the other man asked him, clearly wanting to redirect attention to Fraser's camera.

'Dead men,' Fraser replied, lifting the camera to his eye and squeezing off a few frames.

Munro said nothing, but sat stiffly as the camera filmed him.

'How about yourself?' Fraser asked him. 'There's not much up here to film and the light's not great.'

'Mountains. Munros. That's my name, you see. Munro.' His voice wavered on the last word. He was definitely nervous now.

'There's another coincidence for you.' Fraser's delivery was deadpan.

'What's that?'

'Munro's my name, too.'

'Weird.'

'Definitely.'

'I don't usually believe in coincidence.'

'You're probably right not to.'

'Anyway, I have to be going.'

'Not so fast.'

'What d'ye mean?'

'I mean not so fast. You're going nowhere.'

True enough. Munro appeared frozen to the spot, too frightened to move, bewildered by the turn of events, unsure how to prevent the violence that seemed increasingly inevitable.

'Look, do you want my camera?'

'Aye. It's not all I want.'

'What do you want?'

'*I want to be me.*'

Munro had started to shake. With the cold? With fear?

'You want to be you?'

'I want to be me and you won't let me.'

Fraser stood up suddenly. Munro did likewise, taking a half-step back and falling against the wall of the cairn.

'What's your name?'

'I told you. Munro. Fraser Munro.'

'That was your last chance.'

'What do you mean? That's my name. Fraser Munro.'

'That's *my* name.'

Fraser raised his camera and Munro flinched, lifted an arm to ward off the blow that didn't come.

And then, along with a repetition of the phrase '*my* name', it did come. The camera struck him on the right temple, hard, hard enough to knock him down, and Fraser hit him again as he fell, twice, three times, repeating '*my* name'. He hit him on the ground, still inside the cairn, all the time with the camera and all the time with his fingers clutched around the handle, the soft whirr of the camera's motor the only sound apart from the repeated cracks to the victim's skull and the harsh rasp of Munro's breathing. After a while he stopped hitting him and for a short time he continued to film – then he stopped that as well.

12 · The actress

At the magazine on the Monday morning, people were talking about the discovery of the body and the reports of its having been wrapped in celluloid. Tom the editor had been on *The Big Breakfast* before coming in to work: anything to squeeze a few more sales out of the viewing public. Frank scoured the newspapers for any speculation about a connection between the body and their film.

Virtually no one knew about *Auteur*. It was a genuine underground movie, in that it had never been released, but had acquired mythic status. Did it or did it not exist? Had anyone ever seen it? From time to time, people claimed to have seen it. Some called it by the title the group had given it, which lent their claims some authenticity, while others spoke with great authority about 'that snuff movie' they'd never even seen. There'd been no talk of it for some time and Frank was hoping that no one would think to make a connection.

Jonathan Romney in the *Guardian*, however, dashed Frank's hopes.

'The discovery of the dead body of a man in the foundations of a former cinema just up the road from Central St Martin's School of Art,' wrote Romney in a short piece entitled 'It's a Wrap' in *G2*, 'while bizarrely exciting the imaginations of those obsessed with the question of screen violence, has also breathed new life into old rumours of the existence of a short film depicting an actual suicide.'

Frank felt the blood rushing to his face. He looked up from his desk to see that office life was going on as normal. Christopher, the video reviewer, walked into Tom's office to leave a set of proofs on his desk. Tom was locked into a struggle with the art director over a cover. Siân would be at her desk sifting through cellophane wallets of glossy ten-by-eights. He looked back down at the paper.

'It was reported, by different sources, as long ago as 1985,' Romney went on,

that a group of unnamed students from Central St Martin's had made a short film of a man committing suicide. Very few people can be found who have actually seen the film, if indeed it exists, and of those who do claim to have seen it, not all seem to be describing the same film. Some speak of a dimly lit and badly shot home movie that is not so much a sequence of *longueurs* as one continuous *longueur*, while others praise its economy, its deliberate use of overexposure and its lack of sentimentality in handling a difficult subject. Ira Konigsberg's *Complete Film Dictionary* defines a snuff movie as 'a film, other than a newsreel or documentary, in which human life is actually taken' (Carcanet's *The Language of Cinema*, oddly, does not list the term – a surprising omission by the assiduous Kevin Jackson). 'Such films are supposedly made for the purpose of providing pleasure,' Konigsberg continues. 'Although none of these films have publicly surfaced, their very concept offers the next step beyond the present state of violence and mayhem in the cinema.' Supposing for a moment that *Auteur* – the title given to it by some of those who claim to have seen it – exists, the question arises: is it or is it not a snuff movie? Is filming a suicide significantly different from shooting a murder? Assuming that the film-makers are doing nothing to prevent the suicide, the answer at which we are bound to arrive is that there is no substantive distinction between *Auteur* and a snuff movie.

Romney went on to say that further deductions could possibly be made when more details about the case were released by the police. He ended his piece by pondering the origin of the film used to wrap up the body. Most appropriate might have been *The Mummy*, he wrote, either Karl Freund's 1932 original or Terrence Fisher's 1959 version, although one would not want to rule out Paul Schrader's *Mishima: A Life in Four Chapters*. More likely, he went on, was that the celluloid was discarded leader stock that impoverished film students would have been able to blag from Soho labs. He ended by reiterating that not only was the existence of *Auteur* in doubt, but that even if it did exist, any link between the two things was the very longest of long shots.

Frank needed some air. He took the stairs to the roof, where you went if you wanted to smoke or just hang out. The roof was busy. A few writers squatted with laptops, struggling pointlessly to make out their screens against the sunlight. Girls from ad sales stood in small groups, one arm folded under their breasts, the other pointing straight up from the elbow, holding a cigarette close to the mouth. Tense, nervy designers wiped sweat from foreheads and swallowed quick mouthfuls of Diet Sprite before heading back downstairs to meet impossible deadlines. The magazine shared the building with two others owned by the same company, a fashion rag and a clubbing journal. Jim Cover, the picture editor from the fashion magazine, was conducting a meeting with a model. Jim Cover was very young; everyone who worked on the fashion magazine seemed to be under thirty, while the clubbers thought that twenty-five was ancient. Jim Cover was sitting on a moulded plastic chair smoking Camels and drinking Diet Coke. Frank heard the model tell Jim Cover that her name was Jenny Slade and that she'd brought her book in as he'd asked. He sensed that she thought she was above all this. She looked as if she might be.

Cover placed his Diet Coke on the ground and stuck his

cigarette between his lips as he grasped her huge portfolio and slid it on to his knees. The zip rasped and he glanced at the first picture, then turned the page. He didn't speak as he moved swiftly through the series of plastic pages, each containing prints or pages torn out of magazines. Jenny Slade played with a strand of her dyed-black hair, then moved her fingers slowly over the soft fabric of her white designer top.

Jim Cover looked up at Jenny Slade, squinting through a cloud of smoke as he closed the portfolio and handed it back to her.

She tugged the zip round the rim.

'I'd be interested to see more,' he said, lighting another Camel.

'Sorry?'

'Let me see some more stuff. In a month or two.'

'Yeah, well,' she said. 'Maybe.'

Frank watched the girl walk towards the stairs back to the fourth floor. As she disappeared through the doorway, Frank looked away and caught Jim Cover's eye. He returned Frank's gaze, blankly, then looked down and reached for his Diet Coke.

It was Frank's turn to head for the door. He wanted to see Siân. Even though he couldn't talk to her about Burns and the film, he needed to see her.

Tom and Karl, the deputy editor, were talking to Siân and turned round at Frank's abrupt approach.

'Sorry,' Frank said quickly. 'Just, er . . . wanted to . . .' And he pulled open the nearest of Siân's filing cabinets and pretended to look through the hanging files in search of stills for a particular film. It occurred to him then, as Tom, Karl and Siân renewed their conversation (they were talking about movies starring Robin Williams; Frank made a mental note to ask Siân about that later), that, having reached the chapter in his book where he dealt with films that had Angel in the title, he did need to look for some stills. He closed the F drawer and moved to his left to open the second of the A drawers. He flicked through from the front. *Angel* (good film, fine performance by

Stephen Rea, but not about an angel, as far as he could recall), *Angel at My Table* (would he actually have to watch a New Zealand movie? Then he remembered Vincent Ward's magnificently ambitious *Map of the Human Heart*, which reminded him that Ward's *What Dreams May Come*, with Robin Williams, would be out soon and was actually set in Heaven), *Angel Dust* (Japanese, sounded great, hadn't seen it).

Angel Heart, which he needed for at least one other chapter as well, didn't seem to be present, unless it had got filed in the wrong place. His eyes moved on towards the back of the drawer to see if it was there.

L'Année dernière à Marienbad (didn't Marienbad have a vaguely celestial feel about it?), *L'Appartement* (overrated, contrived), *Aria*, *Assault on Precinct 13*, *Atlantic City* (Louis Malle – enough said, although *Le feu follet* was his), *Au revoir les enfants* (ditto), *Austin Powers: International Man of Mystery* (yes, well), *Auteur*—

A chill blade lodged in the small of his back. He felt hot and cold at the same time and became short of breath. A mistake, it had to be a mistake. Another film with the same title. Had to be. They hadn't checked. Hadn't bothered to check. Silly them.

He took hold of the cellophane wrapper and gingerly withdrew it. The label on the front of the wallet repeated the title, and showing through quite clearly was a picture of the four of them, off set, taken by Kerner at some point before the shoot. Frank swallowed twice in quick succession. Sweat had begun to trickle from his hairline. Aware of their sudden silence, Frank turned to face Tom and Karl and Siân.

'Everything all right?' Tom asked

'Yes,' Frank replied automatically, clutching the stills to his chest. 'I, er . . . no, I just thought of something. Sorry.' So saying, he pushed the drawer shut and turned on his heel, marching down the now endless tunnel of filing cabinets that led back to the rest of the office. On reaching his desk, he grabbed an empty card-backed envelope and slipped the stills inside, then headed straight for the loos. He pushed open the door, saw that there was no one within, and locked himself in a cubicle. He lowered the seat and sat down, felt inside the envelope for the stills and pulled them out with great care.

He was dimly aware of a headache diffusing outwards from a tight knot at the top of his skull.

The first still, as he'd seen, was of the four of them, taken prior to the making of the film, possibly pre-dating Burns's appearance in their lives. He moved on to the next: a portrait of Richard Charnock in Kerner's recognisable, blurry style. This was followed by a shot taken on set: Burns sitting on the old sheet-covered sofa, legs apart, head down. Frank made a fan of the remaining photographs. Stills from another film had been mixed in. A naked actress caught in the middle of a sex scene. A shot of Harry Foxx, then Frank and Angelo together with Harry Foxx and Richard Charnock out of focus in the background.

It wasn't a naked actress.

She was naked but she was no actress.

Frank did the world's slowest double-take on the pictures of the girl.

There were three different shots. All apparently taken during a love scene. Different angles. From beneath, sideways on – both close up. And a long shot, her partner just out of view – you could see part of his leg, but not enough to identify him.

Frank put the photographs back into the envelope and sat still for a moment, blood thumping in his ears. He realised he was going to be sick just moments before the reflex became uncontrollable. Time enough to get up and raise the seat.

It was the look on Sarah's face, a look he knew so well, a look he'd never forget and had no reason to suspect he would ever see again. A possibility occurred to him: that Kerner had somehow spied on them making love, but as soon as he thought this he knew it was impossible. Then, desperate for any way out, he wondered if he could have taken them himself and somehow

erased the memory. But he was certain, he'd never photographed Sarah like that. He'd hinted, once or twice, that it
might be fun, but she'd ruled it out. That was what made it
even worse. She'd let another guy do it. While she was with
someone else.

Harry Foxx spent Tuesday morning lying in bed selectively re-
reading the reviews of *Nine South Street*, which he kept in a big
black ring binder, and thinking about *MPD*, the film that he
and Lawrence seemed unable to get off the ground. Janine was
out at work and Harry had the machine intercepting his calls,
which were all from Lawrence, his voice easily carrying up the
stairs. Harry was increasingly irritated by Lawrence's relent-
lessly upbeat tone. Lawrence had a new plan that couldn't fail.
Lawrence accepted that Ritchie McCluskey had been a bad
move. Lawrence was committed to this movie and Harry should
trust him on this.

Bollocks, thought Harry. The problem was not Harry Foxx
or *MPD*. The problem was Lawrence.

Harry got up, pulled on a dressing gown and went downstairs to lower the volume on the answering machine. While he
was in the kitchen he filled the kettle and flicked the switch.
Then flicked it off again. He switched the transistor radio on
to hear the voice of a politician saying, 'I'm glad you asked me
that question. I'd like to answer that question in three ways.
Firstly—' He switched it off.

From rows and rows of CDs he tried to find something he
wanted to hear, but every one that he slid out to have a look at
he just slid right back in again – even John Foxx's *Metamatic*.
Eventually he settled on something to suit his mood: Stravinsky's
Miniature Masterpieces. He dropped it into the CD player,
skipped forward to track 29, the first of four Études for Orchestra,
and pressed play.

The coffee table was still covered with the weekend's papers,
a couple of them folded open at the story about the discovery

of Burns's body. Harry hadn't needed to hide them from Janine because he had told her about *Auteur* not long after they'd met, casually breaking the vow of silence he'd made with Richard, Frank and Angelo.

Back upstairs, he sat on his side of the bed and looked at the unread books on his bedside cabinet: *Inside Stories: Diaries of British Film-makers at Work*, Conrad's *Heart of Darkness* and a couple of BFI Film Classics – David Thomson's *The Big Sleep* and John Pym's *Palm Beach Story*. Whenever he picked one of them up, a little voice nagged at him that he was supposed to be making his own movies, not reading about other people's.

Harry picked up bottles and jars from Janine's dressing table, revealing circles in the thin film of dust on the lacquered surface. He replaced them carefully and, collecting the ring binder from the bed, wandered into the guest bedroom, where he lay down on the unmade bed. He opened the ring binder, which was filled with A4-size clear plastic pockets. The first dozen contained reviews of *Nine South Street*, organised so that the best ones came at the front and only later did negative comments creep in. The last three or four hadn't found much to praise, but Harry was philosophical: you couldn't expect everyone to understand your work, and really it was their loss. He wasn't making films for the masses; he could leave that to Richard Charnock.

After the reviews came numerous press cuttings about film-makers of a certain kind, writer-directors with a certain edge: Richard Stanley, Christopher Petit, Vadim Jean, Shane Meadows, Paul Mayersberg. There was nothing on Alan Parker, Kenneth Branagh or Duncan Kenworthy – or the *Shallow Grave/Trainspotting* crew for that matter.

There were pages and pages of Frank's journalism, reviews and features, whatever he happened to be writing about and wherever it had been published – Frank covered the well-known film magazines as well as more general titles and the broadsheets.

He carried on turning the plastic pages, going past Frank's stuff, until eventually he came to a cutting from the *Guardian* dated Saturday 29 January 1983. 'Woman found by canal is hit-and-run victim,' read the headline. Harry's eyes followed the lines of print: 'The body of a young woman found in under-growth beside the Grand Union Canal in west London yester-day is believed to have been dumped following a hit-and-run incident, police said. Wounds to the head and legs were found on the body, which was discovered by a man walking his dog on an isolated stretch of the canal near Wormwood Scrubs.' Harry looked away; he knew the story, he'd read it often enough.

Joining his hands behind his head, Harry stared out of the dirty window at the railway line. The line went north to Old Oak Common depot, where Harry wanted to set *MPD*. Every evening a Eurostar train would glide past the window on its way to the sheds. Occasionally there'd be a Connex South-Eastern heading south to Olympia or north to Willesden Junction. Freight services rumbled through in the night. Otherwise, the line wasn't that busy. Beyond the line squatted Hammersmith Hospital and Wormwood Scrubs. Harry smiled grimly at the supposed contrast between his freedom and the incarceration imposed on the patients and inmates of those two institutions, where men lay prone on beds not unlike Harry's, prevented, by either locked doors or physical inability, from walking across the Scrubs to have a closer look at the canal or the sidings beyond. While Harry's door was unlocked and his legs functioned well enough, there were mornings when he couldn't face get-ting out of bed.

He had been staring at the window for some time before his eyes focused on the glass itself and then on a handprint that had never before caught his attention. A left hand, the thumb splayed for maximum support. That he'd not noticed it before didn't mean it hadn't been there since before they'd moved in. He couldn't remember the last time the guest bedroom had been used. The handprint could be anybody's, even his own. He knew he should get up and do some work, but he continued to lie there and stare at the handprint until he was no longer aware that he was doing so.

Richard Charnock pressed his hand against the glass, but Harry Foxx was oblivious. He'd seemed a bit out of it when Richard had rung and asked him to pick him up from the house. But Harry had agreed to come round to Holland Park right away. It was a short ride, but a world away, from Latimer Road. Admittedly, Richard had taken his time getting ready once he'd heard the bark of the Merc's horn signalling Harry's arrival in the street outside, but he surely hadn't taken that long: Harry appeared to be fast asleep in the driver's seat.

Still pressing his palm against the window, Richard used his other hand to rap twice on the glass. Harry jumped and looked round, seeing the hand pressed against the glass, and then Richard's face beyond it.

'What's the matter with you?' Richard asked as soon as Harry had recovered sufficiently to lower the window.

'Tired, I guess. Working too hard.' Harry rubbed his face.

'I worry about you, Harry,' Richard said, opening the rear door.

'Really?' he said, without inflection.

'You don't seem very happy. You should be happy. You've got a lovely wife –'

'Girlfriend.'

'– a good job . . .' Richard settled into the soft taupe leather of the back seat. 'What's this shit?' he asked, pointing to a Thanks For Not Smoking sign.

'What's it look like?'

'The reformed ex-smoker is a cliché, Harry. You are aware of that?' So saying, Richard took a pack of Camels from his pocket, extracted one and lit it.

'I never was a smoker,' Harry pointed out.

'So what were those paper tubes sticking out of your mouth with tobacco in?'

'That's just the point: there was very little tobacco in them. I never smoked cigarettes.'

So saying, Harry lowered the passenger window to create a draught.

'You're taking the piss, Harry.'

Richard averted his gaze from Harry's rear-view mirror and stared at his cigarette while his driver executed a neat, accelerating turn into Holland Park Avenue. Richard was anxious. He'd been anxious for days. Although he'd so far concealed it from Harry, he was strung up. He had the most to lose from any link, no matter how tenuous, that might be established between the exhumed body and the four film-makers. Harry didn't have much to lose, obviously, or he'd be sitting in the back of his own car being driven around by someone else; Frank at least had a job, even if he was just a critic; Angelo had lost the plot so badly he could only benefit from a long stretch, should the four of them go down for assisted suicide. Richard was the only one out of the four who had built up a career in the movies. So what if the critics thought his films were crap? He was the only one out of the four who was making movies. The only one with Jenny Slade's home number.

He thought briefly about the tape in the VCR at his office. He thought about Jenny Slade's acquiescence, the calculated strategy of her undressing for him. It was a game they were both playing.

He knew how critics and film business types thought about him: Michael Winner but no cigar. Richard's view was that it was preferable to be making films that might end up stuffed in a canal-bound sack with the entire *Death Wish* series and a lump of concrete than shooting movies that were so up their own arse they couldn't get screened outside of the ICA and one or two empty art houses in the provinces. People actually went to see Richard's films. They'd made money at the box office *and* popped up on Channel 5, the only terrestrial channel to get the balance right between quality and soft porn.

Apart from *Auteur*, which did not feature on his CV, Richard was proud of never having directed an uncommercial film. He had made his name, controversially, by winning a BBC talent contest for first-time directors in the autumn of 1983. The competition had been conceived as a way of attracting high-quality, high-art film-makers to the BBC and getting them to commit to directing a whole series of films, but when Charnock's film won, it was condemned as trashy, superficial and full of gratuitous nudity. The accusations levelled at the BBC ranged from disingenuously pandering to the lowest common denominator to merely displaying catastrophically bad judgement. The decision stood, but instead of winning the promised contract to direct a number of films for BBC 2, Charnock was bought off. He got good representation and the cash went towards the house in Holland Park.

The BBC might have dropped him, but the sleaze-merchants beat a path to his door. Offers to direct flooded in; he took the jobs that looked least like actual hardcore and soon had a line of product that was like a 1980s variation on the *Confessions* films. *The Night Porter* without the pretension to high art. Or Charlotte Rampling. Ken Russell without the laughs. Indeed, Michael Winner but no cigar.

Meeting Caroline coincided with a hiatus. Caroline, whom he met at one of the members' clubs he joined as fast as they could open, was divorced and came with two children. Her moving in would mean there was someone to look after the house while he wasn't around.

His next film represented a sideways move from the lucrative softcore that had become his stock-in-trade: *NW3* was pitched as psychological drama among the Hampstead set, lightly satirising the chattering classes. *Time Out* called it a 'grotesque comedy of bad sex and bad manners'; the *Sunday Times* said it was simply 'appalling'. But the sex in it worked for the rental market, and Richard Charnock, for all the low esteem in which he was held, remained a bankable director; hence *Little Black Dress*, which attracted the necessary backing without too much trouble. Being a pariah freed him to do what he wanted.

'Good job we never released it,' Harry Foxx remarked, breaking into Richard's reverie.

'What's that?'

'The Burns film. *Auteur*. It's a good job it never got released. We'd be in a lot of bother. I sometimes wonder why we did make it,' Harry mused as he accelerated past the concrete brutalism of the Czech Embassy, 'if we didn't want it to be seen, didn't have something to say.'

'Didn't we make it because he threw himself upon us?' Richard said, his spine uncurling from the soft padding of the seat. 'Because here was a chance to make our first movie and it could be so controversial and dangerous that if we'd stopped to think even for a moment, we'd have realised it could never be released. I think we were all rather in love with ourselves and obsessed by our ambition and we didn't have a clear view of anything that wasn't on the set. We were intense. It was an intense time. Let's face it, we didn't know what we were doing.'

Richard suddenly became aware that the car had stopped at a set of lights on Bayswater Road and that Harry had twisted round in the driver's seat to look at him. Richard had crept forward while delivering this speech and was now perched on the edge of the seat.

'You know what,' Harry advised, 'you should wear your seat-belt.'

Richard recovered his composure and reached for his cigarettes.

'You never wore it,' Harry continued as he faced the front and moved the Mercedes away from the lights, 'even in the old days. Look at Diana. She was in one of these and she wasn't wearing a seat-belt.'

'You're beginning to sound exactly like the kind of chauffeur I didn't want,' Richard said, gazing out of the window at the green blur of Kensington Gardens, thinking about the meeting that was only half an hour away. He didn't know what they could do to keep the story from getting out and he couldn't see what they might achieve by meeting up to talk about it. They'd probably just panic each other. He wondered what it would be like to see the others again after so long and he found it was a question he couldn't answer. Surely, he thought, if he'd wanted to see more of them he would have done. Being a critic, Frank was bound to resent Richard's success. As for Angelo, well . . .

Harry's attitude to his success was obvious, although he strove to hide it. And that was in spite of Harry's having had some small success of his own. In fact, when Richard thought about it, Harry's success had been so small he would probably have been better off without it. To have made a film and have virtually no one see it must be worse than never to have made a film. Accepting Richard's job offer must have been a tough one for Harry.

'I don't like to be constrained,' Richard said vaguely.

'What?'

'The seat-belt,' he explained. 'I don't like being tied down.'

'Yeah, right. Well, it's your funeral.'

At the Troy Club, Frank and Angelo were sitting at a table by the window, their drinks virtually untouched. Frank stood up to shake hands with Richard and Harry; Angelo remained in his seat and gave an awkward wave. Richard ran his hand over Angelo's shaved head.

'Nice,' he said. 'Sleek. How's it going, boys?'

Angelo smiled shyly. Richard noticed Frank staring oddly at Harry.

'Frank,' said Richard, 'you're everywhere. Every newspaper, every magazine I pick up, there's your byline.'

'Not any more,' Frank said, tearing his gaze away from Harry, who was looking uneasy. 'I've taken a staff job with this lot.' A copy of the latest issue of Frank's magazine sat on the table next to his pint.

'Nice one. It's a good magazine. I like it,' Richard lied. What Richard did like about Frank's magazine and *Sight & Sound* and *Empire*, as well as *Time Out* and the broadsheets, was that because their policy was to review all feature films that got released, they had to sit through his movies and find something to say about them.

'Anyway, what about you? You're a big name these days,' Frank declared. 'I'm surprised they let you in here.'

'I suppose I'm a big enough name,' Richard said, 'that if my name crops up in relation to what happened on Friday, it could be bad news. They'll keep digging until they get something.'

'Are you saying,' started Angelo, breaking his silence, 'that you're the only one who could be affected by this? I've got a job to think about, too.'

'No, I'm not saying that, Angelo,' Richard said calmly, 'but what I am saying is that this could get a lot more serious than just worrying about hanging on to your job.'

Instead of looking at Richard, Angelo bent over the table top, studying a square cardboard beer mat. Like all beer mats that get wet and are allowed to dry and then are used again instead of being thrown in the trash with all the other rubbish, it was no longer flat. Angelo laid the mat on the table convex side up and stood his pint on it – the glass perched unsteadily on top. Angelo lifted the glass, flipped the mat and stood the glass on the concave side – the glass rocked from side to side. Finally, Angelo took the glass off the mat altogether and stood it directly on the table top.

Richard snatched up the beer mat and tore it into quarters, tossing the pieces in the ashtray. Frank cleared his throat. Harry looked anxiously from face to face. Angelo stared at his drink. Richard took his cigarettes from his pocket and lit one, then offered the packet around. Frank and Harry declined; Angelo turned to gaze out of the window with a wistful, faraway look. Harry released his fair hair from its pony-tail and raked his fingers through it before gathering the long, fine strands together and reapplying his rainbow-coloured scrunch.

'Look,' said Harry. 'We need to know exactly where we stand.'

'Somewhere really quite uncomfortably close to shit creek, I would have said,' interrupted Frank.

Ignoring this, Harry went on: 'They've found a body. We know that. What we don't know is what condition it's in. Fifteen years is a long time.'

'Not if you cast your mind back and recall what we did with the body,' Richard observed in a half-whisper.

'We wrapped it in film,' Frank said. 'That well-known preservative agent.'

Richard, a pained expression on his face, suggested they mind what they were saying and lower the volume.

'Don't worry about it,' said Harry. 'This is the one place in London we could have this conversation and not have to worry about who's listening.'

Still Richard kept his voice down. 'Does no one remember where we put the body *after* wrapping it in film?'

'There was some kind of vault . . .' Frank frowned.

'Exactly.' Richard lit another cigarette. 'If it was for storing nitrate film, it might have been lead-lined, or at least airtight. I was a bit tight myself by the end of that night. I think we all were. And I can't remember every detail, but I do remember thinking it was like we were burying one of the pharaohs.'

'In other words—' Harry began.

'The body might be quite well preserved. Even very well preserved.'

They fell silent. Frank suggested they get more drinks.

'OK, even if it *is* well preserved,' Harry continued, when Frank had returned, 'that doesn't mean to say it can be identi-fied. Right?' He appealed to the other three. Richard and Frank looked blank; Angelo looked out of the window. 'He didn't have any ID on him. No one really knew him in London, apart from a few projectionists and cinema staff, and they're all likely to have moved on. Fifteen years *is* a long time. His wife lived in East Anglia somewhere. I would say the chances of the body being identified are slim to nonexistent. And, anyway, even if it is identified, there's nothing to connect it with us.'

Angelo glared at Harry. 'I wish everybody would stop talking about "it" and "the body". He had a name; he was a real person.'

'OK, OK,' said Richard. 'Let's not get upset and fall out. As Harry says, there's nothing to connect us with the body – I mean, Burns.'

'What about our film? What about *Auteur*?' Frank interjected.

'It's never been released,' Richard stated.

'People claim to have seen it.'

'Gossips. Film freaks. It's an urban myth. They've seen nothing.'

'What about Jonathan Romney's piece in yesterday's *Guardian*?' Frank said. 'Did no one else see it?'

Heads were shaken. Frank gave a brief summary of Romney's article. Everyone looked deflated for a moment or two.

'That's just one writer,' Harry said at last, 'speculating. No one's going to take it seriously or act on it. And if they did want to act on it, where are they going to get a copy of the film? It's not out there.'

'And even if they did,' Richard took up the argument, 'there's still nothing to connect us with the film. Nothing whatsoever.'

'No,' Frank said quietly, staring into his beer, 'only the stills.'

Everyone turned to look at Frank. The temperature in the room dropped a couple of degrees.

'What stills?' Harry asked finally.

'Stills I found in a filing cabinet five minutes' walk from here.'

'What are you talking about?' Angelo said.

'The picture desk at work has a set of stills.'

'That's impossible,' Richard said.

'You can't have stills from a film that's never been released,' said Harry Foxx.

'I think you'll find,' said Frank, 'that you can. I've got them.' Frank looked around the group, his expression clearly challenging each one in turn. It was Harry Foxx who broke the silence.

'What do they show?' he asked.

Frank returned Harry Foxx's stare and remained quiet for a long time. No one moved. Richard had been lifting his pint – it had come to a halt midway between the table and his mouth. Angelo's head craned so far forward it looked unnatural.

Eventually Frank broke the suspense. 'What do stills ever show? They show the four of us off set, before the shoot. Individually and in various groups. They show Burns on the set, sitting on that old sofa. They come in a bag marked *Auteur*. For all the world like a proper film. A proper film with stills.'

'Well, how did they get there?' Richard asked, flustered.

'And how many other sets are there?' Angelo demanded.

'Good questions,' Frank agreed, still looking at Harry Foxx, 'to which I'm sure we'd all like to know the answers.'

Angelo stood up.

'Where are you going?' Richard asked him.

'Bog.' In the absence of any further challenge, Angelo left the bar to visit the toilet halfway down the stairs.

'Shit,' said Harry Foxx.

'You any idea how these stills came to be there?' Frank asked him.

'Why should I? How do we know this isn't your kind of a joke?'

'Well, someone's having a laugh,' Frank said. 'All we have to do is find out who.'

'They could have been there for years,' suggested Richard.

'I'm sure they have,' said Frank. 'But it would still be nice to know how they got there.'

Angelo returned. They all watched him as he sat down.

'I don't know why you're all looking at me,' he said. 'I didn't have anything to do with it.'

'No one's saying you did,' Frank pointed out. 'But maybe one of us remembers something. Does anyone have anything to say?'

The four looked around. Heads were shaken.

'So we're looking at Kerner,' Frank said.

'But why would he . . .' Richard began.

'I've no idea,' Frank said, 'but he was the stills photo-grapher. Are you still in touch with him?' he asked Richard, who shook his head.

'Haven't spoken to him for years. Don't know if he's still around.'

'Harry?'

'I've no idea, but obviously we need to find out.'

'I already called his old number,' Frank said. 'Unobtainable, so I guess he's moved on. But where? What's his game? Anyone any ideas?'

Silence fell once more upon the group as they lifted their glasses and drank, sombrely. Richard looked from one to another, wondering if anyone knew more than they were letting on. Was Frank the straight-up guy he seemed? Could he be trusted? How out of it was Angelo – was it just an act? And Harry Foxx – he, too, seemed wrapped up in his own problems. Could any of them, in fact, be trusted?

13 · The collector

The day after the meeting in the Troy Club, Angelo went back to the vintage poster gallery. The girl buzzed him in, but whether she recognised him he couldn't be sure. She bent over the smart little desk, her sleek hair falling slowly down over her face like a ruched drape.

He wandered across to where the girl was sitting.

'Hi,' he said.

She raised her head very slowly, loose braids in her hair twisting and somersaulting like eels in a river.

'Do you have a poster for *Eureka*?'

She thought about it. 'I don't think we do.'

'Or *Don't Look Now*?'

'No. Roeg fan, are you? Have you seen *Performance*?'

'Do you mean the film or the poster?'

'I mean the poster. I assume you've seen the film.'

'Both. But I hadn't seen the poster before I saw it here. Can I ask you something? Why are they so expensive?'

'Film posters are only just being recognised as works of art in their own right. At the end of a run, they used to get binned, or burned.'

'I suppose you have to have *Performance*, given where the shop is.'

'Why do you say that?'

'Because Roeg's local. Because the film was shot around the corner.'

'Only the exteriors.'

'But still.'

They were silent, but he sensed that he'd got her interest.

'Do you think it's the case,' he went on, 'that where a film is seen is more important than where it is shot?'

'What do you mean?'

'Location junkies are obsessed with knowing where films are shot. The precise location of a shoot. I think the place where it is exhibited is far more significant, far more important.'

He saw something light up in her eyes. Her mouth opened slowly. He *had* misjudged her. The professional appearance was a disguise. She was a slightly looser cannon than she gave the impression of being. He began to feel excited. Again, she started to remind him of Naomi.

'Round here,' he said, 'what's your favourite cinema?'

She shrugged. 'The Coronet?'

'Too smoky.'

'The Gate?'

'Too hot in the summer. And the front row's too close to the screen. Where do you sit when you go, the front row?'

'Of course.'

'Me too. But at the Gate it's just too close.'

'I used to like the Electric,' she said, looking off to the side.

'It's very sad that it's dark.'

'There's talk of it reopening.'

'It could happen. But I doubt it. It's one of an endangered species.'

'Rep cinemas.'

'Remember the Scala? Soon to reopen as a club. A night-club. The Roxie? Became a novelty shop, then a sandwich shop; now it's empty.'

'The Lumière.'

'Not a rep cinema, but a beautiful space. Closed down. Single-screen cinemas will soon be just a memory. The Parkway and the Plaza in Camden – both gone. The Pavilion, the Palladium and the Galaxy around Shepherd's Bush Green – what are they now?' He didn't know the answer to his own question: the Bush was next on his list. He sensed it was a key area, which was odd because it no longer had any screens at all, and he'd been saving it up. The longer he waited, the more the pressure built up. What if it failed to meet his expectations?

He looked at the girl. The subject of their dialogue was depressing, but the manner of its exchange was increasingly animated. Arc-lights shone in her eyes. Angelo bubbled with confidence.

'It's not all gone, you know,' he said. 'Not quite.'

The girl's mouth opened slowly. The pink tip of her tongue severed a gossamer-thin string of saliva. Her overbite hovered. The Béatrice Dalle lower lip trembled.

'I've got a special collection of my own,' he said.

Her eyes widened.

'I live nearby. If you wanted . . .'

She turned to the wall, thinking, and gazed blankly at an extremely rare poster for Michael Powell's *Peeping Tom*.

At 208 Gloucester Terrace, she followed him up the narrow stairwell.

'Almost there,' he called over his shoulder into the darkness. 'The light doesn't work. It doesn't matter. This is just a transitional place.' Reaching the top, he unlocked the door and pushed it open.

'It's not much, I'm afraid,' he said, pressing himself back against the wall to allow the girl to go first. As she squeezed past him, her hair brushed his face and he caught the smell of old ticket stubs, bare carpets. As soon as she was inside, he closed the door carefully behind them.

She went straight to the window and looked out.

'All those thousands of lives,' she said, watching two trains pull out simultaneously.

Angelo's breathing was fast and shallow.

'I don't even know your name. Mine is Angelo.'

'Claire.'

'Is your hair dyed this colour?'

Standing behind her as she watched the trains, he had taken a handful of her hair and held it against his face. She turned around.

'You wanted to show me something?'

'My collection,' he said, turning towards the white shelves.

She looked at the collection for a moment, taking it in, then started reading the spines on the sleeve inlays.

'*Diva, Les Yeux sans visage, The Shout, The Texas Chainsaw Massacre* – good films, you've got good taste. Am I missing something?'

Angelo took down one of the video cases – Christopher Petit's *Chinese Boxes* – and handed it to Claire.

'It's empty,' she said, weighing it in her hand.

'Don't be afraid,' he said softly, placing his hand on her arm. He took the box from her, held it in his two hands and slowly prised it open, just a crack. 'Smell,' he whispered, holding it up to her nose.

She turned her dark eyes anxiously up at him and breathed in through her nose.

Angelo gently lowered the box and closed it. He turned it over in his hands and showed her the spine.

'*Chinese Boxes*,' she read. 'Roxie, 9.12.86.' She frowned.

'The Roxie closed in March 1987,' he said. 'It's empty now, dark; you can't get in there. But this is part of it.'

Claire turned to look at the rows of video boxes on the shelves.

'All of these boxes are empty?' she said.

'You can tear down the screen and bulldoze the walls, but you can never destroy the space itself. This is a small part of that space.'

'Space?'

'The space between the walls and the floor and the screen and the people watching the films night after night. Do you think that that space can remain unaffected by all of that emotion, all of that drama? It's not invulnerable that space, that air. It mutates. It's organic. Each new screening adds another layer, another infusion, each fresh outpouring of emotion saturates it further.'

Angelo had taken hold of Claire's hair again and was stroking it as he explained. She pulled away.

'And *Chinese Boxes*?'

'*Chinese Boxes* just happened to be the film that was playing the night I carved out my piece of history, the night I sampled the Roxie. Hence naming it on the box. If I open this box, I sense *Chinese Boxes* but I also get the Roxie.'

'Don't you have any real videos?'

'What would I want with real videos?' He gestured to indicate his collection. 'This is a more faithful record of my experience of *Chinese Boxes* than a copy of *Chinese Boxes* itself.'

'But every time you open the box . . . ?'

'I'm careful not to open it too far or keep it open for too long. There are no draughts.'

She smiled.

'Why are you smiling?'

'You're mad,' she said, still smiling. 'But in the nicest possible way. I like that. This is fascinating, but it's making me thirsty.'

He cupped his hand against the side of her face and she rested the weight of her head against him.

'Just a second,' he said, and walked across the room to where the minibar sat forlornly. He withdrew from it a bottle of Scotch and took two mugs from the draining board. He poured two generous amounts. Claire was running her fingers along the spines of his video boxes.

'Do you want to stay?' he asked her.

'Do you think I should?' she asked.

He refilled their mugs.

She stayed. The trains that ran outside ran through his head. Although for once he didn't watch them, he found he didn't need to. The hum of the projector, the crackle of the carbon arcs – the films were screened on his retinas. He directed their love scene like a *maître*, intercutting it with Roegesque snippets of dialogue. They talked about his dream, his belief that all of the old cinema spaces had been saved, either by an agent of the state or by a secret society or by a committed individual, and were stored somewhere, like enormous Rachel Whiteread sculptures in gaseous form. 'I'm close to finding that place,' he said. 'I'm almost there. You can help me. Just imagine it. Every film that has ever been shown on every London screen that has since been torn down plays there constantly and continuously and simultaneously. Each scene is played out at the same time as the next. And each film is reacted to by every audience it has ever had within this city. Every tear that has been shed, every laugh that has echoed around the walls of any London cinema that has ever existed – they are shed over and over and they resound endlessly within the walls of a single building. I have to find that building. You can help me find it.'

Sleep brought dreams that so closely resembled the chaos of his waking life he had no idea when he slipped from one state to the other. He slept deeply and woke to the clatter of the morning trains and an empty space in the bed beside him. He called her name, knowing the only response would be the echo of his cry. He looked at the shelves that held his collection and didn't know whether he was relieved that his first assessment of the girl now seemed to have been correct, or dismayed that his reassessment had proved overoptimistic. In any case, she appeared to have taken only one or two. He studied the spines and soon worked out what was missing – the *Chinese Boxes*/Roxie box he'd shown her, and a *Thundercrack!*/Scala sample he'd particularly prized. *Thundercrack!* always created an atmosphere, even in the freezing-cold cavernous space of the Scala.

As he dressed, he wondered how much of a fool he'd been made to seem. Did it matter that he'd told her about his search for the Museum of Lost Cinema Spaces? At least he hadn't mentioned its name, nor given her any clue to its possible location – not that there were that many clues he could give her. He was confident it would be found in west London, but until he'd done more work on the maps and certain further details had come to light, it was impossible to be more specific.

The *Ghost Train* tapes had been no help in that respect. Angelo heard voices in the static, but they didn't tell him anything about the Museum of Lost Cinema Spaces. They talked to him instead about the trains that ran past his window, who travelled on them and where they were going. When Angelo rode the trains at night, it was because the voices had told him to. They told him which line to take, where to get off and when to return home.

As Angelo stood at the window and looked down at the trains, it sank in just how out of control he'd allowed himself to get with the girl from the gallery. He'd never even told Naomi about the Museum of Lost Cinema Spaces. Her reaction to Rachel Whiteread's *House* had made sure of that. Indeed, it was her reaction to Rachel Whiteread's *House* that had marked the end of their so-called relationship.

It had started in the spring of 1993, when Angelo was a frequent visitor to the benches outside the NFT café. Never buying anything to eat or drink, he used to sit outside, studying the film listings in *Time Out* or poring over a battered *A–Z* held together with an elastic band. One of the bar staff (she turned out to be called Naomi) had stepped out into the cold and asked him why he didn't come inside and have a hot drink and get warm. He replied that he had no money (it all went on empty video boxes and visits to the cinema) and she said that didn't matter – it would be on the house. Angelo followed the girl into the café. Her dark hair, tied in a ponytail, swung like a noose. She told him she'd often noticed him sitting outside.

He told her a little bit about what he was doing, about his interest in old cinemas.

They met regularly and sometimes went back to her shared house in Vauxhall, but never to Gloucester Terrace. They would stay in her room for hours, the warm air thickening until you could have cut a piece out of it and slipped it into an empty video box. Naomi would demand that he massage her all over – full body massage, she called it. Other nights they'd go out with friends of hers and she would cling to his side and introduce him as 'my man'. 'You're so beautiful,' she would say to him later, framing his face in her hands. 'It makes me feel good when they see us together.'

She had never questioned him about his interest in old cinema spaces. She wasn't interested, and Angelo told himself that was fine, she could help him keep his feet on the ground, except that he never really felt they left the ground. His activities seemed perfectly reasonable to him.

If he seemed tired, she thrust out her chest at him. She brushed his groin with the back of her hand in public places. She gazed at him from under her sleek, dark hair and her eyes burned until he, too, felt something ignite and he'd call on reserves of energy he didn't know he had, and they'd go back to Vauxhall by the quickest means available and lock themselves in her room. At breakfast, if anyone else was around, she would stroke the side of his face and say to them, 'Isn't he beautiful? Have you ever seen such a beautiful man?' They'd look bored and not know what to say and Angelo would feel embarrassed.

One night she asked straight out: 'Do you or do you not find me attractive?'

Cornered, Angelo didn't know what to say, so he remained silent, but she didn't give up.

'You never compliment me on my appearance,' she said sulkily.

Later, in a pub, where they'd gone just to break the tension that had settled in her room, she pressed him again.

'I mean, you must like me,' she said, 'because we spend all this time together. But do you actually find me attractive?'

'I think you've got a very interesting face,' he conceded, desperately. Since the Burns episode he was incapable of lying.

At first she was unable to form a coherent response. But finally, in a mixture of hurt bafflement and quiet fury, she managed, '*Interesting*?'

Angelo had begun to sense that it just wasn't happening, or that if it was, it shouldn't be. Very soon after the conversation in the pub, he took her to see Rachel Whiteread's *House* in Bow. This for Angelo amounted to an act of pilgrimage. Bizarrely, it had been Whiteread's *Ghost*, which Angelo had first seen in 1990 at the Chisenhale, that had enabled him to start getting over the death of Burns. The artist obviously shared Burns's obsession with space. In his case it was the space inside old cinemas, in hers the space inside a single room. Angelo saw her as someone who, unconsciously, concretised Burns's ideas – validating them in the most straightforward and stimulating way.

To make *Ghost*, Whiteread had taken a plaster cast of a room in a house like the one in which she had grown up, then eased the plaster away from the walls in sections and reassembled them to form a solid block that mimicked the space inside the room. But it was a space you couldn't penetrate, a negative of the real space. Its effect on Angelo was to make him explore Burns's feelings about space. It was the first time in seven years he was able to think about Burns and not come close to drowning under a black wave of depression, oppressed by grief and guilt, and it prompted him to start his collection, boxing up the atmosphere inside the rep cinemas and independent fleapits that would soon face the challenge of the multiplex. Angelo looked forward to Whiteread's *House*, her notorious 1993 cast of the inside of a condemned home in Bow, like film-goers must have anticipated *The Magnificent Ambersons* after seeing *Citizen Kane*.

He took Naomi to see it. As they approached the ghostly concrete monolith from the south end of Grove Road, the hairs stood up on the back of Angelo's neck. As soon as he set eyes on it, he knew what it would have meant to Burns. It meant the same to him, only more so.

Naomi linked his arm and laughed. 'That's meant to be art, is it?'

He tried not to listen, but she went on: 'It's ridiculous. She's just taking the piss, and as long as there's enough pseudo arty-farty types around to be taken in by it, she'll be laughing all the way to the bank. Hasn't she just won some bloody prize?'

'The Turner Prize,' said Angelo, teeth gritted. Then: 'For someone who's so obsessed by appearances, you show remarkably little interest in something that, in one sense, is nothing but its appearance.'

Naomi stared at him aghast.

'I don't think we're destined for great things together, Naomi. In fact, we're not even destined to travel back on the same tube.'

She slapped him across the face, then turned and marched away. Angelo stepped closer to the railing that separated him, like a rope in a gallery, from the work.

Free of Naomi, Angelo stood and gazed at *House*, allowing his mind to wander. He thought about his collection at home and he thought about the old cinemas he still had to visit, and the dozens he didn't even know about yet, those that had been converted to bars, antiques showrooms, bingo halls and office blocks. If he was able to harvest a cassette boxful, shouldn't it be possible somehow to save the entire space? To do as Rachel Whiteread had done, but without her plaster and concrete.

So began the search for the Museum of Lost Cinema Spaces.

14 · The underground

Scotland/London, 1979–82

Munro dragged his namesake's body clear of the cairn at the summit of Ben More before setting about its disposal. The mist that shrouded the top of the mountain grew denser so that anyone using the path to the summit would have seen and heard nothing. Aware that the removal of every trace of the dead man's identity was essential, Munro did what he had to do and buried the incomplete corpse fifty yards south-west of the summit in a shallow grave. Decomposition would follow swiftly.

Any illusions he might have had that the mountain was his ally were exposed when he began his descent. In the ever-thickening fog he was unable to find the series of cairns marking the route. He veered like a drunk through an alcoholic mist, crisscrossing the path. Visibility was down to less than a yard. When the ground sloped beneath his feet he assumed he had reached the first of the two steeper sections and so accelerated despite the abrupt difficulty of the terrain. In fact, he was heading for a crevasse, but realised his mistake just in time. The mist folded in around him. It provided both isolation and insulation; never before had he felt so cut off from the world and at the same time so wrapped up in himself, so sure of his own identity. He stood absolutely still for an indeterminate time, senses alert for the slightest disturbance in the atmosphere: there was nothing. Beyond him was total absence.

He waited. He didn't know how long he waited. Time made as little sense as space in this new world.

He became aware of movement. The air around him changed, the mist thinned, then swelled again and swirled as a patch was briefly cleared and blue sky appeared. Sliding doors of cloud instantly snapped shut on this vision and Munro turned his head. The light underwent a change, pulsing here and there. Munro was reminded of the time he had been to a dance hall on the island. He had drunk four cans of sweet cider in preparation, but soon realised his error as he lurched through the darkness, tripping from one brightly flashing set of disco lights to the next. Nothing made any sense. The music pounded; girls loomed.

The mist thinned to wraiths as shafts of sunlight jabbed through like huge fluorescent tubes. And then it was gone, away up the mountain, crowning the summit, but vanished from the sodden flanks. Munro gazed in wonder at the sea loch a thousand feet below, the scatter of islands. He felt as if he'd been released and was free to go.

Munro returned on foot to Fraser Munro's rented cottage, using one of the keys he had taken from the dead man's pockets to unlock the door. He didn't delay, clearing the place of everything that belonged to its former occupant and stuffing the bags into the battered Ford Escort left parked on the track between the croft and the road. The keys to the Ford had also been in one of Munro's pockets.

He left the island as soon as there was a ferry and drove directly to Inverness. He unloaded the car and locked himself into the house, where he stayed for a week. For the first two days he did nothing except sit in each room and sleep in the dead man's bed. He tried on some of his clothes, but with one exception they didn't feel right. The exception was a dark blue baseball cap with 'NY' stitched on the front, which Munro instantly took to wearing. The brim had been curled with care. He pulled it down low over his eyes.

He found fifty pounds in cash among Munro's things and used that to get through the next two weeks. He nodded at the few people he passed as he went between the house and the shops, and they nodded back. There was a file in Munro's office containing ideas and notes for films, as well as material pertaining to films that had already been made. At a stroke, Munro's entire back catalogue became his. He worked in the office until late into the night developing some of Munro's half-formed ideas into things he might even have originated himself. He didn't think of it as plagiarism. He thought of it as collaboration.

He emptied the house of everything that could be linked to Fraser Munro. Fraser Munro no longer lived there. Fraser Munro no longer lived anywhere. When he got in the car and released the handbrake, there was only one direction in which he could point the car, and that was towards London. If he wanted to hide, London was the place to do it. Munro had to disappear, slip between the cracks. He had almost to become somebody else. It would be like assuming a pseudonym.

He dumped stuff in roadside bins and burned two suitcases of clothes at dawn beside an unmetalled road in the Borders. He kept Munro's film cans and ideas file, but discarded most of the notes and maps and photographs relating to his existing films.

He spent the night at a motorway services on the M6, sleeping in the back of the car. He woke early, refreshed. He roamed the car parks of the service station, slipping between rows of Triumph Dolomites and Rover 2000s, passing like a shade behind Cortinas and Zephyrs. In the cafeteria he ate breakfast with the drivers of Austin Princesses and Morris Oxfords. He wondered how different from them he was, and they from each other. He spent ten minutes just sitting staring at the large sign bearing the name of the services. Helping himself to a napkin, he doodled on it, repeating two words over and over again.

Eventually he got back on the road and dumped the car in a scrapyard off the North Circular, removing the plates and dropping them in a skip. He made his way on foot to the only address he knew in London, from having watched so much television as a child – BBC Television Centre in Wood Lane, Shepherd's Bush. The immediate surroundings held promise: light industry, waste land and a one-storey abandoned building across Wood Lane from the BBC. It was a simple matter to get in round the back by clambering over a wall and fighting his way through dense undergrowth. It was barely habitable, but there were signs that it had once been lived in after originally serving as office space. Exhausted, Munro collapsed on the floor.

He dreamed that someone was wrapping steel bands around his body from head to foot, and drawing them so tight they cut off the circulation. When the pressure of the steel bands was so great that he could no longer hear the thump of his pulse and he feared he would suffocate, he rolled over and freed his arms from his meagre blankets, pressing his hands against the filthy floor to force himself upright.

As soon as he was on his feet, the ground trembled. Still half asleep, all he could think was that his world was falling apart. Moments after the rumbling and grinding beneath the floor had stopped, a terrible clanging and rattling came from some-where vaguely overhead. His eyes spun this way and that searching for the source of the noise, and he caught a flash of something metallic in the narrow slit of a window. That and the noise and the vibration brought him quickly up to speed.

Trains.

With a longer look out of the window, he saw that there was a railway bridge running diagonally over the road by his building. And there appeared to be an underground line directly beneath it as well.

He went outside to look at the exterior in daylight. It was a disused tube station: the name – Wood Lane – was spelled out in relief above the door. Making his way back to the rear of the building, he saw that he had been lucky the night before not to stumble and fall on to the eastbound Central line, which emerged into a steep-sided cutting only yards from the former station buildings.

He went back inside and sat and watched and listened to the trains while he thought about the days and weeks that lay ahead.

Munro had vanished from sight. He made short films, using Fraser Munro's money acquired from funding bodies and arts organisations, which he withdrew from his account without any trouble, until it ran out, and he got them shown at festivals and small cine-clubs. He operated by stealth and made no personal appearances. The post office box he used as his address filled up quickly. Magazine articles were commissioned, the angle always the same – the abrupt change in Munro's style, from trad to rad, as one blurb writer put it, coupled with his becoming a recluse. Film students tried to track him down, if the gossip was to be believed, and failed. He continued to live in the old station on Wood Lane, which he discovered had closed down in 1947 when White City opened two hundred yards up the road.

Gradually he spent increasing amounts of time either watching and listening to the trains or riding on them – always in the evening or at night. He would take the overground Metropolitan line, as it was then called, to Edgware Road, then switch to the Circle line and complete entire circuits without getting off. He would roam from carriage to carriage, wearing special tight-fitting gloves, and watch people, both those on the train and those he glimpsed in windows as the train passed overlit offices and underfurnished bedrooms. Much of the Circle line, like the Metropolitan, was overground, or, as at Edgware Road, Farringdon and Earl's Court, at a level that corresponded to lower ground: lower than the cars that growled past in angry lines, but still open to the sky and within sight of the lower floors of deserted office complexes and lonely mansion flats.

Munro rode on the trains not for want of something better to do with his time, but because, living where he did, he couldn't escape them. He learned to sleep through the noise and the vibration, but still his dreams were written and directed by the trains. When he drifted into REM sleep around dawn, his dreams were either shot on trains or they involved trains in some way. After some time, they as good as became trains. Or the trains became his dreams. The two became one in his mind. And just as his dreams were indistinguishable from films, so too were the trains, especially those that ran at night, their amber windows single frames, the gaps between the wheels sprocket holes. When they rattled across the points outside Paddington, what Munro heard was the snag of celluloid in the gate of the projector.

In the fading light, he crisscrossed London by overground tube lines. As his train trundled past the rows and rows of Edwardian terraces and Victorian conversions, he got a rare glimpse of his audience. Wherever the curtains had not been drawn or blinds lowered, he was offered a window on to another world, a world where ordinary people lived, a world so remote from his own he could scarcely imagine it unless it was shown to him. A man standing next to a bed in an orange room. A young woman lying on another bed in blue light fully clothed. Two people sitting across a kitchen table eating. Banal but vital images of everyday existence, glimpses of bearable lives.

They all stopped what they were doing and watched the film as it flickered past them.

He also watched the passengers around him, baffled as he was by their efforts to appear real people rather than characters in a film, actors on a set. They ignored the script, getting on or off the train at will. Just as he was viewing them though a framing device made out of his own gloved hands, they'd get up and leave. If he was the director, and they his cast, this was no way for them to behave.

Sometimes he would solve this problem by, having selected a character, leaving the train with them when they changed. In this way he was drawn on to lines he wouldn't otherwise have used, sucked underground, which, through association with the other Fraser Munro, the dead man, made him nervous. He hardly ever thought of his former namesake, and when he did the memories were confused and patchy. But being underground made his mind flip back to a damp, windswept mountainside, and he immediately had to abandon his chase and switch back to an overground line in order to forget.

The Metropolitan – or Hammersmith & City, as a part of it later became known – was OK because you weren't enclosed underground. Its sub-surface sections were close enough to street level that you could breathe easily. There was space around the trains; they even passed each other side by side (which gave Munro an idea for a film consisting of two prints of the same film shown on two projectors simultaneously, one of them running backwards, the pictures overlaid on a screen; at the film's halfway point, a single shot would appear with perfect clarity, before the images would tumble back into chaos. He never made the film. He never made most of the films he dreamed up, not any more).

But there was at least one film he still needed to make and he was reminded of it every time he felt a brick arch close over his head. Munro – the other one, the imposter – had left some unfinished business, which the world had been expecting: his mammoth record of Scotland's mountains over 3,000 feet.

With fifty mountains yet to commit to celluloid, it would be a long and arduous job. To make it a little easier, he bought a second-hand Mini without tax or MOT. He ran it into the ground zigzagging across Scotland to bag the remaining Munros. It might have been part of the original plan to climb each one, but Munro ticked them off with the briefest of visits.

In most cases he took the trouble to get out of the car and set foot on the mountain before rolling the film, but towards the end of the project, when he was sick to death of the country-side's wide-open spaces and itching to get back to the windows and frames of the city, he would satisfy himself with drive-by shootings.

Back in London (the Mini dumped at the bottom of his last Munro like an illegible signature at the foot of a painting), he blagged the use of art-school editing facilities and even added a soundtrack of which Munro would hardly have approved: he recorded his own voice reading the names, addresses and phone numbers of Munros from Scottish telephone directories. Each mountain got one entry and was allotted no more screen time than the ten seconds it took to read it. With almost three hundred Munros to get through, the finished film was close to fifty minutes in length. It was shown at a festival of *avant-garde* film in the Netherlands and won the 1982 Den Haag Prize for Best Nature Film. Munro was not present to receive the award. At the very moment the festival director was assuring his audience that every effort would be made to track down the reclusive Scot to give him his prize (a cheque for three thousand guilders), Munro was riding the Metropolitan line, making a viewfinder of his gloved hands and zooming in on lone passengers in near-empty carriages.

That night, a killing took place on a train between Shepherd's Bush and Goldhawk Road that, some time later, would be retro-spectively viewed as the first of the Hammersmith Tube Murders.

15 · Tx

London, Thursday 16 July 1998

When Frank got into work the day after finding the stills, there was a note stuck to his screen from Siân asking him to go and see her as soon as he got in. The tone was businesslike, peremptory. Feeling anxious, he complied with the note's request.

'Hi,' he said, keeping his voice as normal as possible.

'Hi. Look, I'm sorry about this,' she said briskly, 'but could you just tell me what's going on?'

'Tell you what's going on?' Frank felt cold.

'Yes.' She held his gaze until he had to look away. 'I thought – I mean, maybe I've got the wrong end of the stick –'

'Stick?'

'– but I thought we had something going. You know? The other day? Since when, you've hardly even spoken to me. If you've decided it was a mistake, you could at least let me know.'

Frank looked at her, saw the armour of proud indifference offering little protection to the soft pool of vulnerability in her eyes, and, although ashamed to admit it, felt relieved.

'I don't make mistakes,' he said, squatting by Siân's chair. 'Not any more. My mistakes are in the past. I've been busy, that's all. Had something on my mind.'

Siân indicated for him to go on.

'I can't talk about it. Not now. Listen, why don't we do

something tonight? Although, obviously, I'd understand if it's too short notice . . .'

'Tonight . . .' Siân flicked through her Filofax, while Frank waited, aware that this was her moment. 'Well, I suppose I *could* . . .'

'Good. Soon as the bell goes, we're out of here. OK?'

'OK.'

Frank sat at his desk tapping a pencil against his screen until the point broke off. He noticed Christopher looking at him as he crossed the floor to fill a polystyrene cup with mineral water from the dispenser. Frank grabbed an old press release, turned it over and used the damaged pencil to scribble notes on the reverse side. He picked up the phone to call Harry Foxx, then had second thoughts and replaced it. He switched his machine on, to make it look as if he was around, and left the office, taking the stairs down to the street. No one took the stairs.

At Archway, Frank gazed at a row of toytown houses – minuscule front gardens, black iron railings, bramble-jam driveways, brilliant-white up-and-over garage doors. The entire block containing Kerner's flat had been demolished to make way for this.

Frank had come out here, despite having tried the photographer's number and found it unobtainable, because he suspected Kerner would still be here. Still in the same space but having made a token effort to isolate himself by disconnecting his phone and getting a mobile. But the gentrification of Upper Holloway had claimed Kerner's scalp. Frank knew there was no point knocking on doors. Kerner had gone.

Frank walked back to Holloway Road trying to think of ways to track down his quarry. He stopped at a phone box and tried directory enquiries. The result was predictable. Next, instead of hanging up, he tried Harry Foxx's number. To his surprise, the phone was picked up.

A woman's voice said, 'Hello?'

Frank asked for Harry.

'He's not here. You could try his mobile. Do you have the number?'

After a pause, Frank said he thought he did.

'Do you want me to give it to you?' she asked.

Frank paused again. It was the woman's voice. There was something familiar about it.

'Yes, please. Just in case.'

She reeled off the number and ended the call. He already had the number; he just wanted to hear more of the woman's voice.

Frank walked south down Holloway Road. He needed to think and for that he needed to walk. The tube inevitably killed his capacity to be rational the moment he stepped on to the down escalator. He thought about Siân, whom he was due to see that night. He couldn't ask her about the stills for fear of her making an unhelpful connection. He turned right at the Odeon and walked up Tufnell Park Road. An idea finally occurred to him: he could ask Jim Cover, the picture editor on the fashion magazine, if he knew Kerner or could think of a way to track him down. As he stepped into the elevator at Tufnell Park station, he felt not that he was back at the point where he'd been before discovering that Kerner's flat had been flattened, but that he'd taken a positive step beyond that particular setback.

Then the rubber flanges of the elevator doors snuck together and his mind shut down.

As soon as he got back to the office, he went to see Jim Cover. As Frank outlined his request, Cover's eyes barely left the screen, his finger scarcely ceased to click the mouse. Sweat beaded the sides of his nose; the fingertips of his left hand quivered.

'What's the guy's name again?' he asked, sounding bored.

'Kerner.' Frank spelled it out for him.

'Funny name.'

'German,' Frank said. 'I think.'

'Maybe he's gone back to Germany.'

The girl at the next desk, phone hooked between chin and shoulder, interrupted: 'Jim, that girl you asked to come back – she's downstairs.'

'Tell them to send her up.'

Still he didn't look at Frank.

'He's not German. He's just got a German name,' Frank persisted. 'Look, I was just wondering if he'd ever been in to see you, or sent you his portfolio. You know, looking for work.'

'I see a lot of people.'

Frank looked away.

Cover seemed to pick up on Frank's exasperation. 'I'll ask around,' he offered. 'What's your number?'

Frank gave it to him.

As Frank reached the landing, the doors to the lift opened and a girl stepped out. Frank caught her eye, recognising her as the girl from the roof, the model with the portfolio.

He switched off his voicemail in case Cover tried to call and sat staring at a fax from the BBC: his proposal to adapt the as yet unwritten Heaven book for the *Tx* documentary strand had cleared the first hurdle. The book had not yet been commissioned, but the motivation was not lacking. Even greater than his desire to contribute something to the world of film more meaningful than a co-directed short film of dubious quality and even more dubious morality was his quest for Sarah. Since her death, he'd searched for her beyond a thousand screens. Film had become a medium from which he voluntarily excluded himself, then spent the rest of his life looking back in, searching for a glimpse of where Sarah had gone.

Siân's freckled elbows appeared on his desk. He knew that, as he looked up, his irritation was not masked.

'I thought we were going out,' she said.

He hesitated briefly, aware that if he prolonged the silence he would lose her. She was too proud for this.

'Yeah, sorry. Let's go.'

They rode down in the lift and Frank wished he could think of something reassuring to say. He watched the red numbers of the floors light up as they passed them. On the third floor the lift stopped and two designers got in, causing the atmosphere to ease. As Frank and Siân stepped out on to the street, Siân asked what they should do.

'I don't know,' Frank said. 'Go to a movie?'

They looked at each other a moment, then laughed and said no.

'Let's go and get a drink,' Frank proposed. 'Blue Posts?'

'Where else?'

As Frank instinctively turned to walk north up Wardour Street, he realised he'd forgotten which Blue Posts he went to with Siân.

'Let's go to Newman Street,' he said.

'I didn't know there was one there.'

'Neither did I till recently.'

He'd be safe there, he thought. All he had to worry about there was bumping into Angelo.

They drank steadily and ate crisps.

'I hope you didn't think I was giving you a hard time this morning,' Siân said.

'Why would I? I mean, fair enough. You deserve better.'

She took hold of his hand across the table. 'How would you feel if I said I've never *had* better?'

'I dunno,' said Frank after a pause. 'Under a bit of pressure?'

'I don't want you to feel pressurised.'

'Really.'

'Look, I don't want to get hurt. Again.' She ran a finger round the rim of her glass. 'I'd rather you say now if you don't want to do this.'

'I do, I do. It's just . . .'

'Just what?'

'It's not easy for me.'

'Oh, and it is for me?'

'I'm not saying that. I'm saying it's *really* not easy for me.'

Siân looked away and withdrew her hand. He reached for it, thinking, Why am I doing this?

She let him take hold of her hand, but kept her head turned away.

'I've known a lot of men,' she said, 'who are only interested in one thing.'

'I may be no different,' he said at length.

'So it seems.'

'But not in the way you mean,' he went on.

'So, you do know what I mean then?'

He paused, looked away. 'It's a very long story,' he said at last.

'We've got plenty of time.'

'That's what worries me.'

'What do you mean?'

'I'm not used to talking about it.'

'You spend your life analysing and writing about other people's emotions. Fictional characters. Directors you imagine you've come to know and understand. But you can't talk about your own emotions.'

'Spot on. Maybe I explore my emotions through the work.'

'I'd love to know how writing a review of *The Cable Guy* keeps you in touch with your emotions.'

'That's just something I *have* to do. Not something I *choose* to do.'

'So?'

Frank shrugged. Siân watched and waited.

'What?' he said, looking up at her.

'Tell me.'

'Tell you what?'

'Tell me what's eating you up?'

After a long silence, he said, 'Have you ever lost anyone?'

*   *   *

The week immediately following the Burns episode in 1983, after the filming itself, Sarah and Frank went through a rough patch. It was just a phase, Frank sensed, the sort of thing most couples put up with from time to time. He and Sarah were lucky in that it hardly ever happened to them. But they snapped at each other and Sarah spent a couple of nights sleeping over at a girlfriend's place. Frank decided it had to be related to the filming. Either he was so tense he'd been acting strangely, or Sarah was expressing frustration at her exclusion from the group. By the end of the week he resolved to do whatever it would take to iron out the problem; if that meant taking all the blame and apologising for some phantom slight he wasn't aware of having committed, so be it.

'You've got to imagine it,' he said to Siân. They were back at his flat, a bottle of Absolut vodka to the good. 'We were childhood sweethearts. Never been with anyone else. Married more or less as soon as we could. We were inseparable.'

The day Sarah was due back at the flat, the day Frank had earmarked for his strategic contrition, she failed to show. When he called the girlfriend she'd been staying with, he discovered she hadn't been staying with her at all. The girlfriend had no idea where she was. Frank tried one or two other people, but no one knew where Sarah was or where she'd been. Because they'd been so close, spending almost all of their time together, just the two of them, or hanging out with members of the group, there were few outside friends to try. Frank tried them and got nowhere.

He tried the hospitals. He tried Sarah's parents. Nothing.

Her body was found twenty-four hours later by a dog-walker on the towpath of the Grand Union Canal, near Wormwood Scrubs. An inquest ruled that she had died of head injuries consistent with having been knocked down by a car. No one ever came forward to claim responsibility and it was assumed to be a hit-and-run case with a macabre twist, the driver having recovered the body and dumped it.

Losing Sarah was unbearable. The fact that they'd parted on bad terms made it even worse. Frank was inconsolable. The members of the group saw him individually and expressed sympathy, but that was as far as it went. Immediately after the shooting of *Auteur*, they had all been a bit freaked. Under different circumstances, Frank was sure they would have rallied round and given him more support. There was no one else to turn to. He tried talking to Kerner, the stills photographer, but found him virtually impossible to communicate with. It was as if the Burns episode had drawn a line under that part of their lives and thrown up barriers between them. So Frank turned in on himself. He wrote his scripts, which were all about loss. And some years later he came up with the idea for the book: cinematic visions of Heaven.

'Are you religious?' Siân asked him.

'Sarah was. She was raised a Catholic. We married in a church for her sake.'

'What about you, though?'

'Not really, not in the most obvious way.'

But he had to believe that Sarah had gone somewhere, rather than just disappeared. He knew that *she* hadn't gone into the ground. He had seen her *body* go into the ground, but not her. *She* – her spirit, her character, her soul, whatever you want to call it – must have gone on somewhere, and the name they gave to the idea of the place where she might have gone was Heaven.

So, in the semi-darkness of the cinema, and in the total blackness of his flat, he peered behind every half-lifted curtain, he narrowed his eyes against the bright light that spilled from every door that was ajar, hoping for an insight into the place where Sarah had gone. He knew it was futile, he knew she was dead and never coming back. But he also knew that to survive he had to give his life some meaning when its meaning prior to that point had been destroyed.

'All those videos up there . . .' Siân pointed to the shelves behind the television.

'Heaven films. Every single one of them.'

Siân got up from the sofa where she'd been slumped next to Frank and crossed the floor to read the titles.

'*A Matter of Life and Death*, *Les Jeux sont faits*, *Jacob's Ladder*, *Wings of Desire*. Do you see Heaven in *Wings of Desire*?'

'Heaven. Angels. Whatever. Either I glimpse the place where she's gone, or I look for clues in the faces of angels. Is that fucked up enough for you?'

'Do you really believe she's in Heaven?'

'She would have believed it. What else can I believe? To tell you the truth, I'm not sure any more.'

'*Jacob's Ladder*'s a good film,' Siân said, looking back at the shelf.

'Brilliant film.'

'Isn't it more about going to Hell?'

Frank didn't answer.

'I'm sorry,' Siân said. 'I'm being insensitive. It's none of my business.' She came and sat by him again. 'But if you do want to talk about it . . .'

'It's not that I don't want to. I just can't.'

She took his hand. 'It's all right,' she said, gently pressing his head to her chest. 'It's all right.'

'All these films I've studied over the years,' he said in a muffled voice, 'and there's never been a sign. Not a single clue that that's where she might be. I mean, why can't you make her out in the distance on one of the fairground rides in *Happy Birthday, Wanda June*? Why isn't she sitting between a squadron of airmen and a bunch of Sikhs in that enormous celestial courtroom in *A Matter of Life and Death*? What about the angels in *Wings of Desire* – if they'd seen her around wouldn't it show? Wouldn't Danny Aiello in *Jacob's Ladder* let slip some little detail while he works on Tim Robbins' back? For years I wondered why I never caught a glimpse. Now I know. She didn't go to Heaven at all, she went to Hell. All these years she's been in Hell.'

'Frank, you don't know that.'

'I do. For years it was just a nightmare. Now I know it's true.'

Listening to the sound of his own voice, he was a blaze of mania and delusion, damped down by the occasional splash of irony. He no longer knew what he really believed. But if he had previously believed that Sarah was in Heaven, then it followed that, having died in a state of sin, she must in fact be in Hell.

The only thing he could do now was find out who put her there.

16 · MPD

London, Friday 17 July 1998

As far as Harry Foxx was concerned, what was needed now was a pre-emptive strike. The media needed to have something real to get their teeth into. And film journalists loved nothing more than advance warning of a new British film.

He picked up the phone and dialled Frank's number.

Frank took not only Harry's call, but his bait as well.

'It's called *MPD*. There's a script, but there's no money yet,' Harry felt he had to point out. 'No money at all. Nothing's in place.'

'Don't worry about it,' Frank reassured him. 'A new film from the creator of *Nine South Street* is always going to be a good story.'

'Well, someone needs to fly the flag for the British film industry,' said Harry, but even he was a little surprised when Frank offered to pop round right away with his tape recorder if that would be convenient. He'd never been to Harry's house, he said, but he had the address and he'd jump in a cab.

Harry put the phone down and sat looking at it. It had been a gamble phoning Frank with the story, because he could have approached any number of higher-profile journalists and been sure of the same level of interest, while Frank might have brought along some personal baggage. After all, he hadn't written about *Nine South Street* on its release, despite Harry's having contacted him about it at an early stage. Frank had e-mailed Harry to explain that he'd tried a couple of his usual places and each had already commissioned a review.

So it had been a gamble and he was pleased with the outcome. Now all he had to hope for was that Richard wouldn't call with some ridiculous request, like would Harry please come and drive him two miles down the road because he couldn't be arsed to walk. Janine would probably come home while Frank was there, but that wasn't a problem. He gazed out of the window at the Scrubs and the sidings. They were too far away to see, but he could picture the trains. Sleek blue and-yellow Eurostar babies; the silver bullet of the Heathrow Express. The workhorses – the diesels – lined up ready to be called into service. Beyond them the scrapped engines. Brush 4s and Class 37s waiting out the century, rusting from the ballast up, roofs turning salty white in the sun. It wasn't that he was a railway enthusiast, more that the place itself had got to him. It was the perfect movie location and he wanted to make the perfect movie and shoot it there.

'It's called *MPD*,' he was telling Frank only half an hour later. 'The title works on two levels.'

'Of course,' said Frank, raising one of several bottles of San Miguel that Harry had set aside to lubricate the wheels of the tape recorder.

'On one level it stands for motive power depot, the sheds and sidings where the action is set. Old Oak Common depot is just over there, you know –' he pointed, 'just past the Scrubs.'

'Beyond the canal?'

'No, this side of the canal.' Harry said in a measured tone. 'And on another level,' he continued, 'MPD stands for multiple personality disorder. The main character, the train driver, suffers from MPD, and there's a string of killings, so the spot-light falls on him, you know? But maybe it's not him. We don't know. We'll use subjective camera for the killer's scenes, so the audience don't know who he is. Is it our train-driver hero or one of his "alters", or is it one of the other main characters, or someone else altogether? It's a whodunnit, which appeals to the traditional audience, but it's set entirely on a railway depot—'

'Which appeals, what, to the *Trainspotting* audience?'

'The last thing that I'd want you to think is that I'm exploiting Sarah's – exploiting what happened to Sarah. I know it's close by, but the canal doesn't come into it.'

'Sure,' said Frank, his eyes drilling through into Harry's sockets.

'If anything, it's a tribute to her. This is exactly the kind of film she would have liked, I'm sure.'

'I'm sure you're right, Harry,' Frank said, his jaw set firm. 'Do go on. I derailed your train of thought.'

Harry didn't have a chance to react because at that moment the door opened and Janine walked in. She looked at Harry and Frank and dropped the bag of groceries she was holding and a jar smashed. Fruit spilled on to the floor.

'Janine,' Harry said.

Frank didn't seem to know where to look.

Janine recovered herself and started picking up the scattered oranges.

'Let me help,' Harry said, and got down on his knees to recover the dropped items. 'Janine, this is Frank. Frank, Janine.'

'Hello,' Frank said, a little stiltedly.

'Haven't we met before?' Janine said.

'I don't think so,' said Frank.

Harry looked up at Janine, frowning. 'Have you? No – when would you have met? I'm sure I'd remember.'

'I'm sure you would,' she said, as she presented them with her back and walked away, 'if you were there.'

Harry turned to Frank and shrugged. Frank returned the gesture.

'Look, I'm a bit pressed for time.' Frank gathered his stuff together.

'You have to go already?'

'I have to be somewhere. You can e-mail me about the film. I'll see what I can do. Now, this stills business. I need to get hold of Andrew Kerner – do you have any idea where he might be? I went to his flat. It's been pulled down. His number's unobtainable. You knew him first, didn't you, out of all of us?'

'Yeah, but we were never really close. I honestly don't know where he is these days.'

Frank stared at Harry for ten seconds, then seemed to change the subject. 'Your film,' he began, 'to what extent is it based on real life?'

'What do you mean?' asked Harry quickly.

Frank paused. 'The Hammersmith Tube Murders, of course.'

'Oh, right. Well, I guess they're in my head, in the background, you know . . .'

'Sure,' said Frank.

Frank's manner was beginning to make Harry nervous. He was still faintly worried about the looks Frank had been giving him in the Troy Club. He wondered if Frank really was interested in *MPD* or if there was something else going on. Later – in the middle of the night as he paced the futility room, having been unable to sleep – he would wonder if Frank had been gathering information on *MPD* only in order to undermine it before it got made.

Or if it was even more serious than that.

As soon as he was outside, Frank started to run. It wasn't that he was worried about Janine saying something to Harry. It was more that he was running from what he had done. He'd regretted the incident with Janine – he hadn't even known her name – as soon as it had happened. It had been awkward, pointless and ultimately unsatisfying.

He thought he'd never been to Harry Foxx's house, but of

course he had, one night when he'd got very drunk with a media studies teacher who had engaged him to give a workshop. He hadn't even known that Harry's girlfriend was a teacher. He'd been out of control.

As he searched for a phone box, he wished again he'd bothered to get a mobile. As it was he had to wait until he got back to the tube. He called Jim Cover on the off-chance he'd got a number for Kerner.

'Yeah, wait a sec,' came Cover's voice over the crackly line.

'What? You've got something?' But Cover wasn't listening. Frank could hear him concluding a discussion with a colleague.

Eventually, Cover came back on. 'Got a pen?' he asked.

'Go ahead.'

'It's a mobile number.' Cover read it out.

Frank thanked him just in time before his money ran out.

He dug in his pocket for change, then dialled. It rang several times and was answered by a recorded voice asking him to leave a message.

Leaving the tube at Great Portland Street, Frank was ambushed by *Standard* billboards – 'NEW LEADS IN FILM MURDER'. He bought a copy and read the story walking down Cleveland Street. The 'new leads' were that they'd identified the film used to wrap up the body (there was a quote from Alexander Walker, with his opinion of *Bad Timing*) and they'd established that the celluloid was covered in fingerprints, which had survived fifteen years' entombment somewhat better than the body itself. An autopsy was being carried out and cause of death should be known within forty-eight hours.

He was reminded of Angelo's defensiveness regarding the use of the word 'murder' in the context of Burns's death. But what if the media were right and Burns had been murdered? Was that possible? He could have had a change of heart and revealed it to one of the group when they'd gone in to change the film. But which one? Frank already had his concerns about Angelo and he was no longer completely convinced that Harry Foxx was playing with a straight bat. As for Richard Charnock, how well had Frank ever really known him?

Back at the flat, Frank checked his messages, but there was nothing from Kerner. He remote-checked his voicemail at the magazine, and there was nothing there either. He logged on to the Internet and keyed Kerner's name into a couple of search engines, coming up with two corporate press releases and a family tree, all concerning Kerners in America. Nothing about a photographer. Downloading his e-mails, he noticed one from Harry Foxx, which he double-clicked immediately.

```
Frank

Sorry you had to rush off. Janine's having a
difficult time at work. Sorry if she seemed odd.
Anyway, to business: *MPD* is going to be the
best, cleverest, snappiest, hippest low-budget
British film since - well, let's face it - *Nine
South Street*. A) It's a good gag - motive power
depot/multiple personality disorder. B) If we can
get Old Oak Common, or somewhere like it, it's
going to be a cheap place to film. Very
atmospheric, lots of great big hulking
locomotives, new trains, scrapped engines, etc.
There's this guy who lives there, almost like a
castaway. These places are big and have lots of
out-of-the-way nooks & crannies etc. Pools of
diesel, piles of ballast. The ticking of overhead
wires, the flash of the live rail - I've done my
research. Atmos by the shedload. Ha ha! This guy
lives in the shell of an old engine that's stuck
in the sidings. There's a film crew making a doc
about him, because he won't budge even though the
sidings are being demolished and the trains taken
away. Like *Man Bites Dog* only not set in fucking
```

Belgium, and in colour, natch. There's a girl (of
course). Maybe some kids, maybe homeless kids from
Tent City just down the road, Kurdish refugees,
whatever.

There's a series of murders. Subjective camera
reveals the killer at work, but not who the killer
is. Clearly it's the guy with MPD, one of his
personalities. Say he's got two. What happens is –
and this is based on medical fact – the two
personalities can exist independently of each
other. You can be a killer and not know it.
Because you're *not* actually the killer. This
other personality, that you become, is the killer.
At some stage there can be the beginnings of
mutual awareness. Cracks begin to appear. Light
shows between the cracks and eventually the killer
is revealed to be – who? The prime suspect who
lives in the old train? I don't think so. Too
obvious. One of the refugee kids? Too un-PC. The
girl? Probably not. Maybe someone from the film
crew? OK, so the script needs work, but it's all
there. Filming can begin as soon as we get the
money. I don't like the script to be set in stone
anyway. You know the way I work. I like actors to
improvise. A bit, anyway. I mean, I'm not fucking
Mike Leigh.

This is going to be a neat little postmodern
thriller with just the right amount of
existentialist depth, i.e. not very much. Don't
want to alienate them. Think Alain Robbe-Grillet's
Trans-Europ Express, only our train never leaves
the sidings. I want to keep them guessing. The
thing is, it really could be any of them, even the
guys on the film crew, because you can have MPD
and function perfectly normally with the 'normal'
part of your personality, because it doesn't know

what's going on. All that happens is sometimes you
get forgetful. Big deal. So it could be anyone,
from the obviously mad guy to the apparently
normal, successful types.

I was going to call it *Diesel*, thinking maybe we
could get backing from the fashion company, but
MPD's too good a pun. We might still get Diesel.
That would be a good angle for you, wouldn't it?

John Foxx has agreed to do the music. You know
what that means to me. Must get an underpass into
the film somehow. (Do you remember 'Underpass'?)
Let me know what you think & what you can do. I'll
grant you exclusivity if it helps. That could be
quite a coup for you, when everyone else wants to
get on set. When *Sight & Sound* are calling and
Nick James is desperate to do a major interview.
Dazed & Confused begging to do a fashion shoot,
and *Time Out* want to send Brian Case to do one
of his jazzed-up location reports - and the only
one with an 'in' is your poxy little magazine. No
offence.

Give us a call
Harry F.

Big fucking deal, thought Frank. Exclusivity on a film that
was never going to get made. The phone rang. He picked it up.

'Is that Frank?'

'Yes.'

'This is Andrew Kerner.' The voice was flat, bleak. It could
have been coming from the end of the world. Or the room next
door.

'Fuck. Andrew. Thanks for getting back. I've got a question.'

'I'm doing fine, thanks for asking.' Bitterness creeping in,
like a thread of blood sinking into a glass of water.

'Yeah, right. Sorry. How's it going?'

'What do you want?'

'I need to ask you about some stills.'

'I don't do stills.'

'You used to.'

'A long time ago.'

'Could we meet up?'

Kerner fell silent for so long that Frank thought the connection had been severed.

'Hello?' Frank tried. 'Andrew. Are you still there?'

'I'm still here.'

'Can we meet?'

At length, he responded: 'Tomorrow.' He gave an address.
'Not before one.'

'Whatever. I'll see you tomorrow.'

Frank checked his *A–Z*. Rivington Street was in EC1, near
the Lux.

The following morning he emerged from the tube at Old
Street, still trying to assimilate the morning's news, which
he'd heard on the radio in the flat while making coffee. Of the
various fingerprints on the celluloid used to wrap Burns's body,
only one set had been identified. They belonged, according
to the *Today* programme, to a reclusive *avant-garde* film-maker
called Fraser Munro, who, some years before dropping out of
view in the late 1970s, had been been arrested on a series of
minor charges in Scotland and his prints had remained on file.

The police were anxious to contact Munro and eliminate
him from their enquiries: the discovery of his prints on the film
was by no means a clear indication of his involvement in foul
play. He could have hired the film at any time before it was
put to its ultimate, grisly use. His being a recluse was not
necessarily suspicious either, given that he'd vanished from
public life long before the alleged murder took place.

It was too much to get your head round, Frank was thinking
as he pressed the buzzer Kerner had told him to look for: 'First

Floor' was all it said. One thing at a time, thought Frank. The question of the stills had to be settled before he could grapple with the mystery of Munro.

The buzzer buzzed and the lock clicked. Frank entered a short, dusty hallway. He climbed the narrow, linoleumed stairs at the end and stopped at the first-floor landing, where one of two grease-stained doors stood ajar. He could hear the drip of a tap. A creaking came from overhead: someone moving about on one of the upper floors. He knocked on the door, then, getting no response, eased it open.

He walked straight into a kitchen that doubled as a dark-room. Long strips of negatives hung from lines crisscrossing the room. Ten-by-eights secured by tiny pegs swayed in the draught, curling over on themselves like rays. The light that came into the darkroom from the open door behind him and from the only other way out of the room, a doorway in the wall to his right, allowed him to see many of the pictures clearly enough to get a good idea of their subjects, which were abandoned buildings, dead spaces; shattered glass ceilings, long-disused aircon pipes, upturned desks and scattered contents. Not only were the people who had filled Kerner's earlier pictures gone, but now he was photographing spaces where people had once been and were no more. Frank knew he could be reading too much into a quick glimpse of a small sample of Kerner's work, but he could no sooner disobey the reflex to analyse, to interpret, than he could ignore a call of nature.

He crossed the darkroom slowly to the other door. On the wall by the door there was a noticeboard filled with black-and-whites pinned singly or at top corners. Dusty hospital wards, rubble-strewn stairways, looted stock rooms: the interior archi-tecture of abandonment. No human figures in sight, not even the shadow of the photographer.

'In here,' came Kerner's voice from the room beyond, as expressionless as it had sounded on the phone.

Frank went in. The room looked so much like one of

Kerner's sets Frank decided it couldn't be accidental. An inverted swivel chair dominated the space, a studio that was poorly lit by a high series of narrow windows, one of which had been smashed (shards of glass lay on the wooden floor beneath the window). There was a cabinet with shallow drawers pulled out apparently at random, but Frank suspected that Kerner's was a more controlling intelligence and that the drawers were tilted at those particular angles for a reason. Even the mattress on the floor in the corner, pushed up against the wall, seemed part of some secret design. It had pillows and a grubby-looking duvet, and a pile of books and a camera on the floor by the head of the bed, but Frank couldn't have sworn to its being the place where Kerner slept.

Kerner's carriage had clearly gone off the rails more spectacularly than Angelo's in the fifteen years since they made *Auteur*.

'Hello, Frank.' Kerner was sitting on the floor at the end of the bed. He was holding the back of a camera open and peering inside.

'Andrew. Long time.'

'Yes.' Not looking up, he continued to fiddle with the camera.

Frank walked across the room. 'Your work seems quite different.'

'We all move on.'

'Yes.'

'I'm busy. I'm sure you didn't come here to discuss my work.'

'You're right.' Frank felt a sudden distaste for Kerner, then realised with mild surprise that he had always felt that way. 'You remember doing stills for our film?'

'Stills? What film?' Finally, Kerner looked up at Frank, but his expression was as blank as his voice.

'Fifteen years ago. In that place on Tottenham Court Road. You remember. Me and Richard, Harry Foxx and Angelo. You came on the set and did a bunch of stills. You already had loads of pictures of the four of us. At some point you did some of my wife. Remember Sarah?'

Frank wanted to go right up to Kerner and grab hold of him, but something held him back. Fear – but fear of what? Fear of touching him, perhaps. He looked rancid, derelict, infested.

'I don't know what you're talking about,' Kerner said, then looked down when Frank caught his eye. In that momentary look, Frank saw enough to convince him that Kerner did remember. People had gone from out of his life and from out of his work; he had been abandoned just like any one of the buildings he now photographed obsessively. But that didn't mean he couldn't still remember the old days, the way his mind used to be before falling into disuse. But Frank could also see that Kerner wasn't going to give up what he knew without a fight.

'Look, Andrew,' he said, squatting down beside him. 'I just need to know something about Sarah. It's about some shots you took of her.'

Kerner stared at the floor.

Frank noticed a pile of glossy magazines on the floor. 'What was it?' he asked quietly. 'What was it for you? A sex thing? Or was it art?'

'Sex?'

Frank glanced back at the magazine on top of the pile. He couldn't read the name, but he didn't think it was *Amateur Photographer*.

Kerner stood up. There were thick patches of dust on his torn jeans. He didn't brush them off. But he did put the camera down on the bed.

'You could help me,' he said.

'*I* could help *you*?' Frank snapped.

'I need a model.'

'Doesn't look like you use models these days.'

'Get me a model and I'll see what I can find out.'

'What do you mean, find out?' Frank yelled.

'Everything's in storage. I don't throw stuff out. But I haven't got time to look, especially if I've got to go out and find a model. I want to do some work with a model. You find one for me. Save me a bit of time.' He looked at Frank and added, unnecessarily: 'A girl.'

Frank stared back at him. The look on his face was one he'd seen before. 'I'll see what I can do,' he said.

Frank wasn't a misogynist. If he treated women as objects, it was probably because of Sarah, because of how he had lost her. For a long time after it happened, he never even thought about women, and when he did he never expected one to stay with him again. Not giving them the chance to prove him wrong, he picked them up and quickly dropped them, invariably within twenty-four hours.

Frank loved women. They were fun, good company, easy on the eye. They turned him on and he enjoyed making them happy, or at least satisfied, at the end of the night. Being with women didn't make him feel good so much as gratified. They filled in the blanks, they killed time. But they weren't Sarah.

On the Monday, Frank called Jim Cover again. He thanked him for Kerner's number and asked him for another. Cover gave him the number and Frank called it and arranged a meeting with Jenny Slade, dangling the possibility of some work.

Frank worked it the same way Cover had – got her to come into the office then waited for her up on the roof. She would know where she was going, which might give her the confidence she'd need to accept the job. Especially if he offered her enough cash.

'It might look weird,' he emphasised. 'The set-up. A bit tacky. But he's a good photographer. His name's Andrew Kerner. He does a lot of stuff in abandoned buildings. Normally without models, but he needs a model for this one. He's a bit – driven, I suppose you could say. How's it sounding so far? If you don't want me to go on, just say.'

'Go on,' said Jenny Slade, moving her head to one side. She was cool, Frank acknowledged. She was making it clear who was in charge. Making it clear she could turn down this job if she wanted to.

'It's an unusual arrangement because it's open-ended.'

'As long as I'm getting paid,' she said. 'When would it be?'

'As soon as you can do it.'

'How much?'

Frank named a price, a good one. 'If you're not keen . . .' he went on.

'I'll do it.'

'OK. I'll call him and get back to you.'

'No problem.'

As soon as Jenny Slade had gone, Frank called Kerner and fixed it for the following day. If Kerner was surprised, he didn't show it. Frank stared out of the window and thought about Jenny Slade entering the dead space of Kerner's studio on Rivington Street. Did realising that what he had done was immoral make it in any way more acceptable? Did recognising that he didn't care what happened to Jenny Slade make it any easier to redeem himself? Of course, there was a slim chance that Kerner would simply get her to pose for a few shots in the nearest disused factory and then say thank you very much and shut the door on your way out. But Frank remembered the look in the photographer's eye just as clearly as he remembered the way Kerner had looked at Sarah whenever they'd all been round at the Archway flat in the old days. There had always been an unwholesome look about him.

'He's a bit of an odd character,' he told Jenny Slade when he called her later to give her the details. 'A loner. Possibly a bit sleazy. I'm not sure how relaxed he is around women. If you feel uneasy, just leave.'

'I can handle myself,' the model countered. 'If that's it . . .'

'Yes,' said Frank. 'Oh, wait, there's just one thing.'

'Yes?' Her voice wavered between bored and suspicious.

'He said he'd look out some old pictures for me. Perhaps you could remind him in case he's forgotten. Pictures of a girl about twenty-one, freckled, long auburn hair. Not that you'd be able to tell: they'll be black and white. Like film stills. Pictures from a love scene. I need any pictures he's got of her, especially if there's someone else in the shot. A man. If you can get those out of him, that'd be great.'

'What's her name?'

'Sarah.'

'So you want any pictures I can find of a girl called Sarah.'

Frank left another pause, longer this time.

'Hello?' She was getting annoyed now.

'If you can get a name out of him, there'll be more money in it.'

'What name?'

'The man. The man in the pictures with Sarah. Or just a decent shot of him. One that shows his face.'

'OK, I get it. I'll call you. Jesus, why didn't you just come straight out and say what you wanted from the start? This puts the price up considerably. OK?'

'OK.' The receiver was clammy in his hand. 'Whatever you want.'

'I'll bell you.'

Frank hung up and stared at the phone. Had he gone too far? Made a mistake? All he could do now was wait.

17 · The killing

London, 1982–83

When Munro rode the trains at night, he always wore a short, green zip-up jacket, his tight gloves and dark blue baseball cap, the brim curled over a pair of charity-shop shades, plus camouflage trousers and black trainers. On the tube, travelling in the evening or at night, his outfit ensured that he blended into the background. In the inside pocket of the jacket he carried his foster father's cut-throat razor, over his heart. He occasionally slipped his right hand into the pocket to feel the ivory handle, especially when leaving a train to switch to another line in pursuit of a departing lead actor, but he rarely took it out.

He carried the razor for self-protection. In a film with such a large cast, many of whom seemed to act almost according to their own free will, he felt unsafe without it. Why trust actors, after all? People pretending to be other people. Impersonators. Imposters.

The first time he took out the razor and used it, between Shepherd's Bush and Goldhawk Road, was in response to an actor-passenger who wouldn't stop staring at him. The man was standing by the doors, hanging on to the rail above his head and staring at Munro. As the train left Latimer Road, Munro quietly suggested the man find something else to look at, but the man just continued to stared at Munro, his dark, emotionless eyes seeming to penetrate Munro's shades.

'Stop staring,' Munro repeated. 'Just don't look at me.'

'Who do you think you are?' the man said.

Munro stared back at him from behind his shades.

'I'm warning you,' Munro said calmly. 'Stop staring at me now.'

'I'll say it again,' the man said, leaning forward and edging his chin out in provocation. 'Who the fuck do you think you are?'

The razor was out of Munro's jacket before the man had any idea what was happening. Munro got up from his seat, moving past the man and slashing his throat in a single take. The man fell forward into Munro's vacated seat, spraying blood on to the windows, the seat covers and the floor. His fingers clawed desperately at his throat, legs kicking automatically as his muscles went into spasm.

'It's only a movie,' Munro murmured.

As the train slowed, he looked up and down the carriage. No other passengers were in sight. He stepped closer and bent over the body for a moment, working with his gloved fingers and the razor until the train came to a halt. The doors slid open and Munro stepped out.

CUT TO:

This was the moment, this was the schism.

The damage had been inflicted earlier. The killing of the other Fraser Munro had branded him. And long before that, the experiences at the hands of his foster parents. But it was from this point – the point at which he had two deaths on his hands – that Fraser Munro started to live two lives, his own and that of the pseudonym he had selected on his drive down from Scotland to London. From this point on, he slept in two different places, used two different wardrobes, drew money from two different bank accounts (although little remained in

Munro's). But he mixed with only one group of people and they were those he met in his other life, since as Munro he mixed with no one. As Munro he was a recluse, remaining distant even from his other life. Especially from his other life. Although he – Munro – enjoyed a partial awareness of it – the other life – and what went on in it, he – the other one – knew nothing of Munro when he was the pseudonym. He was playing a part and yet he wasn't, because when he was the other person he had no awareness of its being a role. It was the perfect performance because it wasn't one at all. He was the other person, just as he was Munro, but he was never both at the same time. He was one or the other.

The murder on the train was a catalyst.

The first of the Hammersmith Tube Murders, it took place in the summer of 1982, six months before Harry Foxx, Richard Charnock, Frank and Angelo shot their film. Another killing took place in late September on the Metropolitan line, east-bound, as the train doors opened at Baker Street. Munro had been on the train since Shepherd's Bush, watching one passenger in particular, a short, young man with a shaved head and second-hand overcoat. He'd been watching him because the young man had repeatedly turned to look at him. The young man had a canvas knapsack on the floor at his feet and wore gold-rimmed NHS spectacles. He looked like a student. Or he thought he did. For Munro, his look was too contrived. He looked too much like a student. He was a bad actor and he was staring at Munro.

The carriage was crowded. At Baker Street, Munro got up to leave the train along with a crowd of other passengers. As he passed the young man, who was bending down to pick up his knapsack, he drew the blade across his throat, then quickly covered his face with one hand and took what he wanted, as he murmured, 'It's only a movie.' The act was performed so swiftly and with such sleight of hand that the few witnesses to the act would later fail to agree on the details and none would offer a sufficiently good description of the attacker. Munro was off the train and walking, head down, along the platform, while behind him a hubbub rose and someone pulled the emergency handle.

In the disused station at Wood Lane he built up a little collection. He kept it not in the station buildings, but down in one of the tunnels, on the disused eastbound platform, balanced on top of the wooden frame around the old station sign that read:

WOOD LANE
ALIGHT FOR
EXHIBITION

Although he didn't spend even half his time at Wood Lane, he still regarded it as his space and became very territorial about it. Occasionally people would try to break in – down-and-outs, squatters or just the curious – and mostly they got enough of a fright never to repeat the attempt. Of all the intruders who trespassed on Munro's territory over the years, only one failed to leave: hearing unusual noises one night, Munro slipped out the back way to investigate and came across a photographer hunched over a tripod.

Once he'd finished with the body, he dropped it – and the camera equipment – down the deep drainage well in the old pump house. It took a few seconds to hear the splash.

'It's only a movie.'

18 · The driver

London, Wednesday 22 July 1998

Angelo's search for the Museum of Lost Cinema Spaces, the place where he believed the ghost auditoria of London's disused cinemas were stored, had its own momentum. But a very real sense that time was running out chased him back into the streets not only as soon as he could get away from the office, but during working hours as well. He started turning up at the dispatch office later and later, so that even by mid-July he was barely at his desk before the morning was over.

He left it a week before setting out to recover the cassette boxes pinched by the girl from the gallery, but having left the flat, he headed straight over to the Harrow Road instead to plot the locations of the former Prince of Wales, Coliseum and Regal. He pointed his video camera at the spaces where he believed they had stood. He wound up on Edgware Road and bought a sandwich in the Hubbub Express at number 164, former site of the Blue Hall, and ate it as he looked for the Grand Kinema at numbers 280/284, which had seated two thousand. Any cinema that size nowadays would be a fifteen-screener. But it had gone, demolished to make way for the Westway flyover.

As he headed down Praed Street (pausing to film through the smoked office windows at number 5, formerly the Classic), it occurred to him that the girl from the gallery might have stolen his boxes not in order to make him come and find her, which was the sort of thing Naomi would have done, but to exhibit or even sell them. He was heading in the direction of Talbot Road anyway, so he could go and look.

Angelo could see from some distance away that the place was empty. In fact, until he crossed the street he couldn't tell if the lights inside were on or off. They were off, but the gallery retained a faint luminescence courtesy of its glass roof and pale interior. Angelo peered through the door but could see no sign of life. Nor of his cassette boxes. He stepped back and his eye was caught by the televisions in the TV and audio showroom next door: each was tuned to the same channel and each showed Iain Burns's disembodied, decomposed head rotating on a turntable. Angelo went icy cold, then hot. His stomach went into spasm and his heart pounded. He looked away and when he looked back it was still there. There must have been a dozen TVs in the window and each was broadcasting the same dreadful illusion.

Suddenly the picture disappeared from all twelve screens at once and was replaced by snow. He clasped his hands over his face.

When he next looked, he saw a man inside the shop climbing a stepladder to poke a screwdriver inside a box on the wall. Within seconds the sets came back on. The image was the same, but now Angelo could see it wasn't actually Burns's head. It was close, but it wasn't him. It was an artist's impression based on his skull, and anyone who knew Burns would have no trouble identifying him from it.

'It's always bloody happening.' The man from the shop, now down from his ladder, had opened the door and stepped outside to check that all of his sets had come back on. 'Whole bloody place needs rewiring.'

Through the open door Angelo could clearly hear the reporter's voice: '. . . victim died as a result of a large injection of silver nitrate. It is believed he could have taken anything from two minutes to a quarter of an hour to die. Although there is clear evidence that Burns was suffering from tertiary syphilis, which is known to cause severe mental as well as physical problems, suicide has been ruled out and the police have now launched a murder investigation.'

The news reached Richard Charnock at the same time as it reached Harry Foxx. Harry was driving Richard from one of his Soho meetings for *Little Black Dress* to Shepherd's Bush where he had another appointment. Harry had the radio tuned to Robert Elms on GLR (it beat listening to Richard crapping on). The second story on the news was the coroner's report.

Harry Foxx looked in the mirror and caught Richard's frown.

'What are they talking about?' Richard asked.

'Haven't got a fucking clue. Silver nitrate? Maybe it's a trick.'

'A trick?'

'To draw us out,' Harry suggested.

'Oh yeah, like we're going to stroll into the nearest police station and say, hey, it wasn't silver nitrate, it was insulin. We should know, we fucking killed him.'

'Yeah, except we didn't kill him, Richard,' Harry pointed out.

Richard snorted and looked out of the window. 'I don't think it makes much difference now,' he said. 'We as good as killed him.'

Harry Foxx guided the big Mercedes off the Westway and sat in traffic at the bottom of the M41. He turned to look out of the open driver's window as a high-sided German tourist coach chugged slowly past in the next lane, exhaust fumes swarming towards the Merc. Harry raised the window and noticed Richard's handprint still visible on the toughened glass. He quickly buzzed the window back down again.

'It costs more to replace the window motor on one of these than it does to make a Screen 2,' Richard snapped from the back seat. 'You'll wear it out,' he added when Harry failed to react.

'This job's wearing *me* out, if you want to know the truth,'

Harry Foxx remarked, sticking his elbow out of the window as he sailed through the lights on the south side of the Green.

'Oh yeah? It must be hard work driving two and a half miles every other day. I suppose you've forgotten what hard work feels like.'

Harry ignored the dig. He was trying to figure out a way of getting the handprint from the car window up to the spare bedroom in his house for the purposes of comparison. Did Richard's need to control Harry's life extend to screwing his girl-friend? Should he actually remove the window? Would he ever get it back in? If the prints matched, would there be any need to? He wouldn't be driving Richard's car much longer if he was able to prove the man had been inside his spare bedroom – or, more to the point, inside his girlfriend. In fact, he had a feeling he wouldn't be driving Richard's car much longer in any case.

'What is it you're doing here anyway?' Harry asked, pulling into the left just after the Central line tube station.

'Recce,' said Richard, his hand already on the door handle.

'Oh yeah?' Harry looked in the mirror. 'You won't be doing it alone though, I imagine? Presumably there'll be an attractive young assistant along in a minute to give you a hand, as it were.'

Richard glared at Harry from the pavement. 'I'll call you,' he snarled.

'Yeah, right.' Harry accelerated away from the side of the road, allowing the laws of physics to take care of shutting the rear door.

Richard watched him slip through the red light with a dawning realisation that their business relationship was coming to an end. Then he turned and climbed the steps to the former Exhibition building, where the padlock had been left undone as arranged. He wondered if Jenny Slade had already arrived or if he would have to wait for her.

Angelo didn't go straight home from Talbot Road: he couldn't face a tapeful of answerphone messages from Frank. Instead he

rode the Hammersmith & City line, picking it up at Ladbroke
Grove and going right through to Hammersmith, then waiting
for the first train back to Royal Oak. He sat on the platform at
Royal Oak for several minutes, then hopped on a train going
back to Hammersmith. Just after Latimer Road, at the point
where the tube line was carried by a viaduct over a busy stretch
of motorway, the M41, he stared out of the windows towards
the Holland Park roundabout.

Brake lights gathered at the traffic lights like hot coals in a
fire grate. To the right of the M41, a large patch of wasteland
was occupied by an interconnecting series of long, high-ceilinged
sheds on metal stilts. Beneath these and extending to their
right was a depot for the Central line, sidings and sheds quickly
hidden by other buildings passing in the foreground. Then the
backs of converted houses slid into view: brief lives conducted
like mini-films in tiny 3D cinemas for the benefit of train-
drawn audiences. The tube slowed for Shepherd's Bush. On an
impulse, he jumped off and walked the short distance to the
Green. Three of the buildings down the west side of the Green
had been cinemas in happier times. Angelo took out his notebook. The giant bingo hall was formerly the Pavilion Cinema,
designed by Frank Verity and opened in 1923; renamed the
Gaumont in 1955, then the Odeon in 1962. Angelo slipped
inside and wandered into what had been a vast auditorium seat-
ing three thousand. It had been remodelled for joint use as a
cinema and bingo hall in 1970, and closed as a cinema in 1983.
All they had done was to take the rows of seats out, remove the
screen and fill the raked floor with plasticky booths for bingo
players. Patrons, Angelo imagined, must develop a strange gait,
one leg longer than the other: take them outside on to the
Green and they'd walk round in tiny circles, as if chained to a
post. The attendance was paltry, given the amount of space,
but still the bingo caller called and the players played. Along
the back wall, one-armed bandits gleamed threateningly.

In Angelo's dream of a London transformed, a benign

authority would put the bingo out of its misery and bring back the screen, reimporting the auditorium's spirit from the museum, wherever it was hidden. Pointing his camera into the highest corners of Verity's huge space, he sensed shreds of the cinema's soul still clinging to the plaster, but otherwise he couldn't feel anything. It was dead, sterile, hardly even a ghost of its former self. The new atmosphere was an inert soup of disappointments and anticlimaxes. What did you win if you won? Was it worth winning? Angelo knew the answers. He didn't have to look at the resignation on the faces of players and caller alike; he could taste the desperation, the emptiness with each breath he took. The soul of this place, he knew, would be one of the most vibrant and potent in the museum; the capacity was enough to guarantee it, plus fifty years' accumulated cinema-goers' emotions.

It wasn't just the souls of demolished cinemas that he would find once he located the museum, but those whose buildings still stood, converted to other uses, or were standing empty. Angelo would not only find the lost souls, but somehow, with or without help, he was determined to return them to their rightful homes. The Pavilion Cinema would breathe again.

Inside the Exhibition hall, there was no immediate sign of the model. Nor of the security guard, whose hourly rate was effectively being trebled by his making himself scarce for a couple of hours. Richard Charnock advanced into the old building and climbed the exposed sprial staircase in the middle of the ground floor to the galleried first floor, his feet crunching freshly broken glass into the mildewed boards. Pigeons clattered in the roof space above the collapsed false ceiling as they negotiated a tangle of bust air-conditioning pipes and slewed girders. He wandered into his favourite little room on the right-hand side and looked through the hole in the broken window at the cleared land between the Exhibition halls and the West London line.

While he waited, he thought about the implications of what he and Harry Foxx had heard on the radio. If Burns had been killed by an injection of silver nitrate rather than insulin, then one of the group was responsible. For different reasons they were all pretty desperate characters, and Richard could imagine any one of them being capable of killing by the end of the 1990s if sufficiently motivated, but back in the early 1980s they had all seemed such young innocents with only one thing on their minds – making movies. Which one of them could possibly have been hell-bent on making a snuff movie?

He could understand the sleazy appeal of the transgressive. Some would say the footage he'd shot of Jenny Slade was porn. So he wasn't above breaking through the taste barrier, but snuff was different.

He thought about Harry Foxx and his long-dreamed-of second feature, *MPD*. Did Harry's interest arise out of personal experience, or was it true that if you actually had the disorder there was no way you would know that you had it? Maybe one personality would get the odd glimpse into the life of the other, while itself remaining unknown.

A noise caught Richard's attention. A faint scrape. He looked down and caught a glimpse of a white face floating through the gloom of the lower floor, between the pillars. Jenny Slade. His breathing quickened. She emerged from behind the spiral staircase in combat trousers, heavy-soled trainers and a white top. Richard watched as she walked towards the end of the enclosed ground-floor area looking up at the balcony for any sign of his presence. He stayed hidden, watching her.

Reaching the back wall, she turned round and started walking back, then stopped in the middle and pulled her white top over her head, dropping it behind her on the floor. She knew he was watching.

Richard reached into his top pocket and pulled out a pair of non-prescription blue-lensed glasses. He slipped them on and watched Jenny Slade, who was still wearing the bra-top she always wore. Her breasts were slightly too large for the bra-top. She should have worn a bra that would give them more support. She knew this and he knew this, and he knew that she knew that he knew this. All of which enhanced the eroticism of the display.

As long as Richard kept the blue glasses on, he was doing nothing wrong. He was still looking upon the scene as a director. He made a frame of his hands to emphasise the fact, panning left as Jenny walked across the empty hall. When film-makers had worked exclusively in black and white and they'd wanted to see how a shot would look before committing it to film, they'd peer at it through a square of blue glass. The spectacles were now what saved him from cheating on Caroline. As long as there remained a barrier between viewer and object, he was in the clear.

He watched as she walked as far as the exposed spiral staircase, then climbed it. She disappeared from view but he could still hear the soft thump of her trainers on the carpeted steps. He retreated behind the partition wall, knowing that she would head for the space beyond it. He put his eye to the hole in the wall and waited.

Next door to the bingo hall, the Walkabout pub retained only one reminder of its former glory as the Cinematographic Theatre, opened in 1910 – the name picked out in relief running down the side of the exterior in the cut-through to Pennard Road. Otherwise, it had been transformed into an Australian theme bar. Angelo closed his eyes and imagined it reborn as a five-hundred-capacity cinema running Peter Weir nights and midnight screenings of *Breaker Morant*.

Across Rockwood Place from the Walkabout was the Shepherd's Bush Empire, which had screened its last movie in 1953. As Angelo made his way around the Green, checking out the former location of the Galaxy in the appallingly grim shopping centre on the south side of the Green, he reflected on the evidence that Shepherd's Bush had once been one of London's busiest neighbourhoods for cinema-going. Other picture houses – the Bioscope Theatre and the King's Hall Picture Palace – had operated on the north side of the Green. Angelo reached the Green's apex. Across six lanes of traffic was a huge white building with an arched entrance, disused and fallen into ruin but obviously once a major landmark. It was unknown to Angelo – his notebook drew a blank – so not a former cinema, but a powerful building nonetheless and Angelo crossed the road to get a closer look. The front door appeared to be padlocked and signs indicated that the premises were guarded by a security firm. Fly-posters for gigs, CDs, even books were plastered over the filthy windows. Angelo wondered if there'd been a mistake, if the hard-working compilers of Hammersmith & Fulham's list of cinemas past and present had somehow missed one, a big one. Moving to the edge of Holland Park roundabout, Angelo was able to see how the building extended beyond its fancy entrance: a long white shed with a largely ruined glass roof stretched back fully two hundred yards, then turned a ninety-degree corner and another shed ran west before turning another right angle to head north again. This was the other end of the construction he had seen from the tube. On their metal stilts, the long, narrow sheds marched across a blasted, post-industrial landscape as far as the Central line tube depot.

Angelo felt something shift slowly within him.

Still Richard Charnock waited. Jenny Slade did not appear. He moved back from the wall and wiped his forearm across his brow. Tension had brought him out in a sweat. He pressed his eye to the hole in the wall once more, but there was no sign of her.

Then he became aware of her leaning in the splintered doorway watching *him*.

'No camera?' she said.

'This is my camera.' He pointed to his eyes.

'I met a friend of yours.'

'Oh yes?'

'Photographer.'

'Cinematographer?'

'No. Pictures. Black-and-whites. Funny bloke.'

'I don't know who you're talking about.'

'Andrew something.'

'Oh, him.'

'Yes, him.' The model turned away to kick the loose architrave. 'We had a very interesting talk.'

'Oh yes?'

'About an old friend of yours.'

'Another one?'

'A girl.'

'I don't know that many girls.'

Jenny Slade had now advanced into the room and was circling him.

'This is a girl called Sarah.'

'I don't think I know any Sarahs.'

'Well, no. I don't think she's around any more.'

'What do you mean?' he asked, watching her carefully as she paced.

'You tell me.'

'I'm not sure I like the way this is going, Jenny. What's your angle?'

'Angle?'

'Yes. Angle. What do you want? Money?'

'Is it worth money? How much is it worth?'

Richard stared at her.

'If I wanted to blackmail you,' she said, 'I'd have more than enough for that already. Don't you think?'

'So what's going on then?'

'I'm curious,' she said. 'I'm the curious type. I prefer it when things make sense. When I can see how things fit together. I mean, it's a small world, isn't it?'

'What do you mean?' Richard asked, removing the blue glasses and rubbing his eyes wearily. 'How did you meet Kerner?'

'I was doing some work for him.'

'Modelling?'

'What else?'

Richard heard a noise. He put his finger to his lips and peered round the doorway up and down the length of the shed.

'Probably a pigeon,' he said, sliding the glasses into his top pocket.

'Who was she?' asked Jenny Slade.

Angelo was glad they had discovered Burns's body and he was glad that the truth would come out at last. He had borne the burden of guilt on his own long enough. As he leaned on the parapet over the West London line gazing across at the first two sheds of the unknown building, the bridge supports beneath him rumbled and the air around him was suddenly filled with explosive noise. He pulled himself up to see over the edge of the parapet and a diesel engine burst out of the tunnel directly beneath him, pulling closed freight wagons. He watched as it motored north. In thirty seconds or so it would be causing the windows in the back of Harry Foxx's house to vibrate as it passed by.

When the train had gone, Angelo went back to the main entrance to the arched building. Eyeing it more closely, he saw that the padlock was not securing anything, but hanging free. With barely a moment's hesitation, Angelo pushed open the door and slipped inside.

Richard was growing exasperated. The clock was ticking and the understanding was that Richard should have left the building by the time the security guard returned.

'Does it matter?' he snapped.

'Apparently so.'

Their heads turned at another, different noise from below.

'Security guard,' Richard hissed. 'He's not due back for an hour.'

Jenny looked anxious. 'What are we going to do?' she asked.

'I don't know.' Richard took out his shades and put them back on, his eyes fading into pools of indigo shadow. 'If he's come back early, there must be a reason. We can't risk leaving that way. We'll have to see if there's another way out. Come on.'

He took her hand to lead her out of the little room back into the open-plan first-floor area.

'Which way are we going?' she whispered.

At the far end, a square archway led into the next space.

'What about my top?' she demanded.

He looked down over the rail. Jenny Slade's white top lay crumpled in the middle of the floor. Richard cursed. There was no false ceiling above that section and light from the original glass canopy flooded the well of the hall, making Jenny's top stand out like a flag of surrender.

'We'll have to leave it,' he said.

'It's Gucci,' she protested.

'I can't afford to be seen. And neither can you. Come on.'

They moved, swiftly but quietly, towards the square arch-way. On the wall to the left of the architrave was the biggest, most intricate graffito he'd seen in the building, spray-painted in scarlet, pale blue and canary yellow. Richard's blue lenses thickened the red like dried blood, gave the yellow a greenish cast and rendered the blue almost fluorescent. Scrawled underneath in crazy capitals was the warning 'YA WRONG JUDGMENTS GONNA GET YA HURT'. They passed into the next space, a wide, flat box with a concrete floor, low false ceiling with tiles hanging loose or missing altogether; along the right-hand wall, light poured in through rectangular groups of windows. Because of the angle at which he observed them, the effect was like a series of cinema screens with white light projected on to them. Otherwise the walls were covered with graffiti: 'Fume', 'Niggaz', 'W7' and 'THE'.

'What is this place anyway?' Jenny Slade asked in a low voice.

'Exhibition halls,' Richard answered, looking round to check they hadn't been followed. 'From the early part of the century.'

'Doesn't look that old to me,' she observed, glancing up at the remains of the false ceiling where once there'd been concealed lighting.

'These first buildings were converted to office space at some point. Insurance company. Through there.' Richard pointed to the open doorway at the left end of the far wall.

The next room, which was about the same size again, also had windows like blank screens down one wall. Two lines of pillars broke up the space. The one other detail that distinguished it from the previous room was the lack of an obvious exit at the far end.

'Now what?' Jenny Slade asked. 'Presumably you have a plan.'

'I'm thinking,' Richard retorted, revealing how much of a plan there was.

A noise came from behind them, from beyond the previous room.

Richard grabbed Jenny's hand and led her to one of the windows at the far end. Looking round, he noted with satisfaction that two of the pillars blocked the sightline to the doorway. It wasn't much, but it was a sign that not everything was against them.

'I hope you're not scared of heights,' Richard said as he eased open a window. Traffic growled on the M41; in the foreground, mechanical diggers clawed at the empty land.

'Let's go,' he said.

'Yeah, right,' Jenny said, taking a look. 'If you think I'm going out that window you're an even bigger wanker than I thought you were.'

'Two words: bad publicity.'

'I thought there was no such thing.'

'When *Little Black Dress* is in the can, we need never see each other again. But for now you have to do what I say. It's either this, or kiss goodbye to your acting career.'

There was another noise from back the way they'd come, possibly the next room, and Jenny Slade started climbing out of the window.

'Let me go first,' Richard insisted.

A figure appeared in the doorway as Jenny Slade's head dipped down below the level of the window. Richard closed the window with care; he indicated that they should remain where they were, clinging to the side of the building thirty feet above the ground, until the security guard was out of earshot. They waited until they heard his footsteps recede, then climbed down the fire escape.

As they negotiated the mud hills between the former Exhibition halls and the West London line, Richard called Harry Foxx on the mobile and told him to come and get them from halfway up the M41.

'Can you manage?' Richard asked her as he checked the railway line.

'I can manage,' Jenny Slade retorted, clearly not impressed. Undressing on camera was one thing, stripping for a man wearing blue lenses another, but shinning down fire escapes and stepping over live rails was altogether different. Richard reckoned he'd pushed things with Jenny Slade about as far as they would go.

'How long will it take your driver to get here?' she asked.

'Five minutes or so.'

'Long enough for you to explain about Sarah.'

Richard squatted by the wall between the railway and the motorway.

'What did Kerner tell you?' he asked.

'That her death was an accident, but that you were driving.

Then the body was disposed of. It hardly seems very respectful.'

'That's what he told you?'

'He also explained how it all came about. You and Kerner and Sarah spent an evening together getting out of your heads on some Afghani black you'd got hold of. Frank wasn't there because he wasn't into drugs. He thought dope-smoking was boring and he didn't even like Sarah doing it, so she hadn't told him where she was and who she was with. He thought she was at a girlfriend's. Right so far?'

'Go on,' said Richard.

'You all got completely out of your heads, and after Kerner had taken a bunch of pictures of you and Sarah getting it together, you agreed to give her a lift home. Only somehow you accidentally knocked her down with the car, then for some reason thought it would be a good idea to dump the body by the canal.'

Richard looked away, a half-smile playing on his lips.

'You seem to think it's all a big joke,' she remarked.

'It happened a long time ago and you've got one vital detail wrong.'

'Oh yeah, and what's that?'

Richard lit a cigarette and appraised her defiant, hands-on-hips pose.

'Why do you think I have a driver?' he asked, glancing at the oncoming traffic to see if there was any sign of the Mercedes.

'Because you're a bigshot movie director. Or you think you are.'

'No. I have a driver because I can't drive,' he said quietly.

'Oh yeah?' Jenny Slade challenged him, betraying a little of her lost confidence. 'Maybe you just want everyone to *think* you can't drive.'

Richard Charnock knew he couldn't drive the same way he knew he couldn't walk on water or fly over central London. Driving wasn't on his CV. Put him behind the wheel of a car and he wouldn't know what to do. Hence Harry Foxx, and who-ever might replace him if relations between driver and drivee didn't improve dramatically.

'You want to know what happened? You really want to know?'

'Kerner said he and this film director friend of his,' Jenny insisted, 'spent an evening getting completely fucked up with Sarah, having sex with her, and then later she was accidentally killed.'

'Let me guess the rest,' Richard interrupted. 'You happened to tell Kerner you were working on a movie with me, and between you, somehow, you managed to put two and two together and make five.'

'Let's just say I mentioned your name and he didn't exactly leap to your defence.'

'Jenny, you've got so much to learn. And I thought you were so sussed. Sarah's husband, Frank, had a thing about drugs and couldn't stand her smoking dope. Just as you were told. So she lied to Frank about what she was doing when she wanted to get stoned with her friends. Yes, she did get high on some Afghani black, and Kerner was there, and so was one other person, but it wasn't me. Kerner knew a few people who were film-makers, not just me. In fact, there were four of us, plus Kerner. We hung out together. It wasn't me. I never had sex with Sarah and I never drove her anywhere. Here's our ride.'

The black Mercedes braked sharply on the hard shoulder a few yards ahead of them, its rear wheels spitting gravel.

'Come on,' Richard shouted, grabbing her hand.

He opened the rear door and bundled her in. As Harry Foxx pressed his foot to the floor and gave the power steering a nudge to get the big car back on to the road, with scant regard for the vehicles coming up behind, Richard performed a basic introduction.

'Harry's my driver,' he said to Jenny as the acceleration gently forced him back into his seat. 'He's always been the driver, in a sense, right since the early days. Like Bruce Dern in *The Driver*, or Dennis Weaver in *Duel*, he's very much *the driver*, if you take my meaning.'

Richard smiled at Jenny Slade to drive his point home. She looked from Richard to Harry's rear-view mirror, then back to Richard.

'So, Harry drives the car,' she said, checking.

'Harry has *always* driven the car. Harry probably has sex as well.'

'No offence, but what the fuck are you two going on about?' demanded Harry Foxx.

'Sorry, Harry. Good drugs, that's all. In fact,' he smiled at Jenny again, 'why don't we have some more?' Richard removed a wrap from the pocket of his jacket and unfolded it on a hard-back *A–Z* that he asked Harry to pass him from the front passenger seat. Richard cut up the cocaine into two lines with a bank card he took from his wallet.

'I'd offer you some, Harry,' he said, 'only it's probably not safe to do drugs and drive. We don't want to have an accident, do we?'

Harry made no response.

Jenny Slade nodded slowly as she made sense of it all. Then she accepted a rolled-up twenty from Richard and bent over the *A–Z*. She couldn't have been unaware of the effect her bending over would have on him, especially since the loss of her Gucci top. Again, it was her obvious knowledge of the effect of her display that made it so powerful. Richard's cock was hard even before the coke numbed the back of his mouth. He took the blue-lensed glasses from his top pocket and put them on. Jenny Slade was already grinning with the effect of the drug.

'Where are we going?' asked Harry Foxx irritably.

'Just drive, Harry,' replied Richard. 'You're the driver, Harry. You've always been the driver.'

For one heart-stopping moment it looked as if Harry was

going to take the first left off the roundabout at the top – 'For fuck's sake, Harry, don't leave *London*. I mean, I thought that was obvious,' bellowed Richard – but then he swung the car round to the right and indicated left to join the Westway. As Harry burned into the middle lane and took the speed up to seventy-five, Richard turned to Jenny Slade once more and, leaning forward, said, 'I believe we were interrupted, weren't we? A little unfinished business?'

Jenny Slade grinned again. Would nothing faze her? wondered Richard gratefully as she unhitched her bra-top from one shoulder and reached in with a free hand to release her breast. She didn't get both breasts out, because she understood how the male mind worked, or at least how Richard's worked. For him, this was the pinnacle of sexual arousal. There before him was one breast, in itself an object of such extraordinary aesthetic and erotic beauty. But more powerful even than that visible breast was the deliberate withholding of the other, its invisible twin. It was the promise of its release that aroused him more than anything else. He knew that if he decided to, he could reach across that short distance and free it himself. He could touch if he wanted to, and he did want to, so badly, but his conscience knew it was wrong. He fingered the blue glasses.

He watched Jenny as she moved her fingers over her breast, catching the nipple on the upstroke. She was looking past him, over his shoulder, at a blurred panning shot of Ladbroke Grove.

Fuck it, he thought, reaching across the expanse of taupe leather upholstery between them, and with two hands took hold of the bra top and pulled it up and over her head. Jenny Slade's breasts, straining upwards as he pulled at the grey Lycra, swooped back to their natural position with a grace that reminded him of the pantograph of an electric locomotive falling from an overhead wire back to its cradle. Jenny Slade offered neither reproach nor encouragement. Instead, she turned her head to the front and gazed through the windscreen as Richard moved his hands slowly and firmly over her body. He moved forward and kissed her breasts. She leaned back against the door.

Richard kicked off his shoes and wriggled out of his trousers. He reached into his jacket for another wrap and cut four more lines on the road atlas. He held out the twenty to Jenny Slade. As she leaned forward to snort her share of the drug, he caught her swinging breasts in his hands and massaged them. He accepted the rolled-up banknote and snorted up the crumbs.

'Harry,' he shouted. 'Harry, I haven't got anything.'

Jenny Slade and Richard Charnock collapsed into fits of giggles.

Harry Foxx muttered: 'Jesus Christ.' But he pulled out his wallet and extracted a condom, which he tossed over his shoulder into the back of the car. Richard tore open the pack as Jenny pushed down at her combats and moved into a more comfortable position. As he rolled the condom into place, Richard looked up and saw the curved lines of the cream-tiled former BR building at Warwick Avenue slipping into view. The Mercedes swept past its curiously rounded tower and shattered, graffitied windows at a hundred m.p.h.

As they sank into the dip before the Edgware Road flyover, Richard looked up and happened to glance into the rear-view mirror, where his brain registered a fact so disorienting that his mind took several seconds to catch up: Jenny Slade and Harry Foxx were watching each other in the mirror. The extreme alienating effect of this caused Richard's lust to dwindle, and he moved away from Jenny Slade, somehow managing to be half dressed before they reached the bottom of the flyover on the other side. As the car slowed for the lights on Marylebone Road, Richard reached across and opened the door on Jenny Slade's side.

'Please,' he said simply.

She looked at him as if he'd hit her across the face.

'Please.'

She shook her head, more in disbelief than a refusal to co-operate.

The lights turned green and the inevitable angry chorus started up from the cars behind. Harry Foxx watched in the rear-view mirror, his loyalties divided, and did nothing.

'You have to leave the car now,' Richard insisted.

Jenny Slade gathered her clothes under one arm and stepped out into the road. She shut the car door with a flourish, dropped her stuff on the pavement and stood with her hands on her hips as Harry Foxx, under orders, burned rubber to get across the junction and not collide with the cars that were already crossing from both sides.

Richard twisted his neck to watch Jenny Slade get smaller and smaller as their speed climbed. He could still hear traffic horns, but now they were more of a fanfare than a rebuke.

When he stopped at the next set of lights, Harry Foxx switched off the engine and stepped out of the car. He turned and leaned back in, resting one hand on the headrest of the driver's seat, looking as if he was about to toss the keys into the rear of the car, but then seemed to change his mind and turned and walked away. Richard then watched in open-mouthed dismay as Harry Foxx dropped the keys down a grate on the far side of Marylebone Road, stuck his hands in his trouser pockets and sauntered off down Gloucester Place.

19 · Auteur

London, Thursday 23 July 1998

The phone rang early the next morning in Frank's flat on Tottenham Court Road. Frank picked up on the third ring and grunted. When he heard who it was he became alert and sat up abruptly in bed. Siân rolled over and opened her eyes.

'Give me a name,' he said into the phone. Jenny Slade gave him the name. 'You're sure about that?' She said she was. She started to say something else, but Frank hung up the phone and sat staring into space, as if in a trance.

'It's very early to ring,' Siân murmured. 'Who was it? Angelo?'

Angelo had taken to leaving messages, on an almost daily basis, telling Frank which abandoned cinema he was breaking into next.

'A model,' Frank replied. 'Long story,' he added, turning to Siân.

'Yes, they all are,' she said, turning away from him.

'No, not like that,' Frank said. 'It's nothing like that.'

'No, it never is.'

Siân got out of bed and walked to the bathroom. Frank heard the door being locked. He didn't have time for this. Picking up the phone, he dialled Harry Foxx's home number. There was no answer, and nor did the machine kick in. He tried Harry's mobile, and a recorded message told him it may

have been switched off. Frank didn't know what he was going
to say if Harry had answered.

'Siân,' he said through the bathroom door, 'I have to get
going.'

'OK.' Her tone was brisk, but he didn't have time to worry
about that now.

'You're more than welcome to hang around, but I've got to
go.'

The bathroom door opened and Siân bustled out, dressed
and smelling of toothpaste. 'No, thank you,' she said. 'I've got
to go, too.'

They left the flat together, together in the sense of two
people leaving somewhere at the same time, but in no other
sense. He moved to kiss her goodbye as they hit the street, but
she turned away and walked off towards Soho. Frank hailed a
cab going the other way.

'North Kensington,' he said to the driver. 'Latimer Road.'

For Angelo, the new day was full of promise. He stood at his
window, a soft white ladies' top draped around his neck like a
scarf, watching a Hammersmith & City line train decelerating
before stopping at Royal Oak. He ran his hand over his cropped
hair – he'd given himself a number one with the clippers the
night before, after getting back from the arched building
at Shepherd's Bush – and thought about where the train was
heading after it left Royal Oak: Westbourne Park and
Ladbroke Grove, then Latimer Road and on to Shepherd's
Bush.

How sure could he be about the arched building? What
function had it served in its day? He dressed and slipped the
latest *Ghost Train* tape into the VCR. The screen filled with
snow; static fizzed out of the speakers. He watched and
listened carefully, hoping for a sign, confirmation or denial
that he was on the right track. Nothing. He switched off the
tape. Since the revelation about the cause of death, the voices

had fallen silent. But he no longer needed them, he realised. He knew what he had to do.

The tapes had stopped working the other way as well. The guilt he had shouldered alone was now divided between the four of them and his share was so light he barely noticed it. Burns was finally at rest.

When Angelo had stepped inside the arched building the previous afternoon it had felt like entering another consciousness. He had sensed the atmosphere of the place as soon as the door closed softly behind him. The level of neglect was just what he had been expecting. They would want any intruder to think this was merely an abandoned space, when in fact it was part of the national heritage. It was a bluff, but not one that fooled Angelo. Alert to the slightest sound, he walked past a vacant reception desk on the left and approached an exposed spiral staircase. Instead of climbing it, he walked on into a wide, high-ceilinged space. Graffiti-decorated walls were broken up by gaping doorways into unknown darkness. Angelo kept walking. He heard something that could have been a rat or a bird – or, at a stretch, a human being. But something aglow drew him on, deeper into the great hall. Light that fell from the glass ceiling in this spot pooled in a piece of discarded fabric. He bent to pick it up, surprised at how clean it was – and warm. He held the white garment to his face and sniffed tentatively. Then he buried his face in it and used it to wipe away a brief flurry of tears. Where was its owner? He walked back to the spiral staircase and started to ascend. What was left of the carpet stuck to the soles of his shoes. At the top there was only one way to go. Partially destroyed doorways opened to the left and right. He ignored them and walked on. It was a long building, and he felt drawn into it. At the end of the first space, the glass canopy overhead fantailed to its own conclusion and Angelo passed under a square archway into a long, somewhat narrower room. The windows on the right admitted cascades of silver light, but the overriding impression was of confinement, which Angelo quickly realised could be put down to the low false ceiling. He pictured the empty space above it.

There was only one other way out of the room, at the far end. A doorway without a door. He passed through it and advanced several steps into an almost identical room, when he suddenly became aware of of a figure at the other end. The figure – he couldn't tell if it was male or female, threatening or fleeing – moved fast, but not as fast as Angelo moved in the opposite direction as he turned and ran.

The place had spooked him without his having realised it, and encountering another presence had been all it took to make him bolt. He had trotted down the spiral staircase and slipped past the still-vacant reception desk, pushing open the door to the street. It was only once he was back on Uxbridge Road, walking down to the Hammersmith & City line tube, that he had realised he was still carrying the white top.

An eastbound train had transported him past the BBC, over the abandoned Wood Lane station buildings on the Central line below and over the industrial units of Ariel Way and Silver Road. He looked out at the long white sheds from the reverse angle. They resembled an unfinished game of dominoes.

The train had pulled into Latimer Road, where no one got off. As it pulled away again, heading for Ladbroke Grove, Angelo felt as if the piece enabling the game to be completed might be within his grasp.

So, the following morning, after calling Frank's number and leaving a message explaining where he was going, he rode the Hammersmith & City line westbound, and after Latimer Road he watched the long white sheds as they emerged from behind all the industrial units in the foreground, but instead of getting off at Shepherd's Bush, he went all the way to Hammersmith and walked to the archives of the borough library in the shadow of the West London Ark. There he learned that the mysterious buildings at Shepherd's Bush had been built in 1908 for the

Franco-British Exhibition. Designed to last no more than five years, the long sheds – or Exhibition halls – started immediately behind the Uxbridge Road entrance, which in those days was as elaborate and fancy as a wedding cake, and zigzagged across railway land to Wood Lane station, where a footbridge took visitors across Wood Lane into the White City and the main part of the Exhibition.

Angelo sifted through buff folders full of photographs taken at the Coronation Exhibition in 1911 and at the British Industries Fair ten years later. He pored over ancient, yellowing press-cuttings. Visitors to the Franco-British Exhibition had walked half a mile through the halls that lay between Uxbridge Road and Wood Lane before they entered the White City. There were maps that showed the original layout of the halls. He guessed he'd been inside only the first, possibly the first and second. It was difficult to relate his memories of his brief foray to the diagrammatic representation.

After the White City's brief heyday, the halls between Uxbridge Road and Wood Lane remained in use once or twice a year, until the exhibitions moved to Earls Court. He dug around for information on the halls' use after that. There was mention of them being used as hangars or construction space for gliders; parachutes were made there during World War II; the City Display Organisation used them for many years to manufacture sets for film and television; most recently an American insurance firm had converted the Uxbridge Road entrance and the first two halls for use as office space. Angelo remembered the false ceilings and remains of an air-conditioning system. Nowhere was there any reference to part of the building having been used as a cinema. His feeling about the place, therefore, was either wrong, or—

Or he had finally located the Museum of Lost Cinema Spaces.

He needed to get back inside and explore further. As he walked up to Shepherd's Bush he thought about his unfinished project to map London's cinemas past and present. Should he go back to Gloucester Terrace and seek confirmation from his cartography, or had it served its purpose in directing him to the west? Even the tape he'd watched that morning had resisted interpretation. Was the time for these aids-to-detection really past? Had they finally outlived their usefulness? Was the only recourse left to him direct action? Getting back inside and finding out the truth one way or the other?

When he reached the former Exhibition building, the front door, by which he'd entered the day before, was padlocked. He touched the lock to be certain: it was secure. An electric light showed through a narrow remnant of glass. He'd have to find another way in.

There was no answer at Harry Foxx's house. Frank hadn't really expected there would be, but he had to check. He sat on the doorstep for a while chewing his fingernail, trying to work out the best thing to do. There were no easy answers any more. No longer would sleeping with numerous different women offer a way of sidestepping the truth. Now it had to be faced. It was being faced. But only by Frank. Harry Foxx had to face it, too.

Frank considered breaking in, but didn't imagine it would be all that easy, and he wasn't sure what he would be hoping to achieve. Instead he walked back to the tube and called Harry's mobile from the station. A recorded voice advised him to try again later. He then called Siân to apologise for the way he'd spoken to her that morning.

'Tom's going mad looking for you,' she told him. 'You'll have to come in.'

'What does he want?'

'He wants you.'

Frank headed into town, his mind a blank, as ever, as he travelled on the tube.

'Frank.' The editor was standing by the reception desk talking to Christopher as Frank emerged from the lift. 'Thanks for coming in.'

Frank ignored Tom's uncharacteristic sarcasm.

'I want you to go to the Riverside tonight,' Tom continued. 'They're doing a Fraser Munro thing.'

'I've seen them all,' Frank said.

'Well, see them again. There's something going on. Some kind of special event. They won't say what, and no one else seems to know, but I think it might be worth going along.'

'I'm pretty busy actually. I've got something on.'

Tom replied, 'You'll have a lot less on if you don't do as I ask. Now, I'm supposed to be in a meeting.' Tom left Frank cursing to himself outside the lift. Just then the lift doors rumbled open and the chief sub stepped out. Frank walked into the vacated lift and pressed the button for the ground floor. He had six hours before he had to head down to Hammersmith for the Fraser Munro programme at the Riverside. Possibly enough time to track down Harry Foxx. He walked to Ham Yard. Find Richard, he was thinking, and I might find Harry Foxx. But there was no answer when Frank pressed the buzzer for Richard's office. From a payphone, Frank called Richard's mobile. An automated response told him to leave a message, which he did. He called Harry's mobile again and got the same message as before.

In the next few hours Frank looked everywhere, starting in the Troy Club. He went from there to the Blue Posts on Berwick Street, then decided to cover the other Blue Posts, and by the time he got to Rupert Street he thought that rather than just put his head round the door, he might as well stop for a drink. He trailed around Soho, drinking steadily and getting sufficiently drunk to start asking complete strangers if they'd seen Harry Foxx. He felt an odd mix of emotions that the name meant so little to so many. Even on Dean and Wardour Streets, the heart of the film industry, he encountered only two people from whom the name provoked a reaction. In Freedom, a tired-looking, peroxided actor pressed his card on Frank, insisting he give it to Harry when

he found him. 'We worked together on, what, I can't remember . . .' The actor was even more wasted than Frank.
'*Nine South Street*?' Frank prompted him. 'No,' the actor
replied, baffled. 'Never heard of that. No, some ghastly stud
movie. German, I think.' A younger man appeared, tugging at
the actor's elbow, and Frank left the premises. In the Groucho,
a minor television director stroked his goatee and muttered,
'He's not actually a member, is he?'

With half an hour in which to get to Hammersmith, Frank
staggered on to the Piccadilly line platform at Leicester Square.
When he could keep his eyes open, he scanned the faces in the
crowds, hoping to spot Harry's. He knew, with utter certainty,
that if he saw him now, he would nudge him under a train.

When he emerged at Hammersmith the first thing he saw
was a *Standard* billboard that announced: 'VICTIM NAMED
IN FILM MURDER RIDDLE.' He didn't buy a paper; he
didn't need to. He had a pretty good idea who the victim was in
the film murder riddle.

Siân was waiting in the foyer. The news about Burns's
identification and the fresh air having sobered him up a
fraction, Frank was able to recognise her and ask her what the
fuck she was doing there.

'You're drunk,' she said unnecessarily.

'Well spotted. Got any useful observations to make?'

She gave him a look so dark it would hardly have registered
on film.

'It's about to start,' she said.

'There you are, you see, that's useful.'

Siân held his unsteady gaze for a moment, then turned and
walked towards the stairs that led to the auditorium. He stood
alone in the foyer, vacillating. In the end, he followed her in
and blundered into darkness. The first film had started. On
screen was a faint, vaselined image of a decomposing sheep
carcass. This was Munro's 1980 short, *Counting Sheep*. If it
was any longer than the six minutes at which Frank knew its

running time to be logged, it would almost certainly have the effect suggested by the title. Luckily, he'd already missed half of it. The monochrome image of the dead sheep was slowly burned out by a bright whiteness that enabled Frank to spot Siân three rows down on the left. He slipped into the row and sat heavily in the seat next to hers. She made an indistinct noise of disapproval and transferred her weight to the arm rest furthest from Frank.

'Sorry,' he muttered, leaning towards her.

'Ssh,' hissed someone directly behind him.

'Fuck off,' he said out loud without bothering to turn round.

The man behind tutted and sighed heavily. Frank ignored him.

'I hope it's not that one about fucking mountains next,' he said to Siân.

'Ssh,' went the man behind.

This time Frank turned round. 'Look, mate, if you want peace and quiet, why don't you fuck off outside and jump in the river?'

Siân and the man behind both shushed Frank violently, but he just settled back in his seat and waited for the next film. The lights, which had come up at the end of *Counting Sheep*, went down again and an expectant hush fell over the audience.

Frank was a long way from being prepared for what happened next.

A basic title card filled the screen. It was an imperfect fit, a white splinter of light edging in on one side. In a poorly reproduced serif face that had been fashionable for about two weeks in the late 1970s, all in caps, pink type on a black background, was a single word: 'AUTEUR'.

The title card was followed by a grainy image of a dark, windowless room with a sofa in the centre. A white sheet was draped over the sofa, on which a man was sitting, his head in his hands.

Siân turned to look at Frank. He stared at the screen, hoping it might be a copycat film or some kind of trick, but when the man lifted his head out of his hands and stared into the camera, there was no room for doubt. The perfect opening shot had been selected. The look in Burns's eyes was part self-absorption, part reaching out. Frank also read accusation in its coolness and wondered if that was directed only at the four film-makers or at anyone who might view the film, as if everyone was implicated as a witness.

The effect of seeing Burns again after so many years was to compress those years, almost to remove them altogether, as if they hadn't happened. He felt either as if it were still 1983, or as if 1983 and 1998 co-existed simultaneously, in other words as if time had ceased to exist. So, might not Burns still be alive somewhere?

But he remembered watching the discovery of the body, the news reports, the coverage in the press. To some extent it had all seemed as if it were happening to someone else. Not any more, however. His personal involvement now came home to him with considerable force. He put his fingers to his cheeks and they came away wet.

He watched Burns sitting on the sofa, drinking Scotch and looking around at the last space he would ever see. The 'action' cut between the two cameras, one directly in front of the sofa and the other to Burns's right. The camera on the right provided close-ups of Burns in quarter profile. If Burns changed position, leaned forward or slid along the sofa, he would move out of shot, in which case all you got was a slightly out-of-focus long shot of the doorway at the back of the set by which Frank and his associates had come and gone.

Frank realised with a certain relief that there had been no sign of himself or the other three coming in to change the film, a vanishing act performed by careful editing and switching between the two cameras.

The sound throughout was low and muffled, but because Frank knew what to listen out for he could hear the Satie piano soundtrack from *Le Feu follet* and he was able to identify Art Garfunkel and Harvey Keitel exchanging lines of dialogue in

Bad Timing. Burns looked away to his right for long periods and Frank realised that he was watching the screen on to which the Roeg film was being projected. In fact, he further realised, the projector itself was off-screen to the left, which meant that the hazy, fluctuating light in the air in front of Burns's face was the film's chaotic tumble of images through space.

The chronology was not straightforward. There were long shots of Burns slumped on the sofa near the beginning, and close-ups of him drinking Scotch near the end. But whoever had cut the film had saved the best till last.

CUT TO CU of empty space where Burns should be, only he's not, he's out of shot. Instead, badly lit and somewhat out of focus, Harry Foxx walks on to the set. He's on screen for no more than two seconds, but anyone who knows their low-budget independent British directors will recognise a young Harry Foxx immediately.

In the next long shot, Burns produces a loaded syringe from his bag.

CUT TO CU of Burns, head turning slowly to the right, expression registering discomfort, but it's impossible to say if this represents the moment at which he – or indeed someone else – inserts the needle.

CUT TO LONG SHOT of a dopey-looking Burns, the empty syringe discarded on the sofa beside him.

There is a further selection of close-ups and long shots, the editing getting faster now, and finally a close-up of Burns in quarter-profile. He looks still. It's impossible to say if he is still breathing.

Frank, on the other hand, is breathing fast and shallow.

The same shot of Burns's face is held for the rest of the film, which eventually fades to black. There are no credits.

The lights came up in the auditorium to a shocked silence, which was soon broken by a low-key symphony of exhalations, mutterings, half-whispers and even one or two uncertain out-bursts of applause.

Frank looked down the row. A quick exit was impossible without disturbing Siân. She sensed his need to be elsewhere and led the way out of the auditorium. Once outside, Frank indicated that he was going to the gents'. He managed to lock himself inside a stall before being violently sick. He did something he had vowed he would never do: sat on the floor of a public toilet emptying his guts into the bowl, resting his cheek on the cool seat between bouts of vomiting.

He washed his hands and face, shuddered at his reflection and left the gents'. Siân was waiting for him. He didn't know what to say or do.

'I hesitate to say this,' she began, reaching out to him, 'but you look like you've just seen a ghost.'

So Frank told Siân all about it. He told her everything. And she didn't run to the police, or attack him with a knife, or dump him. She did suggest that it might have been wiser to have told her sooner, but didn't give the impression that by telling her only at this stage he'd fucked everything up.

They had left the cinema and walked down to the river, where Frank leaned on a wall overlooking junk-filled mudflats and told her everything. By the time he'd told her everything up to but not including what Jenny Slade had told him about Sarah and Harry, the rising tide was swirling around the stanchions of Hammersmith Bridge. And then he told her about Sarah and Harry.

'I accept now that I'll never know who was driving the car that killed her,' he said. 'I'll never know who dumped her body by the canal. But at least I know who was fucking her.'

'Harry.'

'Yeah. If he was here now, I'd throw him in the fucking river.'

'He might want you to after that,' Siân said, referring to the film.

Frank gave a bitter little laugh. They both looked down into the river, which was dark and viscous-looking as oil.

'So that man in the film,' Siân said, trying to get it clear in her mind, 'he's the one whose body was dug up on Tottenham Court Road?'

'Yes.'

'And the film was made by you, Angelo, Harry and Richard?'

'That's right.'

'So why's it included in a series of films by Fraser Munro?'

'For the same reason, presumably, that Fraser Munro's finger-prints were found on the celluloid we used to wrap Burns's body in.'

'*Bad Timing*. The film Burns requested you obtain for him and which he watched while you were shooting that film.'

'Right.'

'One of you must know Munro. Is it you? Do you know him?'

'Not as far as I know.'

'So, who knows him? He must be someone's friend.'

'He couldn't get that close to us. No one could. No one else knew about Burns and the film. Apart from Kerner. Everyone knew that Sarah was writing a piece about Munro. If anyone had known him, they'd have said so and offered to put her in touch with him. I mean, we were quite together back then, before we made that film.'

'There's only one other possible explanation,' Siân said.

'What's that?'

'Fraser Munro must be a pseudonym.'

Frank stared into the river.

'One of you is Fraser Munro. It's the only possible explanation.'

'You said that.'

'Who edited the *Auteur* film after you shot it?'

'That's just it, no one. We never did anything with it. I think we knew while we were doing it that that would be the case. How could we do anything with it without getting into trouble? We couldn't. So we forgot about it. I mean, we barely talked to one another afterwards.'

A police launch motored downriver, its wake slapping against the wall thirty feet below where Frank was standing. A heron ghosted past in the opposite direction, its legs trailing like a daddy-long-legs.

'Well, clearly, someone cut the film at some stage,' Siân observed, 'and presumably not in a way that you would have considered acceptable, especially if you're Harry Foxx.'

'Unless Harry cut it himself.'

'So, Harry's Fraser Munro?

'I don't know,' said Frank exasperatedly.

'Who kept the footage after it was shot?'

'*I don't know,*' Frank shouted. 'I had other things on my mind, didn't I?'

'Who out of the four of you has access to editing facilities?'

'I don't know. All of us. Richard, obviously. Harry as well – he's getting a new film together. Even Angelo – he's got the run of the production company where he works.'

'And you,' Siân pointed out. 'You're doing this Heaven thing as a *Tx*. You'll need clips. I presume the BBC facilities are made available.'

Frank looked evenly at Siân and considered his reaction. In the end, perhaps because she offered an apologetic half-smile, he let it go. He had something else on his mind: what to do about Harry Foxx now.

If he was hoping that something else would happen to obviate his needing to take any action, he didn't have long to wait.

20 · The sacrifice

London, Friday 24 July 1998

Iain Burns's funeral was scheduled for eleven o'clock on Friday 24 July at Kensal Green Cemetery, west London. Burns's widow, Penny, was due to attend, and it was down to me, Wim De Blieck, Felixstowe jeweller, to make sure that she got there. Of course, now I wish that I hadn't.

Kensal Green is one of seven big cemeteries built around London in the Victorian era when church bonepits could no longer cope with the rising demand for space. Kensal Green's heyday may have pre-dated the invention of cinema, but among its many graves and mausolea is one honouring Imre Kiralfy (1845–1919), creator and Director-General of the Exhibitions held at Shepherd's Bush between 1908 and 1914. Burials and cremations still take place at Kensal Green today.

Penny discussed with me in some depth the question of where Iain should be buried. Since that occasion in the spring of 1998 when she came into the back of my shop in Felixstowe, for once without any pieces of amber to sell, and told me about the disappearance of her husband, Penny and I have had many conversations. We have discussed a great many things. At first we talked exclusively about her and Iain and their life together. She told me what it had been like for her in the years since his disappearance, how at first she had been possessed of a manic energy and had run around desperately trying to trace him. She had been back to Birmingham to dig up old acquaintances; she'd gone to see Irmin Hegel, Iain's mentor at the Eye Cinema. She told me how, even when she came up with nothing, she refused to stop looking. Iain wasn't a deserter, she felt certain of that, and that certainty meant that she was bound to think it likely that he was dead, because if he was alive he would contact her. But still she wouldn't allow herself to believe that with all her heart. She kept a light burning for him and for a long time, a period of several years, wouldn't give up hope. When the car was fished out of Ipswich docks, the police effectively closed the missing persons file, despite the contradictory evidence of the car's doors being closed and the windows wound up more than halfway. In fact, the car's discovery made her more convinced that he was still alive.

She went to London and toured the hostels for the homeless, she spoke to people camped out under bridges and spent nights with those delivering food and first aid to rough-sleepers. No leads arose.

During all of this time, although she reached out and spoke to many people, there was only ever one subject of enquiry. She never sought help for herself, nor even talked to anyone about her loss. She retreated inside herself in that respect, and soon, as no discernible progress was made, she withdrew from the outside world. If it couldn't help her find Iain, she needn't have anything to do with it.

But the house was full of memories. She would enter the kitchen and expect to see him standing at the window waiting for the kettle to boil. She had to get rid of one of her armchairs because it was the one Iain had always sat in to watch television if she wasn't watching with him; when they watched together, they sat beside each other on the sofa.

So she began wandering on the shore. The Suffolk coastline had a peculiar melancholy that acted as a mirror for her feelings. She saw other women occasionally, looking as lost as her, and she claimed to me that she never actually spoke to any of them, so it's a mystery how she found out about the amber. Maybe there's an affinity between those women, my Amber Girls, that as a man I would never understand. They're all looking for the same thing, interrupted lives trapped in lumps of resin. There's an undeniable feeling you get when you study a piece of amber with an inclusion – a gnat or a beetle, a scuttle fly – that if you were to breathe on the amber and melt it the creature would give its tiny wings a shake and rise into the air as if twenty-five million years had never happened. You feel that the distance between death and resurrection is a very short one.

No one is kidding themselves. They know their husbands are gone for good and nothing will bring them back. But finding a piece of amber that may or may not support the fantasy of suspended animation – only when they bring it to me for polishing will they find out if it contains an inclusion – is some kind of comfort, not a replacement for the man they have lost, but something to be going on with.

Of course, for all the pieces of amber Penny brought to me that she found on the beach, some with inclusions, some without, she hasn't seen the piece of amber whose inclusion is Iain – by which I mean the film, *Auteur*. Neither of us knew about the screening at the Riverside the night before the funeral, although we had both been in London; even if we had known that a film called *Auteur* was to be screened, of course, it wouldn't have meant anything to us. Not at that stage.

I had seen a picture of the reconstruction of Burns's head in the paper on the Wednesday morning and had immediately closed the shop and driven over to Penny's house. I had been trying to persuade her to stay at mine, in her own room, if she wanted, that I would be more than happy to prepare for her, but she insisted on staying on in her own house. I didn't risk pushing it; we moved at Penny's pace.

As soon as Penny answered the door, I saw from her face

that she, too, had seen the picture, and read the accompanying story, which included the revelation that Burns had been suffering from tertiary syphilis. Unless I was mistaken, the look was a mixture of terror and relief, both understandable reactions to the fact that the worst thing imaginable had finally happened. Her husband's body had been found and there could be no more doubt, although the mystery concerning what had happened to him remained.

I, too, had spent time in London trying to track him down. By 1998 the trail, of course, was colder than Southwold beach on Christmas morning. But I was in love with Penny, I was obsessed with her, and wanted to do whatever I could to help. So I had gone to London, as I knew she had done, and I had questioned people under the same bridges. I even spoke to a number of projectionists in some of the rep cinemas, although there were fewer of them than in Burns's day. No one had heard of him. Even if I had visited the Camden Plaza, which I would not have been able to do since it went dark in September 1994 (its final programme was a rerun of Michael Powell's *Peeping Tom*), I doubt the name would have meant anything to them. At that time and even on the day of his funeral, I knew nothing of what had happened to Iain Burns. What I did manage to find out, which I have attempted to relate faithfully in this account, I found out much later after the whole thing blew up and it became easier to play the amateur detective.

For now, though, the day of Burns's funeral, I was as much in the dark as Penny was. On the Wednesday that his likeness was printed in the newspapers, Penny agreed to come with me to London. We phoned ahead, dialling the number that was printed with the story, to tell the police we were coming. The police station was on Tottenham Court Road, a couple of blocks north of the building site where the body was found; it has since been closed down, no doubt earmarked for demolition itself (who knows what might be unearthed when that day comes?). When we arrived, the police interviewed Penny on her own for some time; another officer asked me a few questions, but I was obviously not considered all that relevant to the case. I was, however, allowed to accompany her during the identification of the body.

I was surprised how long she stood looking at him, given the state the body was in. The policewoman made no effort to cut short the moment and as Penny had taken two steps away from my side I could not see her face. I watched her hands, which were so tense and contorted they looked false, but they didn't move. I wanted to reach out and touch her, but didn't in case, like a reflection in a pool, the contact caused her to shatter. Finally, after what must have been five minutes, I heard her utter a very small sound in the back of her throat and she started to turn away. I held out my hand. Her face, dry-eyed, was white as a blank screen. The policewoman was solicitous and softly spoken. As we left the room, I noticed other officers who had been in the background; they were looking at the floor.

When the formalities had been taken care of, we left the police station and Penny said she wanted to sit for a while, so we found a little garden behind Goodge Street and sat there, saying nothing. Some time needed to be put between what we had seen and where we were before it would feel right to speak even to each other.

'You should see your doctor,' I advised her eventually.

'I'm all right,' she said. She could be very stubborn.

'I mean with regard to Iain's disease.'

'Oh.' She shrugged. 'You think I've got it.'

'It would be nice to rule it out.'

'For your sake or mine?'

We booked two single rooms in a chain hotel on Euston Road. Penny had to make arrangements for the funeral now that the police were ready to release the body. We talked about it in the lounge of the hotel. I became disturbed when Penny raised her voice, becoming very matter-of-fact as we discussed the pros and cons of burial and cremation. She thought that Iain would have preferred the former, although they had never discussed it. Kensal Green was chosen not because of Imre Kiralfy, who would have meant nothing to Penny (or to Iain), but because Burns's family came originally from Kensal Rise. Iain's father had moved to Birmingham when he became a minister.

'Are there any of them left?' I asked her. 'His family?'

'No,' she said, 'but still.'

The whole of the next day, Thursday, was taken up with preparations. By the evening we were both drained and Penny said she had no appetite, but I gently insisted we get something to eat. So, while Penny's husband was making his undisputed public screen debut at the Riverside, she and I were sitting in a PizzaExpress on Coptic Street.

As we approached the cemetery the following morning, we noticed several marked police cars outside the gates. One of the officers from Tottenham Court Road stepped forward and told us there had been a development in the case and that he would like to speak to Penny again after the service. He also told us that numerous officers were deployed in and around the cemetery, but that he hoped their presence would go unnoticed. Penny nodded and we proceeded to the chapel. Apart from the police and ourselves, there was only one other attendee; Irmin Hegel, whom Penny had managed to reach by telephone the day before, had turned up despite apparently being quite infirm.

'He was a good man,' Irmin Hegel told Penny as he held her hand lightly in both of his. 'It's so sad what has happened.'

'Thank you for coming,' said Penny. 'You meant a lot to Iain. Indeed, to both of us.'

Penny stood taller than she had for days and glowed with the peculiar self-assurance only grief can bring. I had never seen her looking so beautiful, yet I felt ashamed for thinking it. She was wearing a very simple black dress that she had bought hurriedly the previous afternoon in a department store on Oxford Street.

She cried only once while we stood by the grave. 'It was the ritual,' she said to me later. 'The words of the priest made me realise what we were doing. Burying my husband.' Tears sprang from her eyes and, because she was leaning forward, they didn't roll down her face but fell directly on to the coffin.

Mercifully, what happened next didn't happen until the burial had been concluded. But only just. As we filed away from the grave and began walking back towards the main gate, we became aware of men, ahead of us and to the right, shouting.

Figures dressed in black appeared from behind tombs and mausolea, running between the trees towards the side of the cemetery that bordered the canal. These were the policemen we had been told about, and true enough they had maintained a low profile up to now, but clearly something was happening on the canal. The officer who had been walking just behind Penny and me advanced a couple of steps and pressed an ear-piece into his ear; he spoke into a tiny microphone. Turning to us, he issued a curt but polite instruction to remain exactly where we were and then he, too, ran off towards the canal. As soon as he had gone, Penny started walking in the same direction.

'Penny,' I called, but she didn't stop or look back, so I followed.

We reached the edge of the cemetery, where only a railing separated us from the water. The design for Kensal Green had made a feature of its proximity to the canal and there had been plans to allow water-borne funerals. Funeral barges would sail up the canal and turn into the cemetery through great iron gates envisaged but never constructed.

One hundred and sixty-five years after the inauguration of Kensal Green Cemetery, on the morning of Iain Burns's interment, an *ad hoc* funeral barge sailed up the canal from the direction of Little Venice. Orange and green flames leaped from a pyre burning steadily on the roof of the craft, which was decrepit and barely canalworthy. Still about fifty yards away from us, it made slow progress, its engine sounding very much as if this would be its final voyage. Among the shifting shapes and shadows that made up the sacrificial cargo I glimpsed a number of silver discs. I found out later they were film cans. The dark coils that spilled out of them and caught fire were reels of film. At the centre of the fire, his face alternately disappearing and reappearing behind flashing sheets of flame, was the body of a man.

At first I wondered if the coffin we had just seen lowered into the ground was empty, but then I remembered I'd seen Burns's body and it had been less well preserved than this one.

'Don't look,' I said, holding Penny's shoulders and forcing her to look away from the canal by pulling her close to me. As the barge slid by right in front of us, I held her tighter. To my horror and dismay I knew that even though I could stop her seeing it, I could not prevent her from hearing the sizzling and the hissing and the popping, or from smelling the nauseating barbecue stench of char-grilled human flesh.

For myself, I did not look away. What I saw I'll never forget, but nor will I ever be sure if I really saw certain details or if I expected to see them and so convinced myself I had. Was the head even turned in my direction or did I completely imagine the hollow eye-sockets that seemed to watch me as the barge chugged past?

Police officers ran around us. Some scaled the fence and leaped on to the boat, batting at the flames with jackets and branches torn from trees. But there was too much fuel and the fire continued to burn despite their efforts. It was established later that the body had been doused in petrol, but not set alight. The film cans had contained cellulose nitrate film, old, non-safety film, which is extremely volatile and liable to burst into flames if exposed to a heat source, such as the overhead sun in the middle of summer.

At the time, we didn't know what to make of the burning boat, nor who was sailing on her. The senior officer who had been escorting us returned and asked Penny how she was, did she need him to get her a WPC, could we make it as far as the main gate where a car was waiting? There was nothing to see here, he told us, it was all under control.

At the main gate, the rear door of a patrol car was standing open for us. I let Penny get in then closed it behind her and walked around the rear of the car. On the opposite side of Harrow Road, onlookers had started to gather. Among them I noticed a tall, thin man with close-cropped hair and what seemed a large head in proportion to the rest of his body. He was standing on the kerb, as close as he could get without stepping into the road, and holding a piece of white fabric almost like a comfort blanket. For no reason I could put my finger on, I didn't like the look of him.

21 · Suspicion

London, Friday 24 July 1998

Angelo, carrying the white top he'd picked up in the Exhibition hall, had come to Kensal Green to pay his respects, albeit from a distance. After watching Burns's widow depart in a squad car with an unknown male, he hung around for a while longer. Two fire engines arrived and an ambulance came later. TV crews showed up. Nobody among the growing crowd of rubberneckers seemed to know what was going on. Eventually, just after one o'clock, Angelo left.

Frank didn't get to work on Friday until around lunchtime. Siân, who had obviously been looking out for him, came straight over.

'Where have you been all morning?' she asked him.

'Looking for Harry Foxx,' he said.

'And?'

'He's vanished. Can't find him anywhere.'

'I had to tell Tom about last night.'

'What about last night?' Frank asked sharply.

'About Harry Foxx being in that film. Don't worry, nothing else.'

While talking, Frank had been taking his phone off voice-mail. As soon as he had done so, it rang. He picked up. It was Jenny Slade.

'I've been ringing you all morning,' she said.

'I've been out.'

'Yesterday morning,' she said, 'you didn't let me finish.'

'What do you mean?'

'Harry Foxx.'

'What about him?'

'He didn't just have sex with Sarah.'

'What do you mean?' Frank said again.

'I don't know if you want to know this,' she said hesitantly.

'Then why are you telling me?

'Because I don't want to be the only person who does know this. I don't want to know it if you don't know it.'

'So tell me.'

'He was driving the car.'

'What car?'

'He was driving the car that killed her,' she said. 'Apparently.'

Frank was quiet for a moment. He felt something rising within him. 'I'll kill the bastard,' he said quietly.

'It's a bit late for that, isn't it?'

'Meaning?'

'Do you have access to a TV?'

'Of course.'

'Go and switch it on,' she said, and rang off.

'What?' Siân asked him as he got up from his desk.

'Television.'

Frank led the way to the next floor. The TV room was packed but Frank and Siân managed to squeeze in.

The newsroom presenter could be heard saying that she was handing over live to a reporter at Kensal Green Cemetery.

'Some details are still unconfirmed,' the eager young man said into his microphone, 'but what is beyond question is that the independent film director Harry Foxx was found burned to death on a barge on the Grand Union Canal by Kensal Green Cemetery this morning, where the funeral was taking place of former cinema projectionist Iain Burns, whose remains were found in a building site on Tottenham Court Road two weeks ago today. On the barge with Foxx, as well as a print of the only film he made, *Nine South Street*, were numerous films believed to be the work of reclusive *avant-garde* director Fraser Munro. Indeed, the fire, which seemed designed to resemble a funeral pyre, may have been fuelled or even started by some of Munro's films that he made on cellulose nitrate stock, the notorious pre-safety-film stock from which all films were made before 1950. Nitrate film is highly flammable and Munro attracted criticism for using it in the 1980s—'

'Only for two films,' Christopher, the video reviewer, interjected.

'Ssh,' admonished Tom.

'The two film-makers were linked last night when as part of a programme of films by Fraser Munro being shown at the Riverside in Hammersmith, west London, Harry Foxx made an unexpected appearance in what appeared to be either a documentary about a man's suicide, or, indeed, a snuff movie. It's believed that the subject of the film was Iain Burns, the man being buried at Kensal Green this morning. Fingerprints found on the film wrapped around Burns's remains belonged to Fraser Munro.'

The reporter talked over videotape of Burns's widow leaving the cemetery by the main gates.

'And now back to the studio.'

The anchorwoman linked to a report on *Nine South Street* and the tension in the room eased, as everyone stretched and looked around to gauge others' reactions. Tom, the tallest man there and always the focus, scanned the room with his small dark eyes.

'Frank,' he said, 'I want a piece on Munro. Speculative if you like, but backed up by facts. I want local colour, quotes, interviews.'

'He's a recluse,' Frank pointed out.

'Which is why you'll have to go to Scotland and dig around.'

'Scotland!'

'You know, that place just beyond the Edinburgh Festival.'

'I've got previews on Monday.'

'Christopher can do them.'

'Christopher does video.'

'It's all the same,' said Tom. 'And Christopher, I want a piece from you on Harry Foxx, and then we'll dovetail them together and see if we're talking about the same guy. Are Harry Foxx and Fraser Munro one and the same? We can call it "Double Take" or "Take Two". Whatever. That's what we pay subs for.'

'Aren't the broadsheets going to run all this before we can? Like tomorrow,' said Frank.

'They may do it before us, but they won't do it as well as us, which is why it's worth making an effort and getting your arse up to Scotland. Siân can go with you if that'll make a difference. We're only talking about a couple of days. It's got to go on Wednesday.'

By the time Tom had finished, Siân had left the room.

Frank found her on the roof.

'This is bad,' she said.

'What do you mean?'

'I don't like everyone knowing my business.'

'Look, just forget it. Let's just go to bloody Scotland. It'll be a relief to get out of this place. We can leave this afternoon. It'll be a break.'

'You've got a piece to write.'

'Piece of piss. I've done most of it already.'

Siân was fuming. 'What we do is private, OK?'

'It's not my fault if Tom's a wanker.'

They were both silent for a few moments, until Siân made a suggestion. 'We could go in my car,' she said.

'Great,' Frank agreed. 'Beats going on Richard Branson's trains, and I'm certainly not dying in an air crash for this bloody magazine.'

*   *   *

By Friday afternoon Richard Charnock had a car but no driver.

After Harry Foxx had walked off with the key and dropped it down a grid on Wednesday afternoon, Richard had had no choice but to leave the car exactly where it was, blocking the inner-most lane of Marylebone Road just before the intersection with Gloucester Place. He walked away, confident that within twenty-four hours he'd be able to have Caroline pick it up from the car pound at Paddington.

She collected it after lunch on Friday, hearing the news about Harry Foxx on the car radio driving back to Holland Park. Richard, meanwhile, was sitting in his office in Ham Yard drinking an averagely good single malt and watching videotape of Jenny Slade stripping in the Exhibition halls. Caroline called, on the B-list phone, and told him what she'd heard on the radio. Without bothering to stop the tape, he made appropriate noises, but he was preoccupied by problems relating to *Little Black Dress*. After the episode on Marylebone Road (Harry Foxx's fault, he reminded himself), he'd lost Jenny Slade, and then one of the backers had pulled out that morning; he knew that as soon as the other investors got wind of that, they'd withdraw their support as well. *Little Black Dress* was coming undone.

He kept his glass topped up.

When the tape came to the end, he let it rewind, but couldn't be bothered playing it again, so just left it in the machine and stared at the static that seemed to scour the screen from the inside like electrified wire wool. After a time, he switched the machines off and left the office. He took a black cab to Holland Park and walked across the pavement to the house, where he rang the bell. A strange woman answered the door. The maid? If it was the maid, why did she have two kids with her?

'Did you forget your keys?' asked the strange woman who wasn't the maid because he'd just remembered they didn't have a maid.

'Caroline,' he said. 'It's you.'

'You're drunk,' she said, with a trace of disgust in her voice.

'Where's the car, then?' he asked her.

'What do you think that is behind you?' She backed off and corralled the two boys. 'Come on, boys. Your stepfather's drunk.'

'Stepfather!' he mumbled to himself. 'Wouldn't I need to be married to you to be their stepfather?'

While Caroline and the boys disappeared off to the kitchen, Richard collected a bottle of Scotch and trudged upstairs to the spare room.

In the morning, hungover and disorientated, Richard agreed to join them for a walk in Holland Park.

'We might as well pretend we're a family even if we're not,' Caroline said as the boys ran on ahead. 'Did you sleep well? You seem to spend more and more time in the spare room these days.'

'Do you miss me, then?' asked Richard, rubbing his head.

'Well, I'm aware of you not being there. Let's put it like that. You could be anywhere half the time, for all I know.'

'My film's falling apart,' Richard muttered.

'What film?'

'What do you mean, what film?'

'I mean what film?'

'Do you ever listen when I tell you about my projects?'

'That's just it: you never tell me about them. Sometimes I think we might as well not be living in the same house. I can't remember the last time we slept together.'

'Yeah, yeah.'

'I can't remember the last time I slept with anyone.'

Richard ignored this and stared at the gravel path. The boys were already chasing the white peacocks.

'Can you?' said Caroline.

'Can I what?'

'Can you remember the last time you had sex?'

'Look, what is the point of this? I'm going home.'

'What about Wednesday? Didn't you have sex on Wednesday?'

'Wednesday?'

'Yes, Wednesday. I mean, I didn't check, but I assume that condom in the back of the car was yours?'

'Condom?'

'Don't take the piss. It's not that I haven't thought it before. What else would explain your behaviour? I just haven't had the proof; now I have. You fucked someone in the back of the car on Wednesday and couldn't even be bothered to clean up afterwards. Then you asked me to pick up the car. Either you wanted me to find it, or you just didn't think. I don't know which is worse. You make me sick.'

'Yeah, really?' Richard said. 'So walk away.'

Frank and Siân left the office and went to Frank's flat on Tottenham Court Road so he could get his stuff. The plan was to take a cab to Siân's place and set off from there on their long drive to the north. Frank had packed a bag and was just looking round for his micro tape recorder when there was a knock on the door. It was rare that anybody knocked on the door. Because of the institutional feel of the building, there was little sense of community, and in all the years he'd been living there Frank had made friends with none of his neighbours. There was no animosity, just a cool detachment. Any visitors announced their arrival by ringing the buzzer at street level and speaking to Frank on the intercom. A knock on the door would put Frank's guard up.

Two strangers stood on the threshold. The hallways and landings in Frank's building were not very well lit, but he could see enough to realise they were police officers. He recognised their type not from hundreds of crime movies – the difference between fantasy and reality was rarely so stark as between stylishly crumpled screen cops and real-life filth – but from having had dealings with the police after Sarah had gone missing. Not only had they failed to catch her killer, but they had barely concealed their suspicions that Frank himself was responsible.

'Yes?' said Frank, hearing his voice quaver.

'Mr Warner?' said the younger of the two men. He was ginger-haired and wore a closely trimmed goatee. In any pair of detectives, Frank suspected, one will always be ginger-haired. The goatee was an unwanted bonus.

'Yes.'

'Mr Frank Warner?' said the same man, who was Frank's junior by six or seven years.

'Yes.' The nervousness in Frank's voice had turned to annoyance. He wanted to get out of London before the traffic built up.

'Metropolitan Police,' said the ginger-haired officer, flashing a badge. 'I'm DC Lucas. This is DS Norton.'

'What's the problem?' Frank asked.

'Problem?' said the older man, Norton, speaking for the first time.

'What can I do for you?'

'Perhaps we could come inside?' Lucas suggested.

'Perhaps you could tell me what it's about?' Frank countered.

Lucas turned to exchange a look with Norton, who wore angular silver-rimmed glasses and an open-necked shirt. His hair, brushed back, looked as if it was standing to attention.

'You may have read, sir, about a body being discovered in the building site across the street,' said Norton, larding the 'sir' with the customary irony.

Frank stood very still. 'Yes, I think I did read something about that.'

'Would you have any objection if we came in, sir?' said Norton.

Frank thought hard about the wisdom of refusing them entry and finally stepped back to allow them to walk into his flat. 'This way,' he said, ushering them into the kitchen, which faced the rear lightwell. Siân, who was sitting at the table with a coffee, looked up in surprise. The officers glanced at each other and Norton muttered an apology.

'Do you have a good view of the building site, sir?' asked Lucas.

'Er, I don't really know. I don't have time to sit and stare out of the window, you know. I'm very busy.'

'I'm sure you are,' Norton chipped in. 'This is just a routine enquiry and we don't want to take up any more of your time than is absolutely necessary. But I wonder if we could take a look?' While speaking, Norton brushed his hair backwards and forwards repeatedly.

'Sure.' Frank led the way into the main room.

Lucas went to the window, while Norton's gaze mineswept the room and came up with the zipped-up bag by the door.

'Are you going away, Mr Warner?'

'A work thing,' Frank answered.

Norton's only response was to continue brushing his hand over his hair, producing a sibilant rasp, like a field of corn in a strong wind.

'Just for a few days.'

Frank had been going to elaborate on his assignment until he realised that it would establish an indirect link between himself and Burns.

'What kind of work is it you do, sir?' asked Lucas, coming away from the window.

'I'm a writer.'

'A writer?'

'Yes, a journalist.'

'Work from home, do you, sir?' Lucas turned to look at Frank's desk next to the window.

'Sometimes. I mean, I used to. I was freelance. I have a job now. Full-time.' Frank could feel sweat trickling down the back of his neck and pooling in the hollow of his throat.

Norton and Lucas both stared at Frank, who had begun to

prickle all over the top half of his body. He felt the skin of his face turning red.

'Look, I'm beginning to feel like I've done something wrong,' he said and immediately wished he hadn't. It was, he knew, the very worst thing he could have said, with the possible exception of 'Yeah, I knew the dead man. In fact, I helped make a film of him topping himself.'

'*Have* you done something wrong, sir?' asked Lucas.

Frank tried to laugh it off. 'I'm no worse than anyone else.'

'What do you mean by that?' Lucas snapped, raising his tufted chin to point it at Frank.

'Nothing. Nothing at all.'

Siân had come to stand in the doorway and was watching.

'No worse than anyone else,' murmured Norton. 'What do you suppose that means?' he asked his subordinate.

Lucas stroked his beard. 'I don't know. I just don't know.'

No one spoke for a minute. The two policemen looked at Frank. Siân glared at the policemen in turn. Frank gazed into the top corners of the room, determined not to dig himself in any deeper.

Norton broke the silence. 'It's just a routine enquiry, Mr Warner,' he said suddenly. 'We're talking to all the residents who have a view of the building site, asking if they saw anything unusual, either before the demolition work started or since it began.'

'I didn't see anything unusual,' Frank said abruptly.

'You're sure about that?' checked Lucas.

'Like I said, I'm busy. I don't have time for that sort of thing.'

'That sort of thing,' repeated Norton to himself, running his hand backwards and forwards through his hair. 'Well, if you do remember anything, anything at all, whatever its apparent significance or insignificance, get in touch, would you? The station's just on the other side of the road a few blocks up.'

'I know it,' said Frank.

'Yes, I daresay you can see it from your window,' Norton

said, smiling for the first time since they had entered the flat. 'You might have to lean out, but you'd probably be able to see it. Have a good trip,' he added as he turned to head for the door. 'Where was it you said you were going?'

'I didn't,' Frank said. 'Scotland. It's just for a couple of days.'

'A couple, sir,' Lucas cut in. 'Didn't you say a few before? Is it a couple or a few?'

'I'll be back on Wednesday,' Frank answered, holding open the door and having to restrain himself from bundling the men outside.

'Have a safe trip, sir,' Norton said, brushing his hair a final time. 'I hope we haven't held you up too much.'

'Goodbye,' Frank said, already beginning to close the door.

'Don't forget,' Lucas called back over his shoulder as they walked off down the carpeted corridor, 'get in touch if you remember anything.'

Frank closed the door and turned to lean against it for support, wiping the sweat from his forehead.

Siân looked at him as he re-entered the main room.

'What do they know, do you think?' she asked.

'I don't know.'

He crossed to the window and looked out. Within a minute, the two detectives appeared, leaving the building. They walked off up Tottenham Court Road. Norton turned and looked up towards Frank's flat as he continued walking. Frank backed away.

'Did he see you?'

'I don't know.' Frank buried his face in his hands. 'If it was a routine enquiry and they were talking to all the residents with a decent view, why did they leave immediately after talking to me?'

'Maybe you were the last on their list?'

'It disturbs me I'm on their list at all. Come on, let's get out of here.'

22 · The blue halls

Frank and Siân reached Edinburgh in time for a brief meeting with Bryan Davey, a past organiser of the Edinburgh Film Festival and one of very few people to have spoken to Munro on the phone.

'What's he going to be able to tell us?' Frank wondered.

'Let's just see,' Siân encouraged him.

They met in the Seattle Coffee Company at Waterstone's.

'Bookshops are changing,' Davey observed, stirring his cappuccino.

Frank and Siân exchanged a look.

'You didn't used to be able to get a coffee in a bookshop. It may be American,' he continued, 'but it's very civilised.'

'Do you mind if I ask you about Munro?' Frank pressed him gently.

'Nor did bookshops used to stay open this late,' Davey added, then, catching a look between Frank and Siân, went on to say that he'd never actually met Munro, but that they had spoken on the phone once or twice about availability of prints. Davey couldn't remember which film. 'I could find out for you at home,' he offered. Frank asked what Munro sounded like.

'Softly spoken. Light Scots accent. Difficult to be more precise.'

'Do you believe we've seen the last of him?'

'You mean do I believe that he and Harry Foxx were the same man?' Davey asked, spooning the froth off his cappuccino. 'I've been reading the papers. I don't know. It's pretty weird. We were going to show *Nine South Street* but it fell through for some reason.'

'Harry Foxx didn't have a lot of luck,' Frank said.

'That's right. As to the question of them being the same person, I couldn't say. The evidence seems to point to it and I couldn't put my hand on my heart and say the man I spoke to on the phone wasn't Harry Foxx, but who knows?'

As Frank and Siân had breakfast in their hotel in West Newington Place on Saturday morning, Angelo – four hundred and fifty miles away – was sleeping like a baby, the white Gucci top beside him on the pillow. He slept late. When he finally got up, he made his way slowly over to Shepherd's Bush and spent the rest of the day trying to find a way into the former Exhibition halls. The main door was padlocked and the area around it secure. The only apparent breaches in the building's security were higher up, out of reach: shattered windows lined the east side of the first hall, facing the M41. The roof, visible from the covered footbridge over Uxbridge Road, looked vulnerable. Angelo considered a possible leap from the footbridge to the roof of the Central line tube station, from where it would be an easy task to clamber over the top of the camping goods store to reach the Exhibition halls. He stared down at the twenty-foot drop. It wasn't strictly speaking the idea of his death that put him off, but the realisation that if he did die, or ended up in hospital, he might never find the owner of the white Gucci top.

The Exhibition halls, he now accepted, had become as important to him for being the place where he found the white top as they were to him as the Museum of Lost Cinema Spaces.

Angelo slipped away from the main road into the side streets that crisscrossed the territory between Wood Lane, Uxbridge Road and the Exhibition halls – and the Central line tube depot that lay in their shadow. He clung to the white Gucci top and frequently lifted it to his face to press his nose into it. The layout of the streets seemed unhelpful, counter-intuitive, possibly even designed to thwart him in his desire to penetrate the Exhibition halls. The closest he got was the canopied entrance to the Vanderbilt Racquet Club, which appeared to have taken over some of the halls in the middle. He knew better than to try his luck at what looked an exclusive establishment: while he stood looking up at the gilt tassels and crossed racquets, a new Mercedes pulled up and a woman emerged wearing a designer tracksuit. Because of the zigzag layout of the halls, he was able to get close at one or two other locations, but then the long white crumbling sheds turned away from the buses' turning area or veered obliquely away from the lines of terraced houses. He spent long periods just standing and staring at the halls from different angles. When he could get close enough, he raised his video camera and filmed them. As dusk fell he escaped from the web of claustrophobic, narrow streets into Wood Lane and walked north, past the former entrance to the disused tube station. A gap in the fence allowed him to squeeze through by the arches of the Hammersmith & City line. Then it was a simple matter to jump down on to a branch coming off the Central line that looked as if it must lead to the depot and the Exhibition halls. Twirling the Gucci top into a short scarf, he threaded it around his neck and tucked the ends into his T-shirt.

It was not a long drop and he made a safe landing. To his right were the old station buildings. He couldn't be sure that there wasn't a faint light flickering at one window (squatters, he guessed), so he gave the buildings a wide berth and made his way down to the branch line. He stepped carefully over the two live rails and walked towards a tunnel entrance. The view he'd had from the road had shown him that he would eventually leave this tunnel close to the depot and even nearer to one of the stanchions supporting the Exhibition halls.

Inside the tunnel, with only night at his back, it was black as diesel. He walked slowly, aware that a sudden movement to right or left could result in his being fried. He also remained alert to the possibility that a train might leave or return to the depot at any moment. That the line was in regular use was evident from the good condition of the rails: he could see them shining up ahead in the darkness where they reflected light from the depot. He could make out an old platform on his right, but he could see no detail, nor any sign of the wall that presumably rose up to meet the tunnel's arched ceiling. The other end of the tunnel dilated like the aperture of a camera as Angelo advanced. He felt encouraged by a feeling that what he was doing was right and would take him to where he wanted to be. As he neared the tunnel's end, the light from the depot enabled him to see where he was placing his feet. It also made the nearest of the Exhibition halls, which in daylight were a dirty white, appear blue. Blue halls. Like the chain of cinemas opened by Enrique Carreras in Hammersmith, Edgware Road and Islington at the beginning of the century. These were the Blue Halls at the century's end. The millennium's end. But, although Angelo had dedicated the last five years to locating the Museum of Lost Cinema Spaces, now that he'd found it, he realised it was less important to him for what it was than for what it had revealed to him. His search hadn't been for the museum after all, not for its contents, the old cinema spaces, the atmospheres, the accumulated echoes of laughter and screams, the molecules of sweat and water vapour from the lungs of a hundred years' worth of film-goers, but for the girl who had, for whatever reason, wandered into the museum, leaving a trail for Angelo to follow. It was her scent he was following now as he stepped over long-disused, badly rusted tracks at the edge of the depot to reach the iron stanchion supporting one corner of the nearest hall.

He hugged the flaking, rusty pillar and recovered his breath. Over to his right, diffuse light from the carriage sheds delineated the fan of railway tracks that converged as they approached the twin tunnels that led to White City. A handful of tube staff worked on a train that was sitting half in, half out of one of the two main sheds. Angelo buried his face in the white Gucci top one last time, then lifted his foot on to the first strut and began to climb.

Frank and Siân drove up to Stirling for an appointment with Gordon Pirie, Professor of Anatomy at the university. Frank thanked Pirie for agreeing to see them at the weekend. Pirie, who was in his early sixties, waved his hand. 'Glad to help,' he said. 'Although I'm not sure I can to any great degree. You were keen to know if we had a photograph of Munro, but sadly I can't help you there. In those days there was no system of photographing students for our records. I gather that for a film-maker, in any case, Munro was somewhat camera-shy.'

Frank asked if the university had kept the footage Munro had made in the dissection rooms, which had led to his leaving the university.

'I don't know if we managed to retrieve that,' Pirie said. 'And even if we did have it, I'm afraid I wouldn't be able to let you see it. People donate their bodies to the medical school. The last thing they're expecting is to end up on a cinema screen in, well, that state.'

'Of course. You must remember Munro, though?'

Pirie pulled an apologetic face. 'I never had that much to do with him. Until after the incident, of course, but by then he was gone. I'm afraid I couldn't even tell you what the fellow looked like. So many students come through here . . .' He spread his hands to indicate the department, even the whole campus.

'If I showed you a photograph . . .' Frank began.

'Of this other chap? Harry Foxx? I've seen it in the

newpapers.' Pirie shook his head. 'I'm so sorry. I hope you haven't had a wasted trip.'

Munro had lost him for a few moments against the inky foliage beyond the long-disused and rusted outer ring, but spotted him again as soon as he started to climb. Munro waited. The distance between them was no more than thirty yards.

Munro had been outside, at the rear of the old station buildings, urinating into a bush, when he had heard the intruder emerging from the tunnel. He had zipped up quietly and made his way through the undergrowth in the direction of the noise, soon picking up a dark shadow forty yards ahead and several degrees to the left. He'd come out of one of the tunnels connecting the depot to the permanent way, presumably the tunnel closest to the disused station buildings, or Munro would not have heard him. The fact that the intruder was alone meant that he was not an Underground employee: they travelled in pairs and at night tended to carry lights. The intruder advanced slowly, unsure of his surroundings and anxious not to get juiced by stepping on a live rail. Munro kept him in sight easily while staying far enough behind for his own presence to remain unnoticed. The intruder was already beyond the point at which Munro could have dealt with him in what had become his usual manner. He was within sight of the depot. Letting him proceed unpursued was an option, but Munro wanted to see the intruder off his territory one way or another.

The stanchion the intruder was climbing led directly up to Shed F. Shed F, like Sheds C, D and E, belonged to an exclusive tennis club. In the sixteen or seventeen years that Munro had been living – albeit intermittently – at Wood Lane, he'd familiarised himself not only with the immediate area around the disused station buildings, but also with the Central line depot and with the former Exhibition halls that waltzed across the land on their fancy stilts from Uxbridge Road to Wood Lane. He'd been inside them all, the first two empty halls abutting Uxbridge Road and those taken over by the Vanderbilt Racquet Club, which accounted for all the remaining halls, or, as he'd overheard the Vanderbilt people calling them, sheds. Shed F, the last one standing before Wood Lane, was owned by the Vanderbilt, but it was the only shed of theirs not to have been converted by the introduction of a few indoor courts, wall-mounted heaters and vast green tarpaulins to hide the worst of the dilapidation. He'd heard the staff joke about Shed F. Being sent to Shed F was the punishment you could expect for any misdemeanour. No one entered Shed F by choice.

The spindly figure of the intruder was nearing the top of the stanchion and was only a few feet away from the nearest shattered window through which he would be able to make his entrance into Shed F. Watching as the intruder hauled his lanky frame over the ledge and into the former Exhibition hall, Munro then turned away and walked back towards the tunnel entrances and the old station buildings. He crossed the fan of tracks that led from the depot without having to take great care over where he put his feet. He knew every inch of this ground. It caused him some anxiety that the often proposed – and just as often dropped – plans to knock down the Exhibition halls and build a huge complex of shops, restaurants, cinemas and bars in their place appeared to be very much on again. He had overheard Vanderbilt staff talking of a date by which they would have to move out and relocate beyond the M41. Some work had already started on the massive site. A scrap-metal merchant had taken out a temporary lease and sent in a squadron of mechanical diggers that were turning over the land between the Exhibition halls and the M41. Soon, the short stretch of motorway would have a lane shaved off it to allow for the construction of a slip road into the new development. Munro was already feeling squeezed. Whether or not the development reached as far as Wood Lane, he knew that they'd be knocking down his part-time home. The disused station buildings would be considered an eyesore.

What he would do in that eventuality, he hadn't decided. One option was to abandon his life as Munro and become the Other. Another was to stay and be flattened by the bulldozers. And the third was to get the hell out altogether – to call 'Cut' on Munro, the Other, the whole story. To throw a wrap party.

Saturday night, Jenny Slade had been at a party in Shepherd's Bush. Pennard Road was just to the west side of the green, behind the Empire, the Walkabout and a bingo hall. The host of the party, film producer Ritchie McCluskey, was celebrating having taken out an option on a novel by a hip, bankable author, and Jenny's agent, having got wind of the party, had urged Jenny to crash it. 'I'd come with you,' he'd told her, 'but you know how it is with kids.' (She didn't, particularly, but everyone with kids always assumed that you did.) McCluskey had kids, too, apparently, which was why the party had finished so early, leaving Jenny hanging around Shepherd's Bush Green with time on her hands. It was the first time in years she could remember leaving a party while the tubes were still running, rather than once they'd started up again around dawn.

She walked past the entrance to the Central line, where the grille had already been pulled halfway across in preparation for closedown. The vaulted space beyond the ticket barriers glowed like a cathedral. Passengers and staff moved gracefully around each other as if in some *avant-garde* dance piece. Maybe she shouldn't have dropped that E just before leaving the cab that had taken her to the party, although when she came up in the cosy little back garden with the house on one side and the overground tube line on the other it did make it easier to talk to people. Someone had put on a CD of dance music and the party picked up from there. She drank from a bottle of Evian water provided by the hostess, a tall blonde, whose husband, the film producer, had a stab at dancing with her and asked her what she'd done.

'Mainly modelling,' she said.

'I know *that*,' he said. 'Everybody knows that. But what about acting? Don't you want to move into acting?'

'I was working with a director,' she said. 'Richard Charnock? He's doing a movie called *Little Black Dress*? And I *was* going to be in it.'

'But not now?' asked McCluskey.

'Long story,' she said, but she told him anyway when she went to the kitchen for more water. She told him all about the sessions in the former Exhibition halls and about losing her white Gucci top. She told him about the drive along the Westway and him throwing her out of the car on Marylebone Road. McCluskey said it sounded like a scene from one of Charnock's films, and Jenny Slade said that maybe she should have seen one or two before agreeing to work with him.

'Maybe we could get you to audition for this,' the film producer suggested, gesturing to indicate the excuse for the party. 'It's a great part. I'll call your agent.'

'Yeah, right.'

She was wondering if she was temperamentally unsuited to the film business as she wandered past the entrance to the tube and then the camping goods shop. She was slowly coming down from the E, but languidly, luxuriously so. The entrance to the former Exhibition halls, with its textured collage of vivid flyposters, piss-stained wood and graffitied stucco, looked like something she would usually skip past in the art listings in *Time Out*. She thought about her top, the white Gucci top, possibly still lying in there, towards the back of the first hall, undisturbed on the dusty floor. Or would the security guard have recovered it and hung on to it in case she came back? It was obviously an expensive item. He might have washed it and given it to his girlfriend as a present, or even kept it and worn it himself. Who knows? She found herself knocking on the glass, softly but insistently.

She saw movement inside. A shape shifted beneath the dim fluorescent light. An indistinct voice answered the knock. She knocked again. Suddenly a dark, scarred face appeared at the glass. Jenny started, but then recovered her composure. The scars resembled the tribal markings on a Nigerian she'd dated briefly the year before.

'Can I ask you a question?' she shouted through the glass.

The man frowned.

Jenny gestured at the door.

'Can you let me in? Please? I just want to ask you something.' And she smiled, which seemed to swing it. The man took the key he'd been holding and inserted it into the padlock. He opened the door just wide enough to stick his head out, and Jenny smiled again.

'I lost something,' she said.

'What did you lose?'

'A white top. It's a designer thing, you know. Gucci. Very nice. I wondered if I could come in and look for it?'

He remained silent, just staring at her, but finally opened the door wide enough for her to squeeze in. She felt only mildly nervous when he locked the padlock behind her.

'I don't want to lose my job,' he explained.

She looked away at his little station set up behind the half-demolished reception desk. There was a kettle, a couple of dirty mugs, an empty plastic bag from the Seven-Eleven; a tabloid newspaper opened at the sports pages, a Walkman and a small pile of tapes.

'What are you listening to?' she asked.

'You said you lost something,' he said.

'A white top.'

'How could you lose it here?'

'I was here a couple of days ago with someone. It was all arranged – I think. I mean, I couldn't say for sure. And I accidentally left my top.' She twirled her hair around her fingers. 'It would mean a lot to me to get it back. Do you mind if I just go and have a quick look?' So saying, she pointed into the darkness beyond the spiral staircase.

The man appeared to be concentrating hard. He looked from the desk, where his newspaper waited, to Jenny, who smiled again.

'Five minutes,' he said. 'Must be back in five minutes.'

'You're a star,' she said, leaning closer to bestow a kiss on his cheek.

When she reached the spiral staircase, she looked back. He was watching, so she gave him a wave, then skipped off into the gloom.

By mid-afternoon, Frank and Siân were in Glasgow, where they met Giles Burke, organiser of the pioneering 1979 Aberdeen Film Festival, which had included a couple of Munro shorts. Burke produced a photograph of Munro that had been provided for the festival programme but never used.

'There must be a mistake,' said Frank, handing the photograph back to Burke. 'This can't be Munro.'

'Oh, but it is. I'm sure of it. It's even marked on the back. Look.'

Frank turned the photograph over to look. Sure enough, 'Fraser Munro' was written there lightly in pencil.

Burke offered Frank and Siân a whisky. 'A lovely single malt,' he proposed. 'From the Scottish Malt Whisky Society.'

'But this can't be him,' Frank insisted.

'I don't think I would have made a mistake,' Burke said, splashing the amber liquid into three glass tumblers.

The photograph showed a young man who bore not the slightest resemblance to Harry Foxx. Or Angelo or Richard Charnock for that matter. It wasn't a good shot – no doubt the reason for its exclusion from the programme – out of focus and lacking contrast, but the young man's open, innocent face was not one Frank had seen before. He passed it to Siân, who shrugged as she looked at it.

'We can still use it,' she said. 'If you wouldn't mind us borrowing it,' she appealed to Burke.

'Be my guest.'

Angelo hauled himself over the metal window frame, snagging his army-surplus combats on a miniature mountain range of glass shards. As soon as he dropped down to the floor and remained crouched below the level of the window, he no longer felt as if he was being watched. After a minute, he raised his head and looked out, back the way he'd come. He saw the twin tunnel entrances that led through the old Wood Lane station and on to White City. Nature had reclaimed the land, and somewhere in among the trees and undergrowth were the old station buildings where he'd seen a light burning.

To Angelo's left was the depot. The snouts of three Central line trains poked out of the long, low sheds with lanes numbered from one to fourteen. A turbanned silhouette was visible through the window of a control box that stood between the depot and the tunnels. Angelo turned and stared at the interior of the hall. In truth it was more of a shed. A shed on stilts. Like the others at Uxbridge Road, it was at least four hundred feet long. It was, however, in a far worse state of repair. The floor was a sticky carpet of asbestos dust, pigeon droppings and white feathers. The skeletal remains of a series of tiny rooms lined the east wall. Rusty steps leading up to an unsteady-looking balcony were missing several treads. Long, narrow light fittings hung at crazy angles from the high ceiling like the broken wings of huge birds: their fluorescent tubes lay in a million pieces on the floor, time having worn their edges as soft as the feathers with which they mingled.

Angelo advanced to the centre of the vast hall, where he paused and turned in a circle to examine every rotten ceiling support, each cobwebbed corner. As he stood silently taking it all in, he felt something in the air begin to caress him, something as soft as the fabric of the white Gucci top. It washed over him like a wave. He saw that there were broken windows on all sides of the hall, which would account for draughts of air, but this was something more than just that. He felt a tickling on the back of his neck, a feathering across his cheeks. Was this perhaps the lost space of the Tivoli, the first London cinema to show proper sound films, and the first of the great West End picture houses to be demolished? Angelo's notebook contained the information that its Wurlitzer had been saved, reappearing in Robert Fuest's *Dr Phibes Rises Again*, but now Angelo knew that its soul had been saved too. He felt the mingled emotions of a thousand departed cinema-goers gently buffet him as they endlessly rewatched Roger Corman's western, *Oklahoma Woman*, the last film to play the Tivoli, on a timeless loop.

He took a step towards the far end of the hall and felt the atmosphere shift from the large to the small, to the Eros at Piccadilly Circus, closed in 1985 and turned into a jeweller's. Barely two hundred people had been able to squeeze into its unusual, cramped space, and Angelo now became one of them for a few brief seconds. He felt, for the first time since entering the building, a rush of blood, and he buried his face in the white Gucci top, breathing in its scent. So the Eros had shown sex films for several years, but they were no different to any other movies, which were all about the same thing really. Boy meets girl. Girl meets boy. Boy meets boy. Whatever. It was all Angelo wanted as well, and he now felt suffused by the conviction that his search for the Museum of Lost Cinema Spaces had in fact been, all along, his search for *someone*. He brushed the soft material of the white Gucci top against his cheek and started walking faster towards the end of the hall.

At the end of the hall, Angelo found a heavy, rusty wheel that cranked open a roller door into the next hall. He opened it enough to crawl through and left it open, just in case. Great tarpaulins blocked off his view of the new hall. He pulled aside a flap. Beyond was a full-size indoor tennis court. He remembered the Vanderbilt Racquet Club, whose main entrance he'd seen from the streets behind Uxbridge Road. Running down the full length of the hall were two lines of unbroken skylights, which admitted enough light pollution for Angelo to see by as he made his way along the side of the courts to the far end. He was hoping that security at the other end of the Vanderbilt would not be so tight that he was unable to get into the halls that abutted Uxbridge Road. As he went, he kept his eyes and ears open for any further signs of the buildings' infestation by dead cinema auditoria, but nothing hovered over the tennis net. With part of his mind, he was beginning to accept that what he'd sensed in the derelict hall was a fantasy. The white Gucci top around his neck reminded him of what was real, although as he proceeded from one deserted moonlit court to the next, he was beginning to wonder if his search for the owner of the top had any kind of more substantial connection to reality. As if in response to the news that his flimsy world was coming apart, Angelo began to run, dashing through the articulated passages that joined one hall to another but slowing right down when he reached the admin corridor. The club shop and reception area was a pool of darkness, the light of the neon city blocked by a false ceiling. The ghostly glow from a cold drinks machine humming in a corner was sufficient.

Beyond the reception area, past a coffee table piled high with copies of *The Lady* and *Tatler*, a set of sliding glass doors led to the last converted hall, the one that Angelo hoped would grant him access to the deserted halls at the Uxbridge Road end of the complex. He gently fingered the white Gucci top around his neck, then tried the door.

Frank and Siân headed south from Glasgow. They could have explored further afield and tried to dig up more on Munro, but, having been keen to leave London, Frank was now eager to get back. They made short work of the M74, the steady draining of the light from the Borders sky speeded up by their headlong rush southwards. It was dark by the time they reached Carlisle.

Frank took over from Siân before they joined the M6,

agreeing that a further switch could take place at one of the service stations further south. Frank maintained a steady ninety m.p.h. He preferred to drive, since the concentration required for it meant that his mind was not free to wander on to the subject of Munro.

Jenny Slade advanced slowly into the murky hall. Although she knew the security guard was still at his desk only yards behind her, she felt completely unselfconscious. Her trailing hand caught the underside of one of the exposed steps of the spiral stairway and, liking the smooth feeling of it on her skin, she swung round to the bottom of the stairway and climbed up to the first floor. As she put more distance between herself and the dusty floor below, she felt another wave of euphoria begin to wash over her. Part of her immediately wanted to turn back and find the security guard, to hold him and reassure him that everything was going to be all right. But the stronger part of her wanted to penetrate deeper into the gloomy space and see if she could find her Gucci top, which had begun to assume a significance out of all proportion. Being here without Richard Charnock meant something to her as well. It was an affirmation of her strength as an individual that she was able to come back and not be defeated by the space in which he had, as he thought, humiliated her. She imagined part of the enjoyment for him was believing that she felt degraded by stripping for him, whereas in fact she had felt nothing at all. She had switched off.

She walked along the right-hand side of the upper hall, peering into the abandoned spaces that had once been individual offices but now made her think of booths in a peep show. She imagined the place overrun by police officers conducting a fingertip search, while forensics turned up traces of Richard Charnock's DNA. To banish the image, she crossed to the balcony and looked down into the well of the building where she'd left her top.

She came to an abrupt halt against the rail, heart thumping, breath catching in her throat.

Down below, standing more or less on the spot where she had left the top, was a man. His large head looked as fragile as a dandelion clock, the cropped silvery hair spinning the moonlight into threads. He held a piece of white fabric. She could tell from the folds in which it fell over the edge of his hand that it was her top. But she knew it was her top the moment she saw it not because of the folds in the fabric, but because she felt that there was something right about its being there in the hands of such a beautiful, graceful-looking creature. As he lifted his head and turned his face into the moonlight, he appeared blessed.

She felt the drug surging through her bloodstream with renewed strength and couldn't remain still any longer. The moment she moved, his head turned in her direction. His eyes fastened upon her. In less than a second she saw the hurt in them, but also the hope. She made to go down, but stopped when he called softly, 'I'll come up.'

His long legs covered the distance to the spiral staircase in seconds and he took the steps three at a time. She watched him appear to float towards her. Suddenly he was standing in front of her, head lowered so he could look into her eyes. The black discs of her pupils would be fully dilated. He was holding her top in his hands, offering it to her.

'I found this,' he said.

'Yes, I lost it,' she said. 'Well – took it off.'

'It's yours.'

She couldn't tell if it was a question, but it didn't sound like one.

'Here,' he said. 'Take it.'

She did take it and felt the impossibly soft fabric with her fingers. She held it against her cheek, then she turned her head and briefly buried her nose in it. It smelt of trees and trains and alcohol and sweat. She liked the smell. She was intoxicated by it.

'You keep it,' she said, handing it back. She could tell he hadn't just picked it up, but had had it for a while.

He took it, but seemed uncertain. 'It's you I was looking for,' he said. 'This just kept me company. Maybe I don't need it any more.'

'I'm not sure I do either,' she said. Then: 'Ssh!' She put a hand on his forearm. He lifted his own hands and placed them on her shoulders, his head moving to one side, twitching, alert.

'I heard it too,' he said.

'It must be the security guard,' she said. 'He let me in. He'll let us both out. Come on, let's go.'

She took his hand and led him towards the spiral staircase, but as they reached it, a figure emerged from around the other side, coming up.

Jenny recognised him as soon as he reached the top step, but before she could say anything, Angelo, who had seemed to hesitate for a moment, spoke.

'Richard,' he said. 'Hi.'

'What,' Jenny said, turning to Angelo, 'you know this prick?'

'Yeah. Don't worry. He's all right.'

'Define "all right",' said Jenny.

The last traces of the drug having quickly drained out of her system, everything around her now became very real. The edges of the building became harder, the floors dirtier, the shadows darker. The moon had gone behind a cloud. She could feel her heart beating.

Five miles south of Preston, they passed a sign –

Services
1 mile

'Pull in here,' Siân suggested. 'You need a break. I'll drive for a bit.'

'OK.' Frank indicated left, changed down to third, then second, and rolled the car into the car park. He switched off the engine and they sat for a minute enjoying the relative calm after the havoc of the M6.

'Do you want to use the loo? Get a coffee or something?' Siân asked.

'No, I want to get back.'

'It's still a long drive. We can always stop the night somewhere.'

'Let's see how we go. I'd rather get back tonight if we can.'

From where they were parked they had a direct view of the sign bearing the name of the services –

CHARNOCK RICHARD

They both sat looking at it for a while without really seeing it.

'That's odd,' said Siân at length, and looked across at Frank, who was frowning. 'Hey?' she said, touching his shoulder. 'Don't you think?'

Frank was thinking hard.

'Frank.'

'Yes, yes,' he snapped.

Siân lifted her hand away.

'Sorry,' Frank said. 'Yes, I think it's odd. I think it's very odd indeed.' He looked at her. 'I don't like it. Pass me that road atlas.'

'I mean, it could be a coincidence,' Siân said, handing over the map book. 'There's no reason why there shouldn't be a Richard Charnock. There are other Charnocks. Aren't there?'

'Yes.' Frank was poring over the road atlas. 'There's a writer called Graham Charnock, wrote a story called "Harringay". It was good.'

'Isn't there a dancer? One of those contemporary dance types?'

'Neil Charnock. I think.' Frank held the map up to the light.

'So, you happen to know a Richard Charnock. I mean, it's no big deal. Is it?'

'Look,' he said, pointing at the page. The services were named after a village, Charnock Richard, located a mile east of the motorway, halfway between Preston and Wigan.

'Let's get the fuck back to London,' he said, twisting the key in the ignition.

23 · Cold Heaven

London, Saturday 25 July 1998

'There's no way out back there,' the newcomer said.

'But the security guard . . .' Jenny began.

'The door's locked from the outside. He's doing his rounds.'

'So how did you get in?' asked Angelo.

'I would have thought that was obvious. He let me in.'

'I've got a fucking horrible feeling of *déjà vu*,' complained Jenny.

'Don't worry, we're not going out that way. There's another way. Follow me.'

'So, you two know each other?' Angelo looked anxious, confused.

'Knew,' said Jenny.

'We haven't known each other that long,' Richard told Angelo. 'Jenny was going to be in my next film, but she fucked up. We haven't known each other as long as *we've* known each other. I've known Angelo,' Richard continued for Jenny's benefit, 'since he was a boy, more or less. He was such a beautiful boy.'

Richard put his arm around Angelo's shoulder mock-paternally and started to lead him into the next hall. Jenny trailed uncertainly behind.

'Such a beautiful boy,' Richard repeated. 'Who would have thought he'd turn out to be a callous killer?'

Angelo shook off Richard's arm. 'Fuck off! Get off me!' he shouted, backing away from Richard, who mimed innocence.

'What's he talking about?' Jenny asked Angelo, who moved away from Richard towards her, his expression helpless, imploring.

'It was years ago,' Richard declaimed. 'So long ago practically no one would be interested – but for the fact the poor bastard was only buried yesterday.'

'No!' Angelo moaned, burying his head in his hands. 'Why don't you leave me alone!'

'Come here, Angelo, come to your Uncle Richard,' he shouted over Angelo's pleas. 'Everything will be all right. Come to me.'

Jenny watched over Angelo's shoulder as Richard slipped a hand inside his jacket.

'Angelo,' she shouted.

She grabbed him and together they stumbled past Richard, who made no immediate attempt to follow them, his hand now hanging limply by his side.

Jenny and Angelo reached the far end of the next hall before Richard even moved.

'Angelo, he's coming,' Jenny said. 'Come on, *come on*! How the fuck do we get out of here?'

Angelo appeared to have retreated inside himself. He was still speaking but what he was saying made no sense to Jenny.

'The tapes, the fucking tapes,' he was muttering. 'The bastard. The bloody fucking bastard.'

'Angelo, will you shut the fuck up!' Jenny shouted. 'Just get us out of here. Do we climb out of the window or what?'

Angelo numbly indicated the roller door by which he had entered the abandoned halls from the tennis club.

Jenny could hear Richard moving somewhere behind them. She looked back. He was just passing beneath the square archway between the first and second halls. He was moving slowly, but in their direction.

'Angelo, let's go,' she said.

Angelo lifted his great head and turned his big, hurt eyes on her. He looked baffled and beaten.

'Come on, for fuck's sake!' she hissed, grabbing hold of him. 'We have to get out of here.'

Richard was now close enough that Jenny thought she could see something in his hand flashing intermittently in the poor light as he walked. She wasn't sure, but she didn't want to hang around to find out. Bundling Angelo through first, she then rolled under herself. Angelo had started turning the wheel on their side of the wall to close the door before Richard reached it. She rushed to help. As the door lowered inch by inch, she could hear his approaching footsteps.

Richard's boots appeared in the remaining gap while they were still closing the door. They felt a new resistance on the wheel.

'Come on,' Angelo whispered, and he started to run across the first of the tennis courts. The carpet-like surface cushioned their footfalls.

'Angelo, what's going on?' Jenny panted, as she caught up with him.

'Long story,' he said. 'But it boils down to someone trying to make me assume responsibility for something I didn't do. And now it looks like that someone was Richard.'

'Somebody got killed?'

He nodded. Behind them they could hear the roller door squealing as Richard worked the rusty mechanism from his side.

'Who?' Jenny asked, looking back over her shoulder as she trotted to keep up with Angelo.

'A man I would never have harmed. He was like a father to me, and a friend.'

Angelo stopped walking and raised his head to the vaulted ceiling. The night sky was like a mirror, throwing the light of the city back at the earth. It bathed Angelo's face in a soft purple glow. Jenny bent double, hands resting on her knees, getting her breath back.

'Who did kill him?' she asked.

'Maybe Richard? I don't know. Harry Foxx? It could even have been Frank. It could have been any of us. They're trying to make out it was someone called Fraser Munro. Makes films no one goes to see.'

'Never heard of him.'

'You've not missed much.'

They both heard a piercing squeal from the roller door, followed immediately by a sort of squashy, scuffling sound that they realised was Richard trying to squeeze through the gap.

'Let's go,' Angelo said, grabbing Jenny's hand, and within moments they were in the reception area, then diving into the linking corridor that led to the next set of tennis courts.

'Don't get stopped,' Siân advised.

'I just want to get back,' Frank explained.

Frank hadn't let up since leaving the services at Charnock Richard, his speed rarely dropping below ninety-five.

'It's an automatic ban if you're doing over a hundred,' she stated.

'I know,' he snapped. Then: 'Sorry.'

Siân had reminded Frank that she had a mobile. Was there anyone they could call? Was there even anything to be gained by calling anyone, and what would they say?

Frank used the mobile to call his own machine. He picked up a message from Angelo telling him that he was going into the former Exhibition halls looking for someone.

'What's the problem?' Siân asked, seeing the frown lines deepen on Frank's forehead as he handed the phone back to her.

'Angelo.'

'In danger?'

'Could be,' he said, pressing down harder on the accelerator.

*   *   *

They reached the last hall, the derelict structure by which
Angelo had entered the complex. Richard had remained within
earshot behind them, but thanks to Angelo's having previously
left the first roller door open, they'd still had time to lower
it completely and to wedge a long, narrow fluorescent light
casing between the floor and the wheel that opened the door.
Angelo indicated the window they should aim for. It was about
fifty yards away. To Jenny it seemed like half a mile. She
had suddenly started to feel very tired. Her bones ached. The
feather-strewn floor was soft and inviting, the shattered
windows looked like trouble. She had nothing to fear from
Richard Charnock, after all. Did she?

'Jenny,' Angelo called.

She had slumped to the floor, and violent noises could
already be heard from the other side of the roller door.

'Jenny, come on!'

'You go,' she said, and lay down. 'I've had it.'

Angelo walked back to where Jenny was lying in a shaft of
reflected light from one of the broken windows. As he knelt
down, she watched his large head lower slowly over hers. He
touched his fingers to the side of her face and softly drew them
down her cheek. Although his face was in shadow, she could
make out its soft creases and sharper lines. There was a half-
inch-long scar under his left eyebrow. She saw a fingertip reach
up and touch it, then realised it was her own. Angelo moved his
head slowly from side to side. She slipped her hand behind his
neck and pulled his face down until it was just above hers.

The noises from the next hall got louder, but no gap had yet
been opened between the door and the floor.

'Angelo,' she said softly. 'What a beautiful name.'

'It's a nickname. My real name's Michael; I'm an Antonioni
fan.'

'I think whoever gave you the nickname did so for another
reason: because you look like an angel.' She increased the

pressure on the back of his neck until his face was directly above hers and she only had to raise her own head half an inch off the carpet of feathers and dust to press her lips against his.

'I'm cold,' she whispered. 'It's cold in here.'

At first, Angelo didn't seem to know what to do and he made no response to her opening move, so she held him closer and kissed him less gently and eventually he responded.

As they kissed, she felt another, final aftershock from the E she'd dropped at Ritchie McCluskey's party. It washed slowly over her like a wave breaking on the Tunisian beach where she'd done a swimwear ad earlier in the year. Angelo's caress was soft as a warm breeze. But when they stopped kissing for a moment the feeling persisted and Jenny realised it wasn't the E at all. This was instead that weird thing, a real, immediate sensation. Genuine emotion. She shivered with pleasure.

'Jenny,' he said.

'It's all right.'

'The door,' he said.

'It's OK,' she said, not caring.

She opened her eyes. Her head tilted to one side, she saw the floor of the hall stretching out into the distance. Its softness and spangly glow were not simply the effects of chemicals in her bloodstream. For once, she was actually in a beautiful place where no one wanted anything of her other than that which she wanted to give.

The moon came out from behind a cloud and bathed a section of the floor in a pallid light, so that it took on the blue-white, minutely crenellated stillness of a carpet of snow.

The noise at the door was getting louder.

She moved her head back so that she could look at Angelo. She saw the concern in his eyes.

'We've got to get out of here,' he said.

'It's so lovely,' she said, dreamily. 'But you're right.'

She let him help her to her feet and together they crossed the short distance to the broken windows. Through the jagged glass they viewed a contorted landscape of scarlet and black. Crimson lights burned in irregular patterns broken up by long lines of reflective steel against a dark background. Jenny couldn't make sense of it and it frightened her.

'I want to stay here,' she said, pulling at Angelo's arm.

'Listen.' A muffled thump, repeated over and over again, could be heard coming from the other side of the door. Richard was trying to force his way through. It couldn't be long before he succeeded.

Angelo managed to persuade Jenny to follow him over the ledge and on to the vertical ladder. She looked over her shoulder as she reluctantly climbed down, and the elements began to make sense. Predominant in the trains' livery was red, and a pair of red eyes glowed like hot coals on the back of each end carriage. She knew that half of the dozens of lines spread out before them would be thrumming with electricity. Jenny felt certain that they were descending into grave danger, but at the same time she felt that she could trust Angelo.

When they reached the bottom of the ladder and dropped the remaining five or six feet to the ground, they saw that a gang of railwaymen was working on the track the way that Angelo had wanted them to go. Instead they headed towards the trains and the sheds. Jenny asked Angelo what he had meant by his exclamation, 'The tapes, the fucking tapes.' Angelo explained that over the years someone had sent him video-tapes, with nothing on them but snow, labelled *Ghost Train*. He now knew who had sent them.

On the night they filmed Burns's suicide, once the shoot was done and the others were packing up, while Burns's body was still slumped on the sofa, Angelo had sat and stared at the monitor on which Burns had been watching *Le Feu follet*. He'd watched the dancing snowy picture and tuned out of his surroundings. Frank had come and knelt down beside him, but Angelo had not reacted. A little later, Richard had come and put his arm around Angelo's shoulders.

'I must have started to come out of it by then, because I said something to him. I told him about what my father had called the snow on a TV set. Ghost rain, he called it. He explained it by saying that it was film of rain that had fallen and could therefore never fall again. The reason it didn't look like normal rain was because it wasn't. It was the ghost of rain that had already fallen and somehow it had ended up inside the television set.' Angelo looked beseechingly at Jenny. 'I was only a kid, and probably a pretty impressionable one. I believed whatever my father told me.'

'But he called them *Ghost Train*.'

'Yeah, because he's such a fucking comedian.'

'So whenever he sent you one of these tapes,' Jenny said, 'it reminded you of your father?'

'No, it reminded me of Iain Burns and what we had done to him. As soon as I put one of these tapes in the VCR, I was right back there in that disgusting old place on Tottenham Court Road, with Burns lying dead next to me, and me unable to do anything except wish we hadn't done it. So I just watched the ghost rain.' Angelo lifted his head; the whites of his eyes glowed in the red lights from one of the trains. 'He was more of a father to me, you see, than my own father had been. I loved him, and I couldn't handle him dying, especially the way it happened, with our involvement. I felt guilty. I felt responsible.'

'But why did he send you the tapes?'

'Because he knew what effect they would have. He knew they would destabilise me, make me feel guilty. I don't suppose he could have known about the voices.'

'What voices?'

'I hear voices on the tapes.'

'What, an audio track, sound recordings?'

'No, just voices.'

'Saying what?'

'Telling me to do things.'

'What things?'

'Just things. Things on trains.'

'Did you do what the voices told you?'

'I don't know.'

'Angelo, look!' Jenny pointed up at the black hulk of the hall they had just left. Richard could be seen climbing out of the window, his foot reaching for the first rung on the vertical ladder.

Angelo picked up his video camera and pointed it at Richard.

'What the fuck are you doing?'

'Filming him.'

'We haven't got time for that,' she insisted, but then she looked closer at the camera. 'Angelo, there's no tape in it, is there?' she said gently.

Angelo carried on filming for a moment before lowering the camera with a resigned look and admitting the truth: 'No.'

'Come on,' Jenny said.

They turned away and walked behind the first train. Steam – or smoke – drifted from somewhere. Jenny smelt oil and machinery and something sharper, richer – electricity, perhaps. Beneath their feet the loose rubble of railway ballast gave way to a firm surface.

'We need to get out,' she said.

If they kept going in the direction they were heading, they would enter the shed. Jenny wondered how wise it would be to advertise their presence to tube workers, who would presumably call the police. She didn't need a night in the cells and a police record. But on the other hand, she didn't relish another confrontation with the director, especially if he'd got it in for Angelo, of whom she was beginning to feel ferociously protective. She would prefer to be back with him lying on the feather carpet in the abandoned hall than wandering aimlessly around this maze of trains and tracks and live rails.

'Under here,' Angelo said suddenly.

'Yeah, right,' Jenny scoffed, looking where he was pointing. He wanted her to scramble under the next train.

'There's a pit underneath it big enough for a man to work in,' he explained. 'There's lots of room.'

'Yeah, they call it the suicide pit, don't they, and there's probably a good reason for that,' she said, but followed him under the train all the same and they clambered out the other side, where they found themselves stuck between two more trains, but one lane further away from their pursuer.

'I think we should head further into the sheds,' Angelo said. 'There's got to be a way out at the other end.'

Jenny looked down to check her footing, then heard a noise from behind. She turned round, but could see nothing other than the vanishing perspectives of the trains on either side of her. At the far end was darkness. Because of the strange acoustics, she couldn't tell if the noise was close or distant. When she looked back, Angelo had disappeared. Had he climbed underneath the next train, or somehow put on speed and already reached the front of the train? She hissed his name, but knew it wouldn't carry more than two yards in one of two directions. Then she heard another noise, which did sound as if it came from close to her: a metallic grating noise that could have been a tube worker's wrench knocking the side of a carriage, or a blade scraped along a rail. She could also hear her own pulse pounding in her temple. Her breathing became fast and shallow. When there had been no repetition of the sound within a minute, Jenny started walking again in the same direction. She placed her feet with care. Where was Angelo? Had she been naive to put her trust in him? Were he and Richard working together to some common, banally villainous end? The police cell option began to seem the more attractive one.

When she reached the open area of the shed at the front end of the train, Jenny looked around for Angelo, but there was still no sign of him. Nor was there any sign of Richard

Charnock. She concentrated hard on listening for the slightest sound, but this was London – there was a constant background hum, which made it hard to detect tiny, telltale sounds closer to. There was also the gang of men working on the line near the tunnels – she could hear the percussive echoes of their slow, steady progress, and the ebb and flow of their trackside banter.

Dotted about the shed, dangling down from the ceiling to around head height, were overhead leads jumpers, skeins of electric cables feeding into heavy plugs that were used to power up the trains, since the live rails didn't extend this far into the shed. There seemed to be one set of leads per lane, but their lateral distribution was irregular.

Another sound drifted out of the night beyond the shed. There was a screeching, chalk-on-blackboard quality to it that made Jenny suspect it might be a train making its way up from the tunnels into the depot.

Climbing down into the pits between the rails, she started to edge her way across the shed, keeping close to the front ends of the trains. Not all of the lanes were occupied and the sound of the approaching train grew louder. Then she heard another sound, smaller, but nearer to hand, and she stood stock still, straining to listen.

A dark shape rose up from the pit immediately in front of her. It took two seconds to make sense of the apparition, and by the time she had, Richard Charnock had started to raise his hand. Out of the corner of her eye, as she started to lift her own hand to protect herself, she became aware of another looming presence, and at the same time the sound of the approaching train grew louder. A dark, heavy object swung into view, striking Richard on the side of the head. He collapsed, like a heavy overcoat falling from a broken hook, into the suicide pit directly in front of the oncoming train. The driver's face registered shock and dismay. Jenny looked away, but heard the thudding collision of metal and bone.

The overhead leads jumper swung to and fro like a pendulum between Jenny and Angelo.

Richard Charnock's body lay in a crumpled heap at the bottom of the pit, which was suffused with a red glow from the train's lights.

Jenny looked through the thick glass at the driver of the train, whose face was now buried in his hands. Angelo looked away from the body in the pit to Jenny, who turned her face away from the train and looked directly at Angelo.

In the distance, a siren could be heard. It was soon joined by another, and then several more, as squad cars raced to cover the short distance between Shepherd's Bush police station and the various entrances to the Central line depot and former Exhibition halls. As on squealing tyres they negotiated the illegal, ninety-degree turn from Uxbridge Road into Wood Lane, rather than slog around the Green, the resulting Doppler effect filled the night sky with a skirling cacophony of high-pitched screams that could be heard from Hammersmith Broadway to Kensal Green.

24 · Frames per second

Antwerp, 2000

The first 999 call had been made by Frank as he and Siân sped down to Shepherd's Bush from the North Circular. The train crew manager at White City made the next call after receiving confused reports from staff at the depot. Angelo and Jenny Slade left the scene in separate police cars; Richard Charnock's body was taken by ambulance to nearby Hammersmith Hospital. Having made themselves known to officers, Frank and Siân were taken to another police station, a short drive up Holland Park Avenue.

Everyone went voluntarily and no arrests were made. The police said they would probably need to call people back in, certainly Angelo and Frank, who were advised not to leave London, but no charges were brought for the time being. Jenny and Angelo had each given a straightforward, truthful account of what had happened in the Exhibition halls and depot, thereby backing up each other's story.

A careful search of the land around the Exhibition halls resulted in a gruesome discovery when officers entered the tunnels that led to White City station. They found several pairs of human eyes on the eastbound platform at Wood Lane (Disused). The eyes were in a solution of glycerin and formalin known as kaiserling preservative solution, kept in jam jars lined

up on a ledge, all pointing in the same direction, towards
the track, which was used by trains to get from the depot
to White City station. Tests would later match these to the
eyeless victims in the Hammersmith Tube Murders.

Even more macabre was the discovery made by police in
the disused station buildings, which, it soon became clear, had
been inhabited for years. In a solution of formalin, glycerol and
ethanol they found a pair of gloves made from human skin.
Someone – clearly someone with a degree of training – had
flayed the skin from a man's hands by cutting a straight line
down the middle of the back of the hand and carefully pulling
the skin off the fingers, having first tweezered out the finger-
nails, much like removing a tight-fitting rubber glove.

By keeping the skins in solution when they were not in
use, Munro (police also found film cans bearing his name, and
certain personal papers) was able to preserve them indefinitely.
The chemicals ensured their continued elasticity, so that he
was able to take the skins out and wear them as gloves, tying
them skin-tight along the backs of his own hands with thin
strips of leather.

The prints on the gloves matched those left on the celluloid
used to wrap the body of Iain Burns. Frank volunteered the
photograph of Fraser Munro that Giles Burke had produced
in Glasgow, and a nationwide investigation was launched, which
eventually established that there had indeed been two individuals
called Fraser Munro who had both been film-makers, the
younger having assumed the elder's identity after, presumably,
murdering him. The younger Munro's foster parents were traced
to the Isle of Mull in the Inner Hebrides and much was made
of the revelation that the child's foster father had worked on the
narrow-gauge railway that ran between Craignure and Torosay
Castle. The older Munro had no surviving family, which was
why the younger Munro's assumption of his identity had gone
undetected for so long. There was no one to miss the mountain-
climbing documentary film-maker, at least in his personal life, and

in the world of film, it was assumed that Munro's going underground applied as much to the man himself as to his work.

Frank left the film magazine and went freelance again, but
he maintained his relationship with Siân, who eventually moved
into his flat on Tottenham Court Road, while they started
looking for a bigger place with a different view. He never
wrote his big piece on Munro for the magazine, but turned out
a shorter account of his career for a smaller, edgier publication,
The Third Alternative, just to draw a line under his association
with him. As for Frank's documentary about visions of Heaven
in the cinema, he missed too many deadlines and had to abandon
it, although when I met him he was still intending to write his
book on the subject.

For some time Frank blamed himself for what had happened to Sarah: if he hadn't been so judgemental about her
smoking the odd joint, she wouldn't have needed to resort to
the clandestine arrangement that led to the accident. But it was
all a long time ago, and, with Siân's support, Frank came to
terms with his loss to the extent that he marked his forgiveness
of Harry Foxx by writing a short book about *Nine South Street*
for the BFI Modern Classics series.

Posthumously, Harry Foxx's reputation soared to the kind
of level he would have found entirely satisfactory and *Nine
South Street* achieved the degree of cult notoriety he had always
believed it deserved (its joining the BFI Modern Classics list
would have been unthinkable before Harry's death – unthinkable by everybody except Harry).

Both Frank and Angelo agreed to talk to me, as Penny Burns's
representative, but our conversations were off the record. By
cooperating fully with the police, they avoided having any
criminal charges brought against them with regard to the film
of Iain Burns's supposed suicide. The general perception was
that Munro/Charnock had manipulated the other three, and,
although nothing could be proved, it was widely assumed that
he had murdered Burns. For weeks the Sunday papers were

filled with stories about multiple personality disorder or MPD. As ever when the media tackle a scientific or medical subject, the articles were riddled with inaccuracies, but the message was that some of the time Munro was Munro and lived in the disused station buildings at Wood Lane, while the rest of the time he built up a successful, if never remotely respectable, career as trashy film-maker Richard Charnock. While Munro was partially aware of Charnock's existence as an 'alter', Charnock was never aware of Munro, which explained why the double life remained a secret for so long. The press had never been interested in Charnock anyway, unless it was to pour scorn on his work. And Munro, of course, hid himself away as a recluse, occasionally venturing out in his gloves. A prominent psychologist wrote that he almost certainly would have worn them to commit the Hammersmith Tube Murders, although no useful prints had ever been found at the murder sites. He wouldn't have been trying to avoid detection, but subconsciously hoping to effect a transference of guilt, the psychologist wrote.

The film journalist and writer Kim Newman undertook an in-depth study of Munro's films, and in the course of his work unearthed a lost short in the archives of a Rotterdam university film society that showed an unidentified 'actor' mummified in coils of celluloid. The 'actor' never moved and the camera prowled around him but never got close enough to reveal his identity. The film, having been sent to Rotterdam by Munro in response to a request for work to show in a festival of short films, was never screened.

Angelo left his dispatch job and tried to make a go of it with Jenny Slade, but as her career took off, her previous involvement with Richard Charnock notwithstanding, the pressures on them as a couple became intense, which Angelo found intolerable. He took the white Gucci top back to his bed-sitting room at 208 Gloucester Terrace and to my knowledge remains there to this day. He did at least survive, and I would guess he has found a new obsession to fill his time.

Andrew Kerner, likewise, was not heard of again, not that he'd been at the top of anyone's Christmas-card list in the first place. When picture editors renewed their contacts books, his number would be one that got left out. I presume he broke into one abandoned building too many and fell through a hole in the floor to his death. His body would then become one with the crumbling fabric of the building and probably he couldn't have wished for a more fitting end.

As for myself, I accompanied Penny Burns back to Felix-stowe and we spent a nervous couple of weeks trying to work out if our experience would thrust us together or tear us apart. I spent some time with her at the house she had shared with Iain Burns. She asked me to clear out the attic and get rid of anything connected with Burns. Among the junk stored up there I came across a book, a second-hand edition of Tennessee Williams's *Sweet Bird of Youth*, and a big box full of photo-graphic developing equipment, including a half-empty bottle of silver nitrate. I debated with myself whether or not to tell Penny. She knew that the coroner had found silver deposits in his remains. It wasn't exactly proof that he had actually killed himself after all, but it was as close to proof as anyone was likely to get, with two of the four possible suspects now also dead.

I told her I'd found some old stuff of Iain's and asked did she want to see it. She said she didn't, so I slung it all out.

We talked about what might happen next. There was change in the air. In London, the locations where the drama had been played out were being transformed. A new, glass-sided shop-ping complex started to take shape on the corner of Tottenham Court Road and Hanway Street. The smells of stale beer, salt and vinegar, and the unwashed clothes of middle-aged onanists slipping out of seedy sex dives were to be replaced by the bland, ascetic veneer of high-street brands – Boots, Micro Anvika, Muji, Specsavers, easyEverything, Sainsbury's.

The former Exhibition halls at Shepherd's Bush, long talked

about as a future massive building project, finally got a ticking clock. They were to be demolished in the autumn of 2000 to make way for a huge new development stretching from the Uxbridge Road to Wood Lane that would contain upmarket shops, restaurants and bars, and London's biggest multiplex cinema, with twenty screens. The White City depot would be moved underground and shunted a few yards west.

Early in the New Year, the *Guardian*'s crime correspondent, Nick Hopkins, wrote a feature for the *Guardian Weekend* suggesting that Munro and Charnock were not the same man at all, and that the real Munro, who had committed the Hammersmith Tube Murders and lived, at least part of the time, in the old station buildings at Wood Lane, was still at large. Hopkins proposed the idea, rubbished on the letters page the following week, that Munro had tipped over into one of his alters full time and that we would probably never hear from him again, but that that didn't mean he wasn't still out there.

By this time, Penny and I were long gone, starting a new life together in the Belgian city of Antwerp. Penny had needed a change from Felixstowe, and London hadn't felt right. Since my jeweller's business was transportable and Penny had nothing keeping her in England, I suggested we move to Belgium. Antwerp, of course, boasts a lively jewellery quarter. Whether or not I would continue to trade in amber would remain to be seen. We would be insulated against media intrusion; already, while still in Felixstowe, we had been pestered by tabloid journalists, ambushed by TV cameras. Coming to Antwerp, although in a sense a homecoming for me, was an opportunity for both of us to leave the past behind and reinvent ourselves.

from *The Third Alternative*

Double take

Frank Warner examines the twin-track career of *avant-garde* film-maker Fraser Munro.

The credit, as anyone involved in the film business will tell you, is paramount. And increasingly, since the 1970s, the credit that matters is the director's. Very few films are released these days that are not described thus: 'A David Fincher Film', 'A Wim Wenders Film', 'A Lars Von Trier Film' ('A Film by David Fincher' does the same job, more or less). Even when working under a collective banner, as, to an extent, Von Trier and others have done with the Dogme 95 brand, the director's name retains top billing.

There are exceptions, of course, when the star is perceived as being so important to the project that a movie directed by a newcomer, or an unbankable director, will be trailed as, say, 'Eddie Murphy's new picture'. Whatever. That may happen when the star calls the shots, but essentially the director is the man – or woman – who will for ever be regarded as the 'author' of the film.

This is why directors will remove their name from the credits if they are not happy with the picture that is released. In some cases, the directing credit goes either to whichever uptight producer ended up giving the orders, or to dependable old Alan (or Allen) Smithee.

Given that the name is so important, what must go through

the mind of a new director when he discovers that someone has got there before him with what he considers to be his name? Actors, if they're joining Equity, must come up with a new name, but the Directors' Guild of Great Britain imposes no such rule on directors.

The case of Fraser Munro has been covered exhaustively in the media, but little attention has been paid to the films that bear his name. A regular with the smaller UK and Continental festival circuit since the early mountain shorts, a film director called Fraser Munro first enjoyed public screening of his work at the Aberdeen Film Festival of 1977. Under a programme title, 'Man & Mountain: the short films of Fraser Munro', the festival showed four early shorts, opening with *Pinnacle of Achievement* (1974), a nine-minute film about a crofter from Skye who solo-climbed the mountain nearest to his village at the south of the island (when it still was an island). What was notable about the film was that the crofter had lost a leg in a climbing accident in his youth, but Munro filmed his ascent in such a way that you were barely aware of his disability. Indeed, he made you realise the inappropriateness of the very word 'disability'.

In the same programme, *Touching the Sky* (1976) was an oddly affecting piece about five men from a Highland community who set off one morning prepared to do some mountain-climbing, but as soon as they reach the outskirts of their tiny settlement they split up. The screen goes dark and the next shot is a breathtaking panorama from the top of a high mountain. We hear the sound of effortful approach and one of the climbers comes into view in the foreground. When he reaches the summit, he rests and gazes in the same direction as the camera, which remains behind him. It's a bright, clear day and we see a chain of peaks marching off towards the horizon. The camera holds still, despite its being buffeted by the wind, and our patience is rewarded when, in the distance, we see another climber reach the top of one of the other peaks in the range.

Eventually the other three climbers appear atop three more mountains and then the picture slowly fades to black.

Touching the Sky demonstrates a unique artistic vision but must also have required meticulous planning and organisation, and it has something to say about the relationship between man and his environment: that while these five men can display a certain ingenuity by conquering these peaks more or less simultaneously, the mountains still dwarf the men who have climbed them.

Munro also filmed white witches on South Uist, fishing communities on the east coast of Scotland and a riotous ceilidh in Ullapool. He always worked in black and white on 8mm film. He was compared by one critic to Humphrey Jennings, and possibly, had his career not been cut short, he would have gone on to justify the comparison. The Aberdeen festival programme notes observed that his work belonged to a tradition of Scottish film-making in which landscape was equally as important as character or narrative. If the allusion to Michael Powell's *The Edge of the World* and *I Know Where I'm Going!* flattered Munro, it only did so because he was cruelly prevented from realising his potential.

In 1979/80, three short films emerged bearing Munro's name. *Ben More* (1979), *Carn Sgulain* (1980) and *Bynack More* (1980) were mountain films, but there was a stark difference between these and Munro's earlier, more sympathetic work. In this trio of shorts, Munro intercut extreme close-ups of the mountains in question with extreme close-ups of a partially dissected cadaver or cadavers. At the time, it looked as if Munro had turned a corner and marched off in a completely new direction. With the benefit of hindsight, it is difficult not to draw the conclusion that these were the first films released by the second Munro, although he may have used some of his predecessor's footage. As for the anatomical content, do we assume he 'shot' his unfortunate victim or is this the material he is supposed to have nabbed at Stirling University Medical School? So many questions, so few definite answers.

Counting Sheep (1980) offers the first evidence of Munro's mordant and extremely dubious sense of humour. Smearing as much Vaseline on his lens as has not been witnessed since 1967's *The Wanderer* (Jean-Gabriel Albicocco's extraordinary, hallucinogenic adaptation of Alain-Fournier's *Le Grand Meaulnes*), Munro speeds up a dead sheep's decomposition into six gruesome minutes.

Counting Sheep was followed by Munro's least interesting phase, when he experimented with abstract film; he made at least a dozen unremarkable short pieces that communicated little and yet drew comparisons from various quarters with the work of Americans Harry Smith (and Len Lye before him), the Whitneys, Hy Hirsch, Patricia Marx and James Davis.

His next film was one you could imagine someone taking half a lifetime to complete. The elder Munro had announced the project some years before and had intended to finish the job in a year, with funding from one of the many bodies that dole out cash to arty film-makers, or used to in the good old days before the so-called Young British Artists made life difficult for real film-makers by selling their wacky home videos for huge sums of money to Charles Saatchi and other gullible collectors with deep pockets. It seems likely that he never completed it and that the task fell to the younger Munro. The project was *Munro-bagging* (1981), a celluloid cataloguing of all of Scotland's Munros, a Munro being a mountain over 3,000 feet. Whether Munro had intended to create a series of 300 short films, or one long film with 300 shots, or one *short* film with 300 shots, is not clear.

What finally emerged was very different from anything either Munro had made before. A soundtrack featured a man's voice reading the names and addresses of Munros – that is, people called Munro – from the phone book. There was one per mountain and each shot was cut to the time it took to read the corresponding name and address (not that the connection between the phone-book entry and the mountain was anything other than arbitrary in each case). With a running time of around fifty minutes, it actually seems a lot longer, but it pleased the judges of the 1982 Den Haag Prize for Best Nature Film.

Munro never turned up to receive that prize or any of the others he won. He didn't show his face at festivals. He was never interviewed; the few profiles that were written failed to get underneath the director's skin. We know that Munro managed to get under his *namesake's* skin, but any more than that we can only assume. It cannot now be proved that he murdered him, but it seems a safe assumption given his demonstrated appetite for killing. The interesting question for the film historian is when did he do it, when did he take over sole use of the name? It's possible that the older Munro lived at least until 1983, which was when his prints were left on celluloid wrapped around the former cinema projectionist Iain Burns, who had elected to commit suicide when suffering from tertiary syphilis. But it's likely that Munro dispatched Munro earlier than that: long before *Munro-bagging* was in the can, I would say. The tension between the patient, almost loving attention lavished on the mountains by one director and the brutal cutting and editing practised by the other, I believe, shows that the project's initiator did not get to wrap it up. But the newcomer didn't confine himself to wielding a scalpel and adding a 'witty' soundtrack; I strongly suspect he also filmed some of the mountains, since his predecessor had left the job unfinished.

The closest Munro came to the conceptual artists who started to colonise the grey area between art movies and movies-as-art in the mid-to-late 1990s was in the two short films he made, controversially, on nitrate film. Using nitrate film in the early 1980s – as it still is today – was illegal. Up until the 1950s, all films were shot on nitrate, but it is a highly unstable medium and is liable to burst into flames if exposed to a heat source, such as, unhelpfully, a projector bulb. One way in which Munro could have obtained nitrate stock was by travelling to Brussels and convincing a rogue technician at the Royal Belgian Film Archive to let him have some (all major national film institutes had nitrate restoration programmes, but the Belgians' was one of the most active). One imagines money may have changed hands. Wherever he did go to get the stock, it would have made sense to get the exposed negative processed and printed at the same place. The first film, *Auto-cide* (1984), is a two-minute single take of a burning car crossing a patch of open land before rolling into a large pond or gravel pit. We can only hope that the silhouetted figure in the driving seat is a dummy. The sequence is filmed at night, in black and white, and inevitably we remember the similar scene from *Psycho* as the vehicle tips slowly into the water and begins to sink. The car in Munro's film, however, as well as being a more recent model and on fire, is carrying Belgian licence plates.

The second of the nitrate shorts, *Auto-da-fé* (1984), was Munro's last known film. Running at just under five minutes, it is probably his most interesting work, and possibly his most revealing. The title alone, bringing to mind the burning to death of heretics, begs interpretation. Following the titles sequence, which is basic and stark in its presentation, white lettering on black –

Auto-da-fé

A film by Fraser Munro

– the film fades up very slowly to show an indistinct image of a man's face staring at the camera. Not only is the image blurred and, you suspect, deliberately obscured by having saliva or dirt smeared on the lens, but you begin to wonder, as you concentrate hard on the image, if it isn't a double exposure, if there aren't two faces there. Just as you begin to become convinced that there are two of them, white flickers of flame appear at the bottom of the frame. Some charring occurs and the image, which we had presumed to be in three dimensions, begins to curl up in the heat as if it is a photograph. As it curls, it starts to reveal another, much clearer image beneath it, again of a man's face, but the fire is burning quickly and it whites out the frame before we can get a look at him.

When *Auto-da-fé* was screened at a festival in Hamburg and was billed in the programme as having been shot and printed on nitrate stock, punters vacated their seats in a hurry, believing that a real fire had broken out in the projection booth. Again, Munro provides us with evidence of his morbid sense of humour, but almost certainly he is revealing a great deal more about his own identity than ever before. It is therefore particularly frustrating that all of the known prints and negatives of *Auto-da-fé* (and *Autocide*) were destroyed in a fire in west London on 24 July 1998, the details of which will already be well known to readers.

It is a fact that Munro's career, with its fairly paltry output, it has to be said, will always be overshadowed by the controversy attached to his name. His work, given its essential solipsism and obsessiveness, allows us a tantalising glimpse into the mind of a deranged artist of, frankly, uncertain talent.

Acknowledgements

Thanks to the following for help, support and advice directly related to the writing of this book: Kate Ryan, Jean Royle, Michael Marshall Smith, Paula Grainger, Chris Kenworthy, Chantal Bourgault du Coudray, Conrad Williams, Mike Harrison, Joel Lane, Gareth Evans, Rhonda Carrier, Chris Burns, Mic Cheetham, James Rowntree, Tamara Smith, Russell Celyn Jones, Matt Gilbert, Denis Ryan, Karen Godfrey, John Saddler, David Lee, Lisa Young. Thanks also to Richard Beswick, Antonia Hodgson, Jo Thurman and everyone at Little, Brown; the Film section and my colleagues at *Time Out*.

Generous with their time and expertise were: Johnny Pym, Kris Evans, Tom Bromley, Sushrut Jadhav, Wim Verhaeghe, Tony Falcon; Christine Bayliss, London Borough of Hammersmith & Fulham; Peter Hyatt, London Borough of Islington; Elaine Burrows, BFI; Bill Wrigley, Teaching Services Manager, Bristol University Medical School Anatomy Department; Angie Quinlan & Simon Fox-Hazleton; Amanda Posey, Chris Petit, Tony Peake; James Brooke-Webb, Chelsfield plc; Mary Thomas & Manny Corr, Vanderbilt Racquet Club; Danny Woodward & Brian Butterfield, Central Line, London Underground.

The following publications were referred to in the writing of this book: *The Cinemas of Camden* by Mark Aston (London Borough of Camden); *London's West End Cinemas* by Allen Eyles & Keith Skone (Keystone Publications); *The Amber Valley Gazeteer of Greater London's Suburban Cinemas 1946–86* by Malcolm Webb (Amber Valley); *Amber: the Natural Time Capsule* by Andrew Ross (Natural History Museum).

Chapter three previously appeared in a different version as a supplement with *The Third Alternative* edited by Andy Cox. A text consisting, in part, of sections from chapters eight and thirteen was read at a Foreign Body seminar at the University of Stirling (which does not have, nor has it ever had, a medical school) organised by Nicholas Royle, then reader in English at the University of Stirling, now Professor of English at the University of Sussex and a writer himself, although no relation to the present author. The same text later appeared in *Retro Retro* edited by Amy Prior (Serpent's Tail).